HOW TO CATCH A DEVILISH DUKE

THE DISREPUTABLE DEBUTANTES

AMY ROSE BENNETT

COPYRIGHT

DEDICATION

To my wonderful family for believing in me, always.

To my dear friend Maria for squiffy discussions involving tongue twisters. Those were the days!

To my sweet Buffy. I miss you.

And to my own romantic hero, my best friend, my everything, Richard.

PRAISE FOR THE DISREPUTABLE
DEBUTANTES SERIES BY AMY
ROSE BENNETT

"Bennett makes the Regency historical seem fresh and new through her vividly rendered settings, which display her impeccable command of the glittering world of the ton; her perfectly matched protagonists, whose potent sexual chemistry evolves into sizzling love scenes; and her expertly graceful, tartly witty writing." —*Booklist* (starred review)

"Readers will enjoy this expertly executed Regency with likable characters. A well-written start to a historical romance series full of rakes and the women who love them." —*Kirkus Reviews*

"Bennett delivers a fun start to a new Regency series in which embracing one's bad reputation yields some pretty good results." —*Library Journal*

"Sexy, sweet, romantic, and funny, *How to Catch a Wicked Viscount* will steal your heart away. Amy Rose Bennett is a charming new voice in historical romance." —Anna Campbell

"Amy Rose Bennett's HOW TO CATCH A WICKED VISCOUNT is delightful Regency romance infused with heat, energy and glamour. Bennett effortlessly captures the ingredients that make Regency romance so compelling to readers: sparkling dialogue, passion, and the elegant ballroom manners that mask the danger and risks that lie just beneath the surface."—Amanda Quick, *New York Times* bestselling author

"Amy Rose Bennett is a fresh new voice in historical romance with a flair for historical atmosphere. In HOW TO CATCH A WICKED VISCOUNT she introduces us to a set of lively characters embarking on a fun, lighthearted, tried and true reader favorite romp."—Anne Gracie

"Amy Rose Bennett's *How to Catch a Wicked Viscount* reminds me of just how much fun Regency romance can be at its best. The story is expertly crafted, with lots of heat and humor."—*USA Today* bestselling author Mimi Matthews

"A sweet and spicy read full of sly wit and rich with delicious details that pull the reader into the scene. A delightful confection of ballroom banter and bedroom seduction." —*USA Today* bestselling author Sally MacKenzie

CHAPTER 1

Even though the Season proper is yet to begin, that
doesn't mean the *bon ton* aren't already out and
about Town and getting up to all sorts of mischief.
The Beau Monde Mirror: The Society Page

The Rouge et Noir Club, St James's, London
March 27, 1819
Just after midnight...

Lady Charlotte Hastings's heartbeat hammered
wildly in her ears as the hired hackney lurched to a
halt in a narrow side street in St James's. The entrance to
the alleyway running behind the Rouge et Noir Club—a
gaming-hell-cum-brothel that was highly popular with
the ton's gentlemen—was barely visible through the thick
shroud of scudding fog.

Perfect, thought Charlie as she peered through the
cab's grimy window. Although a hooded mantle of thick
wool shielded her unusual and altogether salacious costume—it really amounted to little more than her unmen-
tionables—she was grateful the roiling miasma would
also disguise her identity to some extent. Well, at least
until she entered the club and had to discard her cloak.
And then she had but a cosmetic mask of face powder,
rouged lips and cheeks, kohl-lined eyes, and an artfully

placed beauty spot at the corner of her mouth to preserve her anonymity.

Heavens above. She prayed with all her heart that she could infiltrate this notorious gentlemen's lair and emerge unscathed. Although, given the morally dubious nature of her mission, she doubted the good Lord would be listening.

Ignoring the censorious look that Molly, her lady's maid, sent her way, Charlie raised a pewter flask to her lips with trembling fingers, then downed a large swig of French brandy. If she was to undertake this entirely foolish but absolutely necessary venture, she needed every ounce of courage—even if it was only Dutch courage—that she could marshal.

She had to go through with this. She *had* to succeed.

Because if she didn't, the consequences didn't bear thinking about.

Her dry throat sufficiently lubricated by the strong liquor, Charlie summoned her voice. "As we discussed, you must wait here for me, Molly," she said as firmly as she could considering her insides were quivering like a barely set jelly. "I've paid the driver well, so you'll be perfectly safe. If for some reason I don't emerge after an hour, you must go to Exmoor House in Grosvenor Square and ask for the duke. He'll know what to do. He's a member of the Rouge et Noir Club and no doubt has some sway with the management."

"Yes, my lady. Only…" Molly's throat worked in a nervous swallow. "What if the duke *isn't* in?"

"He will be. I know he was dining with my brother, Lord Malverne, at White's earlier on, so he should be home by now."

The maid nodded, but even by the feeble light of the hackney's carriage lamp, Charlie detected a worried flicker in her gaze; she wasn't convinced at all that the young woman would comply. "Molly, promise me you won't go to my family," she added in a stern tone. "They cannot know about *any* of this."

"I give you my word, my lady."

Charlie inclined her head. "Thank you."

Indeed, the reason Charlie was undertaking this escapade was to *prevent* her family from ever finding out
the terrible, terrible mess she'd landed herself in. All because of her foolish, reckless choices. To see the disappointment in her father's eyes if he ever discovered the
things she'd already done and would do tonight…

Charlie shuddered. Being expelled from a young
ladies' academy four years ago for unbecoming conduct
was bad enough for the Earl of Westhampton's daughter.
She'd never survive another scandal of such monumental
proportions.

Yes, by hook or by crook, she had to extricate herself
from this new predicament. However, if the very worst
should happen tonight and her plans went spectacularly
awry, she knew without a shadow of a doubt that Maximilian Devereux, the Duke of Exmoor, her older brother's best friend, would step in to help her.

Of course, she might very well expire from mortification if the man for whom she harbored a hopeless *tendre*
ever learned of her shocking secrets…

Charlie shivered again and took another long draft of
the brandy. One thing was certain, if she wished to keep
her secrets just that—secret—she *had* to find Baron
Rochfort and retrieve the notebook he'd stolen from her.
A notebook that contained her most private thoughts and
dreams.

An unexpected loud rap on the carriage window made
her jump and Molly shriek.

"It's Frank," said Molly in a melodramatic whisper.
Cracking open the carriage door, she hissed at her
brother, "Lord love us, Frank. You mustn't sneak up on a
body like that. You've scared her ladyship and me half to
death."

Frank Turner, a tall, thin young man with an earnest
manner, gave an apologetic wince. "I'm sorry, sis." He
sketched a quick bow in Charlie's direction. "Lady
Charlotte."

Charlie recapped her brandy flask and slid it into her
reticule. "No harm done, Mr. Turner," she said with a
smile she hoped was gracious given her face felt oddly

stiff all of a sudden. "And please, let's dispense with formalities. A simple 'miss' will do. I can't afford to share my real name with anyone in the club. Also, before going any further, it would be particularly useful to know if Lord Rochfort is actually here this evening. There's no point in proceeding with this visit if the baron is engaged elsewhere."

"Right. Of course," said Frank. "Yes, Lord Rochfort is here. He was at the *vingt-et-un* table about half an hour ago, and I have reason to believe he's currently consorting with his regular mistress, Madame Erato. I spied them leaving the club floor around midnight."

Excellent. Charlie's pulse quickened. For her plan to succeed, the baron had to be distracted. And what could be more distracting than engaging in sexual congress with a practiced cyprian?

"Thank you, Mr. Turner," she said. "That's very helpful. And I hope this is too." She reached into her reticule and pulled out a coin. "This is to grease the doorman's palm. I trust a guinea will suffice…"

Frank opened the carriage door wider, letting in a blast of cold, damp air before pocketing the coin. "Yes, miss, that will do nicely."

When he bent to let down the hackney's stairs, Molly reached out and squeezed Charlie's arm. "Godspeed, my lady. I'll be praying for your safe return."

Charlie gave the maid a quick nod as she gathered her cloak about her. "Thank you, Molly. All going well, I'll be back before you know it."

The servants' entrance to the Rouge et Noir Club lay at the bottom of a flight of narrow stairs, below street level. An oil lamp cast a weak, yellowish pool of light in front of the sturdy door of black wood fitted with studded iron hinges. As Charlie carefully picked her way down the steps, she tried to dismiss the thought that she was entering some hellish subterranean dungeon of depravity she had no hope of escaping.

At Frank's knock, the door swung open, and the young croupier traded nods with a burly but decidedly bored-looking doorman. Money exchanged hands along with a few quiet words, then Charlie was ushered into the dimly lit interior.

Frank raised a quizzical brow. "Your cloak, miss? You'll stand out like a sore thumb if you wear that in the club."

The doorman grunted in agreement and held out a meaty hand.

Charlie pushed back her hood with shaking hands, hoping that her elaborately curled, Greek-inspired coiffure would pass muster. However, revealing her scanty apparel to a pair of strange men was confronting indeed now that the moment was upon her. To think she would soon be parading through a gaming hell in front of a throng of foxed tonnish gentlemen with money in their pockets and lust on their minds... She gave an involuntary shiver as her fingers ineffectually fumbled with the knotted ribbon ties at her throat.

In hindsight, perhaps she shouldn't have dismissed the idea of donning the disguise of a gentleman. But unless she'd lopped off all of her thick chestnut curls, added another four or five inches of height to her relatively short frame, and was somehow able to flatten her ample bosom *and* squeeze her generously curved hips into narrow breeches, she really didn't have a hope in Hades of passing herself off as a man.

Her fingers stilled. *But there's no doubt I'd be safer...*

Oh, God! What was she thinking?

"Miss?" prompted Frank. He glanced nervously down the corridor to a set of narrow stairs. "I really do need to get back. And Mr. Fudge here doesn't have all night."

At that moment, a narrow longcase clock at the far end of the corridor began to chime the quarter hour after midnight.

Oh, dear. She really couldn't afford to dither about either. Drawing a steadying breath, Charlie ventured, "As I only intend to have a quick word with Baron Rochfort, it might be easier if I just leave my cloak on—"

The doorman, Fudge, gave a snort. "A shy woman in the Rouge et Noir Club. Now that's a novelty. You're sure to attract even *more* attention skulking about in that shapeless sack. Unless..." All of a sudden, his eyes narrowed with suspicion as his gaze traveled over her still-shrouded form. "Hoy, you don't plan on doing Lord Rochfort a mischief, do you?" he demanded. "I 'ope you ain't got a weapon stashed somewhere underneaf there. Letting a young lady of quality like you in for a lark is one fink, but the club owner will 'ave my balls for breakfast if anyfink happens to one of the customers 'ere..."

Oh, no. Being denied entry to the club would be even worse than being leered at. Steadfastly tamping down her bout of missish nerves—failure was *not* an option—Charlie straightened her spine and forced herself to meet the doorman's gaze. "I assure you that 'doing Lord Rochfort a mischief' is *not* my intention, sir," she remarked in a tone that she hoped sounded cool rather than apprehensive. "As I said, I simply need to...to talk to him about a private matter." She shrugged a shoulder and prayed the doorman would believe her outright lie.

Fudge smirked. "Talk? You can call doing the deed whatever you like, miss, but I wouldn't be doin' my duty if I didn't check you were unarmed. Now take it off, or it's back outside wif you." He gestured at the door with his thumb.

Charlie sighed. It seemed there was nothing for it. She was going to have to abandon her dignity along with her cloak. Her stomach aflutter, she roughly yanked at the tie. The knot at last came undone, and she shrugged off the garment entirely.

And then Fudge said, "Cor blimey," and Frank Turner's eyes popped wide open as he blushed to the roots of his hair.

And so did Charlie. Heat washed over her from head to toe.

Good heavens. If she'd provoked such a reaction from the Rouge et Noir's doorman *and* a croupier who no doubt saw barely clad females every single day, what a sight she must look.

She moistened her dry lips. "I trust that my attire is... is suitable, Mr. Turner? Your sister and I only had your rather loose description to go by, after all."

Molly had helped her to assemble the two-piece ensemble—a figure-hugging ivory silk corset that barely contained her bust, and a pair of drawers fashioned from an old fuchsia-pink ball gown that was no longer *à la mode*. On her stockinged feet, she wore low-heeled satin pumps embroidered with seed pearls. Given her face was also painted rather garishly, she looked nothing like a respectable young lady of the ton.

Rather the epitome of a whore from a French bordello. But she supposed it shouldn't surprise her that wealthy, titled men might be titillated by the idea of scantily-clad women being at their beck and call for bed sport, or whatever sort of "sport" took their fancy. After all, most of them believed they owned the world and everyone in it.

Lord Rochfort certainly did.

"Ahem…" Frank tugged at his cravat and looked everywhere but at her. "Yes, I'd say it's suitable, my…miss…"

Fudge simply grinned and didn't even attempt to raise his gaze from her exposed décolletage. "Lady of quality or not, wif tits that big, I'm sure you could get a job 'ere if you wanted to, miss. I could put in a good word wif the manager when I see him later tonight."

"Thank you, but that won't be necessary," Charlie said stiffly. While it was true that her bust was decidedly generous—especially after all the cakes and sweetmeats she'd eaten since Christmastide (and even during Lent)—that didn't mean the man had to make such a crude remark. "As I keep saying, I just need to have a word with Lord Rochfort, then I'll be on my way."

Gathering the last remnants of her failing courage about herself, Charlie followed Frank up the stairs at the end of the corridor. When they reached the landing, he paused by a baize-covered door. "We're about to enter the club's gaming area," he explained in a hushed tone. "I must return to the hazard table, so you're on your own from here on in."

Charlie nodded. "I understand. But perhaps you could tell me how to find Madame Erato's chamber. I'd rather not waste time looking for it." She'd locate the baron, take back that which belonged to her while he was "busy" with the courtesan, and then all would be fine.

Simple. What could possibly go wrong?

Armed with the croupier's directions, Charlie donned an air of nonchalance as she skirted the club floor, heading for the main staircase that led to the brothel area. Massive chandeliers lit a high-ceilinged chamber furnished with plush Turkish rugs and ornate mahogany gaming tables. Groups of well-dressed men—all strangers, thank goodness—milled about, chatting and laughing with a handful of young women wearing attire not dissimilar to her own. Off to the far right, there was another arched doorway swathed in curtains of rich crimson damask. When a footman emerged, Charlie caught a glimpse of two bare-breasted courtesans sprawled upon a chaise longue beside a gentleman smoking a hookah pipe.

Heavens above. The tableau brought to mind the folio of erotic etchings that she'd once discovered in Hastings House's library. Blushing hotly, Charlie hastily looked away. Thank goodness she didn't have to go in *that* direction.

And then anger surfaced at the rampant misogyny on display. She was by no means a prude, but witnessing how these "noble" men thought nothing of indulging their fantasies of subjugating women made her blood boil. If she didn't have to hide the fact that she'd set foot inside the Rouge et Noir Club herself, she'd take her brother to task about his past habit of visiting places like this when he was a bachelor. And she'd jolly well admonish Max Devereux for coming here too.

Even though she kept to the shadows as much as possible, she still managed to attract the attention of a middle-aged gentleman. With a glass of brandy in hand and his cravat askew, he was weaving his way toward a nearby settee. Ignoring his low whistle and clumsy wink, Charlie slightly altered her course to avoid further interaction. She didn't have the time or inclination to fend off unwanted advances from drunken "nobs."

Once she reached the stairs, she quickened her pace, and within a few moments, she'd gained the first floor. Turning to the right as Frank had instructed, she soon found herself in a sumptuously decorated hallway that was thankfully devoid of lecherous noblemen, foxed or otherwise. The soft light of gilt wall sconces illuminated the flocked wallpaper, gleaming oak panels, potted palms, and claret-hued curtains. If it weren't for the paintings of frolicking naked nymphs and a rather well-endowed bronze statue of Bacchus, she could be at home.

But then again, perhaps not. As the hubbub of voices from the main club faded away, other sounds that would *never* be heard in Hastings House became evident—an erotic chorus of rhythmic grunts and moans and cries punctuated with the occasional burst of tittering laughter filtered into the corridor.

Although Charlie tried to tell herself the heat burning her cheeks was simply a result of rushing and nerves, she knew that beneath her discomfiture, she might even be a little aroused. A mortifying and undoubtedly shocking circumstance indeed, that simply listening to the sounds of sexual congress could provoke such wanton and unladylike feelings inside her.

But then, she'd always been a little more wicked than most young ladies. Her mouth twitched with a wry smile. It was her propensity for wickedness that had landed her in this mess in the first place.

Swiftly padding her way down the Turkish runner, Charlie focused on counting off the doors until she reached Madame Erato's boudoir—according to Frank, it was the ninth room along. As she pressed her ear to the cool oak panels of the door to listen—she wouldn't even attempt to slink inside until she was absolutely certain Lord Rochfort was thoroughly engrossed with the courtesan—she suddenly sensed a presence behind her. A large male presence standing much too close.

A hand, warm yet firm, closed about her bare upper arm, and an all-too-familiar baritone grazed the edge of her ear, raising gooseflesh. "Charlotte Hastings. What the devil are you doing here?"

CHAPTER 2

Gentlemen of the ton: what do they like to talk
about? Before you enter the husband-hunting
market this coming Season, be sure to arm
yourself with a range of topics that will fully
engage and charm even the most hardened, hard-
to-catch bachelor.
The Beau Monde Mirror: The Essential Style &
Etiquette Guide

O*h, no! Dear Lord above, no!*
Sucking in a startled breath, Charlie spun
around and came face-to-face with Maximilian Devereux, the Duke of Exmoor.

Her older brother's best friend.

The man who frequently occupied her romantic day-
dreams and deliciously wicked fantasies at night.

A man who was always amiable—perhaps even a little
flirtatious on the odd occasion—but to her unrelenting
disappointment, never *more* than that. Why, in the six
years she'd known him, they'd never even shared a waltz.

The indecently handsome duke planted his large
hands on the door on either side of her shoulders, caging
her in as he stared down at her, a fierce scowl marring his
perfect brow. From beneath a sweep of dark blond hair,
his sapphire-blue eyes seemed to pierce her to her very
soul.

Too flabbergasted to string a coherent sentence together, Charlie stammered, "How…? Wh-what? You're not…" Somehow marshaling her thoughts and her ire—it was one thing to know Max visited brothels, but it was another thing entirely to witness him doing so—she raised her chin and demanded in a furious whisper, "What on earth are *you* doing here? You're not supposed to be here."

"I have more or less the same thoughts about you, *my lady*," he bit out. "Have you gone stark raving m—"

The sound of female laughter—loud and affected—drifted toward them from the direction of the stairs, and Max swore beneath his breath. Because rounding the corner and headed their way, was a courtesan and a ton buck Charlie and Max both knew. Baron Edgerton.

Oh, dear God. If Lord Edgerton recognized her…

As horror and panic whipped the air from Charlie's lungs, Max sprang into action. Seizing her hand, he tugged her across the corridor and after collapsing onto a gilt-legged settee, he dragged her down on top of him.

"Straddle me," he commanded in a hoarse whisper as he grasped her hips. Without hesitation, Charlie complied, moving to sit astride his lap. Even though her back would be turned to the approaching couple, Max's hand came up to cradle the back of her head. "Hide your face in my neck," he urged. "Pretend to nuzzle my ear. Don't let Edgerton see you."

"But I'll smudge my—"

"No buts," Max hissed. "I'm trying to protect you. Just do it. Now."

Charlie immediately dipped her head and pressed her lips to a vulnerable patch of flesh beneath Max's ear.

And almost at once, all of her chagrin and fear, embarrassment and uncertainty began to melt away.

Oh my… Hadn't she dreamed of doing this more than once in the middle of the night? Being this close to Max? Kissing him?

Charlie reveled in the warmth of his skin, the steady beat of his pulse. His delicious scent—a heady combination of his cologne, the starch of his freshly laundered collar and cravat, and another entirely masculine smell she always associated with Max—enveloped her in a sensual cloud, and for a moment, she almost forgot where she was and how much danger she was in.

Yes, danger.

Lord Edgerton called a greeting to Max and Charlie tensed; her fingers dug into Max's shoulders and her breath hitched. But then Max stroked a hand down her silk-clad back as though soothing a restive beast about to bolt. "They've almost passed by. You're doing well," he whispered before he offered the baron a nonchalant greeting in return. "Evening, Edgerton."

Charlie forced herself to breathe. If she played the part of a courtesan with some conviction, she would have less chance of being noticed. Even though she scarcely knew what she was doing, she threw herself into the role. Ignoring the fact she must be smearing away half of her face paint, she burrowed into Max's neck a little more, then dragged her lips along the edge of his sharply chiseled jaw. His taste, the *feel* of him filled her senses again, making her dizzy.

Salt. Musk. Spice. Hardness.

The slight rasp of bristles. Heat.

Max.

When her fingers sifted through the thick, silky hair at the back of his head and she gently drew on his earlobe, the duke shifted restlessly beneath her. "Yes, that's it, sweetheart," he groaned. "Don't be shy."

Good Lord. Was she really stirring Max so much that she'd made him groan? Or was he just pretending? In her heart of hearts, she really hoped he wasn't, because there was no doubt that sharing such an intimate, wholly inappropriate embrace with Max was affecting her in countless, very *real* ways. Her heart beat wild and fast, and desire fluttered to life and gathered in all kinds of secret feminine places.

Dare she trace the curve of Max's ear with the tip of her tongue? She was just about to when Max's hand gripped her nape. "You can stop now," he murmured. "Edgerton's gone."

"Gone?" Slightly dazed, Charlie lifted her head. "Oh, good." She reluctantly climbed off Max's lap and plopped onto the settee beside him. Beneath her relief, disappointment welled as she took in Max's far-from-pleased expression.

"Yes, thank God." The duke stood abruptly as if he couldn't wait to put as much distance between them as possible. "And I expect Edgerton will be otherwise engaged for the next half hour or so. Which means it's the ideal time for us to go."

Charlie sprang to her feet too. "Wait. No."

Max's scowl deepened. "What the hell is wrong with you?" he demanded as he reached for her arm. "I need to get you away from here."

"I…I can't leave." Charlie shook him off and took a step back. "Not yet."

Max reached for her again, and this time his grip was uncompromising as he drew her in close. "Well, one thing is certain," he growled down at her, "you've definitely taken leave of your senses. Come." He began marching her down the corridor, steering her away from the main staircase and toward the very end of the hall. "We'll take the servants' stairs down to the rear entrance."

"No. Stop." Charlie halted her steps, digging her heels in. "Nothing is *wrong* with me. I haven't lost my mind. I'm just in a spot of trouble."

Max spun back to face her. "Oh, and skulking around a brothel dressed up as a prostitute will get you out of it?"

"Please, let me explain," she entreated, placing her hand on his arm. "It's complicated."

His eyes searched hers for one long moment, and Charlie swore she could see his mind making calculations—weighing up the risks if she stayed versus the benefit of immediately carting her off to safety—but then he huffed out an exasperated sigh. "Very well, I'll listen. But make it quick."

He drew her into a nearby window embrasure that was flanked by an enormous pair of potted ferns upon marble pillars. The shadows and feathery fronds partially shielded them from view so they should be safe enough for the moment. Crossing his arms over his chest, Max stared at her expectantly.

Charlie drew a deep breath. How much should she disclose to Max, and how much should she leave out? "The matter involves Lord Rochfort," she began in a low voice. "I take it you know him?"

Max's jaw tightened and a muscle pulsed in his lean cheek. "Yes, I know him. He's depraved through and through. One of the ton's worst blackguards."

Charlie wished she'd known that when she first became entangled with the baron nearly six weeks ago. She'd heard rumors, of course, but had foolishly dismissed them in the face of his practiced charm and sardonically handsome smile. "Well, in case you didn't know, he's here tonight. In fact, I have it on good authority that the baron is with Madame Erato at this very minute. And I was about to sneak into her boudoir when—"

"Sneak in?" Max's eyebrows shot up. "Good God. I'm an openminded sort of fellow, but you weren't planning on joining them, were you?"

"No! Of course not! I know I don't have the best reputation, but do you seriously think that someone like me— a veritable wallflower who's never even had *one* proper suitor—would engage in a…in a sexual threesome with a despicable rogue like him?"

Oh, no. Had she really just said that? Heat scorched Charlie's entire face. Young tonnish misses were *never* supposed to talk about sexual congress, let alone admit they knew about the most licentious types of bed sport.

And it seemed Max might be blushing too. The crests of his cheekbones were stained with a wash of high color as he muttered, "Setting aside the fact you even possess such singular knowledge, at this point in time, I honestly don't know what to think. God in heaven—" Max caught her chin with gentle fingers. Concern clouded his deep blue gaze as he studied her face. "Rochfort hasn't hurt you, has he? Forced himself upon you? Or coerced you to participate in some debauched game for his own perverse pleasure? Because if the bastard has—" Some sort of fierce emotion, something dark and dangerous, flickered like lightning in Max's eyes.

"No...No, he hasn't done anything like that. But..." Charlie swallowed. Her mouth had suddenly gone dry. "He *is* trying to hurt me in another way."

Max's brow plunged into a deep frown. "What way?"

"Some weeks ago, when we were both attending the same rout, he stole something from me. A notebook containing very personal information that I foolishly kept in my reticule. A...a diary of sorts. And I need to get it back. Otherwise..."

"Charlie, what has he threatened to do?" Max's tone was low and taut, laced with barely restrained anger.

A frisson of fear skittered down Charlie's spine. "If I tell you, Max, promise me you won't do anything rash. Make a to-do. If I'm implicated in another public scandal..." Despite her best efforts not to succumb to the urge to cry, tears pricked at the corners of her eyes. "I can't do that to my family," she whispered. "Not again. Not after I was expelled from Mrs. Rathbone's academy. My father will disown me, I'm certain of it. And Nate and my darling sister-in-law Sophie have just welcomed a son into the world. I cannot disgrace the family name all over again. I just can't."

Max's expression softened. "You've known me for years, Charlie, and I promise I'll be the soul of discretion. You can trust me not to make this worse."

Charlie nodded. "All right..." She inhaled a shaky breath while inwardly praying that she was doing the right thing. "Lord Rochfort is blackmailing me. And if I don't keep paying him the sum he's periodically demanding, he'll sell my notebook and all of my secrets to the *Beau Monde Mirror.*"

~

W*hat?*
A white-hot flare of incandescent fury shot through Max before coalescing into ice-cold certainty:

Rollo Kingsley, Baron Rochfort, would pay dearly for his vile, contemptible, and totally reprehensible treatment of Lady Charlotte Hastings.

He wanted Rochfort's head on a pike and his ballocks lopped off. Not necessarily in that order.

He mustn't have schooled his features sufficiently as Charlie laid a hand on his taut-as-an-iron-bar forearm. "Max, you just assured me you wouldn't make things worse, but I can see by your expression how angry you are."

Max forced himself to relax and give her a reassuring smile. "I won't renege on my promise. You have my word. Now"—he drew a steadying breath to direct his thoughts away from committing justifiable homicide at the Rouge et Noir Club—"tell me why you wanted to risk stealing into Madame Erato's room. Are you certain that Rochfort has this notebook of yours with him tonight?"

Charlie sighed heavily. "Of course I can't be *absolutely* certain, but even if he doesn't, I was hoping a quick rummage through his clothing might yield something else useful, like a housekey. You see, several weeks ago, I attempted to bribe my way into Lord Rochfort's townhouse to conduct a search—"

Max thrust his fingers into his hair. "You did what?"

Charlie's generous mouth dipped into a pout. "You needn't look so horrified. It really was the most logical course of action to take. Because Lord Rochfort is blackmailing me, it made me wonder if he might be short of funds and thus underpaying his staff. But I quickly discovered that his servants are all incredibly loyal. Not one of the maids or footmen I approached could be swayed to let me in."

Max snorted. "Thank God for that." Given the rumors he'd heard, Max suspected it was more likely that Rochfort's staff remained loyal to their master out of fear rather than devotion. Just thinking about Charlie creeping about that perverted bastard's house all by herself made his insides clench.

Charlie grimaced. "Well, in hindsight, it wasn't the

wisest plan. The very next day, Lord Rochfort waylaid me in Berkeley Square, right outside Gunter's Tea Shop." She swallowed and a shadow of fear crossed her face. "To say he was unhappy that I'd been trying to nose about his townhouse would be an understatement. In any case, he told me that he always keeps my notebook on his person so I hadn't a hope in Hades of recovering it. Well, at least until he's satisfied that I've paid him enough. And then to teach me a lesson, he doubled his price to stay his hand."

Christ. Max had to unlock his clenched jaw to mutter, "How much has he demanded to date?"

Charlie worried at her rouged lower lip for a moment. "I'd rather not say. But it's more than I can continue to pay on an ongoing basis. I've gone through all of my pin money, and I've had to pawn some of my jewelry"—tears welled in her golden-brown eyes —"and I also gave Rochfort a pearl and diamond brooch that once belonged to my dearly departed mama. But I can't go on this way with this sword of Damocles constantly hanging over my head." She lifted her chin, and her gaze glittered with determination. "So, I decided to periodically follow Rochfort, and when I discovered that he often visits the Rouge et Noir Club late on a Friday evening, well, it seemed I had no other choice but to do what I'm doing tonight. Despite the danger."

"Charlie, I wish you'd come to me soon—"

Without warning, Charlie threw her arms around his neck. "Someone's coming," she whispered urgently. "Quick. Pretend to ravish me."

Pretend to ravish his best friend's sister? Again? Good God. He already felt guilty as hell for dragging Charlie onto his lap and putting his hands all over her the first time. Of course, he'd been trying to protect her, but he *couldn't* do such an outrageous thing twice. Why, he'd known Charlie since she was a sixteen-year-old girl. A chit straight out of the schoolroom.

Although, she was hardly a girl now...

Charlie's spectacular breasts—breasts that he'd been trying very hard to ignore since he'd first laid eyes on her in her scandalous cyprian's costume—were pressed firmly against him. Soft and warm, like two delectable plump pillows. If he glanced downward... Christ, that cleavage... Looking down was the *last* thing he should do.

His hands slid to her waist, which was also a very bad idea as he encountered a sliver of warm, silken, *naked* flesh between the bottom of her corset and the waistband of her drawers. Moving his hands farther south was obviously out of the question, so he placed his palms on her shoulder blades and rested his cheek upon her head, her thick chestnut curls tickling his jaw. It was a platonic embrace, nothing more.

But then Charlie moved, her belly brushing against his hips, and despite his best efforts to remain unaffected, interest stirred within his trousers. *Bloody hell.* To make matters worse, it was clear that a copulating couple in the nearest bedchamber was approaching the climactic end of their amorous ride together—a headboard repeatedly banged against a wall, and a woman was gasping and frantically crying out the name of the Lord and several Christian saints over and over again.

Think of something else, Maximilian Devereux. Anything... His horses. Yes. Max focused on the Thoroughbred filly he would choose to race at Newmarket in a few weeks' time. And then there was that bay Arabian stallion he was thinking of buying to sire—

Damn and blast. Don't think about mating of any kind, in any context.

No, it was best to think about some other innocuous or even unpleasant topic. Like his mother, Cressida, and her infernal griping about his need to enter the marriage mart and choose a duchess. Someone from her carefully composed list of this Season's most eligible debutantes. The thought of wooing some well-bred, well-connected, perfectly groomed, and accomplished chit should be enough to dampen his ardor.

Only he currently had a sweet-smelling, generously curved, too-brazen-for-her-own-good chit in his arms. The very same chit who'd nearly blown his head off when she'd readily sat upon his lap and placed her lips against his neck a few minutes ago. And now she was practically curling herself around him like an affectionate cat.

Oh, devil take him. Max groaned inwardly. Now he was thinking about pussies.

Whoever was in the hallway was drawing closer. He could hear the heavy, unapologetic thud of booted footsteps and the low rumble of a man's voice. A woman's peal of laughter was followed by a sharp slap and a squeal.

God, he wished they'd both bugger off so he could get Charlie out of this den of iniquity. As the minutes ticked by, the odds that she would be recognized by some male member of the ton who knew her were rapidly increasing.

A door slammed, then Max breathed a sigh of relief. Putting Charlie firmly away from him, he said, "You're sure Rochfort is in Madame Erato's room?"

"I am. My informant—a croupier who works here—is the brother of my lady's maid. I have no reason to distrust his intelligence. Only…" She released a frustrated huff. "Only we've been dillydallying about so much, I'm worried Rochfort will have finished with Madame Erato before we've had a chance to steal inside and go through his clothes."

Max cocked an eyebrow. "You are not to set foot in that room. I'll do it. And I wouldn't worry too much. Rochfort strikes me as the sort of man who likes to get his money's worth. With any luck, he's currently balls deep in—"

Goddamn it. Had he really just said that? What was wrong with him? "My sincerest apologies for being so crude. I meant to say, let's hope he's currently…occupied."

Charlie gave a small laugh, her eyes sparkling with mischief. "I think you sometimes forget that I've grown up in a household full of males. Having four brothers—especially someone like Nate, who used to be a thoroughly wicked rake—does mean that one learns rather a lot about the opposite sex. And that includes inadvertently hearing all kinds of improper things. How else do you think I acquired such 'singular knowledge' about taboo topics not meant for a young lady's ears? So, I wouldn't be too concerned. I promise I won't gasp or faint with horror."

Max nodded. "Right. Good. You stay here. This shouldn't take too long at all."

He was about to step out into the hallway again when Charlie suddenly stood on tiptoe and kissed him on the cheek. Her lips were soft and warm and pliant. "For luck," she whispered. "And thank you."

Max tugged at the cuffs of his evening jacket to keep himself from sweeping Charlie into his arms again. Jesus Christ. Where had all his studied, polite nonchalance gone? He'd been practicing amiable indifference around Lady Charlotte Hastings for years. Which was the fitting and right thing to continue to do, despite the rather bizarre circumstances they currently found themselves in. And then, of course, he'd long ago promised Nate, her brother and his former comrade-in-arms, that he'd never go anywhere near Charlie.

Clearing his throat, Max murmured, "No thanks are necessary, my lady. As Nate's friend, it's my duty to see you safe." And he meant it. This injustice, Charlie's ill-treatment, could not continue. He would end it tonight if he could.

"Yes..." Her shy smile slid away before she added stiffly, "Quite."

Setting aside the uncomfortable notion that he'd un-wittingly hurt Charlie's feelings, Max approached Madame Erato's door. Like Charlie had done earlier, he pressed his ear to the wood paneling, then smiled to himself when he detected the unmistakable sounds of frantic fornicating. *Excellent.*

He tried the handle and was not at all surprised to find that it was locked. However, given Madame Erato had conveniently left the key in the keyhole, breaking in would be child's play. After sliding his linen kerchief beneath the bottom of the door to catch the key on the other side, it was but the work of a moment to poke it out of the lock with his narrow-bladed pen knife. Max winced when there was a faint metallic clatter on the other side of the door, but hopefully Rochfort hadn't noticed.

A swift but gentle pull on the kerchief, and the key was Max's.

Steadfastly battering down the urge to pummel Rochfort into dust as soon as he entered the chamber, Max drew a deep breath and stepped inside. Even though the room was filled with shadows—a pair of candles and a dying fire were the only sources of light—he quickly located the baron in the curtained tester bed, going at it hammer and tongs. And thankfully, the dog's back was to the door. When Madame Erato suddenly flung her head back and screamed, "Oh, my lord, yes! Harder, harder, harder," at the top of her lungs, Max suspected the courtesan wouldn't notice his intrusion either.

A few furtive steps across the room was all it took for Max to reach the chaise longue where Rochfort's discarded clothes lay. Breeches, shirt, waistcoat, evening jacket, and boots in hand, Max beat a hasty retreat, then locked Madame Erato's chamber from the outside.

Charlie rushed over to him, her kohl-rimmed eyes huge in her pale face. "You are simply amazing, Max," she breathed. "I didn't even consider that the door might be locked."

Max shrugged. "You forget I've been here before," he said, then winced at the fact he'd all but admitted that he was familiar with the ins and outs of the brothel. Retreating to the window embrasure, he tossed Madame Erato's room key into one of the potted ferns. "Right, let's check these clothes and leave before Rochfort realizes he's been had."

Charlie muttered something that sounded a lot like "damn, bloody damn" when they ascertained that Rochfort had clearly lied to her. It seemed the baron didn't have her notebook on him at all times. They hadn't discovered a housekey in any of his pockets either.

"Now what do I do?" Charlie murmured in a quivering voice. Slumping against the wall, she looked up at

Max with wide haunted eyes. "I *have* to get that book back."

Upon seeing her devastation, a hot wave of anger burned through Max. Frustrated beyond measure, he roughly yanked open the window and hurled Rochfort's clothes out into the street in disgust. "I'll think of something—" he began, but then there was a shout, and a violent blow was leveled at Madame Erato's door.

"Time to go." Grasping Charlie's hand, Max tugged her into the corridor, and they sped toward the servants' stairs. Within a few minutes, they'd reached the back door to the club.

The doorman, Arthur Fudge, greeted Max with a wide grin. "Your Grace," he crowed. "Wha' a pleasure it is to see you again. It's been a while, ain't it?" He then gave a knowing wink. "An' I see you've chosen a fine little ladybird to keep you company tonight."

Charlie stiffened, and Max only just stopped himself from planting a punch in the bruiser's smirking face. "If you don't mind, I'm in a bit of a hurry, Fudge," he said, gesturing at the door.

"Of course. Sorry, Your Grace." The doorman pulled a thick woolen cloak from a peg and held it out to Charlie. "Don't forget this, miss."

"I'll take it from here." Max draped the garment over Charlie's shoulders. As the door opened and lamplight spilled over her face, he caught the shadow of a grateful smile. No doubt Arthur Fudge had said something entirely lecherous to her earlier on. The slimy bastard.

They hurried down the alleyway and into the street, where a hackney waited.

A young woman threw open the door and called out tearfully, "My lady. Thank God."

"*This* is the carriage you took here?" Max demanded as he eyeballed the coarse-looking hackney driver and the fairly dilapidated cab.

Charlie released a frustrated sigh and rolled her eyes. "Really, Max? After all the things that I've done tonight, you now choose to take me to task about my choice of conveyance? It's not as though I could have used my father's town coach."

"I suppose not," Max grudgingly conceded as he handed Charlie in. After instructing the driver to take them to Berkeley Square, he leapt in after her.

"What? You're coming too?" Her expression was aghast as he took the unoccupied seat opposite her and her maid.

Max cocked an eyebrow. "Really, Lady Charlotte? After all the things that I've done tonight, you choose to take me to task about this? As a gentleman and a family friend, it would be remiss of me *not* to see you home now, wouldn't it?"

Charlie gave a disgruntled harrumph and settled back against the torn leather squabs. "I suppose you're right," she grumbled, then directed her gaze out the window to the fog-shrouded London streets. After a brief pause, she added, "I should be thanking you—and I *am* grateful for your assistance, more than you could know—but I'm also cross with you."

"Cross with me?"

"Yes, and my brother and the rest of your friends too. Indeed, all the so-called gentlemen of the ton. How ironic that I once wanted to enter one of your male dominions to see what all the fuss was about. But now that I have, I rather wish I hadn't. Why on earth you choose to frequent places like the Rouge et Noir Club…" She shook her head and emitted a derisive huff. "I mean, gambling is one thing, but cavorting with those poor women who work there..." She shuddered.

"I assure you, all of the women wish to be there and are paid well. No one is taken advantage of."

"Oh, and you'd know, would you?" Her voice was stiff with indignation as she added, "Enduring Fudge's lewd remarks was enough for me."

"I'm sorry he was disrespectful, Charlie, but you shouldn't have been there in the first place."

"And why were you there? Actually"—she directed her gaze toward the streetscape again—"I don't want to know."

"I was in the mood for a game of Faro or *vingt-et-un.* That's all."

"Of course you were."

The thought that Charlie might think less of him sat uncomfortably in Max's gut. Even so, he attempted to justify his behavior and that of other men of his ilk. "Men have needs, Charlie. And at the risk of sounding defensive, perhaps even mean-spirited, I feel compelled to add that even if I had gone to the Rouge et Noir Club to cavort with one of the club's courtesans, it's really none of your business."

"Clearly."

Long, silent minutes passed in which Max studied Charlie. Despite her current prickly mood and earlier display of bravado at the club, he could see that she was deeply troubled. Her fingers were knotted tightly together in her lap. Her posture was rigid and her face drawn.

The peculiar, completely foreign urge to comfort her by drawing her into his arms was back again, but Max ruthlessly pushed it aside. It was not his place to do that. He reminded himself that deep down he was hard-hearted. Unsentimental. He'd been bred that way, and he couldn't be anything else.

Yes, he must keep his distance, just like he'd always done. But that didn't mean he wouldn't do everything in his power to extricate Charlie from the mess she was in. She was his best friend's sister, and it was the right thing to do.

When the hackney drew to a halt outside Hastings House in Berkeley Square, Max leaned forward and touched Charlie's arm. "Don't fret, my lady. I promise you that I will fix this problem with Rochfort. By this time tomorrow night, I will have retrieved your notebook from his townhouse, and then you can put all of this behind you. Forget it ever happened."

"Thank you, Max," she murmured, then met his gaze directly. "And I'm sorry for my waspish outburst. You're right. How you choose to spend your evenings is none of my business. It's not as though I'm unaware of the different sets of rules governing the behavior of the sexes. I might consider them to be unfair, but railing at you won't change how Society works. And the last thing I want is for there to be any discord between us. If you hadn't been at the Rouge et Noir Club tonight, who knows how things would have turned out?" Her golden-brown eyes glistened suspiciously, but then she offered him a bright smile. "I don't know how I can ever repay you."

"A smile like that is all I need from you," he replied. "And your assurance that if you ever find yourself in trouble again, you will come to me for help straightaway. After all, that's what friends are for."

Her expression grew shuttered, and for the second time that night, Max was struck by the uncomfortable feeling that he'd somehow inadvertently upset Charlie by underscoring their friendship.

"Well, given my propensity for getting myself into scrapes, I'm afraid you might regret such an offer." Her tone was laced with a trace of bitterness as she gathered her cloak about herself. "One doesn't acquire the label of 'disreputable debutante' without good reason. But I'll keep your kind offer in mind. Good night, Your Grace."

Without waiting for him to open the door or hand her down, Charlie exited the hackney coach, then rushed up the stairs of Hastings House with her maid scurrying in her wake.

Bloody hell. Max ordered the driver to take him to Grosvenor Square, then slammed shut the hackney's door. Why were women so damned complicated? And Lady Charlotte Hastings was even more unfathomable than most. Brazen, beguiling, and infuriatingly problematic.

Yes, problematic, and not because of this stolen diary and blackmail business.

He'd just stated they were friends. But deep down he knew that was a lie. Because after tonight's escapade, he could no longer deny that he wanted Charlotte Hastings. The smoldering ember of desire that he'd been valiantly trying to smother for so long had suddenly, and most inconveniently, flickered to life.

Damn it.

Somehow, he was going to have to snuff out this lustful spark for Charlie, and quickly. If Nate ever found out that he, Maximilian Devereux, the Duke of Exmoor, was harboring impure thoughts about his sister, he would be a dead man.

CHAPTER 3

The Season is fast approaching, and if you're an aspiring debutante, are your preparations well in hand? Competition to catch oneself an eligible gentleman of means is always fierce, and the wise debutante always plans ahead to ensure she is off to a good start that will put her ahead of the field.
The Beau Monde Mirror: The Essential Style & Etiquette Guide

Hastings House, Berkeley Square, Mayfair
March 27, 1819

"Now, there's no need to look quite so reproachful, Peridot," remarked Charlie as her tortoiseshell cat watched her remove the lid from a box of Gunter's marzipan-coated sweetmeats. "I know it's Lent, so I'm only going to have one."

She chose a tiny cake topped with a glacé cherry and popped it into her mouth. As the rich flavors of butter, almonds, and cherry brandy flowed across her tongue, she almost moaned with delight. Of course, such treats were but a temporary antidote to the ever-present anxiety buzzing through her veins—especially tonight, given her thoughts kept straying to Max and what he might be doing right now. And whether he would be successful in his quest to retrieve her damning notebook.

Hating that she felt so powerless, Charlie focused on the box of sweetmeats again. "All right, Peridot, I'll have two at the most." She licked her sticky fingers and perused the delectable array. "Definitely not more than three."

She was just about to choose her fourth treat when a knock at her sitting room door made her start with guilt. After replacing the lid, she hastily pushed the box beneath a silk cushion on the settee between her and Peridot. Ignoring her cat's disgruntled frown, Charlie called, "Come in."

It was her father.

"Well, aren't you complete to a shade this evening, Lord Westhampton?" observed Charlie as she took in his rather dapper evening attire which included a paisley satin waistcoat in rich shades of crimson and cobalt blue. "If I didn't know you better, Papa, I'd wonder if you were trying to impress someone."

Her father made a pretense of polishing his monocle on the sleeve of his smartly tailored Savile Row jacket, perhaps to hide the dark flush stealing across his cheeks. "Do you think it will invite too much comment?" he asked. "Wearing such a bright waistcoat rather than something a little more sedate? It *is* Lent..."

Ah, so he *was* avoiding the topic of whether he did indeed wish to impress someone. *Interesting.* Rising to her feet, Charlie gave a small snort. "I'm sure you can get away with it. I would be surprised if your sartorial choices became the subject of the latest on-dit." Although, *who* the very eligible Earl of Westhampton was accompanying to the theater tonight might become fodder for newspapers like the *Beau Monde Mirror* and the ton's insatiable gossipmongers.

Her father emitted a short chuckle. "I suppose you're right." After tucking his pristinely polished monocle away, he focused his attention on her. His brow creased with a frown as he noted her rather disheveled appearance: her undressed hair, her crushed wrapper, and the plain muslin morning gown that she had in fact been wearing since she'd breakfasted with him. "Are you sure you won't change your mind and come to Drury Lane with me, Charlotte?" he asked. "This evening's concert is a celebration of Handel's hymns. Viscount Wyatt, his wife, and their daughter, Lady Tilbury, are sharing my box."

Ah, so the lovely young widow, Eleanor, Lady Tilbury, was the woman who'd snared her father's interest at long last. Charlie was nothing but pleased for her father. He'd been a widower for almost sixteen years now, and it was about time he began to court again. He deserved to find happiness. "I'm quite sure, Papa," she said, making an effort to smile. "Besides, I'll take far too long to get ready and only make you late." Even though she would very much like to make the acquaintance of Lady Tilbury— who by all accounts was intelligent, agreeable, and the epitome of refinement—her mind would be elsewhere.

"Hmm." Her father's frown deepened. "Don't think I haven't noticed how you've been closeting yourself away since your aunt Tabitha left Town. I think a change of scenery will do you good."

Charlie batted away his observation with a flick of her wrist. "I'm perfectly fine, Papa," she lied, feigning a nonchalance she certainly didn't feel. "And not lonely at all, if that's what you are concerned about. Indeed, tomorrow I plan on spending a good deal of the afternoon with Nate and Sophie, and darling baby Thomas. Besides, you know Handel's oratorios are not really my cup of tea. I'd be sure to fall asleep and snore during the performance." She affected a little laugh. "Now *that* would invite comment and make the papers. Aside from that, I'm certain Lord and Lady Wyatt and their daughter would be far from impressed."

Her father gave a heavy sigh of resignation. "Very well, my dear girl. If you're set on staying home, so be it." He gave a wink, then nodded at the settee. "Although I would appreciate it if you saved me a sweetmeat or two. I think I'd rather fancy one with a glass of port when I return."

Oh, darn and drat, and double damn. Peridot had shifted, and the cushion concealing the box from Gunter's had fallen down. Her face flaming with mortification, all Charlie could do was acquiesce. "Of course, Papa," she murmured. "I'll leave the box on your library desk."

After her sitting room door swung shut behind her father, Charlie flopped back onto the settee and groaned. Her appetite had well and truly fled now.

She must be the worst daughter in London, if not all of Christendom. Not only was she devouring decadent treats during Lent, she was also telling her father bald-faced lies.

Because truth to tell, she *was* lonely. Aunt Tabitha had departed over a month ago to help care for her dear friend, Lady Kilbride; they were currently taking the waters in Bath, and Charlie wasn't sure when her aunt would return.

Two of her closest friends whom she'd bonded with during her time at Mrs. Rathbone's Academy for Young Ladies of Good Character—Arabella and Olivia—were also absent from Town. Arabella was presently busy in Edinburgh establishing an orphanage with the help of her besotted husband, Lord Langdale, and his mother, Caroline. And Olivia, who was now happily married to the deliciously gruff marquess, Lord Sleat, was currently far away on the Isle of Skye.

Of course, her own dear sister-in-law, Sophie, was nearby. She and Nate had taken up residence in a grand townhouse in Park Lane just before Christmastide. But while Charlie adored playing the doting aunt—Thomas had made his entrance into the world only a few short weeks ago—she didn't wish to encroach *too* much. After all, her brother and Sophie were still very much newlyweds. And if she were honest with herself, seeing them together and so much in love was a bittersweet experience. It made her even more aware of the fact that for the most part, she was viewed as an unsuitable match by most of the ton's ranks. Over the last four years, the number of times she'd been whispered about, sniggered at, snubbed, and worse besides... Charlie shuddered. She'd truly lost count.

Yes, despite the elevated position of her father, aunt,

brother, and friends, it seemed her ruined reputation followed her about like her own personal dark cloud of shame, forever casting her in dismal shadow. A target for the most sanctimonious, unkindest members of "polite" society.

Unmarriageable. Disreputable. These were the less vicious barbs aimed her way.

Fast. Loose. Hoyden. Slut. She'd heard those words too, and often from the tongues of supposed "gentlemen" when she'd refused their lewd propositions in quiet corridors and shadowed corners.

To make matters worse, she'd believed Lord Rochfort was different.

What a fool she'd been to be gulled by his false flattery and easy smiles. His kisses and whispered words of praise.

But then the predator had struck. And she still had no idea why he'd chosen her as a victim.

Charlie's eyes burned, and she dashed an angry teardrop away from her cheek with impatient fingers. If only she could brush all of her horrid memories and cares away so easily. While she missed Aunt Tabitha and spending time with her dearest friends, it was also a relief that she didn't have to constantly pretend that nothing was amiss in her world.

But it most certainly was.

After depositing the box of sweetmeats on her father's library desk and spending the next hour fruitlessly searching the shelves for a book to capture her attention, Charlie returned to her sitting room empty-handed. A current of dread still hummed through her veins, even though she'd drunk a nip of her father's brandy.

As she slumped onto the settee again, her gaze strayed to the mantel clock. It was almost half past nine. She suspected Max wouldn't want to sneak into Lord Rochfort's townhouse *too* early. Even if the baron was at one of his clubs or elsewhere, there would be far too many servants about. But Max wouldn't want to conduct his search when it was too late either, because Lord Rochfort might be home.

Gah! Charlie thumped a fist into the silk cushion, earning another reproving look from Peridot.

"Sorry, puss," she murmured and patted the cat's silky head. Sitting around fretting about what Max may or may not be doing right at this moment was giving her heart palpitations.

And then another, altogether disquieting thought filtered through the fog of her anxiety. Max had no clue at all what her notebook looked like. Its size, the type of cover. What, if anything, was printed on the outside. How could he possibly conduct a swift search if he had no idea what he was actually searching for?

And if he *did* happen to find it, well, he would undoubtedly open it up to check that it was indeed her notebook. He'd peruse the contents...

Oh, God.

Charlie flew across the room to the bellpull to summon Molly.

∾

Exmoor House, Grosvenor Square, Mayfair

Little more than half an hour later, Charlie stood on the front doorstep of Exmoor House.

As to whether Max was in, Charlie couldn't be certain. All the curtains were drawn, but slivers of light spilled out from between the chinks in the heavy fabric. Thank goodness he lived alone. His mother, Cressida, the formidable Dowager Duchess of Exmoor, resided in nearby Curzon Street with Max's widowed sister-in-law, Diana. At least she would only have to contend with Max's perennially flustered but amiable butler, Chiffley, when she summoned the courage to knock on the door.

One of Hastings House's footmen—a strapping young man named Edwards—waited on the pavement below, shifting nervously from foot to foot. She beckoned him closer. "Once I'm inside, you may go back to Berkeley Square," she instructed.

Edwards frowned. "Of course, my lady... Only, I'd be

happy to wait until you are ready to return to Hastings House. I know it's only a ten-minute walk, but it's dark and rather late…" He trailed off uncertainly, his gaze skipping away into the shadows.

Ordinarily, Charlie would have been irked by a servant questioning her orders, but she realized Edwards was simply motivated by concern for her safety.

"No, that won't be necessary." Her tone was kind but firm. Whatever the outcome tonight, Max would provide her with a suitable escort to see her home.

As Charlie expected, Chiffley failed to contain his surprise when he discovered who was visiting at such a late hour.

"Lady Charlotte," he exclaimed, his bristle-brush eyebrows darting up toward his receding hairline. "At the risk of overstepping, and if you don't mind me asking, is everything all right?" His gaze darted behind her to where Edwards waited before returning to her face. "His Grace had not informed me that he was expecting any calls this evening."

Irregular calls late at night from single young women was what he really meant.

"Yes, I do apologize for making an unscheduled visit," said Charlie. "And to answer your first question, nothing's wrong." Of course, that was a lie, but she wasn't about to explain herself to Max's butler. No doubt the man was wondering why she hadn't a suitable chaperone. On the few occasions she'd been a dinner guest at Exmoor House, her aunt Tabitha, Nate, and her father had accompanied her.

Stepping into the elegant entry hall that was a study in marble, polished wood, and gleaming brass, she slid back the hood of her cloak. "However, I do need to speak with His Grace—if he's at home, of course. And if he isn't home"—she lifted her chin, hoping a show of confidence would get her what she wanted—"I'll wait."

"Oh…" Chiffley's spiky brows plunged downward. "I see." He glanced in Edwards's direction again, but the young man had disappeared into the night. "Harvey here"—he nodded at a nearby footman—"will take your cloak, my lady. And then if you would care to wait in the front parlor"—he gestured to an oak door to the right of the entry hall—"I can send one of the maids along with a pot of tea if you like."

Charlie forced herself to tamp down her impatience. Tea and the chaperonage of a chambermaid would not do at all. Not when her whole future hung in the balance. "So, I take it the duke *is* at home?" she asked as she shrugged off her cloak and handed it to the waiting footman.

Chiffley's Adam's apple bobbed above his perfectly tied neckcloth. "Ah, I would have to check, my lady…"

The butler was clearly lying. If Max wasn't at home, the servant would have told her straightaway. She narrowed her eyes. "He's in the library, isn't he?" With determined strides, she started across the black and white parquetry floor toward the hall leading to the back of the house. "Or his private study?"

Charlie swore she heard Chiffley groan before he muttered, "In the library, my lady. I shall send your tea there."

"Thank you," Charlie called over her shoulder as she hastened down the hall. Although she doubted she'd drink it. She was sure Max would at least have sherry at hand, even if he was reluctant to serve her brandy.

∼

As Max leaned back in his favorite leather wingchair, he yawned and scrubbed a hand over the bristles on his jaw. Good Lord, he was tired. After last night's escapade at the Rouge et Noir Club, a ride through Hyde Park this morning, several bouts of bare-knuckle boxing at Gentleman Jackson's, followed by a prolonged session at his club to try and discreetly gather intelligence on Rochfort, he was spent.

But he'd promised Charlie he'd recover her notebook, and he wouldn't let her down. Because if he did, God only knew what further trouble she'd get herself into.

And then of course, he so very badly wanted to trounce Rochfort.

He sipped his cognac and stretched his booted toes toward the fire's leaping flames, idly studying the play of light across the polished black leather. According to the oak longcase clock in the corner, it was just after ten o'clock, which meant he'd best set out for Rochfort's townhouse in Bedford Square within the hour. All going well, he'd have Charlie's dashed notebook back to her by midnight.

Not for the first time, he wondered what on earth she'd written that was so damned incriminating. Not that it was any of his business, of course. But there must be something scandalous within its pages, otherwise Rochfort wouldn't have anything to hold over Charlie's head.

Charlie's observation the night before floated into his mind. Yes, she did indeed have a singular propensity for getting herself into scrapes.

She was definitely trouble...and in more ways than one.

A knock at the door had him straightening in his seat and frowning. He'd instructed Chiffley that he wasn't to be disturbed tonight unless the matter was urgent. "Yes?" he called. "What is it?"

When the door opened to reveal Lady Charlotte Hastings, he nearly dropped his cognac.

"Charlie." Discarding his drink, he sprang to his feet. "Is everything all right?"

A brittle laugh escaped her. "Aside from the deep pickle I'm currently in, yes," she said as she closed the door, then joined him at the hearthside. "Although, I was rather hoping that you had already managed to retrieve my notebook and I'd been unpickled, so to speak. Now wouldn't that be wonderful?"

Max winced as guilt pinched. "I wish I did have good news for you. But no, not yet."

"Considering you hadn't sent word, I suspected as much." She removed her gloves with a few impatient tugs, then deposited herself in the wingchair opposite his. "To be perfectly frank with you, sitting around Hastings House, not knowing what is going on, waiting to hear from you—it's pure torture. In any case, I do hope you can forgive me for invading your bachelor's sanctum at such a late hour."

Max reclaimed his seat. "Of course. I can appreciate how difficult this situation is for you. Although"—his voice held a gruff edge as he added—"I hope to God you didn't make your way here on your own."

She gave a small snort. "I'm not a complete widgeon. A footman escorted me. And my father is at the theater, so you don't need to worry that I'll be missed at home. Indeed, no one of consequence knows I'm here at all." She eyed his brandy on the occasional table beside his chair. "Chiffley is sending a maid with a tea tray—I suspect he's concerned for my reputation and will ask her to stay and act as chaperone—but might I have one of those instead?"

Max arched an eyebrow. "It's cognac. Are you sure?"

She rolled her eyes. "Yes, I'm sure. I'm not a child, Max. I know what I like." Her shoulders dropped with a sigh. "I'm sorry. I shouldn't be so shrewish. I'm just…I'm so tired of being on tenterhooks. Over time, it tends to wear one down."

"Perfectly understandable," Max said gently. "And no offense taken." He crossed to the sideboard where he kept a tray of spirits and poured a measure of cognac into a cut-crystal tumbler. "Actually, I'm surprised Chiffley let you in at all," he observed over his shoulder. "He's become quite protective of me lately. A veritable guard dog."

Charlie gave a huff of laughter. "Protective? Of you, the powerful Duke of Exmoor? The man with five sprawling estates, including a castle in Devonshire and heaven knows how many properties in London? A distinguished former officer in Wellington's army who's rumored to be richer than Croesus?"

"As strange as it may sound, yes." Max returned to the fireside with her drink. As he passed her the tumbler and his bare fingers inadvertently brushed hers, he tried to ignore the disconcerting reaction of his body. The tingle of his flesh and the surge of heat in his veins. He might be a battle-hardened duke with untold property, wealth, and influence, but right now, he felt quite inexplicably randy like a callow schoolboy. Giving himself a silent rebuke, he resumed his seat. "Actually, I think you'll find the whole situation rather amusing."

"Oh, do tell." Charlie's eyes gleamed with expectation as she regarded him over the rim of her glass. "It will take my mind off my own trials and tribulations."

Max retrieved his own cognac. "I don't know if you've heard any of the latest on-dits about Town, but word has recently got out that my mother is putting pressure on me to take a bride by the end of this year's Season."

"And is she?"

Max grimaced. "She's recently compiled a list of eligible debutantes. Not that I'm interested in becoming leg-shackled. Not for another five years at the very least. In any event, the result of all this gossip doing the rounds is that young women are beginning to 'seek me out,' shall we say? Vie for my attention. And it's all rather disconcerting."

Charlie laughed. "So, marriage-minded young women are throwing themselves at you, are they? Oh, you poor, poor thing."

"It's dashed dangerous, that's what it is," said Max. "And yes, they are quite literally throwing themselves at me on occasion. Why, only this morning when I was riding through Hyde Park, a woman quite recklessly ran onto Rotten Row, waving her arms at me, urging me to help her find her lost hound. But then her leashed dog charged out from a nearby copse, dragging her footman along behind him. At first I thought the footman had simply located the runaway animal, only he began to apologize to his mistress that the dog wouldn't stay and was impossible to hold. The young woman blushed bright red and thrust her card at me, but as I rode away, she let loose a tirade of abuse at the footman, accusing him of ruining everything."

"Goodness," said Charlie, mirth still dancing in her eyes. "That does seem a tad dangerous. And desperate. I won't ask who it was."

"But it gets worse." Max pointed at his desk. "See that pile of correspondence on the end? In the past week, I've received an inordinate number of perfume-drenched poems and letters from 'secret admirers'. One of the missives even had a silk ribbon garter pinned to it, and another contained a lock of hair. And this evening, while I was out at my club, my valet discovered a young woman in the lime tree outside my bedroom window. Whether she hoped to gain entrance to my room or just wished to spy on me, I have no idea. In all honesty, I feel like I have a huge target painted on my back at the moment. I swear the battlefield of Waterloo was less fraught with danger."

A sad smile curved Charlie's mouth. "Oh, Max. I do sympathize. I do. I recall last year's Season when Nate was desperately trying to avoid the Duke of Stafford's daughter, Lady Penelope, because my father had suggested that they might make a suitable match."

Max sighed. "I believe she's at the top of my mother's list."

Charlie shuddered. "Perish the thought. She's really not as perfect as everyone claims. Well, at least that's been my experience. But that's a story for another day."

She took another sip of her cognac, and Max noted that she barely grimaced as she swallowed the fiery liquor. When she saw that he was watching her, her fulsome lips twitched with a wry smile. "Just add my taste for strong spirits to the list of 'unladylike habits of the far-from-perfect Lady Charlotte Hastings'."

Concern for Charlie softened Max's tone. "I cannot even begin to imagine how difficult the last few weeks have been for you. And I would be a hypocrite for passing judgment on you given my own fondness for brandy." He raised his own glass to make a point, then promptly drained it.

"So…" Charlie ventured after a quiet pause. "To return to the reason for my impromptu visit… When do you plan on breaking into Lord Rochfort's house? I take it you've been waiting for a suitably late hour."

"Yes," Max replied. "I intend to set out shortly. Word about White's is that Rochfort intends to attend the cock fights at a public house at St. Andrews Hill before moving on to Birchmore House, a notorious brothel in Soho Square. That should keep him busy until the wee small hours. After his household servants retire for the night—and I imagine that will be quite soon—I'll be able to break in and search safely without any interruption."

"I'm grateful I caught you, then." Charlie's gaze met his. "You see, it occurred to me that you have no idea at all what you are looking for. I'm sure Lord Rochfort has simply piles and piles of ledgers and journals and notebooks scattered about his house. You could be rummaging through his things for hours."

Max gave a huff. She was right, of course. And he was annoyed that he hadn't thought of that himself. He prided himself on formulating thorough, precise plans, and he couldn't fathom why he'd suddenly turned into such a dunderhead. Unless his concern for Charlie had addled his thinking... Now *that* was something he really didn't want to think about. Not wishing to openly acknowledge his unforgivable oversight, he said, "You could have sent me a note with a description."

"True," she acknowledged with an incline of her head. "But I wasn't sure if you'd still be home, and as I said earlier, sitting about and waiting for news is far too agonizing for words. Aside from that"—she sat up straighter, and there was a determined glint in her eye as she continued—"I want to come with you. To help."

Horror blasted through Max. "No. Absolutely not." He slammed his open hand down on the table. "It's far too dangerous. I won't have it."

Undeterred, she edged farther forward on her seat until her knees almost bumped against his. "Many hands make light work. Two heads are better than one. The more the merrier..." She arched a brow. "I could go on, but I think you gather my meaning."

Max ground his back teeth together. Damn it. She *did* have a point. Nevertheless, ingrained chivalry and the fear Nate would have his guts for garters if he ever found out about all of this made him say, "You can argue your case all night, Charlie. I won't be swayed."

"Oh…" A sigh shivered out of her and her gaze dropped to her glass of cognac. "Very well," she murmured. "I suppose you're right." Her bottom lip trembled and a tear slipped from beneath the thick sweep of her lowered lashes.

Oh, bloody, blazing hell. He'd made Charlie cry, and the sight tore into his chest like the sharp thrust of a bayonet. In fact, he'd never seen her so defeated and miserable before.

In all the years he'd known her, Lady Charlotte Hastings—despite all the slings and arrows hurled her way—was never ever anything *but* vibrant and bold and cheerful.

He couldn't bear to see her like this. He spent a moment evaluating the risks versus the benefits of each plan. Calculating the odds of success versus failure. If Rochfort came home, if his servants discovered both of them… God, what an utter disaster it would be. But Charlie's arguments were also sound; the sooner they were in and out of the baron's townhouse, the better.

Max released a deep sigh. At least she was suitably dressed for the occasion in a dark green gown with some kind of black military-style frogging across the bodice. Sensible footwear of black half-boots. Black kid gloves. Even her wild chestnut curls were suitably restrained for once.

Despite his bone-deep reservations, he relented. "All right," he said, his voice rough with feelings he didn't wish to examine. "You can accompany me to Rochfort's residence. But"—he adopted his most ducal expression—"you must do everything I say, no questions asked. At once. Do I make myself clear?"

Charlie nodded, her eyes now alight with eagerness rather than tears. "Of course, Max. Absolutely. We'll be in and out in a jiffy, and then this will all be over."

CHAPTER 4

Was there a commotion in Bedford Square last
night?
There have been unconfirmed reports of shouts,
screams, and shadowy figures in and around one
of London's most prestigious addresses. One
wonders what went on...
The Beau Monde Mirror: The Society Page

Bedford Square, London

"My goodness, Max, I had no idea you were so adept
at breaking into houses," whispered Charlie as
she huddled against the wall by the servants' entrance of
Lord Rochfort's residence. Given the deep shadows, she
couldn't discern a great deal, but she could definitely hear
faint metallic scraping sounds as Max worked at un-
picking the lock. "Wherever did you acquire such skills?"

Max, who was squatting on the ground, emitted a
quiet chuckle. "I'd rather not say," he murmured. "You
might think ill of me if I confess my secrets. Chalk it up
to a misspent youth."

"I very much doubt that I would ever think ill of you."
Charlie pushed back the hood of her cloak and leaned
down, squinting at what Max was doing, wishing she
could see more. In the wash of moonlight filtering
through the branches of a nearby plane tree, his bare

hands were as pale as an apparition's, the movement of his long fingers controlled and delicate. "Indeed, I'm sure your misspent youth couldn't be any worse than mine, given my expulsion from Mrs. Rathbone's academy. As far as I'm aware, you were never expelled from Eton or Oxford."

"True, but I'm certainly not a saint. And you know as well as I that many of my scandalous exploits have appeared in gossip columns far and wide." Max jiggled and twisted his tools—a thin-bladed penknife and lockpick. "Talking of scandalous exploits and secrets, you still haven't given me a description of this troublesome notebook of yours."

Charlie sighed. "For a troublesome notebook, it's quite small, actually. Palm-sized and easy to fit into a reticule. And the cover is a lovely deep crimson leather with an embossed gold filigree pattern around the edges. My aunt Tabitha gave it to me on Saint Valentine's Day— a parting gift before she left for Bath a few days later. She wrote a sweet little farewell note to me on the endpaper at the front of the book. If Lord Rochfort takes it to some horrid newspaper…" Charlie shuddered. "There's no mistaking who it belongs to."

There was an encouraging click—the sound of the lock tumbling—then Max rose to his feet. He tucked his knife and lockpick into a pocket of his coat, then leaned forward to gently grasp her elbow. "Well, very soon it will be safely back in your hands," he murmured, his warm breath softly brushing against her ear. "Are you ready, my dear Lady Charlotte?"

Charlie's pulse began to race, and it wasn't just because she was about to do something both illegal and dangerous. Even though Max's nearness was playing havoc with her senses, she shouldn't misinterpret his attempt to reassure her as a display of affection or any indication that he wanted her at all. "Yes," she whispered back. "I am."

"Good." Max turned the handle, and the door swung open on silent hinges. "Stay close to me," he said. "We'll try Rochfort's library first. Fingers crossed it's easy to locate."

They stepped into a barely lit corridor. All was silent save for the sound of Charlie's quickened breathing and the furious pounding of her heart. The rustle of her skirts and the slight creaking of the floorboards beneath their feet as they crept toward a darkened stairwell at the very end. The only door that was ajar revealed a kitchen—a dull glow emanated from the banked fire—but nothing and no one stirred except a tabby cat who blinked at them sleepily from the hearthrug.

"Let's hope the servants are all abed," whispered Max as they began to climb the stairs to the next floor. "But just to be safe, we'll take extra care near the front door in case there is a footman still on duty."

"Eminently sensible," agreed Charlie, picking up her wool skirts so she wouldn't trip.

When they reached a closed door at the top of the staircase, Charlie's heart was in her mouth, and it felt like a swarm of butterflies had taken up residence in her belly. She prayed Lord Rochfort was indeed out. She didn't wish to see the man ever again, let alone be caught in the act of breaking and entering his house.

Max paused on the landing and pressed his ear to the door's wooden panels before cautiously opening it a fraction. "All clear," he murmured before stepping into the corridor and beckoning. The light of a nearby wall sconce glanced off his artfully ruffled dark blond hair. There was no fear in his eyes, and as his wide mouth tilted into a slight smile, Charlie was oddly reassured that everything would be all right.

Shadowing Max, they padded swiftly down the Turkish runner in the center of the hall, checking doors as they went. Several were locked; one led into a darkened room containing a billiard table, and then they came upon a high-ceilinged entry hall. With a brisk hand gesture and a jerk of his chin, Max silently urged Charlie to stay behind him before he peered around the veined marble column flanking the arched doorway.

Turning back, he whispered, "There's no night footman," and Charlie released the breath she'd been holding.

Standing on tiptoe to peek over Max's wide shoulder, she surveyed the entry hall too. The candles in the chandelier burnt low, but there was sufficient light to ascertain that there were two sets of grand double doors—a pair either side of the central marble staircase—that they would need to try.

"So, my lady," murmured Max, "Where should we look first?"

"I vote we try the doors closest to—" Charlie broke off as the sound of footsteps on creaking floorboards directly above their heads penetrated the quiet night.

Max cursed beneath his breath. Before Charlie could blink, he'd tugged her behind a nearby set of heavy velvet curtains concealing a window embrasure. One strong arm circled her waist, and he pressed a long finger to her lips. Charlie nodded to indicate she understood the need to be absolutely silent and stared into his deep blue eyes. A silvery shaft of moonlight caressed the strong planes along one side of his too handsome face, and just like the night before at the brothel, she was transfixed. By the shape of his perfectly chiseled lips; the line of his nose and his high-cut cheekbones; the sharp angles of his square jaw and the small cleft in his strong chin; his intoxicating masculine scent. She forgot where she was and how much danger she and Max were in. For the space of several heartbeats, she allowed herself to pretend that this noble, charismatic, powerful man was hers. That they weren't merely friends or temporary partners in crime, but lovers.

No, more than just lovers. That they *loved* each other. Truly. Passionately. Deeply. That Max wanted her—despite her myriad faults and tainted reputation—for his wife. His duchess forevermore.

Max stared back, his gaze intent. Heavy and somehow hot. And when his attention slid to her mouth where his finger still rested, burning the tender flesh of her slightly parted lips, Charlie's breath caught in her chest.

Kiss me. Please kiss me. His thumb brushed a barely-there caress over her bottom lip, and without conscious thought, her gloved fingers curled into the lapels of his coat.

How long had she dreamed of a romantic encounter just like this? Max holding her close in his arms, looking at her as though he wanted her the way she wanted him. That he ached for her and her alone. That if he didn't kiss her right now, this minute, he might die—

The sound of a door snicking open broke the spell. And then a woman spoke, her harsh whisper close by. "Hurry, Nancy," she urged. "We don't want Mrs. Phipps to notice wha' we're up to."

"All right, all right, Ruth. The 'ot chocolate ain't going anywhere. And Phipps is snoring 'er head off. How else do you fink I got the key to the pantry? Let's just 'ope the master don't come back early."

Light, rushing footfalls approached then passed by their hidey-hole, and Charlie let out a shaky exhale. Relief they were safe and disappointment she and Max's intimate moment had been interrupted welled inside her in equal measure.

"It sounds like Ruth and Nancy are headed to the kitchen." Max's expression was shuttered, his manner all business again as he released her from his embrace. "We'd best find the library before they return."

"Agreed."

The closest set of double doors opened onto an elegantly appointed drawing room. The second set on the opposite side of the entry hall led to the library.

Thank God. Charlie offered up a prayer to heaven as Max quietly shut the oak-paneled doors behind them.

The banked fire offered little light, so Max swiftly lit a pair of candles while Charlie crossed to the ornately carved desk on the opposite side of the room.

"One thing that strikes me as odd, is that for a man who is blackmailing me for money, Lord Rochfort doesn't *seem* short of funds," remarked Charlie as she began to sort through a pile of books on one edge of the leather blotter. "I mean, his townhouse and all its furnishings"—she gestured at the enormous mahogany desk with its bronze lion's paw feet and the preponderance of gilt Egyptian-style ornamentation and artifacts scattered about the room—"well, they're very fine indeed. We could be in Hastings House."

"Yes." Max approached with the candles and placed them on opposite corners of the desk. "It is odd. I haven't heard any rumors that Rochfort is in debt."

"My notebook's not here." Charlie tried but failed to stop a note of panic creeping into her voice as she pushed the pile of books away. The only other items on the desk were an elaborate brass inkwell set, a jeweled snuff box that resembled a scarab, a letter opener with a vicious-looking dog's head—presumably Anubis—at the end of the handle, and a neat stack of papers. Her gaze traveled over the cabinets and towering bookcases lining the walls and Lord Rochfort's impressive collection of leather-bound tomes. If he'd hidden her notebook somewhere on the shelves—Charlie swallowed hard—she and Max would never find it. Not before Rochfort returned home, anyway.

Max moved behind the desk, flicked out his coattails, and claimed the baron's chair as if he owned it. "Fear not," he said as he began to try all the drawers. Then he huffed out an exasperated sigh. "Damn it. They're all locked. But not for long."

Flashing a grin at Charlie, he seized the letter opener, then wedged the slim blade between the edge of an upper drawer and the top of the desk. A quick wiggle, a thrust, and a twist, and there was a click.

Charlie joined him as he pulled open the drawer. A swift rummage revealed nothing but papers, a penknife, sealing wax, and a few pencils.

"Blast," muttered Charlie. According to the Boulle mantel clock, it was almost half past eleven. "I do hope your intelligence about Rochfort's movements tonight is correct, because this search is going to take a lot longer than I thought."

"There are still eight drawers to go," said Max as he began to lever the next one open. "Perhaps you could look through the shelves in one of the glass-fronted bookcases by the fireplace."

Charlie lit a branch of candles on the mantelpiece and set to work, carefully checking the spine of every volume upon each shelf. But no palm-sized notebooks covered in crimson leather leapt out at her. With each passing moment, her anxiety kicked up a notch.

And then she heard Max release a low whistle. Charlie spun around, hope flaring inside her chest. "Have you found it?"

"I'm sorry, no," said Max, his tone grave. "But I've discovered something else of interest." His gaze was riveted to the piece of parchment he was in the process of unrolling. A document, perhaps.

Curiosity pricking, Charlie approached the desk. "What is it?"

"It's a deed." A muscle twitched in Max's lean jaw. "To a townhouse not far from here. In Bloomsbury Square."

Charlie frowned. That didn't sound terribly interesting, but Max's reaction to his find certainly was. She'd never seen such a grim expression upon his face. She propped her hip upon one corner of the desk and folded her arms. "I suspect there's some sort of story associated with this property, then?"

"Yes." The light in Max's eyes was hard and unflinching as his gaze met hers across the desk. "It belonged to a young woman—and I hope you'll forgive me for being indelicate—who was once a paramour of our mutual friend, Hamish."

"Euphemia Harrington," murmured Charlie. Olivia, Hamish's new wife, had told Charlie a little about her last year. "She's the mother of Hamish's former ward, Tilda, isn't she? And I believe she's now employed at one of your country homes?"

"Yes. As a housekeeper at Lynton Grange in north Devon. But what you *might* not know is that the reason Mia Harrington felt compelled to give up Tilda was that a man had threatened to harm her young daughter if she didn't sign her townhouse over to him, and indeed everything else she owned. The poor woman was so terrified of this man, she would not divulge his identity to Hamish or myself. But little Tilda had informed your friend Olivia that her mama referred to this blackguard as 'the baron.'"

"Oh my God," breathed Charlie as horror lanced through her. "So, do you believe this despicable baron character is Lord Rochfort?"

"Based on the fact he has the deed to Mia's townhouse in his possession, it would seem so."

"Oh." Charlie felt the blood drain from her face, and her knees were suddenly as insubstantial as water. "Oh. That's… Oh, he's vile. I wish I'd known all this last month when—"

Max's gaze sharpened. "When what? What did Rochfort do to you, Charlie?"

Charlie swallowed. "Nothing I haven't already told you."

"Are you sure?"

Heat scalded her cheeks. "Yes," she lied.

Max gave a humph. "Now, why don't I believe you? I think you'd best tell me the unvarnished truth, Lady Charlotte Hastings."

Charlie sighed. "I don't think we have time for the unabridged version. If we could just find my notebook, this will all go away."

Max crossed his arms over his chest. "The abridged version will do. I want to know exactly what I'm dealing with here. As your brother's friend—and yours—I deserve nothing less."

Ugh. Why did he have to keep reminding her that they were nothing more than friends? Charlie shot him a mulish look. "Very well. Before my aunt Tabitha departed for Bath, she persuaded me to attend a Saint Valentine's masque at the Earl and Countess of Penrith's residence. She was convinced it would be good for my spirits—and it was true they had been flagging a little, given Olivia and Arabella were far away, and Sophie had just entered confinement."

Max frowned. "I'm sorry, Charlie. I had no idea you'd been so lonely."

She waved his comment away, determined to put on a brave face. The last thing she wanted was Max's pity. "Really, it's neither here nor there. In any case, I attended the masque with my aunt, and the evening was progressing rather swimmingly." Another lie, but Max wasn't to know that. It was too humiliating to admit that for most of the evening, she'd been a wallflower. And even though she'd worn a domino mask, anyone who was anyone in the ton recognized the disreputable Lady Charlotte Hastings and kept well away from her. Unless they wanted to have a sly little dig at her. Or proposition her. Which was nothing out of the ordinary.

"However, at one particular point, I realized I was quite tired. Too much dancing, I suppose." She feigned a little laugh. "In any case, I repaired to my hosts' library, and as I rested my feet"—another lie; her feet hadn't been sore at all—"I decided to take the opportunity to record some of my thoughts in my brand new notebook. Aunt Tabitha had actually presented it to me in the carriage on the way to Penrith House, and I was just itching to use it." This part wasn't a lie, at least. "But then I discovered I wasn't alone."

"Go on," said Max. His tone was gentle, even if the light in his eyes was hard.

"Lord Rochfort had been sitting in a shadowy corner of the library drinking Lord Penrith's cognac. I only became aware he was there when he went to refill his glass. Of course, I was startled at first, but then we struck up a conversation"—she omitted the part where she'd boldly asked for a glass of cognac too—"and then..." Willing herself not to blush, she met Max's gaze. "Rochfort was exceedingly charming. I knew who he was, and of course I'd heard he was quite the rakehell. Perhaps even a little dangerous. And I suppose that's why I stayed in the library with him. Because..." She lifted her chin. "You may condemn me for being a reckless fool and worse, but it was Saint Valentine's Day, and I wanted an adventure. I... I'm twenty-two years old, all my friends are married, and I too wanted to feel what it's like to be admired, perhaps even desired. And even though it was imprudent, I let him kiss me. I *wanted* to be kissed. Only," she let out a derisive huff, "it seemed Lord Rochfort had another agenda."

"Clearly." Max's expression was unreadable.

"It wasn't until he'd quit the library that I realized my notebook was missing. At first I thought it had slipped behind one of the cushions on the settee we'd shared. Or that it had fallen on the floor. I searched high and low for my notebook, but of course to no avail because *he'd* taken it. It wasn't until the following day when he sent a note to Hastings House that I discovered what he was really about. And you know the rest…"

"Yes." To Charlie's surprise, Max reached out across the desk and took one of her hands in his. "Charlie, I want you to know that I don't think any less of you, and I would never 'condemn' you, as you put it. Unrepentant rake that I am, I would be a hypocrite to do so. But that doesn't mean I can't condemn Rochfort for all he has done. To you and others like Mia Harrington."

There was something about Max's manner, his grim tone, that sparked alarm inside Charlie. "Max, I really hope that condemning Lord Rochfort doesn't involve you taking some sort of rash action to exact vengeance, like calling him out. Because that would invite all kinds of unwanted attention and speculation. As I keep saying, if we can just find my notebook, all this nonsense will end. Avoiding another scandal is of paramount importance."

Max's expression grew colder than a frosty winter's day; his blue eyes glittered with a strange hard light. "Are you suggesting that Rochfort shouldn't be held to account for all he has done to you? By God, when I think of that depraved excuse for a man being anywhere near you, let alone touching you—" Max pounded his fist on the edge of the desk so hard, it shook. There was a soft metallic snicking sound—like the rasp of a latch coming undone—and Max's gaze dropped to the open drawer in front of him. "Well, well, well," he murmured, shifting the papers aside. "What do we have here? A secret compartment, perhaps?"

Charlie rushed to his side. Excitement leapt about inside her like sparking fireworks. "Is there anything there?" she asked as she watched Max lift a small slat of wood on the bottom of the desk and reach into the compartment below.

"Yes," he said with a triumphant grin. "A small red notebook with a gold filigree border."

"Oh, my Lord. Oh, sweet heaven." As soon as Max brandished the book in the air, Charlie snatched it up and hugged it to her chest. Joy and undiluted gratitude—more potent than any French brandy—washed through her veins, making her dizzy. "I'm so relieved, I could faint."

Max replaced the wood slat and pushed the drawer shut. "I'm rather hoping that you don't because carrying you out of here might prove to be a bit tricky. Now that you have your notebook, we'd best be on our way."

"Yes, you're quite right," agreed Charlie. Although, the thought of Max sweeping her up into his arms made her feel like swooning all over again.

As Max set the rest of the desk to rights—putting away the deed to Mia Harrington's old townhouse, along with papers, books, and other miscellaneous items— Charlie took the opportunity to quickly flip through the opening pages of her notebook. Everything appeared to be the same—all the pages were intact. Her single entry that she'd made with a pencil during the Saint Valentine's Day masque hadn't been altered or erased.

When she looked up, she discovered Max was studying her, a speculative light in his eye. No doubt he was wondering what she'd written that was so damning, but he was too much of a gentleman to ask. "I trust everything is all right?" he said, then licked his fingertips and snuffed out the candles on the desk one by one. There was a faint sizzle, and wisps of smoke drifted in the air between her and Max.

"Yes. Perfectly fine," she said, offering Max a genuine smile for once. When she retired for the night, she would sleep soundly like a wee untroubled babe. It would be the first time in weeks.

"Very good, then." Max closed the last desk drawer. "I suggest we leave by the front door if it's still unmanned.

Hopefully a key has been left in the lock. I'd like to be well away from here before—"

"Before I return home, Your Grace?"

Charlie's gaze shot to the library doorway, and her heart all but stopped. Lord Rochfort lounged on the threshold, one wide shoulder propped against the doorframe. With his jet-black hair, hooded eyes, and saturnine good looks, he reminded Charlie of a savage beast feigning nonchalance right before it went on the attack.

"Lady Charlotte." His deep, cultured voice, a voice that Charlie had once found appealing but now she loathed, had a mocking edge as he straightened then sketched a bow in her direction. "I'd ask you to what do I owe the pleasure of this visit, but that would be rather disingenuous of me now, wouldn't it? I trust you found what you were looking for?"

"Yes, and as you heard, we were just leaving." Max's voice was as hard as forged steel. "So, I'd suggest you move aside and let us be on our way."

Rochfort affected a sigh. "I suppose I should concede defeat graciously. It seems the game is well and truly over, Lady Charlotte, and you've won." He shrugged a shoulder and his obsidian eyes glittered, but he didn't step away from the doorway as Max had requested.

Despite the unease prickling along her nape because Lord Rochfort still barred their exit, fierce anger flared inside Charlie. The baron thought this was all a game? How...how *dare* he?

Stiffening her spine, she skewered him with her gaze. "Actually, before we go, I have a question for you, Lord Rochfort. Where is the diamond and pearl brooch I gave you? Or should I say, you extorted from me? Do you still have it? Because if you do, I'd like it back."

The baron's mouth twitched with amusement. "As a matter of fact, I do still have it in my possession, my lady."

He took a step forward, but Max held up a hand. To Charlie's surprise, the baron halted immediately, his eyes widening momentarily before narrowing into a dark fulminating glare.

"Wait there, Rochfort," drawled Max, rounding the

desk. "You'll forgive me if I don't trust you." That's when Charlie noticed that Max had a rather deadly looking flintlock pistol trained on the baron.

Good Lord. Charlie had had no idea that Max had been armed this whole time. But right at this moment, she was rather glad that he'd had the foresight to bring a weapon. The currents of enmity rippling around Lord Rochfort and across the room were forbidding indeed.

Thine eyes shoot daggers... Had an expression ever been so apt? Charlie was only just beginning to fathom how dangerous Lord Rochfort really was, and that Max was far more ruthless and fearless than she'd ever imagined.

"Now, now, Your Grace. There's no need to behave in an uncivilized manner," said Lord Rochfort in a silky, menacing tone that set shivers racing across Charlie's skin. "There's a lady present, after all."

Max's blue eyes flashed, but his manner was smooth and unhurried, perhaps even a little bored as he said, "Stop equivocating. Just tell Lady Charlotte where her brooch is, Rochfort. That's all you need to do."

The baron gave a dramatic sigh. "Very well." His unsettling gaze moved to Charlie. "It's in a silver casket inside the lacquered cabinet behind the desk, my dear. Top shelf. Neither are locked."

Charlie bristled. "Just so we're clear, I'm *not* your dear," she bit out before retrieving her mother's *en tremblant* brooch. Her heart swelling with relief and gratitude, she ran her fingertips over the delicate floral spray wrought in silver, and the diamond and pearl inlaid blooms trembled for a moment before she slid the treasured keepsake into the pocket of her cloak.

Turning back to Max, she caught his eye. "I have it," she said. "We can go. I gather the front door is unlocked…" This remark she directed at Lord Rochfort.

"Actually, I have the key right here." The baron began to reach for the inner breast pocket of his evening jacket.

Again, Max bade him stop. "I don't know what you have concealed in there, Rochfort. If you'd be so kind as to remove your coat slowly, then toss it onto the floor near Lady Charlotte. She can check it."

Rochfort shook off his coat of black superfine with a violent shrug, and once Charlie had retrieved the key, Max jerked his chin in the baron's direction. "Move into that far corner, Rochfort," he directed, his pistol hand as steady as the tick of the mantel clock marking the last ten minutes to midnight.

Rochfort rolled his eyes but nevertheless complied. "Is this really necessary?"

"Yes, it is." Max's tone was so cold, clipped, and positively ducal, it was evident that he was accustomed to being obeyed without question. "Lady Charlotte, if you wouldn't mind stepping out into the entry hall, the baron here is about to part ways with the rest of his evening attire." He smirked. "Again."

"Ha! So, it was you who stole my clothes last night," growled Rochfort. "You prick."

"You mean, 'you prick, Your Grace,'" Max amended, droll amusement lacing his voice. "But needs must when the devil drives, as they say. Charlie…" He cocked an eyebrow. "I'd suggest you leave this very minute so you don't see rather more of Lord Rochfort's person than you'd like. Perhaps you can make sure that the key does indeed work. I'll be with you shortly." To Rochfort he said, "Strip."

The baron began to tug at his cravat with rough movements. His dark eyes blazed with fury. "I'm not going to give chase," he spat. "I've already conceded defeat."

"And as I said before, I don't trust you."

With the key and her notebook in hand, Charlie beat a swift retreat to the entry hall and unlocked the grand double doors that led out to Bedford Square. "The key works," she called out to Max.

"Excellent," he called back. Another minute passed in which Charlie could hear Lord Rochfort muttering all kinds of foul imprecations, then Max emerged with a bundle of clothes under one arm. He gave the library door a decisive kick shut, then hastened over to Charlie.

She couldn't help but laugh as he dumped the baron's

clothes on the front doorstep. "Oh, Max. You are too wick—"

At that moment, a female shriek and a loud bellow erupted from the depths of Rochfort House. Max pulled the front door closed, then caught Charlie's elbow. "I suspect poor Nancy and Ruth have come upon their master *en déshabillé*," he remarked as they hurriedly descended the short flight of stairs to the square below. Max's carriage waited on the other side of the private park.

"Oh, dear." Charlie had to rush to keep up with Max's long strides. "At least they got to enjoy a cup of hot chocolate beforehand."

"I, for one, am going to enjoy a celebratory tipple of brandy." Max pulled a pewter flask from his coat as soon as they were settled in the carriage and on their way. He raised an eyebrow, smiling in invitation. "Would you like a sip or two, my lady?"

Charlie laughed again as she took the flask. "Heavens. What else have you got stashed away in that coat of yours? You think of everything."

"I like to be prepared," he said with a grin. "I always have a contingency plan to increase my chances of success. A strategy for making a safe exit up my sleeve. One can never be too careful."

"Well, I appreciate your attention to detail and dedication to the cause." Charlie uncorked the flask and raised it in the air. "To you, Maximilian Devereux," she said with a heartfelt smile. "I'm truly grateful for everything you've done for me tonight. And last night. You've removed a terrible millstone from around my neck, and for that, I shall be forever in your debt." She took a delicate sip, then handed the flask back to Max.

She felt as weightless as a cloud, and for once, she didn't wish to blunt her emotions with spirits. She no longer teetered on the dizzying edge of ruin. The torturous, ever-present worry that Lord Rochfort might expose her, subjecting her to ridicule and miring her in shame, was gone. No one—not her family or friends, nor society or Max—would ever know her innermost secrets. She was free.

CHAPTER 5

Portraits… Have you ever considered sitting for
one? If you are a member of Polite Society, it goes
without saying that your likeness should be
preserved on canvas for generations to come.
Look no further than this article for a
comprehensive list of London's preeminent
portrait artists…
The Beau Monde Mirror: The Fine Arts

Westhampton House, Park Lane, Mayfair
March 28, 1819

"He's simply gorgeous, Sophie," murmured Charlie as
she sat upon a damask settee, carefully cradling
her drowsy month-old nephew, Thomas Nathaniel Hastings, in her arms. A pale shaft of afternoon sunlight filtering through the silk gauze curtains at her back softly
illuminated his little face; his chubby cheeks were flushed
with sleep, and his brow was squished into a slight frown.

Her sister-in-law, who sat beside her, smiled, and her
blue-as-a-midsummer-sky eyes shone with maternal
pride and tenderness. "He is, isn't he? I'm quite transfixed
by how perfect he is."

"While I'd like to think you're talking about me, I suspect it's baby Thomas who has you both turned about his little finger," remarked Nate as he sauntered into the drawing room and winked at his wife.

Looking up as he approached, Charlie couldn't help but roll her eyes. "How perceptive of you, dear brother."

"Now, now, you two," said Sophie, ever the peacemaker. "I think we all can agree that Thomas is a lovely healthy boy and that's all that really matters."

"As always, you are absolutely correct, my love," said Nate, his brown eyes glowing with warmth as he gently ran a hand over the light red fuzz atop Thomas's tiny head. "Although, I will add that the reason he is so perfect is quite obvious…" His gaze lifted and connected with Sophie's. "He takes after you, my dear Lady Malverne."

A flush of pleasure suffused Sophie's fair complexion. "Won't you sit down and take tea with us?" she murmured and gestured at the low table by the settee where a delectable array of cakes and sandwiches was assembled along with a fat china teapot and a silver coffee pot. "Charlie and I can hardly eat all of this. And look, I had Cook make your favorite strawberry tartlets with clotted cream."

"Mmm, I'm sorely tempted," replied Nate with a lopsided smile that Charlie could tell was meant only for his wife. "But I'm afraid I have an appointment with my man of affairs. Egads." He scrubbed a hand through his thick auburn hair. "Look what you've done to me, Sophie. Turned me into an upstanding fellow who not only takes his responsibilities seriously but tends to them with alacrity. This time last year I would rather have stabbed myself in the eye with my cravat pin than attend such a meeting."

Charlie had to suppress a wistful sigh before she observed, "She's effortlessly transformed you into a blissfully happy husband and doting father, that's what she's done."

"For once you and I can agree, dearest sister," replied Nate. His adoring gaze met his wife's once more before he leaned down to bestow a gentle kiss on Thomas's tiny forehead. The babe's brow wrinkled, he squirmed a little, then he planted his minuscule thumb firmly in his cherub-like mouth.

Nate gave a soft chuckle. "Why don't you join us for dinner, Charlie? It feels like ages since we've had a good tête-à-tête."

"Oh yes, please do," said Sophie. "Nate, I can send a note round to Hastings House to invite your father too, if you like."

"That's a capital idea." When Nate rounded the settee then bent to give Sophie a kiss, Charlie had to look away. While she was over-the-moon happy for her best friend and brother, she couldn't help but feel a small pang of envy whenever they displayed their affection for each other so overtly. It made her own heart yearn to find the same kind of romantic connection and idyllic domestic contentment with someone too.

Someone like Max.

As if Sophie was attuned to her private thoughts, her friend said, "Perhaps we could also invite Max to dinner. It seems like forever since he's visited us here at West-hampton House." She cast a sly look at Charlie before continuing, "He would even out the numbers for dinner quite nicely."

Nate leaned down and picked up a strawberry tartlet. "I'm afraid he won't be able to," he said as he dolloped a large spoonful of clotted cream on top of the plump strawberry. "I saw him this morning at Gentleman Jackson's, and he was lamenting the fact that he's obliged to attend a dinner party at Devereux House. It seems his mother has arranged it, and we've all heard what a virago the dowager duchess can be. Apparently, Lady Penelope Purcell, along with her brother, Lord Mowbray, and their parents, the Duke and Duchess of Stafford, are on the guest list."

Sophie's fine black brows dipped into a frown. "Lady Penelope Perfect? Oh, dear. That doesn't augur well. It sounds like Max's mama is attempting to matchmake."

Nate grimaced. "Yes, it would appear so. Poor sod."

"Well, I, for one, still haven't forgiven Lady Penelope for publicly insulting you so dreadfully last year, Sophie," said Charlie with a huff. "And to think that the whole exchange ended up in the *Beau Monde Mirror*. I can't believe that his mother would even consider such a match for Max." Jealousy flickered and fused with a smoldering ember of indignation. "Although Lady Penelope might have a remarkable pedigree and possess a host of accomplishments, she most certainly *isn't* perfect. Not by a long shot. Max could do much better."

"Mmm. Agreed." Nate popped the strawberry tartlet in his mouth, chewed with gusto, then swallowed. "Delicious," he said, changing the subject, then swooped down to kiss his wife's cheek in farewell. "And thank you, sweetheart. You know how much I love the flavor of strawberries. Now I must be off. I promise you that I won't be late."

As her brother quit the room, Charlie noticed that the tips of Sophie's ears had turned bright pink. Even though she wasn't sure why, she rather suspected it had something to do with Nate's remark about strawberries.

Best not to think about that.

Little Thomas began to stir and fuss, so Sophie rang for his nurse. As her friend began to dispense the tea into elegant Wedgwood cups, Charlie helped herself to one of the strawberry tartlets and silently concurred that they were indeed delicious.

Her thoughts strayed to what Nate had just disclosed, and she added another tartlet and a cucumber sandwich to her plate. She wasn't at all surprised, given Max had complained last night about his mother's machinations. But still, the knowledge that Lady Penelope had been invited to dinner, and that she, Charlie, would never be good enough for Max—at least in the eyes of the dowager duchess and Polite Society in general—smarted.

She released a sigh and nibbled at the sandwich. If only Max would stop looking upon her as just his friend's younger, bothersome, and clearly far-too-brazen sister. The hope that had sparked in her breast when they'd hidden in that moonlit window alcove at Rochfort House had all but fizzled out by the time he'd dropped her home at Berkeley Square. After she'd handed back his brandy flask in the carriage, he'd become withdrawn and had barely spoken a word to her other than goodnight.

The initial elation she'd felt at recovering her notebook had dimmed too. When she'd been safely tucked up in bed with Peridot at Hastings House, she'd perused the pencilled notes she'd made during the Penriths' Saint Valentine's Day masque and realized how futile many of her fantasies were, how silly her list of "Secret Wishes and Dreams".

So, she must find new dreams and different aspirations, she decided as she added two sugar lumps to her tea and gave it a vigorous stir. Another purpose. Reinvent herself. Fashion a brand-new Lady Charlotte Hastings who wasn't lonely or bored or ashamed or lovesick. Yes, she was utterly weary of foolishly mooning over a man who seemed determined to leave her in the "do not ever touch" category forever.

If, after all this time, Max Devereux felt nothing at all for her and couldn't view her as a prospective wife, well, he could just jolly well go and jump in the Thames.

"Penny for your thoughts, Charlie?" Sophie said softly. "Is everything all right?"

Charlie hastily swallowed her pique along with a quick mouthful of her tea before she replied. "Oh yes. Never better." She was pleased that for once her pronouncement wasn't an outright lie. She put down her cup and glanced at the Ormolu mantel clock. "My apologies for being so distracted, but I need to keep an eye on the time. As much as I'd like to stay until dinner, I have another appointment in an hour. In Half Moon Street, so not far."

"Oh?" Sophie arched an eyebrow, and her eyes twinkled with mischief. "Something exciting, I hope."

"Well, yes. It is a little." Charlie felt her cheeks grow warm with an uncharacteristic blush. "Would you like to come along? I'd value your opinion, actually."

Sophie beamed. "Absolutely. I'd love to."

∾

17 Half Moon Street, Mayfair

"Heavens, Charlie, I had no idea that you'd been up to something as exciting as this. I'm quite…speechless. Flabbergasted, in fact. And also in awe." Sophie gazed with wide-eyed wonder at the series of charcoal sketches fanned out upon the polished rosewood table in the elegant parlor of Madame Louise de Beauvoir, portrait artist extraordinaire. "I mean, how did all this come about? How did you hear about Madame de Beauvoir?" She touched a finger to one of the pictures. "She's quite talented, isn't she? You look…you're breathtakingly gorgeous."

Charlie laughed. "You're too kind, my dear friend. And to answer your questions, it was Aunt Tabitha who arranged the sittings. Just before she quit Town."

Sophie patted her now flat belly beneath her smart walking gown of blue velvet. "Ah, while Nate and I were still rusticating at Deerhurst Park." She fixed Charlie with a narrow-eyed look. "It seems you've been keeping secrets from me."

To hide her guilt, Charlie gave an arch smile. "Only the most scandalous ones. Now, in all seriousness"—she directed Sophie's attention back to the sketches—"which one do you like best? I have to make a choice this afternoon so Madame de Beauvoir can begin work on my portrait. I'd like it to be finished before Aunt Tabitha returns to London."

Sophie sifted through the drawings and chose one in which Charlie wore a low-cut dress and her curls were piled high on her head. "What about this one? The style of the gown suits you well. It's very Grecian. And with the elegant marble colonnade in the background, and the way you're balancing that urn on your hip, you could be Circe. Or one of the three Graces."

"You don't think I look a little too…Rubenesque? You see, after Christmastide, I discovered I needed a new wardrobe." Charlie affected a laugh. "You were increasing because you were with child, but I was increasing because I'd eaten too much cake and pudding and too many sweetmeats. In any event, when Aunt Tabitha noticed how down in the doldrums I was because none of my clothes fit properly—particularly across the bust—she dragged me off to the modiste as soon as we returned to London. And before she departed for Bath, she also decreed that I should have my portrait painted *à la* Lady Hamilton so I could see that I wasn't as frightfully plump as I thought I was."

"Plump?" exclaimed Sophie. "What a thing to say! You and your curves are divine, Lady Charlotte Hastings. I've only seen a few portraits of Emma, Lady Hamilton—all by George Romney—and while she is pretty, I would venture to say that you are even lovelier."

"You don't think these sketches are a little...well, as the French would say, *risqué*?" Charlie picked up another sheet of parchment. "I mean, this one for instance. I'm supposed to be a water nymph, and I'm not wearing any undergarments beneath my white silk muslin gown. At all." She'd posed side on, bunching up her skirts so that her bare lower leg was exposed and her toes were pointed, as though she were about to dip her foot into a pool of water. "Madame de Beauvoir also insisted that I rub oil into my skin, then her assistant dampened the muslin so that it clung *everywhere.*" The side of her breast, the cheek of one buttock, her thigh. "I'm worried it's a little *too* salacious..."

Sophie took it from her and studied it. "I like it," she pronounced after a thorough inspection. "Very much. It's tastefully *risqué* rather than ribald like Thomas Rowlandson's etching of Lady Hamilton. Now *that's* the epitome of a salacious picture. She hasn't a stitch on."

Charlie raised her eyebrows. "You've seen it?"

Sophie laughed. "And more besides. Why do you think a folio of Rowlandson's etchings was stashed in your father's library at Hastings House? The folio you brought to our very first meeting for the Society for Enlightened Young Women at Mrs. Rathbone's academy? It was Nate's." A telling pink blush suffused her cheeks as she added, "He reclaimed it long ago."

"Ah, well, I rather suspected that it might be his."

Charlie gave her friend's arm a playful nudge. "I told you he was wicked."

Sophie's blush deepened but nevertheless she smiled. "Exceedingly. I think that's why I love him so much. Now…" She placed the tastefully *risqué* etching back on the table then tapped her chin. "I've decided. This one is my favorite. Because we only see part of your profile and you're looking down, and the way your curls fall across your cheek, it gives you quite an ethereal air. You're both beguiling and mysterious. It's cleverly done. If it were featured in the Royal Academy of Art's Annual Exhibition, everyone would be abuzz with excitement as they tried to guess who the artist's muse might be."

"Oh, Madame de Beauvoir is an excellent artist, but this won't be displayed in any art gallery. Just my private sitting room. And even then, I might have to have it enclosed in a special cupboard," said Charlie. "Or hide it behind curtains. I hate to think what my father would say if he saw it." A shiver of horror passed through her. "He might never speak to me again."

"Oh, stuff and nonsense. The ambiguity of the subject is so marked—your identity so well-concealed—I'm sure you would be able to display it in the entry hall or indeed the drawing room of Hastings House and no one would even raise an eyebrow."

"Are you certain?" Charlie wasn't at all convinced.

Sophie gave an emphatic nod. "Most definitely."

"Very well. I will ask Madame de Beauvoir to paint this one."

"Wonderful." Sophie sifted through the other sketches. "You know, I'm feeling a little left out. Considering Arabella is her husband's muse and now your likeness has been captured so becomingly, I rather think I should have my portrait painted. For Nate." She glanced up. "How is it that your aunt became acquainted with Madame de Beauvoir? You didn't say."

"Ah, that's an easy question to answer. Late last year, the Mayfair Bluestocking Society invited her to give art lessons to its members. Aunt Tabitha and I both attended,

but I'm afraid to report that my efforts were quite woeful.
But it was not through want of trying."

Sophie laughed. "I'm sure my efforts would have been
far worse. The art tutor at Mrs. Rathbone's academy
would have happily set fire to all of the appalling abomi-
nations I created."

"But my dear sister, you are accomplished in so many
other ways," countered Charlie. "Aside from being a talented novelist, you're a devoted wife and mother. Olivia
can sing like an angel. And Arabella is clever beyond
words and a dedicated philanthropist. Whereas I..."
Charlie picked up one of the discarded sketches and
sighed. "Aside from getting into mischief, I suppose I'm
quite adept at balancing a porcelain urn upon my hip,
don't you think?"

"Oh, Charlie." Sophie enveloped her in a warm hug.
"You're perfect just the way you are. You bring untold joy
and fun and laughter into the lives of everyone who
knows you. To my way of thinking, there can be no finer
accomplishment than that."

∾

Devereux House, Curzon Street, Mayfair

"Maximilian."

Max winced inwardly as he helped himself to
a large brandy from the crystal decanter that graced the
satinwood sideboard in the drawing room of Devereux
House. "Yes, Mother?" he said without turning around. "I
do hope that you're not going to chide me for my intem-
perate ways. Because you know I'll just leave, given I
don't particularly wish to be here anyway."

"Good heavens. There's no need to be so rude or
dramatic."

Max turned around, propped one hip against the sideboard, and took a long, deliberately slow sip of his
brandy. "I didn't think I was being either of those things,
Mother. Just honest and matter-of-fact. And I'm not in
the mood for your sniping."

"Really, Maximilian." His mother stalked across the room to the fireplace, her ice-blue silk skirts fluttering and whispering about her ankles. The firelight glanced off the diamonds at her ears and throat as if it wanted to be somewhere else too. "All I ask is for you to behave in a civilized manner tonight"—her cool, appraising gaze slid over him—"even if you don't dress like a gentleman of your rank should. You should hire a new valet."

Max scratched the evening stubble on his jaw. "Smedley does a sterling job. And bristles are all the rage, didn't you know? As are stylishly rumpled cravats and unkept hair. I hear young women are particularly wild about ton bucks who look as though they've just stumbled out of someone's bed. Which is rather the point of this evening, isn't it? Don't you want Lady Penelope to be all moon-eyed whenever she casts a glance my way over the roast guinea fowl at the dinner table?"

His mother pinned him with a frosty glare. "There's no need to be vulgar. And I know why you're doing this. It's your rather puerile attempt to put off the Duke and Duchess of Stafford. To ruin your chances with Lady Penelope, even if she's partial to"—she waved her hand in his general direction— "poorly dressed men."

"You give me far too much credit," Max drawled. "The simple explanation is that I just couldn't be bothered to make an effort. I really don't give a tinker's damn about the Duke or Duchess of Stafford's opinion of me, or Lady Penelope's, or Lord Mowbray's, for that matter. And unlike you, Mother, I don't spend every waking hour plotting and scheming. I'm all for expediency. I have far better things to do with my time."

His mother bristled. "Yes, like drinking and whoring and gambling and Lord knows what else. The number of times your name has appeared in newspapers, you'd think you'd have learned your lesson by—"

Max held up a hand. "Spare me the lecture. Next you'll be telling me how I should try to be more like my dearly departed brother. Or how disappointed Father would have been."

His father. Even now, after all these years, Max still

felt his shade. It was as though he was here in the room, hovering at the edges of his vision. Waiting. Judging.

Sneering.

His mother lifted her chin. "Well, you *should* be more like Anthony," she rejoined. "He took his ducal duties far more seriously than you. Why, by your age, he'd taken Diana to wife. Indeed, I would have at least one grandson by now if he hadn't—" She broke off and her hands curled into tight fists as she attempted to tamp down what she'd consider an unseemly display of emotion. "All I ask is that you seriously consider marrying someone suitable sooner rather than later. You're almost nine-and-twenty, Maximilian. And since your father died—God rest his soul—you've had years and years playing the role of licentious rake and 'war hero', sowing your wild oats far and wide. It's time for you to settle down with someone like Diana. And I happen to think Lady Penelope Purcell fits the bill."

Diana. His brother's widow. A sliver of guilt pierced Max's armor-plated heart whenever he thought about the circumstances surrounding his brother's death nearly four years ago. Diana, who had no immediate family left to speak of, still resided with her mother-in-law here at Devereux House. The two were on amicable terms, and Max suspected that his mother really did wish him to wed someone exactly like the quietly confident and agreeable young widow. Indeed, his mother had hand-selected the well-bred debutante for Anthony six years ago, so when he, Max, had decided to do his duty for King and Country and joined Wellington's army, it wouldn't have mattered if he'd perished on the battlefield. The dukedom was in safe hands. Anthony would sire an heir and several spares with Diana.

As if his thoughts had conjured her up, Diana appeared in the drawing room's doorway. As fair and slender as her mother-in-law, she was attired in a gown of dove-gray gauze and satin with pearls at her throat and in her hair.

"Good evening, Maximilian. Cressida," she said softly

before advancing into the room with elegant, measured steps. "I hope I'm not interrupting…"

"No, of course not," replied the dowager duchess. "I was just telling Max—"

"Mother was just extolling the virtues of Lady Penelope Purcell in an effort to convince me the chit is worth courting."

With studied grace, Diana lowered herself onto a gilt-legged settee. "She does have much to recommend her. I believe she's very accomplished. And attractive as well as amiable."

"Amiable?" Max sipped his brandy. "She wasn't particularly amiable when she encountered Lady Charlotte Hastings's friend, Sophie, in Gunter's Tea Shop last year."

His mother's gaze could have cut glass. "Lady Charlotte Hastings is a shameless hoyden. And from what I hear, the new Viscountess Malverne is little better. By all accounts, she's a veritable nobody who just happened to possess sufficient guile and a pretty enough face to ensnare Lord Malverne's interest. But everyone knows how fickle he is. Now that he has his heir, undoubtedly his attention will wander."

"Careful," growled Max. "You will not insult Lord Malverne, his wife, *or* his sister in my presence. You do not know them like I do."

His mother sniffed. "And I do not wish to. Thank goodness you've never shown any real interest in Lady Charlotte. If you ask me, Lord Westhampton should have taken her in hand long ago. But then, her low-born mother, Elizabeth, didn't have much to recommend her either. And by all accounts, her aunt, Lady Chelmsford, has radical views. No wonder the girl has turned out the way she has."

Further discussion on the "management" or lack thereof of Lady Charlotte was precluded by the arrival of his mother's guests.

Max managed to bury his chagrin and greeted the Duke and Duchess of Stafford, their son Nigel, Lord Mowbray, and Lady Penelope with due deference. Several

other well-heeled ton families arrived—again, acquain-
tances of his mother's—and when they all trooped through
to the dining room, there was not a seat to spare at the mahogany table which had been set with twenty places.

His mother had clearly decided to dispense with the
usual formalities at dinner. Although that didn't mean she
hadn't put a great degree of thought into the seating
arrangements. Indeed, every guest was positioned as
strategically as any chess piece upon the board. Lady
Penelope took her seat to Max's right at the very end of
the table. Lord Mowbray was to his left. The duke and
duchess had pride of place at the far end, where his
mother presided.

Although Max had steadfastly tried to ignore
thinking about Charlie all day—especially after he'd almost lost his bloody head and nearly kissed her last
night—now, as he attempted to make pleasant yet idle
conversation with Lady Penelope, he could think of
nothing and no one else. Comparisons kept leaping
about in his mind like damned randy jack rabbits, distracting him.

Even though Lady Penelope was certainly pleasing to
the eye—flaxen-haired and blue-eyed, her neat, slender
form was attired in a tasteful gown of pale pink silk—it
seemed Max couldn't stop envisioning Charlie in her
shocking harlot's costume. The way her luscious curves
had all but spilled from the confines of her tight corset.
How his hands still itched to cup her magnificent breasts.
Seize her generous hips and drag her onto his lap again.
He wanted her lips sliding along his jaw. To feel the
humid fan of her breath against his bare finger when he'd
pressed it to her ripe-as-a-summer-plum lips. If he'd
done the unthinkable and *had* kissed her last night at
Rochfort House, would she have tasted sweet or tart or a
mixture of both?

He kept recalling what she'd told him in Rochfort's
library: that she *wanted* to be admired. Desired and
kissed.

And yes, he'd wanted to kiss her in that moonlit alcove. He shouldn't desire her, but he did. Since that night

at the Rouge et Noir Club, he seemed to be caught in a fever dream that he couldn't wake up from.

Lady Penelope was speaking, and Max reluctantly refocused his attention on the poised young woman who reminded him of one of the fine porcelain figurines sitting upon the marble mantelpiece in his mother's sitting room. Effortlessly elegant, eye-catching, polished, and utterly devoid of warmth.

She was talking about her excursion to the theater last night and how much she'd enjoyed the oratorio. It was an entirely appropriate but entirely bland topic, rather like the white soup that had been served earlier and the blancmange that sat untouched upon Max's gilt-edged plate now. Both were pleasant enough, but he had no appetite for either of them.

Max nodded, only half-listening to Penelope as she continued to chat about the composer Handel and his blasted hymns. His mother was right, curse her. He had no doubt that Lady Penelope had been carefully trained and would fulfill the role of duchess admirably. She would do her duty. She'd know her place. She'd run her husband's household smoothly and efficiently. She'd be an impeccable hostess, her conversation always light and easy and superficially entertaining just as it was now.

He glanced across the wide expanse of snow-white linen, cut crystal, and gleaming silverware to where his mother sat, holding court. She was smiling and nodding regally at something Diana had just said.

In many ways, Lady Penelope was simply a younger version of his own mother and his sister-in-law. Max couldn't suppress a shudder of horror. It seemed his mother was determined for him to marry a woman in her very own image so that he might beget a stable of blond-haired, blue-eyed children to continue the Exmoor line.

Lady Penelope paused to take a breath, and Max took the opportunity to wave over a footman to replenish the port wine in his glass. As he picked it up to take a sip, the candlelight from a nearby candelabra momentarily illuminated the golden-brown depths, and he couldn't quite decide if the hue reminded him more of Charlie's eyes or her wild chestnut curls. Or perhaps the deep amber shade of his favorite brandy would be a better match—

"Your Grace, I believe you have a first-class stable." This time it was Lord Mowbray who spoke. He'd obviously given up on trying to charm the stuffy countess to his left. "My sister likes to ride." He gave a wink, then added, "Don't you, Penelope?"

"Yes. I adore it." Lady Penelope's pale blue gaze connected directly with Max's. "Although it might be frowned upon by some, I do like to ride hard and fast. Especially in the mornings. A bout of vigorous exercise first thing is most refreshing. Wouldn't you agree, Your Grace?"

Sweet Jesus. Max nearly choked on his port before he managed to respond with a non-committal answer of, "Quite."

Did the chit know what she was saying? He studied her face for any hint of guile, and saw a momentary flash of triumph in her eyes. Her rosebud mouth twitched. Yes, she'd said something deliberately provocative to recapture his wandering attention. And it seemed her brother was in on the plan because he was the one who'd introduced the topic and prompted her to respond.

The whole idea that the pair had premeditated and then coordinated such an exchange suddenly made Max feel quite ill.

Penelope's slippered toe brushed his ankle beneath the table as Lord Mowbray reclaimed his attention with another question about his horses and an upcoming sweepstakes.

Good God, the girl was determined to test the waters. Max pushed away his port and tucked his own foot farther beneath his chair, out of reach. It seemed she was more brazen and dangerous than he'd hitherto thought. He'd best be on his guard for the rest of the night, because the last thing he wanted was to be "caught" in a compromising position with Lady Penelope Purcell.

She might be poised and perfect and amenable and amiable, but Max suspected it was all for show, that deep down, Lady Penelope was another kettle of fish entirely—

manipulative and calculating. As ambitious and cold-hearted as his mother.

As cold-blooded and ice-hearted as he'd become. All superficial charm and no care for anyone or anything except his horses, and his former brothers-in-arms, Nate Hastings, Hamish MacQueen, and Gabriel Holmes-Fitzgerald. And he was determined to keep things that way despite the fact he couldn't seem to get his best friend's sister—a hoyden with brandy-hued eyes—out of his damned head.

CHAPTER 6

My List of Secret Wishes and Dreams:
1) Sneak into a 'Gentlemen's Club' to see what all the fuss is about;
2) To be kissed, with passion, in the moonlight by a rake;
3) Or in the rain (either will do);
4) Ride hell-for-leather down Rotten Row at least once (preferably not in the rain unless there's any chance said passionate kiss happens straight afterward);
5) Sea bathe, naked;
6) Sit for a licentious portrait à la Lady Hamilton;
7) To be thoroughly ravished in a carriage;
8) Waltz the night away at Almack's;
9) To experience a Grand Passion that I will remember long into my dotage;
10) The man (or should I say duke?) of my dreams falls in love with me.

Hastings House, Berkeley Square
March 29, 1819

Charlie yawned, stretched, and rolled over in her wide tester bed, dragging the amber silk counterpane with her. Smiling, she hugged a fat fluffy pillow to her chest. All was right with the world, and this morning she was going to be an unashamed slugabed.

Eventually, she'd ring for Molly to draw back the curtains to let in the spring sunshine, and after the fire was restoked and leaping merrily in the grate, she'd send for a breakfast tray stacked with her favorite things—hot chocolate, buttered and honeyed crumpets, and perhaps a fruit bun sprinkled with cinnamon sugar. She'd peruse the mail and the papers, maybe wallow in a steamy hot bubble bath until she resembled a prune, read a novel from cover to cover while petting Peridot...and she would *not* have a single thought about that vile black-guard Lord Rochfort or wonder when she'd next see the steadfastly invulnerable Duke of Exmoor.

An hour later, all was going to plan; she was propped up in bed with her breakfast tray, sipping hot chocolate, and she was smiling because she'd just read several heart-warming letters, one each from her younger brothers Jonathon, Benjamin, and Daniel, who were all due to quit Eton and come home for Easter. She couldn't wait for the halls of Hastings House to ring with their boisterous laughter, even if it was only for a few short days.

The Countess of Langdale's letter was characteristi-cally succinct and no-nonsense: Arabella mentioned that she was still as busy as could be setting up her orphanage in Edinburgh, but that both she and Gabriel hoped to be in London by mid-April at the very latest. Charlie de-cided that as soon as Arabella returned, she would seek her out and ask if there was some way that she, Charlie, could become more involved in philanthropic endeavors during the Season. After her chat with Sophie yesterday, she realized she was far too indolent and hoped that en-gaging in charity work—being useful—might help to fill the void in her life.

Charlie opened the Marchioness of Chelmsford's letter and began to eagerly peruse the contents for all of her aunt's latest news...and her heart fell. Charlie had been so looking forward to her aunt's return, but it seemed she would be staying in Bath for the foreseeable future to help with Lady Kilbride's convalescence. How-ever—Charlie quickly turned the page—all going well, her aunt was proposing a trip to the Continent in the summer with another set of friends from the Mayfair

Bluestocking Society, and she would love it if Charlie joined their traveling party.

Charlie put down the letter and worried at her bottom lip. She wasn't sure how she felt about such an invitation. It was so unexpected, and Europe was so very far away. Of course, her father would acquiesce to such a proposal, so that wouldn't be a problem.

There really was only one thing to do. Charlie helped herself to another cup of hot chocolate, retrieved her crimson notebook and a pencil from her bedside table, skipped past her "List of Secret Wishes and Dreams", and began to record a brand new list of all the pros and cons for embarking on such a trip on a fresh new page.

Cons: if she went, she'd miss her family and friends; she'd miss Peridot; and as much as she didn't want to admit it, she'd probably miss Max.

Blast him.

Pros: she'd have some wonderful adventures, and she might meet another eminently eligible gentleman. A man who didn't give a fat flying fig about her past and would fall madly in love with her. Sweep her off her feet.

Someone who really *would* make her forget all about Max Devereux and his sapphire eyes, his heart-stopping smile, and the way he made her laugh.

It wasn't *that* far-fetched an idea that she could meet and fall head-over-heels in love with someone new. After all, darling Arabella, who'd been steadfastly against the idea of marrying, had met her wicked-as-sin Gabriel on a Grand Tour last year. And look how that had turned out. In the meantime, planning a trip to the Continent would give Charlie something to look forward to.

Yes, perhaps a jaunt abroad was exactly the tonic she needed to fully restore her *joie de vivre*.

Mind made up, Charlie snapped her notebook shut and reached for the newspapers sitting in a neat stack on her bed. *The Times* didn't hold her interest for very long. Nor did *The Morning Chronicle* or *The Morning Post*. There was the latest issue of *Ackermann's Repository of Arts*, and at the very bottom of the pile, the *Beau Monde Mirror.*

She really shouldn't peruse the infamous scandalmongering rag. In fact, she sometimes wondered why her father still bothered to subscribe to the paper as he rarely looked at it, especially now that Nate had settled down and his outrageous antics no longer appeared within its pages. It was likely an oversight, *or* perhaps he also suspected that Charlie liked to secretly catch up on all of society's gossip.

In any event, the newspaper was there, waiting for her. Tempting her like a plate of her favorite cream buns or a box of fondant bonbons.

She reached for it, flicked it open.

And then her throat closed over and her heart froze.

Stopped.

A strange buzzing sound filled her head.

Oh, dear God. Oh, sweet heavens above.

No. Oh no, no, no.

This couldn't be true. Couldn't be real.

But it *was.* For there, plastered in big bold letters upon the front page of the *Beau Monde Mirror,* was her list.

Her secret, scandalous list. The list contained within her stolen notebook that no one was *ever* meant to see.

Her private thoughts. All her hopes and dreams.

Exposed. For everyone to read and laugh at.

It didn't matter that her name wasn't explicitly printed in the paper. Or Max's. Everyone knew who "the former disreputable debutante, Lady C." was. And given the fact Nate and Max were such firm friends, the ton could easily guess the true identity of the unnamed "duke of her dreams".

And Max would know too. How could he not?

Humiliation and horror washed over Charlie in a huge suffocating wave. She was drowning in it. Couldn't move. Couldn't breathe.

How?

Why?

She choked in a much-needed breath, then another as she tried to make sense of what had happened. She and Max had rescued her notebook. It was right there beside her, the crimson cover standing out starkly against the deep golden counterpane.

Somehow, the voice of reason rose above the clamoring, riotous thoughts whirling about in her mind and made itself heard. *Lord Rochfort deceived you, Charlie. When he threatened to go to the papers with your notebook, perhaps he already had. Days if not weeks ago. And he was simply waiting for the right moment to wield the hammer. To plunge the knife.*

You humiliated him. Thwarted him. And just when you thought you'd bested him, he decided to teach you a lesson.

And oh, what a lesson.

She was ruined. Utterly. Entirely.

Irrevocably.

Lady Charlotte Hastings wasn't just a "disreputable debutante" anymore. Now she would be forever branded a brazen slut.

And the ton would never, ever let her forget it.

≈

Gentleman Jackson's Saloon, 13 Bond Street, London

W hen Max strode into Gentleman Jackson's boxing saloon, he wasn't just looking for a fight.

He was looking to maim someone.

A specific someone by the name of Rollo Kingsley, Baron Rochfort—although filthy swine, gutter bastard, depraved snake, or even "scum of the earth" were monikers that would serve equally as well. "Not long for this world" also sprang to mind.

Even though Max believed his intelligence was accurate—it hadn't taken more than a few coins and a few short sharp words for one of Rochfort's footmen to cough up his master's whereabouts—it wasn't the baron who he first ran into on the floor of Gentleman Jackson's.

It was Nate. Curse him.

"What's wrong?" asked Nate as he waved away his sparring partner and wiped the perspiration from his brow with his bare forearm. "You look…livid."

Max swore beneath his breath and drew closer. "You

haven't heard? Or seen the *Beau Monde Mirror* this morning?"

Nate frowned and flexed his cloth-bound knuckles. "No. I don't subscribe. Although I have been getting some rather strange looks since I arrived here." His face suddenly paled. "Why? What's happened?"

Bloody hell. It was clear Nate didn't know about any of this blackmail business. Or what Rochfort had just done to Charlie. Or the horrific scandal headed his family's way.

Max swallowed and gripped his friend's sweat-slickened shoulder. "I think it's best if we go somewhere quiet. One of the rooms out the back, perhaps." Already, other men were watching their exchange with interest. A viscount who Max vaguely recognized from White's—Loxley, perhaps—smirked.

Rochfort was nowhere in sight, but perhaps that was for the best at the moment.

Once they reached the relative quiet of one of the private changing rooms, Max drew a deep breath. "A few days ago, Charlie came to me for help," he began and then proceeded to tell his friend a highly edited version of all that had ensued. It wasn't the absolute truth, but Max didn't see the sense in making things worse by sharing every unvarnished detail. He especially didn't wish Nate to suspect that he had been lusting after Charlie ever since that highly charged night at the Rouge et Noir Club. Or that she'd been with him when he'd broken into Rochfort's townhouse.

When Max disclosed what he suspected Rochfort had done in retaliation after his blackmailing scheme had been foiled—that he'd instructed the *Beau Monde Mirror* to go ahead and publish Charlie's scandalous list of desires to humiliate and punish her—Nate's dark eyes turned black with fury.

"I'll kill him," he muttered, heading for the door, but Max caught him by the shoulder.

"No. You won't." His voice was low, urgent. He had to make his friend see sense. "You have a wife and son now. Your duty is to them. So, let me enact vengeance on your family's behalf. It will be my way of repaying the debt I owe you."

Nate shook him off, but he released the door handle. "You owe me nothing. What I did, I did because we are friends. There is no debt to be repaid."

"Yes, there is. You went above and beyond the night my brother died, so let me do this. For you and for Charlie. I may be a self-serving, ruthless bastard at the best of times, but you know how much I loathe injustice. Of any kind. Rochfort must be punished for his despicable acts."

Nate's eyes narrowed with suspicion. "What do you plan on doing?"

"The only thing I can do in a situation like this. Call Rochfort out."

"No." Now it was Nate gripping Max's shoulder. "You can't. You will only make things worse. For yourself and for Charlie."

"How could it possibly be any worse for Charlie? You know this will destroy her socially. Your father, who has always striven to maintain an impeccable public record and prides himself on his standing in Parliament, will be devastated too."

"Are you sure you're only motivated by friendship?"

"Whatever do you mean? Your sister has been wronged most grievously."

"Yes, but that's the point," asserted Nate, his expression grim. "She's *my* sister. You do realize what will happen if you go down this path, don't you? When word gets out that Rochfort was behind this story in the paper and that you sought vengeance? There will be speculation. People will wonder why you decided to step in and become Lady Charlotte Hastings's champion."

"I know." An uncharacteristic feeling—guilt, perhaps —cramped Max's gut. A few days ago, he'd promised Charlie he *wouldn't* make this worse, but that's exactly what he was about to do. He would be feeding the scandal. Turning it into a raging bonfire.

Unless... A mad idea suddenly occurred to him. Max's jaw tightened as he braced himself for Nate's reaction to what he would say next. "However, I have a plan."

Nate listened and by the end, he indicated his agreement with a short sharp nod rather than the bare-knuckled facer Max had been half-expecting. "I'll hold you to your word," his friend said, his voice edged with steel. "And so help me, if you go back on it, I will be obliged to call *you* out."

"I understand, and knowing you as I do," Max said with suitable gravity, "I wouldn't expect anything less."

"Good." Nate blew out a heavy sigh. "You know I'll be your second."

But Max shook his head. "I can't accept. Must I remind you yet again that you have other, more important familial responsibilities? I'll ask Edgerton. He's a good shot and can be counted upon."

"I concur." Nate snagged a towel off a nearby bench and blotted his face and neck. "So, when do you plan on confronting Rochfort?"

Max paused a moment, gauging his friend's mood before he answered. "Now. Word is that Rochfort is here. But I take it you haven't seen him?"

Nate's nostrils flared, and he cracked his knuckles. "No. Although if I do, I wouldn't mind darkening his daylights."

Max understood perfectly.

As they both quit the changing room and stepped into the hallway leading to the main saloon, the devil himself appeared in the doorway at the head of the corridor.

And Max saw red. Blood red.

In the next instant, he was storming down the hall with swift strides, throwing off his coat as he went.

Rochfort smirked, put his head down, and charged.

They crashed into the wall, grappling, pushing, grunting, then stumbled into the main saloon and fell to the ground. Max managed to gain the upper hand; pinning Rochfort to the wooden floor with the weight of his body, he drew back his fist, then drove it into the dog's jaw with an almighty crack.

Rochfort's head snapped back, then Max pushed his forearm against his windpipe. "You filthy, despicable cur." His words were little more than a hiss as he forced them through clenched teeth. "I demand satisfaction for what you've done to Lady Charlotte. And I'm setting the rules." Rochfort's eyes bulged and he clawed at Max's arm, but Max only pressed harder. "Pistols at Hampstead Heath. You know the place. I'll see you there with your second in three hours' time. At dusk. No excuses. We fight until one of us can no longer stand. Because as much as I'd like to end you"—Max pushed on Rochfort's windpipe again, enjoying the fact that the baron's face was beginning to turn an alarming shade of purple—"I'd rather not be tried for killing you. A pound of flesh will suffice."

Rochfort bucked. They rolled once, twice, and then one of his fists landed a glancing blow across Max's cheek. Then several pairs of hands were on Max's back, gripping his shoulders, and he and Rochfort were prized apart and dragged away from each other.

Barely restrained by two other men, Rochfort swiped a hand across his split lip and spat on the floor. "I'll be there, Exmoor," he snarled through bared bloody teeth. "And the only one who will be stripped of any flesh is you."

"I wouldn't be so cocksure." Max shook off the hands holding him. "You forget that I was at Waterloo and lived to tell the tale. I'm certain the most action you've seen has been here at Gentleman Jackson's. I hope you're ready for the sound arse-whipping you so roundly deserve."

With that he accepted his discarded jacket from Nate, stalked from the saloon, and strode down Bond Street in the direction of Grosvenor Square. He had better things to do than trade barbs with Rochfort. He needed to make sure his affairs were all in order in case the worst should happen despite his bravado. He had to speak with Edgerton, check his brace of Manton dueling pistols, and he had to procure a surgeon.

As much as he wanted to see Charlie, to see how she was faring and reassure her that everything would be all right, their meeting would have to wait until after the duel.

His resolve was as strong and sure as his aim. One way or another, Rochfort would pay.

CHAPTER 7

Hampstead Heath…a rural idyll on the outskirts of London. A playground for poets, writers, and artists. Why not escape to the "country" this Season for a picnic, to take Hampstead's medicinal waters, or to simply admire the arresting views? After the hustle and bustle of Town, no doubt many of our readers will find such leisurely activities to be a restorative tonic for the soul. (Just beware of the duelists…)
The Beau Monde Mirror: General Health & Medical Miscellany

Hampstead Heath
Dusk…

The light was only just beginning to fade into a muted purple twilight when Rochfort's carriage drew to a halt in the lane adjacent to Max's dueling ground of choice, a secluded glade within the environs of nearby Kenwood House. Situated at the northern edge of Hampstead Heath—a vast and ancient wooded parkland just outside of London—the shadowy clearing was exactly forty paces across and the perfect place for men to settle matters of honor away from prying eyes. By all accounts, it had been the scene of many a duel for centuries.

Max knew the place well. Not because he made a

habit of dueling. No, it was simply because he owned a nearby property—Heathcote Hall was only half a mile away.

"Thank you for being here, Edgerton," said Max as he watched Rochfort alight from his conveyance with his second, Viscount Loxley. "I really do appreciate it."

"Think nothing of it, Exmoor," replied the baron, his eyes dancing with good humor. "London is frightfully boring this time of year, and there's nothing like a good bit of blood sport to liven things up. Aside from that, everyone knows Rochfort needs a good ballocking. Given all the rumors about his unsavory tastes and unscrupulous dealings, I'd say he's had it coming for a long time."

Max's interest was piqued. "You know something of his business dealings? His financial affairs?"

Lord Edgerton shrugged, then brushed something off the cuff of his well-cut redingote. "One hears things. He's not short of blunt by any means. But he did inherit a less than profitable estate six years ago, so of course, speculation is rife about how he managed to turn things around so quickly. Even though I haven't any proof, I suspect he owns shares in some sort of shady but profitable business. In any event, even if you kill the arrogant arse, I'm sure you'd get off scot-free."

"Hmph." Max removed his beaver hat and tossed it onto the ground at the foot of a nearby oak tree. "Hopefully it won't come to that. As much as I'd like to end him, I'd rather not get hauled before the courts. A bit of bloodletting—Rochfort's blood, not mine, of course—should satisfy me."

"And me as well."

Max turned and scowled into the gloom of the trees. "Nate. What the hell are you doing here?"

"I didn't want to miss out on all the fun," he said, drawing closer. "Although I know you're an excellent shot and I hear Edgerton is too"—he nodded at the baron —"it doesn't hurt to have someone else you can trust at your back."

Max inclined his head. "Thank you. I appreciate your support."

Nate's mouth quirked with a wry smile. "Besides, to be perfectly honest, I'm worried that Charlie will kill me if I don't look out for you. You know how protective she can be of her friends."

Charlie. Max's heart constricted with a peculiar sensation he suspected was a combination of sympathy and regret. Sympathy that she was suffering and regret that he hadn't been able to stop Rochfort from publishing her highly personal list of desires. Desires a gently bred lady should never admit to in public. It didn't matter that she was only referred to as Lady C. Given her past history, anyone who was anyone would believe Lady Charlotte Hastings was the author.

Somehow, some way, he had to make everything better. And punishing Rochfort was but the first thing he intended to do.

Rochfort's second stepped into the clearing and beckoned Lord Edgerton over. Edgerton nodded and took Max's brace of pistols with him for the other man to inspect. All the while, Rochfort waited in the shadows of a beech tree, sending a glowering stare in Max's direction. If the baron hoped to unnerve him, it wouldn't work. Max's father had used a similar bullying tactic on him so many times in his youth to intimidate and "toughen him up" that Max had become inured to it.

"I'm pleased to see you have Mr. Havers standing by." Nate nodded in the direction of the surgeon who stood several yards away, near his own carriage in the laneway.

Max nodded. The surgeon had stitched up their friend Hamish MacQueen after he was grievously wounded at Waterloo, and Max firmly believed the man had saved the Scot's life. "He's also offered to give the signal to fire. Shouldn't be long now."

"It had better not be," rejoined Nate. "Or soon it will be too bloody dark."

Obviously satisfied with the condition and quality of Max's firearms, Loxley called Rochfort over to choose his weapon. Max followed suit, and after Edgerton reminded both combatants of the agreed upon conditions—that shots would be exchanged until one of them could no

longer stand—Rochfort and Max both retreated to opposite ends of the clearing to wait for Mr. Havers to give the
signal with the drop of his kerchief.

As Max checked his weapon one last time and took up
his position, he centered his anger. It sat like a cold hard
stone, deep in his gut.

Uncompromising. Unwavering.

Charlie deserved so much more than the hand she'd
been dealt, and Max would do this for her because...

He swallowed. He didn't have time to be distracted by
useless, mawkish sentiment. He was doing this because it
was the right thing to do. That was all.

If he felt fear, he was not aware of it. Tension tightened his muscles and sharpened his senses as he drew a
steadying breath and raised his pistol. Took aim at
Rochfort, who stood at the ready, his firearm trained
steadily upon Max. Attired all in black save for his white
cravat and high-point collar, his opponent's frame almost
blended into the shadows of the dense copse at his back.

Time slowed down. Stretched. Max could measure its
passing in heartbeats, breaths, but there seemed to be a
century between each one.

And then Mr. Havers gave the signal. His snow-white
kerchief began to flutter to the ground, and Max pulled
the trigger.

The sharp crack of weapons discharging rang out, and
in the very next instant, Max was reeling backward, stag-
gering to keep upright.

Fuck. Devil take me. He'd been hit. Winged. His left
upper arm was ablaze. But as he clutched at the wound,
pistol still in hand, he became aware of activity at the
other end of the clearing.

Rochfort was down. On his knees. Gripping his
shoulder. His pale face glowed with a strange spectral
light above his perfectly tied cravat.

And just as Havers and Loxley reached his side, the
baron toppled over.

≈

Hastings House, Berkeley Square

"My lady, my lady." Molly was rapping at the door of Charlie's bedroom, lightly but insistently. "My lady, you have a visitor. Lady Malverne. My lady?"

Groaning, Charlie rolled onto her stomach and dragged a pillow over her head. She had no idea what time it was, but she'd let Molly draw the curtains, light the candles, and stir the fire to life several hours ago. While part of Charlie wanted to see Sophie, her soul was still too raw, too crushed and humiliated, to even seek comfort from a dear and trusted friend.

Why wouldn't the ground open up and swallow her whole?

In fact, the only person Charlie had seen today—besides Molly—had been her father. Lord Westhampton had visited her rooms in the early afternoon, and while he hugged her and patted her back ineffectually, she clung to his superfine-clad shoulder like a limpet, offering incoherent apologies between wracking sobs.

When her fit of crying had eventually abated, he'd mentioned that he would speak to his man of affairs about the possibility of suing the *Beau Monde Mirror* and Lord Rochfort for libel—Charlie had confessed who she thought was behind the ruinous article—but her father doubted it would come to much, given the paper had been careful not to actually print her name in full. And if anything, bringing legal proceedings against the publication would undoubtedly prolong the life of the scandal. A public court case might drag on for months and months, and her father would understand if she couldn't abide it.

Because he'd been so sweet and understanding and not angry at all, it had made Charlie feel doubly worse. Her anguish and guilt were so smothering, so heavy and overwhelming, she wasn't sure if she'd ever be able to fight her way through to the surface and breathe freely again.

And now sweet Sophie was here. When it was clear that Molly would keep knocking until she was ordered to go away, Charlie flung off the pillow, sat up…and then the door opened.

"Charlie. Oh, my darling friend." Sophie entered the room, her blue eyes soft with love and understanding. "Please say you'll forgive me for the intrusion. But I just had to see you." A shadow crossed her countenance, and her expression shifted into one of concern. "I…I have news."

A frisson of panic rippled through Charlie. *What else could possibly go wrong?*

"What is it?" she asked. Rising from the bed, she took a step forward and brushed a tangled lock of hair out of her eyes. "Is everything all right with you and Nate and Thomas?"

"Yes, yes, we're all perfectly well." Sophie crossed the Aubusson rug and took both of Charlie's hands in hers. "Nate and I are worried about you, of course. And I'm so angry that the *Beau Monde Mirror* has impugned you so maliciously. But the reason I've come is…" She drew a deep breath. "It's about Max. He's fine…"

Charlie frowned in confusion. "Why wouldn't he be fine?" The alarm flickering inside her burst into flame. "What's happened?"

Sophie squeezed her hands. "As I said, he's fine, and I'm sorry that I'm not explaining this very well." She glanced at the bedroom door to make sure it was closed, then drew Charlie over to the bed. "Let's sit."

"Now," she continued, her expression still grave. "Earlier today, when Nate was at Gentleman Jackson's, Max arrived, looking for Lord Rochfort. And yes, Nate and I now know what that wicked, contemptible man has done to you, Charlie. I can't even begin to understand the pain you've endured."

Charlie's vision blurred with tears, but she dashed them away. She'd cried enough today. "Thank you," she murmured. "I won't lie. It hasn't been easy these past few weeks, pretending everything is quite all right when it hasn't been. The last thing I wanted was for Lord Rochfort to do the unthinkable and reveal my private, innermost thoughts to the papers for everyone to see. And I hate that he's not only shamed me, but you, Nate, Father, and the rest of our family."

Sophie gathered her into a warm hug. "Do not worry about the rest of us. It's you who needs our support right now." Drawing back, she studied Charlie's face. "But I digress."

"Yes, you were telling me about Max, and that he was looking for Lord Rochfort…" Charlie gasped. "Oh, my God. I'm almost too scared to ask what happened. *Did* Max find him?"

Sophie nodded. "Yes…and he challenged him to a duel right in the very middle of the boxing saloon, and Rochfort accepted. Pistols at Hampstead Heath at dusk. They've…" She winced. "They've already fought."

"Oh…" Charlie was suddenly very glad she was sitting down. Incomprehension warred with wonder and a modicum of anger. "Oh…I cannot fathom… How…?" She closed her eyes for a moment and tried to organize her riotous thoughts and emotions. "Max shouldn't have. What a completely noble yet entirely idiotic thing to do. If he'd been killed…because of me and my stupid list." She pressed a hand to her stomach, not even wanting to contemplate such an outcome. "But you said Max is all right, didn't you?"

"Yes, both he and Rochfort agreed that the duel would end when one of them could no longer stand. Max has a relatively minor injury. A bullet graze to his upper arm."

Charlie inhaled a shaky breath. "And what of Rochfort?"

"Max's bullet lodged in Lord Rochfort's shoulder but didn't hit anything vital according to the surgeon who attended him at the scene. Word is, he should recover. Although"—Sophie's mouth twitched with a wry smile —"Nate suspects Rochfort's pride might not."

Charlie shivered as she recalled the murderous look the baron had shot her way and Max's when they'd invaded his library two nights ago. Max might have attempted to defend the slight to her honor in the manner preferred by many a gentleman, but Rochfort didn't seem like a man who let go of his personal grudges easily.

"I can't believe Max took it upon himself to do this," she whispered. "He…"

Oh, no. Charlie's stomach pitched. "Word will get out about this too, won't it? If Max challenged Lord Rochfort in the middle of Gentleman Jackson's, the gossip will spread. Everyone will soon know that the Duke of Exmoor fought a duel to defend my honor. They'll think he's the mysterious duke of my…" She couldn't say it.

Sophie winced. "I'm afraid so."

Charlie sprang to her feet. "I must go to him. See him this minute." *Give him a piece of my mind for feeding the ton's scandalmongers even more humiliating fodder. Try to convince him he's not the duke of my—* Gah! Even in her mind, she couldn't bring herself to say it.

She raced about the room, looking for a shawl or a wrapper. Molly had dressed her in a pale blue gown earlier this morning, but she'd been curled up in bed for most of the day. The silk muslin was hideously rumpled, but right at this moment, she didn't care.

She pulled a crimson cashmere shawl out of a drawer in her dressing room, and as she quickly thrust her feet into slippers, she called out to Sophie, "Did you come here in a carriage?"

"Yes, I did. And Nate is downstairs waiting for you. He thought you would want to visit Max when you heard all that had transpired."

Charlie emerged, suddenly suspicious. "He did?"

"Yes." Sophie held her gaze steadily. "He knows how much you esteem Max and thought you would want to see for yourself that he is, indeed, all right."

"Oh. That's very considerate of him."

"Are you ready?"

Charlie dragged her hands through her unbound curls, her fingers catching in the snarls. "Yes," she said. Her hair might be a bird's nest, but she didn't want to waste time calling for Molly to brush and arrange it. Not when the man she cared about had fought a duel for her, and in doing so, had inadvertently deepened her predicament. "Let's go."

CHAPTER 8

"It is a truth universally acknowledged, that a single man in possession of a good fortune, must be in want of a wife."—Jane Austen, *Pride and Prejudice.*
But what if that man is an inveterate rakehell…?
This month, the *Beau Monde Mirror* will be giving our readers who are budding debutantes—or even perennial wallflowers who are perhaps beginning to wilt—tips to capture the eye, and perhaps the heart, of that most prized but often elusive creature—a monied ton bachelor.
The Beau Monde Mirror: The Essential Style & Etiquette Guide

Exmoor House, Grosvenor Square

The footman had barely let down the steps to Nate's carriage before Charlie was scrambling out of it and racing up to the front door of Exmoor House.

Chiffley, the butler, opened his mouth to protest when she barged inside, but Charlie cut him short. "Where is he?" she demanded. Even if he was in his bedroom, she would demand admittance. After all, her reputation couldn't get any worse.

"He's, ah… Let me check…" Chiffley's gaze darted away, but when Charlie took a step closer and pinned him with her most imperious look, he emitted a sigh of resignation. "He's in the library, my lady."

"Thank you."

"My pleasure, my lady."

Swift steps carried Charlie across the marble floor of the vestibule and down the hall leading to the library. Without bothering to knock, she pushed open the double doors and advanced into the room. "Max," she began without pre-amble, "we need to talk. I appreciate what you did today, I truly do, but you promised me that you wouldn't make the situation worse, and—" She broke off, stunned to silence as she finally registered the scene before her.

Max was standing by his desk, his back to the door, wearing nothing but buckskin breeches and top boots. A liveried servant, perhaps Max's valet, hovered nearby with a cobalt-blue silk banyan draped over his arm, and another gentleman—middle-aged and well-dressed—was carefully wrapping a linen bandage around the duke's bulging bicep.

"Lady Charlotte," Max said, glancing over one impos-sibly broad shoulder. "May I introduce you to Mr. Havers, physician and a fellow of the Royal College of Surgeons here in London?"

"I, ah… Of course." Charlie inclined her head as a burning blush marched across her cheeks. How she must look, barging in unannounced without a chaperone, dressed like a slattern. "Mr. Havers."

But despite her embarrassment, her gaze immediately drifted back to Max and his lean, muscled, *naked* back. To his narrow hips and firmly rounded buttocks encased in that figure-hugging leather. He was… She swallowed, her mouth suddenly dry. He was too magnificent for words. Perfect. A veritable work of art. Indeed, he reminded her of one of the Elgin marble statues she'd seen at the British Museum. An ancient Greek god come to life.

The surgeon, Havers, put the finishing touches to the bandage, turned to face her, and bowed. "My lady."

It was only then that Charlie noticed that the doctor's fingers were slightly stained and that there was a pile of bloody linen—towels and washcloths, perhaps—upon the desk by a bowl and ewer. She reached for the back of a nearby wingback chair as the reality of what Max had done for her—what he'd risked for the sake of her already besmirched reputation—hit her full force. Her knees trembled and her chest felt far too tight. All the air seemed to have been sucked out of the room.

Max could have been killed. And all because of me and my silly list.

After Max declined Mr. Havers's offer of Kendal's Black Drop, a laudanum concoction to reduce the pain of his injury, he thanked the surgeon then bid him farewell. The manservant was dismissed too. After draping the banyan over the back of another chair when Max waved it away, the servant then collected the soiled linen and Max's discarded coat, shirt, and waistcoat, which lay in a rumpled pile at his master's feet.

As the double doors shut behind him, Max, still shirt-less and apparently oblivious to his scandalous state of undress, crossed to the sideboard where his tray of spirits sat. "I'm having a cognac, Charlie. After the day I've had, I certainly need one. Would you care for one before we have our much-needed talk?"

"I…ah… Yes, thank you," she murmured as heat scorched her cheeks yet again. She really did need a slug of something strong to restore her equilibrium.

Inwardly admonishing herself for behaving like an in-coherent, blushing ninnyhammer, she joined Max. Which was a mistake. A sideways glance sent her pulse racing, and another wave of breathlessness assailed her. Max's naked front was even more entrancing than his back. Be-fore she looked away, she had a fleeting impression of swelling chest muscles, a scattering of light brown hair, tightly bronzed nipples like ha'pennies, a ridged torso, and another tantalizing trail of hair descending into the waistband of his breeches.

Good Lord. Somehow, Charlie dragged in a much-needed breath and gathered her wayward thoughts. "But before I partake in a tipple—and berate you for allowing your misplaced sense of chivalry to cloud your judgment —I must ask if I can take a look at your arm."

Max frowned down at her. "Whatever for? The wound is quite superficial, all things considered. And Havers has an excellent reputation."

"I'm sure he does. And yes, Nate and Sophie told me it was only a graze. But did Mr. Havers apply alcohol to the wound before he bandaged it? Something strong like whisky or brandy?"

Max scowled as he dispensed a decent measure of his cognac into two crystal tumblers. "What? No. Why would anyone waste good alcohol on treating a wound?"

Charlie lifted her chin. "Arabella once told me that doing so helps prevent purulence. Her grandfather, also an esteemed physician, used to recommend such a practice. Arabella doesn't know why it works exactly, but she assures me that it does. I'd hate to think what would happen if infection set in."

She caught his gaze and gave him a reproving look as she added, "It's either that or I can apply a hot poker, Your Grace. Apparently, that works too. Your choice."

Max grunted. "All right, then. Brandy it is. But not cognac. I'm not wasting that."

Charlie discarded her shawl on the way to the desk to retrieve a clean cloth. When she returned to Max's side, he'd already removed Mr. Havers's bandage.

She winced as she took in the sight of the stitched graze. It looked angry and red and puckered, and rather than a neat straight line, it was jagged. "You'll have a decent scar," she remarked as she reached for the bottle of brandy, uncorked it, then poured some onto the folded linen washcloth. "And describing it as a superficial wound seems like a gross understatement. Rochfort's bullet seems to have taken quite a piece out of you."

"Yes..." Max glanced down and examined it. Screwing up his nose, he added, "All right, it's a sizable graze. But it will mend." He caught Charlie's gaze. "Shall we get this over with, Dr. Hastings?"

She laughed at that. "Are you ready?" she asked as she gripped his bare shoulder—to steady both herself and him—before lifting the soaked cloth. "I suspect this will sting a bit."

Max nodded. "Go ahead."

When Charlie applied the poultice to the stitched wound with a firm hand, he winced and let fly a string of such strong curses, Charlie was mightily impressed.

"Don't be such a baby," she chided gently when he'd run out of invectives and perhaps breath. "Anyone would think I'd just cut your arm off."

"You're accusing me of being—" He broke off, shaking his head, clearly incredulous. "Lady Charlotte, you are a wicked she-devil sent straight from hell to torment me, aren't you?"

She couldn't help but laugh as she ended his torture and removed the cloth. "Perhaps. You have the wicked part right, at any rate. At least that's what most of society will believe after today."

"Yes." Max offered her one of the tumblers of cognac. "About that..."

"The time for talking has arrived?" she asked, arching an eyebrow.

Max's deep blue gaze was steady. "Yes."

Charlie took a fortifying sip of her cognac. "First, let me restore your bandage, then we'll retire to the fireside. Oh"—she nodded in the direction of his banyan— "might I also suggest that you put on more clothes, Your Grace? I wouldn't want you to catch your death of cold."

"Well, if you invade my bachelor's sanctum without invitation, you must take me as you find me, my lady. And consider yourself lucky that I wasn't wearing less. Because that's been known to happen on occasion."

"Wearing less? In the library?" Charlie shook her head as she gathered up the discarded bandage and began to unravel the knots. "I just think you're a terrible tease and trying your hardest to set me to the blush, Your Grace."

"Perhaps. But I don't think I'm the only one in this room who isn't dressed appropriately," said Max dryly as Charlie began to wind the untangled strip of linen around his arm again.

Charlie wrinkled her nose. "All right, I'll concede I

came here in a rush and my hair is a mess. There's no need to rub salt into the not-insubstantial wound of my embarrassment."

Max's eyes twinkled with amusement. "It's not really your hair that's the issue. The just-tumbled-out of-bed look suits you. It's your shoes."

"My shoes?" Charlie glanced down. *Oh, no.*

In her hurry to get dressed, she'd put on mismatching slippers that didn't go with her blue gown at all. One pale lemon toe in satin and one in buff-brown leather peeked out from beneath her skirts.

"Well," she said stiffly as she tied off the ends of the bandage. "At least I'm wearing *enough*. And might I add, it's not particularly gentlemanly of you to point out my fashion faux pas? Or to make mention of my 'bed hair'. Or your apparent habit of parading about your library sans clothes."

"Lady Charlotte. When have I ever laid claim to being a gentleman *all* of the time? That would be far too much effort for a scoundrel like me."

"Hmph. I suppose you have a point," she said, picking up her cognac and retreating to the fireside. "Just as I cannot really lay claim to being a true lady *all* of the time, despite my honorific title."

She chose a leather wingback chair and nursed her cognac between her hands. But as Max took the seat next to her, she frowned.

"What?" he said, raising his eyebrows. "I put my banyan on."

He had indeed. The contours of his wide, well-muscled shoulders were highlighted to perfection by the fall of the rich blue silk. Even though he'd secured the robe loosely about his hips with a gold tie, it sagged open, revealing far too much of his chest and long, lean torso.

But that's not why she was frowning.

"The right side of your face is bruised. Terribly bruised," she said. The crest of his cheek was swollen and empurpled. She supposed she hadn't noticed it before because he'd had his back to her when she'd first arrived, then she'd been standing to his left at the sideboard. And well, he'd been half-naked. And she'd been tending to his wounded arm.

Max touched his fingertips to his cheekbone and winced. "Yes. I'd almost forgotten about it. It's nothing, though."

"It doesn't look like nothing to me. How did you come by it?"

Max waved his cognac in the air. "I might have sparred a bit at Gentleman Jackson's earlier this afternoon."

Charlie snorted. "Sparring? Is that a new euphemism for trading blows with Lord Rochfort?"

Max sighed. "Let's just call it another instance of chivalry run amuck. In any case, it hardly signifies now."

"Well, I hope you landed a good punch or two on Rochfort's person."

Max's mouth kicked into a grin. "I may have."

"Excellent," Charlie said. "While I'm still miffed with you for endangering your life to defend my already dubious honor, I'm also grateful that you cared enough to do so. According to Nate, Rochfort took a bullet in the shoulder." Charlie's frown deepened. "Speaking of Nate... where is he?"

"You were expecting him?"

"Well yes, considering Nate and Sophie brought me here. But it's only just occurred to me that they haven't joined us...which is decidedly odd. We both know Nate has always been quite touchy about you and I spending too much time together."

"Yes, about that..." said Max.

The smoldering ember of suspicion inside Charlie flared anew. "I have this horrid nagging feeling that something is going on." She narrowed her gaze. "What are you up to?"

"I think you must have an idea," said Max. "When you first burst in here, you accused me of making the situation worse for you. And you're quite right. I did, despite my promise that I wouldn't. Suffice it to say, my anger over Rochfort's betrayal—the injustice of the whole situation—got the better of me. In any event, because I took it upon myself to publicly challenge Rochfort to a duel to defend your honor—and then went through with it— there *will* be speculation as to why I did so. There will be talk that I am, indeed, the duke of your—"

Charlie held up a hand. "Stop. Don't say it. It's humiliating enough to know it's printed in a newspaper. And just so you're perfectly clear, you are *not* that man. When I penned that list of silly romantic fantasies, I…I had an imaginary duke in mind. I mean, I hate to sound like all those other husband-hungry debutantes that you are trying so desperately to avoid, but doesn't every young tonnish miss imagine she'll wed a duke and become a duchess one day?"

Max swilled his cognac, his expression non-committal. "So I've heard. My mother would certainly agree. In fact, she's counting on quite a few tonnish misses lining up like potential brood mares for me to inspect."

"You see? There you go," said Charlie, warming to her argument. "I may have the occasional lapse in judgment, but I would never be so foolish as to set my cap at a marriage-averse rakehell like you, Maximilian Devereux. No offense intended, of course." She had no idea if he'd believe her lie, but she had to try to salvage some remnants of her shredded dignity. If Max suspected for one moment that she really *did* harbor a deep and abiding affection for him… That she desired him, might even love him in spite of the fact it was becoming clearer by the moment that he didn't feel the same way…

Oh, the horror.

Max's mouth twitched. "Or course. Be that as it may, it won't stop everyone else from assuming the worst— that I actually *am* that duke. So…" His gaze caught hers. Held. "Given all of that, the most logical course of action —and indeed the best and *only* way to restore your reputation in the eyes of the ton, in my opinion—is that we… you and I…hammer out the terms of a mutually beneficial fixed-term arrangement."

"What on earth do you mean by that? A mutually beneficial fixed-term arrangement sounds rather like a business transaction or..." *Oh, no.* Charlie shook her head. "Surely you aren't suggesting that you and I, that we..."

"Yes, I am," said Max, his expression as solemn as could be. "We should enter into a faux engagement for the duration of the Season. It would solve both your problem and mine."

"A faux engagement," Charlie repeated. How utterly lowering to receive such an unromantic proposal. Not that she expected Max to fall at her feet and profess his undying love. He might have fought a duel for her, but that really didn't mean anything.

Men fought duels over all sorts of inconsequential matters. Things like cheating at cards and whose dog started a fight. She didn't doubt that Max cared about her well-being, but to expect anything more from him after all this time would be beyond foolish on her part.

She'd already played the fool far too long.

She retrieved her cognac and took a decent sip. Then another. As the fiancée of a duke, perhaps she would not be so openly snubbed by society, and of course, she was very keen to reduce the impact her fall from grace had upon her family.

Her father had only just begun to court again, and the thought that he might retreat into his lonely shell because of his wayward daughter made her want to weep. And who knows what teasing her brothers might have to endure at Eton about their disgraced older sister.

The question was, if she *did* take up Max's offer, would she be able to protect her heart? Because that was the real danger of his proposal—that she'd fall even more in love with him if she spent an inordinate amount of time in his company over the next few months.

*But...*it would also give her the opportunity to test the waters once and for all. Max had just suggested that they could "hammer out the terms" of this arrangement.

Hmmm. She suspected small, careful steps were required so she didn't scare Max away.

"Charlie, your silence is beginning to worry me. What are you thinking?" Max's brow had furrowed into a frown. "I know it's a lot to take in and mull over. And of course, you are free to turn me down—"

"You mentioned an engagement would solve a problem for you too," said Charlie, pinning him with a narrow look. "What did you mean by that?"

"Well"—Max cocked an eyebrow—"one would hope that it would effectively stop this Season's crop of debutantes and their matchmaking mamas from hunting me down. And it would certainly stop my mother from trying to engineer an engagement with someone from her god-awful list. If I'm no longer an eligible commodity on the market, I won't have to watch my back every time I step outside."

Charlie couldn't deny that his reasoning was sound. "And when the Season ends, I suspect you have an exit strategy, so to speak…" She trailed off and studied Max, trying to detect any flicker of feeling for her. But she found none. His noble countenance was a study in cool, ducal neutrality.

"When the Season ends, I will leave it up to you to decide what to do," he said matter-of-factly. "You could quite safely jilt me, and if you claim it's because I'm a scoundrel, everyone will believe you, given my rakish history. Or you and I can wed, and we could look upon it as a marriage of convenience. I might not be the man you dreamed of marrying one day, but I like to think a union with me would not be an altogether disagreeable prospect. We do rub along rather well together. And I would be a generous husband. But as I said, I will leave the decision as to whether we wed or not entirely up to you."

"Oh, well, that makes all the difference as to whether I accept your entirely practical, perfectly sensible proposal. Or not." Charlie couldn't hide the bitterness in her voice. "But I think there is a glaring flaw in your plan. My father might give his consent to our betrothal, but what of Nate? He's always been against the idea of you and I…" She released a heavy sigh. "He thinks that you and I will not suit because we want different things. You don't really wish to wed, and when you do, I'm sure you have an accomplished young woman with a pristine reputation in mind. And wicked hellion that *I* am, I'm foolishly holding out for a love match with a duke who doesn't exist anywhere but in my fantasies. So, I can't imagine that Nate will be happy about it. Are you willing to ruin your long-standing friendship—"

"He already knows."

"What?"

"I've already spoken to him about the prospect of you and I entering an engagement-in-name-only, and he is amenable to the idea if you are. He agrees that such an arrangement might help to dissipate the scandal. Which can only be good, all things considered."

"Oh…" Charlie abandoned her chair and stalked over to the fireplace. Lifting the poker, she jabbed at the logs, and sparks flew up the chimney. "It seems it's all been decided, then."

"Of course it hasn't. I've made an offer—and I know it probably isn't the one you've always dreamed of—but it only has to be a temporary arrangement, if you so choose."

"I see." Charlie put down the poker and wrapped her arms about her middle. Despite the fact she was standing right by the fire, she suddenly felt chilled to the bone. "If I accept your proposal, Max, your mother will be furious. She's never liked me. And after today…" Charlie shivered. Memories of scathing looks Cressida, the formidable Dowager Duchess of Exmoor, had sent her way flitted through her mind. The woman had blue eyes, but unlike Max's, hers were as hard and frosty as Arctic ice.

Max followed her over to the fireplace and leaned his uninjured arm against the black marble mantel. Charlie was conscious of the fact his robe had fallen open, so she kept her gaze carefully fixed on the burning logs and the leaping flames.

"I'll make sure my mother lends you nothing but her full and unstinting support," Max said gently. "She's one of the *bon ton's* doyens. She can ensure Polite Society's doors are opened, rather than shut against you. And so can my sister-in-law, Diana. She is quite amiable, and I've been led to believe well-liked with wonderful connections. Between them both, I'm certain they can smooth the path for your re-entry into Society."

Charlie thought she'd much prefer to walk barefoot across broken glass than down any path supposedly cleared for her by Cressida or Diana Devereux.

Nevertheless, she couldn't deny that yet again, Max was doing his very best to sort out this awful mess they both found themselves in.

She looked up from the fire and studied him. The way the flickering light illuminated all the strong contours and planes of his handsome profile. How his deep blue eyes drew her in, tempting her to drown in them forever. How she wanted to reach out and brush a light caress over his bruised cheek and say thank you for caring about her honor. And her family's honor too.

For a brief moment, she allowed herself to imagine what it would be like to be married to the Duke of Exmoor. To spend every single day with him, laughing and talking about anything and everything. To join him in the marriage bed every single night. To kiss him and run her hands over his hard, sleek body, exploring. Worshipping him with her own body...

Desire flared, bright and burning. Max was proposing an "engagement in name only", but he was a man with strong passions. She recalled the look in his eyes in the moonlit alcove at Rochfort House as he'd pressed his finger to her lips and she'd sensed he'd been tempted to kiss her. Would he be able to resist temptation once they were betrothed? Or would he go behind her back and continue to visit places like the Rouge et Noir Club? Would he continue to seduce widows or even married women when he thought she wasn't looking?

Of course, she knew he'd practiced such habits for years. That he'd bedded countless women, and all the while she'd watched from the wings, waiting and hoping one day he'd pick *her* to join him. And that when he did, she'd be more than just a passing fancy.

But if they were engaged, surely she could strike a bargain with him. After all, he'd said they could negotiate the terms of their arrangement. "Max, before I give you an answer, I need to ask you—"

The door opened, and a crisp, clear voice sliced through the air. "Maximilian. What in heaven's name is going on? The gossip is rife. The town is abuzz."

Charlie jumped and whirled around. Chiffley hovered just outside in the hallway, his face as red as a beet as the Dowager Duchess of Exmoor swept past him and entered the room like Boadicea advancing into battle. Drawing to a halt a few feet away, her disdainful gaze skimmed Charlie from the top of her disheveled head to her mismatched toes. "Oh, good Lord. Who let *that* impudent hussy inside?"

Impudent hussy? Well, so much for Max's pronouncement that Cressida would lend her support.

"Mother," drawled Max. When Charlie chanced a glance his way, she noted that he'd at last cinched his banyan tightly about his waist. "I'll thank you not to insult Lady Charlotte. In fact"—he suddenly reached for Charlie with his uninjured arm, and after threading his fingers through hers, drew her to his side— "I insist you apologize this minute, or I'll ask you to leave."

The dowager duchess sniffed. A tall and elegant woman, she reminded Charlie of a perfectly carved marble statue, beautiful but in an austere way. Hard and cold and unyielding. "And why should I deign to offer an apology to someone who is so far beneath my notice—"

"Enough," barked Max, and his mother started. "Apologize to my fiancée or get out."

"Fiancée?" The dowager duchess paled. "So, the rumors *are* true. That you fought a duel on behalf of this… this piece of bag—" She broke off and fixed her son with a look which might pass for imploring if it contained a speck of warmth. "Oh, Maximilian. How could you? She's simply not worth it. I know it. You know it. The whole of the ton knows it."

"Of course she's worth it, Mother." Max squeezed Charlie's hand, then added, "She means far more to me than Lady Penelope or any of those other bird-witted chits on your list of prospective wives ever could. And as you still haven't done as I've asked and said sorry to Lady Charlotte, I'll once again ask you to go. Chiffley?" He called through the still open doorway. "If you'd be so kind as to escort the dowager duchess out? I have some unfinished business to discuss with Lady Charlotte."

"Maximilian," erupted his mother. Bright color flagged her cheeks. "I beg you to reconsider. Think of the family name. Think of me. What would your father have—"

"Don't." Max's voice was colder and sharper than a midwinter gale. "Do not *ever* speak to me of my father again. He's dead and gone, and unless you can change your ways and stop your infernal meddling, I will sever all ties with you. Are we clear?"

To Charlie's utter astonishment, Cressida bowed her head. "Yes, my son. We are." Lifting her gaze, she turned to Charlie. "And Lady Charlotte, I do hope that you'll accept my sincerest apology for my rude outburst and disparaging remarks. I have no excuse other than I was not thinking clearly. When I heard Maximilian, my only surviving child, had fought a duel in your name, I was quite overwhelmed and…" She gave a tight smile. "It won't happen again, and I do hope that in time, you will see your way to forgive me."

Charlie inclined her head; she couldn't bring herself to curtsy. Not for one minute did she think the dowager duchess's apology was sincere. "Thank you, Your Grace," she returned stiffly for the sake of appearances.

"Yes. Thank you, Mother," added Max. "I bid you good night."

∽

As soon as the door shut, Max turned to Charlie. Guilt twisted his gut. "Oh, God. I'm so, so sorry for what just transpired. And after all those things I'd said about my mother." He shook his head. "Her behavior is inexcusable. Unforgivable."

"You're not responsible for her opinions or what she

says or does," Charlie said softly. "But I'm also quite certain that she's not alone in her low opinion of me."

"Well, I don't see you that way. My opinion of you couldn't be higher."

"Thank you." A soft, rosy blush tinted Charlie's cheeks, and her full lips curved into a small smile that didn't quite reach her eyes.

Max still hadn't let go of her hand, and she hadn't made a move to remove it either. The unfamiliar urge to draw Charlie into his arms and offer comfort flickered through him. To cup her face in his hands and kiss away any lingering sadness. To slide his palms over her lush curves and plunge his fingers into her wild, tumbling curls…

He swallowed. No. He couldn't do that. He'd promised Nate that he wouldn't seduce Charlie. This engagement was all for show.

But she hasn't said yes… And he needed her to, for both their sakes.

"Charlie," he said gravely, "I also owe you an apology. I told my mother that you were my fiancée. But you hadn't yet accepted my offer. And before my mother so rudely interrupted, you were about to ask me something."

"Yes." Charlie blushed again. Now she did let go of his hand and retreated to the hearth. "You're ostensibly making this offer so that this dreadful scandal in connection with my name goes away. But"—she inhaled deeply as though steeling herself to continue— "I need to know that you too will do your utmost to avoid any kind of scandal during the Season. I do not wish to come across as a harpy before we've even begun—and I know you are under no obligation to be faithful to me when our arrangement will only be temporary—but if you continue to frequent places like the Rouge et Noir Club, or pursue other conquests, and if your lack of interest in your fiancée is noted by others…" She shrugged. "I suppose what I'm trying to say is that our engagement should *appear* real, even if it isn't."

Max blew out a sigh. He hadn't thought that far ahead. "You are absolutely right, of course. In fact"—he placed a hand upon what remained of his heart—"I solemnly swear that I will stay true to you from this day forth and throughout the Season if you consent to my proposal. No one will have cause to suspect that our betrothal isn't genuine."

Some emotion Max couldn't quite recognize flitted across Charlie's face. But then she smiled. "Very well, Your Grace. I will say yes."

He smiled back. "Excellent. I will speak to your father in the morning so we can make it official."

"Well…" Charlie clasped her hands behind her back and took several steps forward. In that attitude, her fulsome breasts pushed against the restraints of stays and bodice, and the firelight caressed one long tendril of her unbound hair as it snaked toward her cleavage.

Good Lord, she was lovely. Did she know how tempting she was? If he hadn't promised her brother to keep his hands to himself, he'd drag her into his arms right this minute and kiss her senseless. With a Herculean effort, he forced himself to focus on her eyes as she began to speak again. "We're engaged, but as it's in name only, Max, I'm not sure how we should plight our troth. Shaking hands seems far too formal, but then kissing doesn't seem appropriate either, considering the circumstances."

"No…" Devil take him, why did she have to mention the very thing he was trying to resist? Before he could stop himself, Max's gaze fell to Charlie's damnably delectable mouth. She was so close, her perfume teased him. The fragrance wrapped around him like silken ribbons, tangling him in the scent of sweet summer blooms—orange blossom and honeysuckle, and jasmine, perhaps. To stop himself reaching for her, he clasped his hands behind his back too. He winced as he pulled the stitches in his arm. The graze began to throb in earnest.

Charlie's brow creased with concern. "I should go so you can get some rest."

"Yes, I think that would be best," conceded Max, not trusting himself to spend any more time alone with

Charlie. "Nate informed me earlier that he would leave his carriage here to take you home."

Charlie gave a disgruntled snort. "I really must have a talk with my brother," she muttered before retrieving her discarded shawl. "Men are always complaining about managing females, but I seem to have London's most managing brother."

Max followed her movements, watching as she flipped her hair over one shoulder and wrapped the shawl about herself. "He only wants what's best for you."

She sighed at that. "Yes. You're right. Well…" She returned to the fireside, and before Max knew what she was about, she slid a hand around his waist, then reached up to kiss his cheek. Her lips brushed so close to his, if he turned his head just a little…

"Good night, Max," she murmured, her breath a teasing caress along his jaw. Her fingers lingered at his waist for a moment longer, her gentle touch searing him through the thin silk of his robe. Max forced himself to curl his own hands into fists so he wouldn't seize her and do what he really wanted to do. What he was beginning to suspect she wanted to do too…

It was only when the door closed behind her that Max could breathe freely again. He topped up his cognac, tossed it back, then poured another measure.

Dear God above. What had he got himself into?

The next few months would be sheer hell. Being so close to Charlie on a regular basis, pretending they were as besotted as a pair of lovebirds, but then not being able to touch her… It made him want to gnash his teeth and howl in frustration. Since he'd assumed his ducal title, being denied something he really wanted was a novel experience for him. And he didn't like the feeling. Not one little bit. Because it reminded him of times past, when wanting something with a passion was seen as a weakness. When the things he cared about were taken away.

He poured another cognac to blunt his emotions and dull the pain in his throbbing arm before returning to his favorite chair by the fire.

The strange thing was, he was certain that sticking to the terms of Charlie's bargain—avoiding any form of dalliance with other women—wouldn't be a problem. Because for the first time in his life, ever since that night at the Rouge et Noir Club, he couldn't seem to think about anyone *but* Charlie.

Damn it. Perhaps this inconvenient obsession, this incessant hunger inside him had blazed to life simply because he was being denied forbidden fruit. But if he gave into temptation and seduced Charlie to satisfy his craving, he'd feel so bloody guilty for going against his word, he didn't think he'd be able to live with himself.

He might not care deeply about many things, but if he made a promise, he meant to keep it.

CHAPTER 9

Betrothal rings… While not a necessity by any means, who wouldn't like to be presented with a token of affection to celebrate such a momentous event? A little hint dropped now and again in the vicinity of one's fiancé certainly couldn't hurt…
The Beau Monde Mirror: The Essential Style & Etiquette Guide

Hastings House, Berkeley Square
March 30, 1819

The weather was dismal. Cold and raining, in fact, but Charlie was in good spirits. Well, relatively good spirits, all things considered as she welcomed Sophie into the drawing room to share a spot of tea in the early afternoon.

"Congratulations on your engagement, darling Charlie," Sophie cried and gathered her into a warm hug as soon as she entered the room. "Nate shared the good news this morning after Max dropped by on his way here to speak to your father. I'm so, so happy for you. I knew it was meant to be."

Yes, she, Lady Charlotte Hastings, was now officially engaged to Maximilian Devereux, the Duke of Exmoor. And Max, true to his word, had visited Hastings House first thing this morning to ask for her father's blessing and to arrange the marriage contracts. Charlie had only seen her fiancé briefly when her father had summoned her to the library to make sure she did indeed wish to be betrothed to Max.

When she'd stepped into the room, she'd been assailed by an unexpected bout of breathlessness and uncharacteristic shyness as Max had greeted her with a gentle buss against her temple. Despite the nasty bruise upon his cheek, she'd never seen him looking so handsome, and she wondered if he'd taken extra care with his appearance. His cravat was knotted in such an elaborate design it must have taken his valet an age to tie, and his azure-blue satin waistcoat brought out the color of his eyes to perfection.

While it was easy to summon a smile for Max, lying to her father, pretending their engagement was genuine and not a "mutually beneficial fixed-term arrangement" was one of the hardest things she'd ever had to do in her life. The only way she'd been able to profess that she was as happy as a lark in spring was to remind herself that the subterfuge both she and Max had agreed to perpetuate might help. That it might lessen the damage caused by yesterday's scandalous *Beau Monde Mirror* article. Of course, her father's parliamentary colleagues and their wives would no doubt whisper about the Earl of Westhampton's thoroughly disreputable, if not entirely dissolute, daughter and her sudden and unlikely elevation. And there would be plenty of speculation about whether the betrothal would last—because how could the Duke of Exmoor truly abide being married to such a wicked, wanton creature? But at least no one would dare to openly sneer or laugh at her father.

One thing Charlie wouldn't do, though, was lie to Sophie.

Once they were settled upon one of the settees by the cheerfully blazing fire with steaming cups of fragrant tea in hand, Charlie gathered her courage. "I have something to confess," she said carefully. "Something about Max and me."

Sophie's blue eyes shone with excitement. "He made

you his own, didn't he? Last night at Exmoor House? Oh, I'm so thrilled for you, Charlie. I know how long you've been dreaming of this—"

"No, that's not it," said Charlie dolefully. "In fact"—she put down her cup and saucer on the low table in front of her—"we didn't even kiss."

"*What?* Whyever not?" Sophie's finely drawn black brows dipped into a frown. "Don't tell me Max wants to do the noble thing and wait until the end of the Season to introduce you to the delights of sexual congress? To be perfectly honest, I'm not even certain why you both want to wait so long to get married. A special license would be easy enough for him to procure."

Charlie sighed and fiddled with the gold fringing on the end of her paisley shawl. "There is a reason," she said. Drawing a steadying breath, she continued, "As much as I hate to admit such a thing, I can't pretend everything is all moonlight and roses. Max and I have agreed to enter into a faux engagement."

Sophie's mouth dropped open. "What?" Her cup clattered against its saucer as she too put down her tea. "Surely you jest."

Charlie had to blink away a sudden rush of tears. "Oh, my dear friend. With all my heart, I wish I was." She confessed all to Sophie in a great breathless, watery outpouring of what had transpired the night before and all the details of her and Max's arrangement. That Nate knew about the transactional nature of it, but their father didn't. And that at the end of the Season, it was up to her to decide if she was ready to settle for a marriage of convenience or wanted to end things. If it was the latter, she intended to scarper off to the Continent with Aunt Tabitha in the hope that her broken heart would mend faster with a complete change of scenery.

At the end, Sophie's eyes were darting blue fire. "I'm speechless, Charlie. I can't believe that your brother...that my husband..." She closed her eyes and started again, "That Nate would deign to meddle in your affairs. Ugh." She leapt to her feet and began pacing back and forth across the hearthrug, her skirts flaring and swirling about her ankles in agitated fury. "And Max. Chivalry is all well and good, but surely he knows how you feel about him. It's cruel of him to dangle the thing you want so badly right in front of you but never let you have it." She stopped and folded her arms over her chest. "I'm cross with him too. Why are men such idiotic asses at times?"

"Max doesn't know how I feel," said Charlie. "Last night I lied to him. I told him he wasn't the duke of my dreams. That when I wrote that list, I was simply musing about some imaginary nobleman like all young women do. Because I really couldn't bear it if Max knew the truth. He might care about me a little—well, enough to care about defending my honor—but he doesn't love me."

Sophie pinned her with a narrow look. "Balderdash. I think he must care about you quite a lot, Charlie. He didn't have to help you when you were trying to retrieve your notebook. He didn't have to call Rochfort out. Fighting a duel is *not* a trifling matter. And when I return home, I intend to tell Nate that he must mind his own business and stop warning Max off."

Charlie sighed. "The problem is, I'm beginning to think Nate has a point. Perhaps he has good reason to be concerned that Max and I don't suit. Yes, all things considered, I think it's best to be circumspect. I've been smitten with Max since I was sixteen years old, and for years I've held onto the hope that one day he would confess that he loves me too. That he's simply been waiting for the right time to tell me. But six years have passed, and if he wasn't able to declare his feelings for me last night and offer a genuine marriage proposal, will he ever be ready to do so? I'm afraid it's time for me to face the cold hard truth, Sophie. I want a love match. A Grand Passion. But my love for Max is unrequited. And I fear it always will be so."

"Oh, my dear friend. Please don't despair." Sophie returned to Charlie's side upon the settee. "You've given me, Arabella, and Olivia such sage advice in the past. You know as well as I that falling in love can be a frightening prospect for a rakehell. Perhaps Max just needs a little more time. If he stops seeing you as Nate's little sister, someone he can't have, who knows what might happen?" She clasped Charlie's hands in hers and squeezed them. "Promise me that you will not give up," she said fiercely. "You have three whole months to nudge Max in the right direction and help him realize he's being an absolute dunderhead. And if he doesn't…"

Charlie summoned a smile. "If he doesn't, I have a Grand Tour to look forward to and new horizons to explore."

"Exactly," said Sophie.

A tray of afternoon tea things arrived; Charlie had again succumbed to the temptation of ordering a box of tiny cakes and pastries from Gunter's. One of the footmen also bore a gilt-edged missive.

Curiosity nipped at Charlie as she picked up the thick cream sheet of parchment from the silver salver. The blood-red wax seal bore the Dowager Duchess of Exmoor's coat of arms. She worried at her lower lip.

"Is everything all right? Who is it from?" asked Sophie anxiously.

"It's from Max's mother," said Charlie. She didn't know whether to open the letter or cast it into the fire. "She hates me, you know."

"Hates you?" Sophie frowned. "I could understand that she might be a bit standoffish, considering all the gossip she's no doubt heard. But surely she doesn't really hate you."

"Well, I'm certain she does. For one thing, I'm not perfect like Lady Penelope Purcell." Charlie explained that according to Max, Lady Penelope had been at the top of his mother's list of this Season's most eligible debutantes. And how she'd called Charlie an impudent hussy when she'd dropped by Exmoor House to see how Max was faring after the duel.

"Max made her apologize, but as you might expect, I'm a little nervous about opening anything written by her. Who knows, maybe she's used poisoned ink to pen her poisonous words."

Sophie laughed. "I can fetch some kid gloves if you like."

"No, it's all right." Charlie sighed. "I'm just prevaricating because I'm nervous." She cracked the seal and unfolded the parchment. "It's...an invitation. She'd like me to join her and her daughter-in-law, Diana, for afternoon tea at Devereux House next week." She looked up at Sophie. "Do you really think she's offering me an olive branch?"

"One would hope so," said Sophie. "She *is* a duchess, and as your future mother-in-law, it's the right thing for her to do. And you'll never know unless you attend."

"Very true," agreed Charlie. "And I *would* like to meet Diana. It's sad indeed that she lost her husband at such a young age. I believe she and Max's older brother, Anthony, were only married for two years before he passed away."

"Oh, dear," said Sophie. "At the risk of being insensitive, do you know what happened?"

"Only the scantest details. According to Nate, it was a riding accident. Anthony received a nasty blow to the head when he fell from his horse."

"How utterly tragic," murmured Sophie.

"Yes." Charlie twisted her teacup back and forth on its saucer. "You and I both know how much the loss of our older brother, Thomas, affected Nate. The circumstances are different, of course, but I do wonder how grief might have changed Max. He always conveys such a cool, unruffled air and is a master of using charm and humor to deflect how he really feels. Even though I've known him for years, in many ways, I don't really know him at all." She gave a mirthless laugh. "He's quite adept at keeping me at arm's length, and he seems determined to keep on doing so."

Sophie's eyes twinkled with mischief as she picked up her tea. "Come now, Charlie. One thing you've never lacked is spirit. Or guile. I'm sure you can change his mind. As I suggested earlier, you'll just have to help him see you in a different light."

～

When Max arrived back at Hastings House midafternoon, he discovered he was uncharacteristically tense; his stomach was in knots, and his pulse was elevated. It was a most disconcerting sensation. If he discounted his entire childhood or how he'd felt before entering the fray of battle, he couldn't recall the last time he'd experienced such a bout of nerves. But here he was, lingering in the vestibule of Hastings House, procrastinating because—he eyed himself sternly in a gilt-edged mirror by the drawing room door—because he didn't trust himself to do the right thing when he was alone with Charlie, despite his promise to her brother. All day he'd been thinking about her and all the things they could do if this were a *real* engagement…

But it wasn't real. He wasn't a besotted fiancé. He was… He passed a hand through his rain-damp hair, adjusted the folds of his cravat, and scowled. He was confused, and he didn't like the feeling. At all.

Telling himself he was wasting time and that he simply needed to wrest back the reins and take control—he was a twenty-eight-year-old duke, for God's sake, not a lust-ridden adolescent—he drew a deep breath and indicated to the footman waiting nearby that he could knock on the drawing room door.

A young maid opened it almost immediately. "Edwards…" she said, addressing the young footman. "Oh, I mean, Your Grace." She blushed and bobbed a curtsy.

"Who is it, Molly?" called Charlie. "I wasn't expecting anyone."

"I hope you don't mind receiving an impromptu morning call from your fiancé," replied Max as he entered the room. Charlie was sitting by the fire with her sister-in-law. "My dear Sophie." He tilted into a gentlemanly bow before adding, "I apologize for the intrusion, dear ladies. I can return to speak with you later, Charlie, if you would prefer."

"Oh." Charlie put down her teacup with a clatter and rose to her feet. "Oh, Max, what a lovely surprise. And no, you don't need to leave. Please come and join us for tea."

"Actually…" Sophie stood too. "I should be on my way. I can't bear to leave Thomas for too long. He's been a little fractious of late." She reached for Charlie's hand and gave it a squeeze. "Remember what we talked about," she said in a low voice. Turning to Max, she smiled. "And before I depart, may I offer you my heartfelt congratulations on your engagement, Max? Nate shared the wonderful news with me this morning. And I, for one, happen to think you two are perfectly matched." She winked at Charlie. "I will speak with you soon."

Charlie elegantly subsided onto the settee and patted the vacant space next to her. "Come and sit, Max, and I shall pour you some tea. Or would you prefer coffee?"

"Ah, tea is perfectly fine."

"Are you certain? It's no trouble at all. Molly…" Charlie addressed the maid who was waiting by the door. "Please go to the kitchen and ask Cook to send up a pot of coffee for His Grace, just in case he changes his mind. Then I'd like you to return to my rooms and finish mending the flounce on the leaf-green sprigged muslin. I'd like to wear it this evening. I'll ring if I need you."

"Yes, my lady." The maid curtsied, then promptly quit the room.

Charlie began to prepare his tea just the way he liked it. "Why are you hovering over there, Max?" She looked up and gave him a mischievous grin. "I won't bite, you know."

He laughed at that. Crossing the room, he claimed the opposite settee; he'd have selected the nearby wingchair, but Charlie's impudent cat, Peridot, was curled up on the seat. "My reluctance to sit by you has less to do with my fear of being bitten and more to do with the fact it's been raining all day and I'm concerned my muddy boots might stain the hem of your lovely gown." And indeed it was lovely; the light apricot silk was the perfect foil for her creamy skin and chestnut hair.

"All right, your compliment makes up for the snub," she replied and dropped a lump of sugar into his tea before stirring it. "How is your arm?"

"Sore, but no worse than yesterday, so I'm beginning

to think there might be some merit to Lady Langdale's unconventional treatment. Thank you." Max reached out to accept his cup of tea from Charlie, but he nearly dropped it when his gaze accidentally fell on her spectacular bust. As she leaned across the table, the scooped neckline of her gown gaped lower, revealing a great deal more than he'd expected.

Good Lord. Max hastily looked away and focused his attention on taking a sip of tea. Had Charlie decided to play the part of minx today? When he dared to look up, she was smiling at him innocently enough, although her fingers were toying with a heart-shaped gold locket that sat just below her collarbones. Hmm, she wasn't as naive as most tonnish misses, so perhaps she was deliberately drawing attention to her décolletage again just to tease him. She'd never done so before, but then he recalled the provoking kiss that she'd brushed against the corner of his mouth last night. The way her small hand had lingered upon his waist…

He took another, larger sip of tea.

"So, to what do I owe the pleasure of this visit?" asked Charlie as she reached for a plate of tiny cakes and leaned even farther across the table to offer him one. Her gown's neckline sagged even wider, and Max nearly choked.

Now, *that* couldn't have been an accident. Max swallowed hard and cleared his throat before selecting a tiny iced cake with a glacé cherry on top. "I wanted to let you know that our engagement will be announced in tomorrow's papers across Town, so everyone will know it's official."

"Oh…" She cast her gaze downward, then sipped her own tea. "I'm glad. I imagine there will be quite a to-do at first, and many will look askance at me, wondering why on earth the Duke of Exmoor proposed to the disreputable Lady C."

"No doubt there will be whispers," said Max, placing the untouched cake on a nearby china plate. "But everyone also adores a love story and a happy ending. It's my hope that the gossips will soon be twittering away about how romantic it all is. That the disreputable Lady

C. did indeed catch her duke. And to that end"—Max reached into the inner breast pocket of his tailcoat and withdrew a small box covered in dark red velvet—"I hope you will accept this small token of my esteem and affection. And when you wear it, no one will be able to dispute the fact that you *are* the Duke of Exmoor's fiancée."

Charlie placed her cup on its saucer very carefully. Her eyes glowed like sunlit honey as she took the box from him. "My goodness, Max. I certainly didn't expect anything like this. You've already done so much for me. More than enough."

"Open it," he said with a grin. "Tell me what you think."

Charlie removed the lid, then gasped with delight. "Oh, Max. It's divine." With trembling fingers, she removed the enormous rose-cut diamond ring from its bed of white satin and slipped it onto her ring finger. It was a perfect fit. "You really shouldn't have," she murmured, her gaze connecting with his across the table. "But thank you."

Max shifted restlessly in his seat. He'd never given such an extravagant and meaningful gift to anyone before, and it was a novel sensation. His chest seemed to be flooded with a strange warmth. "I know betrothal rings aren't all that common, but as I said, I think it's important that everyone knows you're mine."

Except she isn't really. This isn't a real *engagement,* he reminded himself.

Although the way Charlie was smiling, a petal-pink blush blooming across her cheeks, it *almost* felt real. But not quite. Because if this was a genuine betrothal, he would have slipped the ring onto Charlie's finger, and, muddy boots or not, he would be beside her right at this moment, capturing her face in his hands and kissing her generous mouth until they were both breathless. And then he would gently push aside the curls grazing her neck and taste the warm silken flesh where her pulse fluttered. He'd slide her gown off her shoulder, and after he'd whispered in her ear exactly what he'd like to do to her next, he'd push her down upon the cushions and make slow, sweet love—

Jesus Christ. What the bloody hell was wrong with him? Max leaned back in his chair and flexed his suddenly twitchy fingers on his thighs. Fantasies were all well and good, but he wasn't that man. Could never be that man, a man who "made love".

He might be unfailingly loyal to his friends—on occasion he might even seek to right the wrongs that threatened them if it was within his power to do so—but in all other matters, he was a calculating, cold-hearted realist. Unsentimental. Unromantic. He couldn't afford to be anything else.

He wouldn't allow it.

A footman arrived with a silver coffeepot, and Max breathed a sigh of relief when the man didn't immediately leave the room. Good. He had time to regroup. Shore up his defenses. Marshal his runaway thoughts into some semblance of order.

Charlie dispensed a steaming cup of black coffee, and this time he leaned across the table to take it before she could do so.

"Your mother has invited me to take tea with her and your sister-in-law at Devereux House," she remarked as she helped herself to a pastry.

"I'm pleased to see she's attempting to make amends," managed Max, suddenly transfixed by the sight of Charlie popping the bite-sized cake into her mouth and chewing it with obvious relish. He sighed inwardly. So much for his resolve to remain unaffected. "She also sent me a note this morning mentioning that she would like to hold a house party at Heathcote Hall to celebrate our engagement. After Easter, when my Parliamentary schedule allows for it."

Charlie licked a tiny crumb off her lower lip, and Max almost groaned aloud. "Heathcote Hall?" she said. "I don't think I've heard of it."

"It's a property I own at Hampstead Heath. Although my mother has laid claim to it in recent years. She says it affords her a little escape to the country without having to travel all the way to Exmoor Castle in Devonshire."

"It sounds wonderful. Heathcote Hall and the house party." Charlie's expression changed, her mouth curving with a knowing temptress's smile. "You haven't tried your cake yet. They're from Gunter's. I know it's Lent and I should be good, but sometimes I cannot help being a little wicked."

Good God, the minx *must* be teasing him and with malice aforethought. He didn't want to think about Charlie being wicked in *any* way, shape, or form. To satisfy her and distract himself from thinking about his own unsatisfied carnal appetite, he slid the cake into his mouth, and then he did indeed groan aloud. Devil take him, it was good. Damn good. *Sinfully* good. Rich and bursting with the flavor of almonds, liqueur, and cherries.

"Would you like another?" she asked, proffering the plate again. "It's impossible to have just one. These little round ones with the gold leaf on top have a walnut and chocolate-flavored filling inside. They're pure decadence."

Max couldn't resist and had to agree Charlie was right. "Which one is your favorite?" he asked when he'd finished chewing.

"Oh, I love them all."

"But if you *had* to choose? Which one would it be?"

"Hmm." Charlie idly played with the gold locket again. "That's a hard question. Gunter's sometimes makes a lemon and blackberry cake that reminds me of the end of summer. But aside from that, I do adore the almond and cherry ones."

A cake that reminded Charlie of the end of summer. Max reached for his coffee cup. He'd never thought about food in such a way before. He enjoyed a good meal, of course, but Charlie seemed to have a keener sense of taste than he did. He was suddenly a little envious of her ability to live in the moment and fully relish the flavor of whatever she ate.

But that was something he'd always admired about Charlie. Her zest, her passion, her impulsive and mischievous nature. In many ways she was completely opposite to the type of woman he imagined that he would marry one day. Someone like Lady Penelope, his mother's choice.

At least his no-strings-attached arrangement with Charlie would save him from that fate.

"Well"—Max glanced at the Boulle clock upon the mantel—"as much as I would like to tarry away the afternoon with you, I'm afraid I have another appointment." He wanted his man of affairs to appoint an inquiry agent to begin investigations into the *Beau Monde Mirror* and to keep an eye on Rochfort. Lord Westhampton had mentioned he'd contemplated suing the paper for libel but had discarded the idea when Charlie had entreated him not to add fuel to scandal's fire. But that didn't mean Max couldn't find out more about the company—its owners and who drove its dubious practices. And he wanted to know more about Lord Rochfort's finances, of course. It still bothered him that the baron had been extorting property and other assets from his victims for no apparent reason.

"Oh, no. That's such a shame," said Charlie. "But I understand how busy you must be. My father's hardly ever about for the same reason…" She straightened her shoulders. "Not that I'm complaining. Far from it. When your schedule permits, you must come for dinner. I'll invite Nate and Sophie too."

"Of course." Max stood. "I would love to."

Charlie followed him to the drawing room door. "Thank you again for the betrothal ring." Her voice was soft as she placed her hand on his arm. "I love it."

Before Max could stop himself, he caught her bare fingers and raised them to his lips. Feathered a kiss across her knuckles. Her eyes widened and her lips parted.

"Max," she breathed, "I know we agreed that this engagement should be in name only, but—"

Max squeezed her fingers gently, then released them. "Charlotte, even though I'm not the sort of man who feels tender emotion, I *do* care enough not to ruin you. It would be wrong to act on my desire if I'm not capable of giving you what you truly want. The last thing I want to do is hurt you. And no doubt your brother would want to castrate me if I did. So, all things considered, I do think it's best if we keep to the terms of our arrangement."

Her gaze hardened then. "And I would counter that what Nate doesn't know can't hurt him. I'm a grown woman and quite capable of deciding what risks I'm willing to take. Perhaps you need to think about *that*, Maximilian Devereux."

The door slammed behind him, and Max huffed out a sigh. Damn it. Just as he'd suspected last night, the next few months were going to be harder than he'd originally thought.

His mouth quirked with a wry smile as he started toward the stairs that would take him to the family's private suites. A *lot* harder, judging by the discomfort in his trousers.

It didn't take Max long to locate Charlie's sitting room. He'd been a guest at Hastings House on many occasions in the past, and he knew her rooms weren't far from Nate's old bedchamber. Charlie's maid looked up in surprise when he poked his head around the door.

"I have just one quick question for you, Molly," he said. "But you must promise to keep it a secret."

CHAPTER 10

Spring is in the air!
Read all about the latest fashions so you can make
a splash this Season.
The Beau Monde Mirror: The Essential Style &
Etiquette Guide

Devereux House, Curzon Street, Mayfair
April 5, 1819

The Dowager Duchess of Exmoor's drawing room was very much like the woman herself, decided Charlie as she made herself sit ramrod straight upon a pinstriped shepherdess chair. The gilt-edged furniture and enormous sash windows were adorned with rich fabrics in shades of wintry blue and ivory, and upon the white marble mantel sat a pair of dazzling crystal vases filled with slender-stemmed hothouse lilies. Even the two footmen stationed by the drawing room doors were attired in blue and ivory livery with gold frogging and gilt buttons.

Everything was elegant and pleasing to the eye, yet the atmosphere was decidedly chilly.

"And how do you take your tea, Lady Charlotte? With lemon or without?" asked Cressida Devereux. Her light blue gaze drifted over Charlie before returning to the tea things—a silver urn, an ornate tea caddy, and a fine bone-china teapot precisely arranged before her on the elegant satinwood table.

With milk and two lumps of sugar, but I can see that's *not on the cards,* thought Charlie. It seemed the dowager duchess liked to take Lent *very* seriously. "With lemon, thank you, Your Grace."

"And would you like a Prince of Wales biscuit?" asked Diana Devereux. A maid waiting nearby extended a Spode china plate toward Charlie. "Cressida has these ordered in from Fortnum and Mason."

"No, thank you," replied Charlie politely. The biscuits might be sporting a stamp of the Prince of Wales's feathered heraldic badge, but they looked plain and dry and hard enough to crack her teeth.

"They're very good," remarked Cressida. "But rest assured, I'm not offended. I understand you might be watching what you eat at the moment."

What? Charlie's mouth almost dropped open. How... how *dare* Max's mother suggest she might need to lose weight? And here she was thinking she looked quite fetching in her new day gown of white muslin trimmed with daffodil-hued satin ribbon.

Lifting her chin, she countered, "More often than not, I find that I need to watch what I say." And then she inwardly winced.

Oh, dear. Trading barbs with Cressida was *not* going to end well. She really should have bitten her tongue.

Cressida's mouth curved into a superior smile as she handed Charlie her cup of tea. "Yes, well, that's hardly surprising. But in all seriousness, I do believe it's quite sensible that Maximilian has decided you won't wed until Season's end. Considering most of the ton already has a... shall we say, certain opinion of you, rushing down the aisle will only reinforce that." She paused to stir her own cup of tea, quite unnecessarily considering she hadn't even added lemon to it. "And then, of course, you'll have several months to lose a few more pounds." Her gaze flicked over Charlie before she picked up her cup. "I'm sure you'll want a new wardrobe once you've trimmed down a little."

This time, Charlie's mouth did drop open. Heat burned her whole face. *My God.* Max was wrong, so wrong about his mother.

She was a spiteful witch. A cow. A…sharp-tongued virago. A bat, and another word that began with "B" and rhymed with her first thought.

Diana cleared her throat. "Lady Charlotte, I've been meaning to ask, who is your modiste? I do love the Mameluke sleeves on your gown. Or are they Marie or Juliette sleeves?" She gave a little laugh. "I can never quite work out the difference. In any case, the style suits you well. And the colors remind me of spring."

Charlie swallowed to loosen her tight throat. "Thank you," she murmured, surprised but grateful indeed that Diana had not only complimented her but had deftly nudged the discussion in a different direction. "And to answer your first question, my modiste is Madame Boucher. Her boutique is in Conduit Street. My aunt, Lady Chelmsford, uses her too."

Cressida adjusted the folds of the linen napkin that lay upon her lap. "I have not seen your aunt lately, Lady Charlotte. I trust she is well…?"

"Exceedingly," replied Charlie. "Although she's currently in Bath. Her friend, Lady Kilbride, has been under the weather lately, so she's following her physician's recommendation to take the waters there for a few months."

"Oh, I'm sorry to hear that." Cressida's gaze sharpened a little. "I have a memory—and perhaps you can correct me if I'm wrong—but isn't your aunt a member of that odd little society with rooms somewhere on Park Lane?"

Odd little society? The nerve of the woman. "I gather you mean the Mayfair Bluestocking Society," Charlie said. "I'm a member, and most recently my dear friends, the Marchioness of Sleat, Viscountess Malverne, and the Countess of Langdale have become members too." *There, take that.*

"Lady Langdale…" Cressida pursed her lips. "Wasn't there some dreadful to-do involving her last year? A kidnapping around Seven Dials? I recall reading something in the papers…"

The dowager duchess was clearly fishing for gossip about Arabella and her new husband, Gabriel, but Charlie would not divulge a single detail. "Perhaps the article was in relation to her charity work at the Seven Dials Dispensary," remarked Charlie, hoping to steer the conversation toward a more neutral topic. "Lady Langdale is quite progressive in her thinking. In fact, she's been working with the Mayfair Bluestocking Society to raise funds for additional dispensaries for the poor here in London. And parish schools for girls. And most recently, she opened a brand-new orphanage in Edinburgh. Aside from supporting philanthropic endeavors, I'm proud to say the society does much to promote the advancement of women. A most worthy cause as well."

Cressida made a scoffing noise. "Don't tell me you're all proponents of that utterly dreadful woman, Mary Wollstonecraft? The views she espoused in *A Vindication of the Rights of Woman* are beyond the pale."

"Well, I would be lying if I said that we *haven't* discussed Mary Wollstonecraft's views on occasion," said Charlie. "And with much spirit. I, for one, do believe that *all* women should receive a sound education. And that we are not intellectually inferior to the male of the species. The Mayfair Bluestocking Society has certainly given its very own members the opportunity to participate in pursuits that are often deemed the sole province of men. Why, I've learned to fence and drive a curricle. And on one occasion, when we had an excursion to Putney Heath, we had a pistol-shooting lesson, and I discovered I'm actually quite a good sh—"

Charlie broke off. *Blast and damn and blazing hell.* Judging by the pernicious twinkle in Cressida's eyes, she'd certainly said far too much this time, despite her earlier resolve not to. So much for her pronouncement that she watched what she said.

Diana sat forward, her soft gray eyes aglow. "That sounds like such fun, Lady Charlotte. I've tried my hand at archery in the past, and I consider myself quite a good shot too. If I were a little more daring, I might consider joining the Royal British Bowmen Society." Turning to her mother-in-law, she added, "Perhaps we can add archery to the list of activities our guests might enjoy during the house party at Heathcote Hall. Of course, if you agree, Lady Charlotte. It is very much your party, after all. Yours and Max's. I, for one, cannot wait."

Again, Charlie sent Diana a grateful smile. The young woman could only be a few years older than herself. She was very attractive—pretty, even—with a heart-shaped face, pale blonde curls, and a pleasing figure displayed to perfection in her well-cut gown of lavender muslin. Charlie suddenly wondered why she hadn't remarried after the passing of her husband. And why she'd chosen to remain living with Cressida, her mother-in-law, rather than members of her own family. "I think that sounds like a wonderful idea, Your Grace."

"Please, do call me Diana," the young duchess replied. "After all, we'll be sisters very soon, and I don't know about you, but I fear there will be so many 'Your Graces' flying about, we're all bound to get confused."

Charlie couldn't help but laugh. "As long as you call me Charlie—" she began, then broke off when there was a knock at the door.

Cressida called, "Come in," and another liveried footman entered, proffering a note upon a silver salver. The dowager duchess perused it, then her lips tightened. "If you'll excuse me," she said, putting aside her tea and napkin before rising to her feet. "I just have a small matter to attend to. I shan't be long."

In the split second before the drawing room door clicked shut, Charlie caught a glimpse of a balding, be-spectacled gentleman with a leather portfolio tucked beneath one arm who bowed as Cressida approached. She didn't have time to ruminate any further on who the man might be as Diana began to ask who Charlie would like to invite to Heathcote Hall.

"Cressida and I thought that we shouldn't invite more than forty guests for the four-day event, lest the party becomes too unwieldy. And an intimate affair is always nicer, to my way of thinking. But of course, on the night of your betrothal ball, you and Max can invite as many guests as you li—" She broke off as her stomach emitted a rather loud rumble. "Oh, pardon me." She placed a hand upon her belly, and a rosy blush colored her cheeks. "I'm so, so sorry."

Charlie waved a dismissive hand. "Think nothing of it," she said. "But perhaps you should have one of Cressida's biscuits…"

Diana made a moue of displeasure. "You were wise not to have one. They're quite horrid." Her stomach protested again, and this time a laugh escaped her too. "I know it's wicked of me to say so, but I really can't wait for Lent to be over so I can have something decent to eat," she murmured in a conspiratorial fashion.

My goodness. Diana sounded like she was positively famished. Charlie reached for her reticule. "Would you like a bonbon?" she asked. "I carry a tin about with me. The toffee is quite hard, but they're delicious all the same."

Diana's eyes lit up. "I would love one." After selecting a hazelnut praline, she popped it into her mouth, closed her eyes, and moaned. "Oh, my word." The sugared sweet filled the left side of her cheek, and her next words were little more than a mumble as she added, "This is so good. I could eat ten. Perhaps a dozen. A baker's doz—"

The drawing room door swung open without warning, and Charlie and Diana both jumped in their seats. As Cressida swept toward them, Diana's whole countenance turned bright red, and she looked as guilty as a child who'd just been caught raiding a jar of sweetmeats. Or, in this particular instance, a tin of bonbons.

Cressida's gaze narrowed as she took in her daughter-in-law's cheek and its odd, squirrel-like protrusion. "Are you all right, Diana?" she asked as she sank with regal poise onto her chair.

Diana nodded. "Yes. Char—I mean, *Lady Charlotte* offered me a comfit. To settle my stomach."

"Yes," agreed Charlie, lifting up the silver tin. "Of course, you're welcome to have one too, Your Grace. They're clove, cinnamon, and ginger flavored, but the texture is a little hard and gritty. I fear the apothecary did not grind the spices and apricot kernels up as well as—"

Cressida held up a hand. "No, thank you. My tea will suffice."

Diana cast Charlie a thankful look, and Charlie sent a small smile back. She'd been dreading this call for an entire week, and she was nothing but relieved that she might have found a friend in Diana. Navigating Society's fraught waters suddenly seemed far less daunting a prospect if she had an ally like the Duchess of Exmoor by her side.

When Charlie arrived back at Hastings House an hour later, she was greeted by a mewling Peridot and the sight of an enormous bunch of yellow and white roses that smelled divine. Molly had placed them on display on a mahogany table in the center of her sitting room.

Another gift from Max, no doubt. For a man who professed he was incapable of feeling tender emotion, he was certainly playing the part of besotted fiancé to perfection. In fact, he'd been sending fresh bunches of roses—her favorite flower—and boxes of Gunter's treats to Hastings House every few days. Because the hue of the blooms often matched the color of her day gown, Charlie was beginning to suspect Molly was sneakily sending him intelligence about her sartorial choices.

In any event, perhaps Max thought such extravagant gifts would make up for his absence. They didn't. Charlie hadn't seen him since the afternoon he'd presented her with a betrothal ring, and then she'd gone and slammed the door on him in a fit of pique. Such a silly, childish way for her to have behaved. But then, the man's commitment to "doing the right thing" *was* beyond infuriating.

She released a disgruntled sigh as she plucked the small card from the flower arrangement. As usual, Max's handwritten note was sweet but brief.

Dearest Charlotte,
I hope these make you smile.
Yours,
M

Ugh.

Charlie cast the note aside. She didn't want the gentleman. She wanted the rake. The hot-blooded, take-what-he-wants-whenever-he-wants-it-duke of her own wicked dreams.

She scooped Peridot into her arms and wandered over to the window seat. She shouldn't really be so miffed with Max. Not when he was making such an effort to spoil her. But when all was said and done, she only wanted *him*. His smile. His conversation. His kisses. His touch…

Sweet heaven above, how she yearned for his touch. After that night at the Rouge et Noir Club, all she could think about was the feel of his large hands at her waist, on her hips. The heat of his hard body and the taste of his skin.

Even though it seemed Max was determined to continue with this "engagement-in-name-only" arrangement for the foreseeable future, something else he'd said to her at the end of their last meeting wandered through her mind. *It would be wrong to act on my desire…*

If only you would, Max, Charlie thought as she sank onto the chair and began to tickle Peridot beneath her chin. *If only you would.* She'd tried to flirt with him over afternoon tea, but he'd been steadfastly oblivious to all of her advances.

But he did *admit he desires you,* she reminded herself. *And he's never done that before. Ever. And you have until the end of the Season to change his stubborn mind.*

Well, she was equally stubborn. And as Sophie had pointed out, Charlie didn't lack spirit. Or guile. It was about time she fully deployed her arsenal of feminine wiles.

"'Faint heart never won fair rake' should be a proverb too," she murmured as she continued to pat a purring Peridot. "And of course, 'all is fair in love and war'. So, Max Devereux, you had better watch out, because I'm not going to give up on you just yet."

❦

Exmoor House, Grosvenor Square

"I'm afraid all reports indicate that Lord Rochfort has taken a turn for the worse, Your Grace."

Max leaned back in the chair behind his desk, affecting an air of nonchalance in front of the inquiry agent. Sadly, maintaining a neutral expression in the face of troubling news—or anything untoward at all—was a skill he'd perfected by the age of fourteen. "Go on. I don't need coddling, Mr. Hunt," he said. "I need specifics. That's what I pay you for."

The man, a former Bow Street Runner, simply tilted his head. He never seemed ruffled by Max's direct, no-nonsense attitude, and Max liked that. "Of course, Your Grace. According to one of Rochfort's footmen, the baron's physician had to aggressively debride his shoulder wound several days ago because it had turned purulent. Aside from the infection, there have been other complications too…"

Irritation at the inquiry agent's prevarication made Max impatient. "Out with it, man."

"It appears the additional procedure has resulted in some sort of nerve damage. My source tells me that Lord Rochfort has lost most of the movement in his left arm and that he suffers from bouts of 'nerve pain', a burning, shooting pain in his arm that is quite debilitating. He's begun to quaff laudanum likes it's water."

"Will this be a permanent condition?"

"No one knows, Your Grace. It's too early to tell."

"Hmm." Max couldn't say that he was sorry considering all the grief Rochfort had caused Charlie and Euphemia Harrington. In Max's opinion, if the man ended up with some sort of permanent impairment, it was just deserts for his unconscionable behavior. In contrast, Max's own bullet wound was healing well. In fact, his own physician was due to remove his stitches later on in the day. Perhaps Charlie's friend, Lady Langdale, was right, and there was some merit in using alcohol to cleanse a wound.

Max had one more question for Mr. Hunt before he

dismissed him. "And what have you learned about the *Beau Monde Mirror?*"

"So far, only what is available on the public record. The paper is produced by Juno Press, and its head editor is a gentleman by the name of Erasmus Silver. Another company called Fortuna Trading owns the publishing house. But as to who owns Fortuna Trading…" Mr. Hunt shrugged. "Unfortunately, it is run by a group of silent partners. I suspect they must have some status and influence but wish to keep their identities secret. And as I've reported before, the baron does not seem to be in any obvious financial strife. In fact, he appears to be swimming in funds. His motive for blackmailing and extorting money and property from others is not clear."

Interesting. Max was beginning to wonder if Rochfort was the kind of man who engaged in such practices just for the perverse enjoyment he derived from manipulating others. From controlling them. His own father had been such a man.

Max turned his attention to the other gentleman in the room, his man of affairs. "And what have you learned about the Bloomsbury Square townhouse? The one Rochfort effectively stole from Euphemia Harrington?"

Mr. Woodleigh pushed his spectacles farther up his nose and sat up straighter. "It appears Lord Rochfort's ownership is all above board. It will be difficult to prove that Miss Harrington was coerced into giving up her property unless she is willing to come forward and make an official statement to the authorities. And even then, it would be her word against the baron's if it went to court."

Max nodded. "I thought as much. It looks as though the only way Miss Harrington will have her property restored to her is if I purchase it and gift it back to her. Would you be able to arrange the purchase via a third-party, Woodleigh? I fear that Rochfort won't sell if he knows who's behind the acquisition. And I'm also prepared to offer a good deal more than what the property's worth if Rochfort seems disinclined to let it go. I trust that in the end, his greed will win out."

Woodleigh bowed his head. "Very good, Your Grace. I will have an intermediary begin discreet inquiries."

"Excellent."

Max dismissed both Hunt and Woodleigh, but after his man of affairs exited the library, Hunt turned back. "There's something else I wanted to mention to you, Your Grace, but I think it's best that I disclose this particular piece of information to you in private."

"Of course." Curiosity mingled with uneasiness as Max watched the inquiry agent shut the door and approach the desk again. "It sounds like it's intelligence of a sensitive nature."

"Yes." Hunt met his gaze directly. "My men have been keeping up a round-the-clock surveillance of Rochfort House. The majority of the comings and goings have been inconsequential, but one of the baron's recent visitors might be of interest to you."

Max frowned. "Who is it?"

Hunt flinched slightly. "I'm afraid your mother was observed visiting Rochfort House two days ago."

What the hell? Max couldn't hide his shock this time. Why on earth would his mother visit Lord Rochfort? "You're absolutely certain that your man hasn't made a mistake?"

"No, Your Grace, he hasn't. I should also add that one of the baron's footmen, a younger fellow who's been quite happy to take my coin in exchange for information, also confirmed it this morning."

Max rubbed his temple. He could almost feel a megrim coming on. "Thank you for telling me, Hunt. I appreciate your discretion. Keep up the good work."

As soon as the inquiry agent took his leave, Max summoned his personal secretary to inform him that he would be out for the next hour or so. Then he donned top hat and gloves and strode the half mile from Grosvenor Square to Devereux House in just under ten minutes. He found his mother in the vestibule, putting on an elegant bonnet.

"I can't receive you right now, Maximilian," she said

tersely as she checked the ribbon beneath her chin in a large, gilt-framed mirror.

"This won't take long, Mother," he said grimly. "And I'd suggest we repair to somewhere a little more private for this discussion." He nodded toward a nearby parlor.

She arched a brow. "Has your fiancée already come bleating to you about how I upset her during our afternoon tea together? Considering she only left half an hour ago, she certainly didn't waste any time."

"What the deuce? What did you say to her?"

His mother shrugged a shoulder. "That she could do with losing a few pounds before your wedding. Now, don't scowl at me like that, Max. You know it's true. Plump girls are not your type."

"Don't presume to think you know what sort of woman is 'my type', Mother," growled Max. If he didn't have to question her about Lord Rochfort, he would have turned on his heel and quit Devereux House straightaway. "Although I would love to take you to task right this minute and demand you issue Lady Charlotte with a sincere apology for insulting her yet again, that's not actually the reason for my visit."

His mother sniffed, then turned to face him. "Very well, Max. You can have five minutes." Waving away the pair of kid gloves a nearby footman held, she marched across the polished parquetry floor to the parlor.

Max followed and shut the door. "I have it on good authority that two days ago, you paid a visit to the home of one of London's worst scoundrels. I want to know why."

"I take it you're referring to Lord Rochfort," his mother said, adjusting the cuff on one sleeve of her pale blue pelisse.

"Yes, of course I'm referring to Lord Rochfort. Or do you make a habit of calling on worthless dogs?"

"And you accuse *me* of issuing insults."

"Stop obfuscating. Tell me why you visited the man I called out because he grievously insulted the honor of Lady Charlotte."

"As if Lady Charlotte has any hon—"

"Enough," Max snapped. "Answer the question."

"Now, there's no need to shout like a bully," his mother said stiffly. "The reason I called upon Lord Rochfort was simply to check if he was in any danger of expiring. I'd heard that the man's condition had deteriorated, and if he were to die, you'd be in deep trouble, Max. You'd have to leave the country or else stand trial for the man's murder. And I couldn't have that. I know we have differences of opinion on occasion, but the dukedom—*you*, my son—must be protected at all costs."

Suspicion prickled along Max's spine. "How? How did you know Rochfort had taken a turn for the worse?" he demanded. "I, myself, only heard this a short time ago."

"I have my own sources of intelligence, Max. I certainly shan't divulge them to you. In any event, you needn't worry that anyone will remark upon my visit. It occurred during broad daylight, and Diana, her maid, and a footman accompanied me. It was all terribly mundane, all things considered. We even took a fruit basket. Come to think of it, you should be thanking me for smoothing things over with Lord Rochfort, not berating me."

Max ground his teeth so hard, he was surprised they didn't disintegrate into dust. "Mundane? Visiting a man like Rochfort is anything *but* that, considering the circumstances. I forbid you from undertaking such a foolhardy venture again. What if it ended up in the *Beau Monde Mirror*'s gossip column?"

"Pfft." His mother flicked a hand. "It would hardly signify."

"Really? For a woman who's always fussing about appearances and maintaining a pristine reputation…" A horrible, altogether chilling thought occurred to Max. His gut tightened with foreboding. "How well do you know Rochfort? You're not in any trouble, are you?"

"Trouble? Of course I'm not in trouble. What are you implying?" His mother raised her chin, her expression glacial. "I don't like your line of questioning, Maximilian."

"And I don't understand why my mother would be cultivating a far-too-familiar association with a black-hearted blackguard. That man is dangerous."

His mother's eyes darted blue fire. "How dare you insult me in such a fashion. And how dare you spy on me! I've told you why I paid Lord Rochfort a visit. If you wish to ascribe an indecent, ulterior motive to my actions, I cannot stop you. But I will most vehemently object to you voicing such vulgar thoughts in my presence. Now I'll thank you to leave."

"And I'll thank you to heed my warning, Mother. Because if I hear you've been dropping by Rochfort House, supposedly delivering fruit baskets again, I'll cut off your allowance and pack you off to Exmoor Castle's dower house so fast your head will spin. And the same warning applies to insulting my fiancée. I won't have it. Do I make myself clear?"

His mother's mouth flattened into a mutinous line. But then she inclined her head. "Crystal."

"Good."

When Max returned to Exmoor House, the first thing he did was dash off a note to his inquiry agent. As much as he didn't like the idea of having his mother watched, he was highly suspicious of her reason for seeing Rochfort. If the baron had somehow got his claws into her, or if she had some sort of sick romantic tie with the cur… Max's gut roiled. Surely not.

But then Charlie had been tempted by the man's dark and dangerous aura…

In any event, he would not let his guard down. Rochfort's health might be ailing, but that didn't mean the viper wouldn't strike again. Max was quite certain that vengeance, not blood, ran through the man's veins.

CHAPTER 11

"In April's bower thy sweets are breathed…"
Read an exclusive preview of John Anster's poem,
The Everlasting Rose.
The Beau Monde Mirror: The Literary Arts

Hastings House, Berkeley Square
Easter Sunday, 1819

"Gah, Benjamin and Daniel," grumbled Charlie as she balanced her overflowing basket of flowers on her hip and bent down to scoop up a discarded, cracked Easter egg at the bottom of the main stairs. "Indoor pace egging is all well and good, but you need to be more careful. Someone—me, for instance, or dear Sophie here—could have broken her neck."

"Sorry, sis," called Benjamin over his shoulder as he bolted into the library with his twin brother at his heels. "Daniel missed one."

"It doesn't matter who missed—"

The library door slammed, and Charlie rolled her eyes. While she loved having her three younger brothers —Jonathon, aged eighteen, and the twins Benjamin and Daniel, aged fifteen—home for Easter, she certainly didn't love the chaos they invariably created. After the entire family had all trooped back from church that morning, it had started pouring with rain, so Daniel and

Benjamin, clearly bored, had decided to challenge each other to an Easter egg rolling contest around the house like a pair of restless eight-year-olds. Charlie swore adolescent boys could turn just about anything into "sport" especially if wagers were involved.

"Is Jonathon about?" asked Sophie. She transferred her flower basket to one hand and picked up her skirts with the other before gingerly negotiating the last few steps; no doubt she was looking for any stray Easter eggs that might trip her up. After the church service, she had offered to help with preparations for the rest of the Easter celebrations at Hastings House, and Charlie was grateful indeed.

"He's reading. In the library." There was a shout and Charlie winced. "Well, he *was* reading." She shook her head. "I just pray that the three of them don't break anything before tonight's dinner party. Their horseplay is"— there was a crash, then a whoop of laughter. She sighed— "rather exuberant. But I suppose I can't blame them. Not when they've been cooped up at Eton for weeks on end. And they'll have to return after Easter."

"I rather suspect Daniel and Benjamin take after Nate," observed Sophie. "He doesn't take well to being cooped up either. Which reminds me…" Sophie glanced at the longcase clock by the stairs. It was almost two o'clock. "He should be back from his ride in Hyde Park soon. He wanted to escort me back to Westhampton House."

Come rain or shine or Easter Sunday, Nate would never miss a ride. Charlie idly wondered if Max had joined him. Her missing-in-action fiancé had been invited to dinner tonight, and while he had accepted the invitation, she was also rather hoping that he would drop by Hastings House a bit earlier. Which he might do, if he'd gone riding with her brother…

In any event, she really should get on with her preparations. She had a romantic battle plan to execute, and there was no better time than the present to lay the groundwork.

"I'm sure this will work, Charlie. You're ingenious,"

remarked Sophie as they watched Edwards and another footman stringing up an elaborate garland of flowers above the drawing room door; the roses, peonies, hyacinths, and tulips had been threaded with pink satin ribbon and tendrils of ivy, and Charlie thought they were as pretty as could be.

"I certainly hope it does," replied Charlie. "But you might have to distract Nate at some point if Max doesn't put in an appearance before dinner. I dare not put my plan into action if my brother is about. The last thing we need is blood on the Aubusson rug on Easter Sunday."

"Rest assured, when you give me the signal, I'll make sure my husband is occupied." Sophie glanced about the vestibule of Hastings House. "So how many of these spring kissing boughs are you going to put up?"

Charlie laughed. "As many as I can. But in all seriousness, I asked the florist to create ten arrangements. Aside from this garland here, I plan on hanging a kissing bough above the doors leading to the dining room, library, morning room, and the terrace. And then these"—she lifted her basket that contained smaller balls of blooms —"will be suspended from the chandeliers, including this one here in the entry hall."

Sophie gave Charlie a little nudge. "The poor man doesn't stand a chance."

"I hope not," agreed Charlie. "Because if this doesn't work, I have no idea what to do."

"If what doesn't work?"

Charlie turned around to find her father standing behind her and Sophie. Oh, dear. How much had he heard? With any luck, nothing about kissing.

"Oh, Papa, I was just remarking to Sophie that if these blooms don't brighten up the house enough, I don't know what I shall do at this late stage," she said, hoping that he wouldn't notice the blush heating her cheeks. "We have so many guests for dinner tonight. And I'm sure you're keen to impress Lord and Lady Wyatt and their daughter, Lady Tilbury, just as much as I am."

"The house already looks wonderful," replied her father, moving forward a pace to stand on her other side.

"And the menu you've chosen for this evening is sure to be a triumph. But I appreciate the extra effort you're going to." He gave her elbow a little nudge. "No doubt you're keen to impress your fiancé."

"Well, perhaps a little," confessed Charlie. But she doubted it was in the manner her father was thinking of. "Although, after observing how much Daniel and Benjamin now eat, I am beginning to worry that I haven't ordered in enough food. I'm sure they could devour a leg of lamb and a Simnel cake each."

Her father smiled. "I'm sure everything will be perfect." A resounding bang, a thud, and a chorus of raucous laughter emanated from the library, and he swung around, frowning. "Egads, Charlie, I swear Daniel, Benjamin, and Jonathon are going to be more of a handful than Nate. And that's saying something," he muttered. "I'd best intervene before they bring the house down around our ears."

"Good luck," called Charlie after him as he marched across the vestibule.

"Boys," her father began as he threw open the library door. "What the devil—"

The door slammed behind him, and Sophie gave her a sympathetic smile. "I suppose we should leave the library until last."

"Yes," agreed Charlie. "Lord knows what they've done in there."

The footmen had just finished hanging the last kissing bough from the chandelier in the entry hall when Hastings House's butler, Mr. Abbott, approached. "My apologies for interrupting, my lady…"

"That's quite all right, Abbott," Charlie replied, but her eyebrows shot up as she took in the sizable bundle the butler held in his arms—two enormous boxes with another round bandbox balanced on top. "What on earth have you got there?"

"It's for you, my lady. A gift from the Duke of Exmoor. I believe there's a note tucked into the ribbon of the bandbox."

"Oh…" Charlie took it and examined the wax seal on the back. "It *is* from Max. How wonderful."

"And romantic," sighed Sophie. "You must open it at once."

"Yes." After Charlie directed Edwards to help Abbott take the parcels upstairs to her sitting room, she cracked the seal and unfolded the small sheet of parchment.

Dearest Charlotte,
I hope you'll accept this small token of my esteem and
affection.
I've missed you, and I look forward to seeing you very
soon.
Yours,
M

Charlie showed the note to Sophie, and her friend smiled. "Well, that's encouraging. He says he misses you."

"Yes…" Charlie wasn't sure whether she believed Max or not, but she was touched all the same. "Shall we go and see what's in the boxes?"

"Of course." Sophie clapped her hands together. "One thing is certain—you cannot fault Max's generosity."

Indeed, Charlie was in complete agreeance with Sophie as she opened the largest box. "Good heavens," she breathed as she lifted the most exquisite promenade gown she'd ever seen from its tissue paper wrapping. The dusky pink silk muslin was trimmed with chocolate brown ribbon. "Max must have spent a small fortune."

Sophie reached out and reverently stroked one of the sleeves. "It's divine, Charlie. And it looks like it will be a perfect fit. I wonder if he's had a word with your modiste."

"Yes, I suspect he might have done that too. It *looks* very much like Madame Boucher's work." Charlie tore open the next package to reveal a matching spencer in chocolate brown velvet and a pair of buttery soft gloves in fawn kid leather. The band box contained a beautiful poke bonnet adorned with an abundance of brown satin bows and silk roses in shades of soft pink and ivory.

"*I* think the Duke of Exmoor wants to take his gorgeous fiancée promenading about Town this afternoon," said Sophie with a knowing smile. "It's a good thing it's stopped raining."

"Yes." Charlie couldn't hide her own excitement as she hugged the gown to her chest. "I think you might be right. I must try all of this on."

"Yes, you must," agreed Sophie. "At once."

Sophie's pronouncement that the attire would be a perfect fit was correct. As Charlie admired her reflection in the long oval looking glass in her dressing room, she couldn't help but smile.

"Do you think I should wear a chemisette?" Charlie caught her friend's eye in the mirror. "The neckline of the gown *is* a little daring." Indeed, there was a good deal of the tops of her breasts on display... Although, it might work to her advantage if she managed to entice Max beneath one of her strategically placed spring kissing boughs. He might steadfastly pretend that he didn't notice her bust, but she rather suspected he would.

"Oh, I don't think so," said Sophie, drawing behind her. "There's nothing wrong with a daring neckline. I think the cut of the bodice is simply perfect. And the spencer should keep you sufficiently warm when you are outside. This afternoon you'll be the belle of Hyde Park. Just you wait and see."

Charlie smoothed her hand along one of the spencer's sleeves. "You know, this will be the first time I've been out in public since that horrible *Beau Monde Mirror* article came out," she murmured. "Or since my engagement to Max was announced. I'm not sure..." She met Sophie's reflected gaze. "I'm not sure how I will be received. What if..." She swallowed, unable to voice her fears. Dread curled through her at the thought that she might be snubbed or openly laughed at or labeled something even worse than "disreputable debutante". Names that made her feel both angry and ashamed.

Sophie wrapped her arms about Charlie's middle and rested her chin on her velvet-clad shoulder. "I understand you're nervous, my darling friend. But Max will be with you. No one will dare to insult you or give you the cut direct with the Duke of Exmoor by your side. I'm sure of it."

Charlie squeezed one of Sophie's hands. "Let's hope so. In any case, I suppose this will be a good way of testing the waters before Max and I attend any larger social events together."

An hour later, Charlie was impatiently idling about on the terrace in her new gown and spencer. Her Easter bonnet and fawn kid gloves sat on the wrought-iron table along with a small tea tray. Whenever Max arrived, she would be ready.

If he arrived...

She released a small sigh and tapped her booted toe on the stone flags. Patience was *not* one of her virtues. At least the weather held fair, so if Max *did* happen to show up and invite her to promenade during the "fashionable hour" in Hyde Park, her new ensemble wouldn't be ruined.

A light breeze pushed pale gray clouds across the powder-blue sky and lifted the pages of the novel Charlie had tried to peruse. Sophie had departed a little while before in Nate's company. To Charlie's disappointment, her brother had returned from his ride alone and had been infuriatingly vague when she'd questioned him about Max's movements for the rest of the day.

After Charlie had consulted with both the cook and housekeeper about that night's elaborate dinner preparations—all seemed to be well in hand—she'd decided to take tea *without* cake or sweetmeats. For once she was too on edge to eat anything. All she could think about was Max and whether her spring kissing bough contrivance would work.

In all of history, had there ever been a more elusive, kiss-shy rake than Max Devereux?

Charlie twisted her diamond betrothal ring about her finger and scowled into the dregs of her cold cup of tea. She seriously doubted it.

The garland hanging above the nearby French doors shivered in a gust of wind, and a soft, fragrant shower of flower petals floated to the ground and drifted along the terrace. Another disgruntled sigh escaped Charlie. At this rate, this particular kissing bough would be completely denuded before this evening.

And then the gauze curtains in the doorway parted and Max appeared. Attired in buff pantaloons, gleaming black Hessians, and a swallowtail coat of navy blue, he was, as always, heart-stoppingly handsome.

As soon as his gaze connected with hers, he shot her a dazzling smile.

"Charlotte." His voice was filled with warmth as he crossed the terrace toward her in a few swift strides. "You look wonderful. Simply breathtaking."

"Do…do you really think so?" she asked as he took her hands in his and helped her to her feet. Her pulse was racing so fast, she almost couldn't draw enough breath to speak.

In all the years she'd known Max, he'd never once made a comment about her appearance. Well, unless it was to tease her about something that was amiss like her messy hair or mismatched shoes or a dusting of pow-dered sugar upon her nose.

"Of course I do." His appreciative gaze traveled over her gown and spencer, and Charlie felt her cheeks grow warm with pleasure. "The colors suit you well."

"Thank you. I certainly wasn't expecting such an ex-travagant gift, and I'm most grateful," she murmured, suddenly as bashful as a giddy chit about to attend her first assembly. "And I feel thoroughly spoiled."

"And so you should be. Spoiled, that is. And often…" His expression changed, and a shadow of remorse crossed his features. "I must apologize for being absent for so long. Life has been rather hectic of late. But this af-ternoon and this evening, you shall have my undivided attention, my lady."

"Oh, I like the sound of that. What did you have in mind"—Charlie looked up through her eyelashes at him —"for this afternoon?"

"Well, I rather think it's time to show off your new Easter bonnet. So, if you agree, I'd like to take you for a ride about Hyde Park in my new high-perch phaeton. It's waiting outside in the square."

"I would love to." Charlie tugged on her gloves, scooped up her bonnet, and took the arm Max offered. They crossed the terrace, but as he began to draw back the curtains, shielding the doorway, Charlie hesitated. Butterflies began to dance about in her belly.

"What is it?" he asked, raising a quizzical brow.

"Oh… It's just that…" Charlie inhaled a deep breath. They were alone. Max was being as attentive as could be. Come what may, *this* was the moment to ask for a kiss. "It's just that we've stopped beneath the spring kissing bough."

"Spring kissing bough?" A slight frown knitted Max's brow. He looked up. "You mean to say this garland of roses and whatnot is akin to a ball of mistletoe?"

"Yes. Exactly. This year the Hastings household is instituting a new family tradition. Because why should kissing boughs be confined to the Yuletide season? It's spring. A time for rejoicing. A time for celebrating new beginnings."

Max lowered his gaze and his frown deepened. "I don't think you can just create a new tradition out of thin air and expect everyone to go along with it, Charlie."

"Well, I don't see any harm in it," she added defensively. Her mouth was suddenly as dry as could be. If Max rejected her… No, she didn't want to think about that. Ignoring the tripping of her heart, she drew another bracing breath and lifted her chin. "I mean, Nate isn't here. Or my father. And we *are* engaged. So, why not? After all, there has to be a first time for anything that is to become a tradition, even one that involves the exchange of a simple kiss." She bit her lip, deliberately playing the coquette because at this point, what did she have to lose? "What harm could it do?"

A muscle worked in Max's jaw, but amusement and something hotter gleamed in his deep blue eyes. "Well, when you put it like that, my dear Lady Charlotte…" He raised a hand and cupped her face ever so gently. Tilted her head a fraction and leaned in. His breath fanned across her lips as he murmured, "Who am I to stand in the way of tradition?"

He pressed his mouth to hers, and Charlie's insides melted like a lump of sugar in her hot chocolate.

Yes, Max. Yes...

Her bonnet fell to the ground unheeded as her fists gripped his lapels and everything else that wasn't Max faded away. All she was aware of was the gentle press of his firm lips. Their silken, sinuous, languid glide. Her own lips parted on a sigh, and his tongue swept into her mouth, the intimate caress as soft as warm velvet. His mouth gently brushed against hers again...and then, to her disappointment, it was over.

Max drew back, and his hand slid from her jaw to her shoulder. "There. Will that do, my lady?" he whispered, his voice low and husky and almost as delicious as his kiss.

Charlie swallowed. "I... It's a start," she managed. Tremors of desire still fluttered in her belly, and she seemed to be having trouble arranging her thoughts and feelings. They ricocheted between the urge to demand more kisses and the wild impulse to dance a little jig because at long last, Max had actually kissed her. And it had been wonderful and sweet and—

To Charlie's amusement, Max gave a disgruntled harumph and cocked a brow. "A start?"

"Well, when you kiss that well, Your Grace, you can't expect me to be satisfied with just one." She let go of his jacket, even though her knees were still as wobbly as jelly. "But you've fulfilled your obligation. The custom has been observed. We may now continue on our way."

"Not quite." Max bent down and retrieved her Easter bonnet. "You've forgotten this, my dear Charlotte." He very carefully placed it upon her head and tied the chocolate-brown bow beneath her chin. The heat of his fingers brushing the sensitive flesh beneath her jaw made Charlie shiver with longing all over again, but somehow she managed to keep herself in check. She dared not press him for another kiss. Perhaps later that night she could snatch another quiet moment alone with Max beneath another one of her strategically placed kissing boughs...

Offering his arm once again, Max said, "Shall we?"

Charlie readily slipped her hand into the crook of his elbow. "We shall."

CHAPTER 12

Dear ladies of the ton, it's time to don your Easter
bonnets!
The Beau Monde Mirror: The Essential Style &
Etiquette Guide

Hyde Park, London

Max had made some very bad decisions in his
twenty-eight years, but his decision to kiss
Charlie beneath her spring kissing bough would have to
be one of the worst. Because ever since that moment, he
could think about nothing else *but* doing it again. And
again. Until he'd kissed her senseless and she was panting
for more.

God, how he wanted more.

Of course, doing such a thing, right here, right now in
the middle of Hyde Park, was out of the question.

Keeping his matched grays under control and steering
the phaeton through the fashionable-hour traffic had
kept his attention occupied for a short while, but when he
drew the open carriage to a halt beneath a willow tree beside the Serpentine and Charlie turned in his direction to
observe the lake, he found he couldn't tear his gaze away
from her mouth. With the lovely oval of her face framed
by her new bonnet and her golden-brown eyes illumi-

nated by the late afternoon sun, she was breathtakingly pretty.

Her lips, as soft and plump as ripe plums, were slightly parted, and when the breeze coming off the water lifted a tendril of her rich chestnut hair and blew it across her cheek, caressing the corner of her mouth, he was hard pressed not to give in to the urge to stroke the errant lock to one side and place his own mouth there instead.

Damn. Charlie had been right. One kiss wasn't enough to satisfy him either. He'd initially given in to temptation because her contrivance of a kissing bough had amused him, and he'd mistakenly thought that perhaps one light bussing of his lips across hers would be enough to sate his craving and hers. Of course, that reasoning had turned out to be utterly foolish, especially after he'd surrendered to the impulse to taste the honeyed recess of her mouth.

Max almost groaned aloud as he recalled the flutter of her tongue against his, the silken press of her plush lips, the tiny moan she'd made at the back of her throat…

Charlie's kiss was like a goddamned box of sweetmeats from Gunter's. He could gorge on the entire contents of that box, and it still wouldn't be enough to satisfy his hunger. If anything, his craving had sharpened. It was no longer just a gnawing pang but a wild need. A slavering, ravenous beast that longed to seize Charlie and—

Max stifled another groan of frustration. Yes, thank God he and Charlie were promenading in Hyde Park. Because it was Easter Sunday, there were members of the ton everywhere, constantly casting curious glances their way or even tipping their hats and raising hands in acknowledgement as they passed by. Because if they weren't in a public space—

Charlie's gaze connected with his. "Don't tell me you're thinking what I'm thinking," she murmured, a mischievous smile playing about her lips.

Max swallowed guiltily. "And what would that be, Lady Charlotte?"

A rich, throaty laugh tumbled forth, and her elbow nudged his. "I know you asked me to be your fiancée to

repair my reputation, but the wicked part of me can't resist the idea of giving the ton something else to talk
about, even if it's only a kiss that sets tongues wagging. I
mean, I don't know about you, but I might as well be
hanged for a sheep as a lamb."

Max shook his head. "Charlotte Hastings. What on
earth am I going to do with you?"

Her eyes gleamed and when she murmured, "Whatever you like," in a low, husky voice full of sensual promise, Max's cock stirred in appreciation. Lust slithered and
curled through his belly.

Dear God, this minx—no, this woman—would be the
death of him. Valiantly harnessing the urge to flick the
reins and send his horses barreling straight for Exmoor
House so he could really do everything he wanted with
Charlie, Max reached for her gloved hand and captured it
in his. "You're playing a dangerous game," he warned. "I
know you claim to know what you want, but have you
really thought this through? What would happen if we
both succumbed to temptation and the possible consequences that might follow? I don't want to hurt your feelings, but I may very well do just that if we go too far and
we *have* to wed. While I would endeavor to be a good
husband, I know I won't be able to give you what you
want. I…I'm not like Nate or even my other friends,
Gabriel and Hamish." He deliberately hardened his voice.
"They might be rakes who fell head-over-heels in love,
but I'm different. I'm fundamentally flawed in that regard. I'm simply not capable of forming close attachments, and never have been."

Charlie's full bottom lip jutted out in a determined
pout. She didn't look convinced, so he prepared another
argument.

"See those swans over there?" He nodded at a pair
floating serenely by, their necks intertwined like lovers.

She sighed. "Yes."

"The male finds a partner, and they mate for life. It's
within a swan's nature to do that. It's not within mine.
I'm more like a—"

Charlie arched a brow. "Tomcat?"

Max grimaced. "I was going to say lone wolf. But yes, tomcat would fit just as well."

Gold sparks of challenge flared within Charlie's eyes. "How can you be so sure that you cannot love? I sometimes feel that when we're together, there could be something more. The way you look at me. The sweet things you do for me..." She touched her fingers to the elaborate bow of her bonnet. "You fought a *duel* for me, Max."

"I've known you for a long time, Charlie, and it would be a lie if I said that I didn't feel a...a deep and abiding fondness for you. As for the rest..." He drew a deep breath. "It pains me to admit something so disrespectful, but it's lust. Pure and simple. And it would be unconscionable if we...if you and I became intimate but I ultimately disappointed you because I cannot give you the lifetime of love that you so clearly want. And deserve. I won't be that selfish cad."

"But—"

"No buts. I've never been in love with a woman before. I've never shared a close bond with anyone at all, for that matter. You know my mother; she's aloof at best. Always has been. And my father...he was far, far worse. Anthony and I were rivals most of the time. I grew up in a cold, loveless household, Charlie. I cannot change who I am. How I think. What my heart feels, or to be more precise, what it *doesn't* feel. I might feel strong emotions like passion or anger when I see an injustice perpetrated, but I am also inured to the absence of warmth or affection. I do not crave intimacy of any kind. I was brought up that way."

Charlie nodded. Beneath the bow of her bonnet, her delicate throat worked in a swallow. "Yet you've formed a close bond with my brother and Gabriel and Hamish."

"Nate and I became friends at Oxford. And all of us— your brother, Gabriel, Hamish and I—were brothers-in-arms at Waterloo. Male bonds of friendship are entirely different."

Charlie lifted her chin. "I don't know if they are, Max. I suppose we'll have to agree to disagree on that score."

They lapsed into tense silence for a minute, and Max

wondered if he should give the reins a flick to return to Hastings House. But then Charlie gave a wistful sigh and said, "I'm sorry to push you, Max. Although a lady shouldn't admit this, I seem to be suffering from a most unseemly bout of lust too. Of course, impulsive creature that I am, I often say and do things without thinking them through. But I do understand your reticence to pursue a relationship of a more intimate nature with me, and from now on, I'll make a concerted effort to behave with a greater degree of decorum. Besides"—she shrugged a shoulder—"there are only so many times I can throw myself at you before I appear utterly foolish and as desperate as those other debutantes who were chasing after you. I won't be that annoying ninnyhammer. I don't want you to grow to despise me."

Max squeezed her hand. "You must know I could never feel that way about you. And you don't need to pretend to be someone you're not, Charlie. Don't ever do that."

Her mouth twitched with a wry smile. "To thine own self be true?"

"Something like that."

"Hmm. If only my true self were a little less impetuous and prone to wicked thoughts." She sighed and withdrew her hand from his. "While we are exchanging confidences…just out of interest, what sort of wife *are* you looking for, Max? You told me once before that you anticipated on marrying five years from now. If you do not want a love match, what *do* you want?"

He frowned and fiddled with the reins. "This will sound dreadful and terribly shallow, but I always imagined that I would wed someone a little like Lady Penelope Purcell. Someone who is agreeable, and who can manage my household. Someone who will be content to share my bed until I have my heir and a spare. Someone who will make my life easy, I suppose." He winced. "Good Lord, does that sound as bad as I think it does?"

Charlie smiled. "A little. But for someone in your position, it also sounds eminently sensible. No one could fault your reasoning. Oh, no. Speak of the devil," she muttered.

Max looked up, and sure enough, Lady Penelope was headed their way in the company of her brother, Nigel, Lord Mowbray. The marquess was driving a nicely sprung curricle.

Wonderful.

"Hey, ho," called Lord Mowbray as his vehicle drew close. "Fancy meeting you here, Exmoor. Oh…" His light blue gaze slid to Charlie, and his smile widened as he added, "And your charming fiancée. Lady Charlotte." The marquess tipped his top hat. "Happy Easter. And may I offer my congratulations to you both on your engagement? Such an unexpected but no doubt felicitous union."

"Yes, Happy Easter, Your Grace, and congratulations," echoed Lady Penelope. The smile she turned on Charlie was as false as the clusters of enormous silk peonies on her Easter bonnet. "Lady Charlotte, you must be very happy."

Beside him, Max felt Charlie's body stiffen, but nevertheless, she returned the young woman's smile. "Yes, thank you. I am. Over-the-moon happy."

"I say, I'm rather looking forward to your betrothal celebrations later this week, Exmoor." Lord Mowbray winked at Charlie. "I'm sure you are too, Lady Charlotte, eh? There's nothing quite like a house party to lend some excitement to the Season. Why wait until summer when we all quit Town?"

"Yes," drawled Max, only just restraining the urge to plant a facer in the vicinity of the marquess's nose. He didn't like the way the man was looking at Charlie. "Quite."

"It was so kind of your mama to issue our entire family with an invitation, Your Grace," purred Penelope, drawing Max's attention. "I've heard Heathcote Hall is lovely. I can't wait to explore the gardens. Perhaps we could take a turn about the grounds sometime, or even venture onto the heath…" A tinkling laugh escaped her. "That is, if you can bear to let your handsome fiancé out of your sight, Lady Charlotte. He's quite the catch, isn't he?"

"Yes," replied Charlie with a smile that didn't reach her eyes. "He is."

Max reached for Charlie's hand. "I'm afraid I must beg to differ with you, Charlotte," he murmured. "You're the one who's the catch, my sweet." Raising her gloved fingers to his lips, he held her astonished gaze as he glanced a gentle kiss across her knuckles. "I consider myself the luckiest gentleman in London, indeed the whole of England, to have you as my bride-to-be."

Charlie blushed, but she didn't look away. "I think the feeling is mutual, Your Grace. I mean to say, I feel lucky too."

Max threw her a deliberately rakish, lopsided smile. Lord Mowbray cleared his throat. "Yes. Well. What say we bid these two lovebirds adieu, dear sis?"

"Yes," agreed Lady Penelope. The smile on her face looked decidedly fixed and icy now. More of a forced grimace. "I think I spied Lord and Lady Bartlett on the other side of the park earlier on. We should pay our respects."

"Tallyho, then." Mowbray lashed the haunches of his matched bay geldings, then they were off, careening down the bridle path at breakneck speed.

Max groaned. "Dear God. I take back what I said earlier. I don't wish to wed *anyone* like Lady Penelope."

Charlie laughed. "I'm relieved to hear it. And while I also appreciate your display of support and kind words just now, you might also be relieved to know that it's not a foregone conclusion that we will wed. That is, in case you are worried you're well and truly caught in the parson's noose."

Max arched a brow. "It sounds like you've already made up your mind about what will happen at the end of the Season. But I want you to know that I will do the honorable thing and gladly, if that is what you want."

"I…" Charlie straightened her shoulders. "To be perfectly frank, I'm not sure what I want, Max. You see, a little while ago, I received a letter from my aunt Tabitha inviting me to accompany her on a Grand Tour in the summer. And I would like to see the world. Very much. And who knows"—her mouth curved in a bright smile that didn't quite reach her eyes—"Arabella met Gabriel in Switzerland. Perhaps I shall meet my love match on the Continent too if you and I don't… Well, what I mean to say is, I have options, Max. So you needn't worry that you're destined to become leg-shackled to someone like me—a woman who isn't overly agreeable and who's bound to make your life difficult rather than easy. It wouldn't be fair to either of us if our union was forged on a foundation of fleeting lust and obligation and that alone. I know we would both do our best to maintain an amicable relationship, but as you've said, in the end, we both want different things from marriage." She gave a little laugh. "No doubt your mother will be glad to see the back of me. Unfortunately, I think I might have cemented her bad opinion of me when I shared afternoon tea with her and Diana."

The fact that his mother had insulted Charlie about her figure made Max's gut tighten with anger. Resisting the urge to scowl lest Charlie misconstrue the reason for his temper, he asked in a deliberately mild tone, "Why, what happened?"

Charlie winced. "I let slip that I know how to fence, drive a curricle, and shoot a pistol. Not ladylike—let alone duchess-like—accomplishments at all."

Max gave a snort of laughter. "I would have liked to have seen her face. Her expression would have been priceless."

Charlie blinked at him. "You're not shocked? That I can do all of those things?"

"Of course not. I knew you fenced. I've heard you talk about it before. And there's nothing wrong at all with being able to drive a curricle. Many women do. And as for being able to use a pistol, well, to my way of thinking, it's nothing but practical. Knowledge brings power, after all."

"Well, I'm relieved you agree," said Charlie. "Although, I might have told your mother and Diana a tiny white lie about my shooting skills. I intimated that I'd only used a pistol once. But in actual fact, Nate has taken me shooting at our father's estate many times. During the summer holidays, when we were both bored. Although I've never shot at anything but a fixed target. Mainly empty champagne and brandy bottles, actually. I can't abide the idea of hunting."

Max gave her a wry smile. "Remind me never to get into your black books, Lady Charlotte Hastings. If you decided that running me through wasn't sufficient punishment, it sounds like you could also run me over with a curricle, then finish me off with a pistol."

Charlie laughed at that. "Yes, you'd best remember that, Your Grace. I'm not someone to be trifled with."

Max's smile widened to a grin. "Oh, I know, my lady. I know."

"In any event, despite my penchant for less than genteel activities, Diana didn't seem to think ill of me," she continued. "In fact, I rather think that given a little time, we could become firm friends. When your mother began to discuss the arrangements for the house party at Heathcote Hall and our betrothal ball, Diana asked for my opinion on anything and everything. I truly appreciated her support."

"Well, I'm glad," said Max. And he truly was. "And it's my fond hope that other members of the ton with influence will change their opinion of you and will be singing your praises to all and sundry very soon. I'm sure this house party and ball will only be the beginning of your acceptance back into Society's fold."

Charlie's nose wrinkled. "I pray that you are right, Max. Even if I continue to be the subject of speculative whispers, I would like the overt slander to die down. For my family's sake more than anything else."

"I'm sure it will," said Max. "And I'm sure excursions like this will help too. Between now and the house party, I'll endeavor to take you promenading again. The more you and I are seen together, the better."

"I shall look forward to it," replied Charlie softly. "And I promise to behave. You were right to refuse my presumptuous proposal earlier. If we kissed in the middle of

Hyde Park on Easter Sunday, I'm sure I'd be lambasted in the papers again for unbecoming conduct, which would defeat the purpose of our engagement-of-convenience. And I don't want to do that. Not after all the trouble you've gone to, and are going to, for me."

"You know I wouldn't be doing this if I didn't want to, Charlie. And as I said before, you don't need to pretend to be more ladylike or decorous or duchess-like. I like you just the way you are."

It wasn't a lie. In fact, he liked Charlie far too much. But regrettably, not in a way that was remotely gentlemanly or appropriate, given the way his gaze kept wandering to her delectable mouth...and lower to the swell of her generous bosom beneath the soft brown velvet of her spencer.

Hell and damnation. Eyes up, man. He was almost as bad as bloody Mowbray. Flicking the reins, Max urged his horses onto the path. He'd take Charlie on another circuit of the park, then he'd head back to Hastings House before he did take her up on her offer and kiss her.

Now more than ever, he was certain that the brief kiss they'd shared beneath the kissing bough would plague him for days. And nights. Thank God no one was privy to his innermost thoughts, the ones in which he had Charlie all to himself and he laid bare her luscious body. When they both had all the time in the world to explore all kinds of bed sport. How he'd love to learn all the ways to bring her pleasure and hear her scream his name...

And there was the rub. Charlie *shouldn't* be the object of his libidinous fantasies. She deserved so much more.

If only his heart *was* capable of more. Because if he could give Lady Charlotte Hastings his love, he would. While he would undoubtedly miss her company if she did take up her aunt's offer and go abroad at the end of Season, in the long run, it was probably for the best.

For both of them.

CHAPTER 13

What if you were to learn that a certain
bluestocking society with headquarters at a
prestigious Mayfair address was not only
fomenting seeds of political dissent among its
female membership, but also promoting unseemly,
perhaps even dangerous activities?
Curricle driving? Fencing? Pistol shooting? What
is the world coming to?
Is this the fall of "Polite Society" as we know it?
The Beau Monde Mirror: The Society Page

Hastings House, Berkeley Square
April 14, 1819

The morning room of Hastings House was quiet save
for the crackle of the fire, the tick of the Boulle
mantel clock, and the mad drumming of Charlie's fingers
upon the mahogany tabletop.

Grrrr. Charlie threw the *Beau Monde Mirror* down beside her half-eaten crumpet with a huff of disgust. If
Max's mother, sister-in-law, or someone else within the
environs of Devereux House—a traitorous servant perhaps—wasn't responsible for this blatantly derogatory
story, she'd eat her Easter bonnet, flowers and all.

Now she was in a bad mood, and according to the
mantel clock, it was only a few hours until Cressida sent

her carriage round to Hastings House to pick her up and ferry her to Heathcote Hall at Hampstead Heath. The house party wasn't due to begin until the morrow, but the dowager duchess wanted to arrive the day before to make sure all of the preparations were well underway, and everything was in order. And apparently, she wanted Charlie to help oversee things too. Of course, Charlie had been pleased to be included, but now…

She scowled at the paper over the rim of her teacup. Now she'd be out of sorts and wondering who was spying on her and leaking intelligence to London's worst scandalmongering rag the whole time she was at Heathcote Hall. Rather than enjoying the affair, she'd have to mind her Ps and Qs and take care never to put a foot wrong the entire time. For four whole days. Ugh!

So much for being myself…

But then again, she'd have Max and other close allies by her side. Nate and Sophie were staying for three days, and all going well, Arabella and Gabriel would be back in London in time for the betrothal ball too. Charlie had received a letter from Arabella two days before and she couldn't wait to see her friend and swap news.

However, all that aside, what worried and hurt Charlie the most was the idea that her initial impression of Diana Devereux might have been incorrect. It would be both sobering and hurtful indeed if it turned out that the young duchess was really that duplicitous. There'd only been a handful of people in the drawing room of Devereux House that day she'd taken afternoon tea—Diana, Cressida, two chambermaids, and a pair of footmen—and it could have been any one of them who'd tattled on her.

As much as Charlie hated to broach such an uncomfortable subject with Max—that someone within his mother's household must have betrayed her—she supposed she ought to. Perhaps he could have a word to Cressida about the possible breach of confidence. And really, wouldn't Cressida want to know if someone on her staff *was* selling gossip to the papers?

But what if it's actually Cressida?

A shiver of apprehension slithered down Charlie's spine, and she pushed her lukewarm tea and crumpet aside. Her appetite had suddenly disappeared. She knew the dowager duchess disliked her, but would the woman actively try to undermine her son's fiancée? Surely such underhanded tactics were beneath a woman of her social standing.

At least the *Beau Monde Mirror* hadn't explicitly mentioned the disreputable Lady C. on this occasion. But still, Charlie hated to think that her private disclosure had discredited the Mayfair Bluestocking Society. Especially when its dedicated members put so much effort into supporting worthwhile charities.

With a sigh, Charlie wrapped her cashmere shawl about her shoulders and got to her feet. Sitting about fretting and brooding wouldn't help matters. She had things to do. First, she had to change into her new carriage gown of claret-red velvet and squeeze in a visit to Madame de Beauvoir's studio. The artist wanted her opinion on her half-completed portrait, and Charlie was most excited to see it. Thank goodness Cressida didn't know about *that*.

On her return to Hastings House, she would then need to check that Molly had her valise and traveling trunk in order. While Heathcote Hall was only five miles away, she didn't want to have her maid, or Edwards, the footman, running back and forth between Berkeley Square and Hampstead Heath because she'd forgotten something.

She'd already bid her father farewell. Busy as always, he'd been exiting the breakfast room as she'd arrived. But it wouldn't be long until she saw him again. He had promised to attend the betrothal ball along with Lady Tilbury in two days' time. Charlie smiled to herself as she climbed the stairs to her room. Lady Tilbury was delightful, and Charlie swore she'd caught a glimpse of her father and the attractive widow beneath the spring kissing bough in the library right before dinner on Easter Sunday.

Perhaps there might be another engagement in the family before too long.

But at this rate, there would only be one wedding by Season's end.

Charlie frowned at her reflection in the mirror as Molly attempted to tame her unruly hair into some semblance of order with a red velvet ribbon and a battalion of hairpins. After their promenade in Hyde Park on Easter Sunday, Max had adroitly evaded her strategically placed spring kissing boughs as though they'd been strung with stinging nettles and deadly nightshade. Throughout dinner and the rest of that evening, he seemed steadfastly and infuriatingly determined to play the part of the perfect gentleman yet again. No doubt Nate's presence, and her father's, had quelled his ardor to some extent.

But then, Charlie had also sensed a shift in his regard. An increased intensity in his gaze which seemed to alight upon her more often during dinner and afterward, when they'd all gathered in the drawing room and she and Lady Tilbury had taken turns entertaining them with tunes on the pianoforte. Charlie swore there was a simmering heat, a hum of awareness that hadn't been there before whenever Max looked her way.

Yet still he avoided any and all of her kissing boughs, even going so far as to depart with Nate and Sophie so they wouldn't be alone in the entry hall of Hastings House.

Curse him and his innate sense of chivalry.

Two hours later when Charlie received word that the Dowager Duchess of Exmoor's carriage had arrived, she reminded herself that at least she would be spending several days and nights in Max's company during the course of the house party. While she wouldn't throw herself at him again, she also hoped there would be further opportunities to be alone with her determined-to-keep-his-hands-to-himself fiancé.

Somehow, she had to subtly convince him that giving into his lustful urges wouldn't be a bad thing. She wasn't a naive girl. She knew there were precautions they could take to avoid the situation Max had alluded to—one in which they *had* to get married if they went too far. It was a risk she was more than willing to take, because in her mind, how could their friendship blossom and grow into something more if Max kept her firmly in the do-not-ever-touch-my-friend's-sister category?

Well, the Duke of Exmoor might be obstinate, but she was obstinate too. Charlie pulled on her fawn kid gloves with a determined tug.

After the one kiss they'd shared, as far as she was concerned, this battle of hearts and wills was only just beginning.

$\approx$

Heathcote Hall, Hampstead Heath

Heathcote Hall, a three-story whitewashed mansion set against a backdrop of verdant parkland, was absolutely beautiful…and absolutely enormous. Charlie quickly discovered this fact when Cressida assigned her the task of making sure that the state of all thirty-two guest bedrooms was up to scratch.

Charlie had barely settled into her own chamber—a small but prettily furnished apartment on the third floor —when Heathcote's dour-faced housekeeper, Mrs. Entwhistle, came to knock on her door with "Her Grace's request." A young, fair-haired chambermaid hovered behind the middle-aged woman with an expression that suggested she'd rather be someplace else.

"Oh really?" said Charlie after she'd listened to Mrs. Entwhistle's relayed message. "She wants me to do this right now?" The dowager duchess had not mentioned anything of the sort in the carriage ride to Hampstead Heath. In fact, Cressida had been talking to Diana about having a spot of luncheon on the terrace as they'd drawn up before Heathcote Hall's grand, marble-pillared portico.

"Yes," answered Mrs. Entwhistle through lips so

pursed, Charlie wondered if the woman had been tasting lemons. "She does. She was very clear. You are to accompany me on my final inspection of each room, and I will make a note if anything is amiss. Her Grace has very exacting standards. Everything must be spick-and-span." Her small, bird-like eyes ran over Charlie, and Charlie had the distinct feeling she'd somehow failed the housekeeper's very own spick-and-span test. "And she'd like a full accounting sooner rather than later." For added emphasis, she waved a large leather-bound notebook in the air.

Charlie barely suppressed a disgruntled sigh. So much for joining Cressida and Diana for luncheon. But what else could she do but comply with her hostess's request? Putting aside the fact that Charlie was, for all intents and purposes, a guest as well, it would be discourteous of her not to. Besides, she was curious about the room Lady Penelope had been allocated. Ever since their encounter in Hyde Park on Easter Sunday, she'd been wondering about Cressida's motives for inviting the Duke of Stafford's daughter to the house party. The young woman clearly had designs on Max. At least he'd been indifferent to her obvious attempts at flirting.

By the time Charlie had reached the second floor and had entered the second to last bedchamber over an hour later, her feet were sore—her new leather half-boots were pinching her toes—and she was dying for a cup of tea. So far, everything had been perfectly in order, and Charlie had begun to suspect that Cressida was trying to send her a message—*you are in my house and you will do as I say. And you clearly don't need luncheon.*

"And who will be staying in this room?" Charlie asked as she looked about the chamber with its own dressing room and sitting room. It was spacious and furnished with elegant satinwood pieces, including a wide tester bed with curtains of sage-green damask. Plump pillows in shades of pale rose and ivory adorned the head of the bed, and a thick Aubusson rug in matching tones carpeted the gleaming wooden floor. The arched windows overlooked a wide swathe of manicured lawn with a glimpse of lake and woodland beyond. Indeed, it was grand enough for a duchess.

Mrs. Entwhistle consulted her list while the chambermaid quite unnecessarily rearranged the pink roses within a vase upon a gilt-legged table. "Lady Penelope Purcell, I believe, my lady."

"Oh, I see…" Charlie frowned. "But a moment ago, didn't you inform me that the duke's suite of rooms is next door?"

Mrs. Entwhistle met her gaze unflinchingly. "Yes, my lady."

"So, let me see if my understanding of the situation is correct… I'm the Duke of Exmoor's fiancée, yet I've been allocated a bedchamber on the floor above at the far end of this wing. And Lady Penelope, a single young woman with no close ties at all to His Grace, is occupying the bedroom adjacent to his?"

The housekeeper's mouth flattened. "It would seem so, my lady."

Cressida. Cressida had to be behind this.

Tamping down a surge of temper, Charlie aimed for an aloof arching of one eyebrow instead. "Tell me, Mrs. Entwhistle, is there a jib door connecting this room and the duke's suite?"

The housekeeper blushed beet red. "I…I wouldn't know, my lady."

"You wouldn't know," Charlie repeated flatly. She ran her gaze over the patterns of peonies and butterflies on the silk wallpapered panels beside the bed but could see no obvious signs of a hidden door. "Now, why do I find that difficult to believe?"

She started forward, and the housekeeper followed. "Yes. There is a jib door," the woman said with a mulish glint in her eye. "But it's locked, and only the dowager duchess, the duke, and I have a key. So, if you are suggesting even for one minute that Lady Penelope would do anything untoward to try to enter His Grace's—"

Charlie held up a hand. "Excuse me, Mrs. Entwhistle, but are you questioning *my* right to question the highly irregular nature of this arrangement? And who made you the authority on what His Grace or Lady Penelope may or may not do in any given situation?"

The woman's mouth opened and shut like a landed trout. "Well…I…I would never…"

Charlie took a step closer and held out a hand. "May I see your list, Mrs. Entwhistle?"

The woman swallowed and passed the notebook to Charlie. "Of course, my lady."

"And may I have your pencil?"

The housekeeper handed that over too.

"Right." Charlie glanced over the list of entries, and sure enough, it looked as though Lady Penelope had been allocated the Rose and Peony Room, right next to the Duke of Exmoor's apartments. She marched over to a nearby dressing table and crossed the young woman's name out, replacing it with her own. Then she found her own name, drew a line through it, and wrote Lady Penelope's in its place.

"Here you are, Mrs. Entwhistle." She handed back the notebook. "Something *was* amiss, but now the problem has been rectified. Lady Penelope will now be sleeping in the Lilac Room on the third floor." Turning to the chambermaid who was openly gaping at her, Charlie said, "Hannah, isn't it?"

The young maid bobbed a curtsy. "Yes, my lady."

"If it's not too much trouble, would you be so kind as to run upstairs and inform my lady's maid, Molly, that she will need to repack my things as her mistress is relocating to the Rose and Peony Room."

"But…but you can't do that," began the housekeeper, her expression aghast. "Her Grace will not stand—"

"Mrs. Entwhistle," said Charlie firmly. "May I remind you that very soon, I will be the Duke of Exmoor's wife, and thus, your new mistress. But rest assured, I will inform Her Grace of the new sleeping arrangements myself, and furthermore, that you have had nothing to do with the change of plan. Besides, given the fact that Lady Penelope's brother, Lord Mowbray, and the Duke and Duchess of Stafford are also staying on the third floor, I think it's a far more appropriate arrangement, don't you?"

"Yes, of course, my lady." The housekeeper dipped into a reluctant curtsy, then barked at the chambermaid who still lingered by the roses. "Hannah, hop to it, girl. You heard Lady Charlotte. Go and speak with her maid. And offer her a helping hand to repack her ladyship's things. I'll summon two of the footmen to ferry everything downstairs."

"Wonderful. Thank you, Mrs. Entwhistle," said Charlie with an incline of her head. "Now, where might I find the dowager duchess? Last I heard, she was taking luncheon on the terrace with her daughter-in-law."

∽

As it was, Charlie didn't end up joining the irksome, meddlesome dowager duchess for luncheon. Upon quitting the Rose and Peony Room, Charlie noticed one of the doors to Max's suite of rooms was ajar, and the soft sound of a muffled sob then a sniffle floated out into the hallway.

What on earth?

Mrs. Entwhistle frowned and approached the doorway but then retreated. "I shall see how Hannah is getting on, Lady Charlotte," she said. "And then I'll organize the removal of your things down here. If that is all right with you, of course?"

"Yes, of course. And thank you, Mrs. Entwhistle," replied Charlie, curious as to who might be crying in Max's chambers. Surely it wasn't Cressida, which meant it must be Diana. Because if it had been a maid, surely the housekeeper would have entered to check on her.

Mrs. Entwhistle hastened away toward the servants' stairs, and Charlie moved to the door. Pulling it open a little farther, she peeked in, and sure enough, it was Diana. The young duchess sat upon a window seat on the far side of the chamber, a very masculine sitting room. She seemed oblivious to Charlie's presence as she crossed the thick Turkish rug.

"Diana…" Charlie murmured, and the young woman jumped.

"Lady Charlotte. Oh…I'm sorry…" Diana hastily dashed away the tears from her cheeks with trembling fingers. "I…I'm sure this must look very odd. I assure you I'm not usually a watering pot. And I'm not in the habit of frequenting my brother-in-law's rooms." Bright color flooded her cheeks. "I mean, I don't even visit them infrequently. It's just that… Oh, fiddlesticks. I'm not making any sense."

"That's quite all right." Charlie gestured at the seat beside her. "May I join you?"

"Yes. Of course." Diana moved her skirts of pearl-gray silk. "Please do."

Charlie sat and studied Diana's flushed, tear-stained countenance for a moment before transferring her gaze to the view outside the window. "I take it this used to be your husband's sitting room," she said softly.

Diana gave a shaky exhale. "Yes. Yes, it was…" Her gaze flitted about the chamber but darted away from the open bedroom door that showed a glimpse of a majestic four-poster bed beyond.

Max's bed.

Charlie blew out a breath and looked away too. "I have a little understanding of what it's like to lose someone you love. I lost my oldest brother, Thomas, and my dear mama, Elizabeth, passed away when I was only six years old. My poor father has grieved for his son and his wife for such a long time. And the sorrow never really goes away. You learn to cover it over and hide it, to go on, but then something happens, or you see something that brings it all back, and all of that sadness wells up to the surface again. There's no way to control it."

Diana reached out and squeezed her hand. "Yes, that's exactly what it's like. Only…it's not just sorrow that I feel. It's…" She closed her eyes and swallowed. "It's anger. Especially when I'm here at Heathcote. You see, this is where Anthony died. During another house party, not unlike this one."

Charlie opened her mouth, then shut it again. She

wasn't sure what to say. She'd heard—well, all of the ton had heard—about Anthony Devereux's untimely death almost four years ago. But Charlie hadn't known it had been at Heathcote Hall. No wonder Max hadn't made mention of the property until recently. Eventually she managed, "I'm so sorry, Diana. I had no idea. And I can't even imagine how difficult it is for you to be here right now."

A small smile trembled about Diana's mouth. "As difficult as it is, please know that I'm very happy for you and Max, and I would never want you to think that I do not wish to be here. I always experience such a tangle of emotions whenever I visit this place. But after I've had my initial bout of tears, I'm fine." She met Charlie's gaze. "I suppose you've heard that it was a riding accident that took Anthony's life."

Charlie nodded. "Yes… Well, I'd heard he'd fallen from his horse. But nothing more."

"I don't blame him at all. That's not what I'm angry about. Accidents happen. What I can't forgive him for is —" Diana broke off and her eyes glittered with tears again. "What I can't forgive him for is the fact that he was unfaithful to me. And even worse, his…his lover was one of the guests at our house party. I still love him, and I miss him, but I'm so, so angry that he…that he betrayed me. When I discovered what he'd done…to me. To us…" She shook her head. "The worst part is, I never got to confront him about it. To ask him why he would do such a thing. I thought he loved me…" She bit her lip and wiped away another tear that had slipped onto her cheek. "I'm sorry, I'm weeping again."

Shock stole Charlie's breath. "Oh, Diana," she whispered. "That's so heartbreaking and awful and—" On an impulse, she gathered the young woman into a hug. "I don't know how you bear it. Coming here. Having to revisit it all. It must be absolute torture."

"Yet still I come back. And I visit this room. It's almost as though I enjoy pressing on the bruises inside me." Diana drew back from Charlie's embrace and sighed deeply. "I'm such a fool."

Charlie touched her arm. "No, you're not. Not at all. You loved him even though he hurt you. It's only natural that you would miss him and grieve for all that you once had, and for all the hopes and dreams that were taken from you."

Diana gave a watery sniff. "Thank you for listening, Charlie. And for your understanding. I would say that virtually no one knows about Anthony's infidelity. It's not something one generally tends to talk about during morning calls or when making polite chitchat at a ball or soiree. Or even with one's mother-in-law. Indeed, I've never really spoken about this to anyone before today."

Charlie smiled. "I'm touched that you feel comfortable enough to confide in me, given the short time we've known each other."

"It's funny, but yes, I do feel that way. Comfortable. I haven't any immediate family of my own to trade confidences with; I was an only child and both my parents passed away soon after Anthony and I wed. And most women in the ton are…" She shrugged a slender shoulder. "I can sense you're different, Charlie. And for some reason I cannot explain, I believe I can trust you." Her mouth curved in a smile. "Perhaps it's because I've always liked Max and I trust his judgment. He's an honorable man at heart. Despite what the scandal rags say."

Charlie pressed her lips together. "Hmm, the scandal rags."

A shadow of remorse passed across Diana's face. "Oh, Charlie. I didn't mean to imply… I shouldn't have mentioned those dreadful publications. They print the most horrid rubbish. And now that I've met you, I can see that the gossipmongers are quite wrong about you. You're lovely and sweet and you have such…spirit. I admire that about you. And I will do what I can to restore your good standing in the eyes of Polite Society."

"I…I'm quite overwhelmed. Thank you, Diana. I appreciate your support."

She waved an elegant hand. "Think nothing of it. To be perfectly honest, I've never been that fond of Cressida's first choice for Max."

Charlie cocked an eyebrow. "Lady Penelope?"

"Yes…" She leaned closer in a conspiratorial fashion. "I've always thought that that young woman is all superficial prettiness with no real substance to her. A bit like that Delftware vase over there." She nodded at the gray marble mantel where a blue and white patterned porcelain urn stood.

At that moment, Charlie's stomach emitted a long low growl, and she clapped a hand over her belly. "Oh my goodness. I beg your pardon."

Diana laughed. "Think nothing of it." But then her expression changed. "Don't tell me you've had nothing to eat since you arrived. When Cressida and I took luncheon on the terrace, she mentioned you were tired and had asked for a tray in your room."

Charlie didn't know what to say. "I… No, I haven't had anything," she said carefully. Cressida was such a nasty— Oh, she really didn't want to say it, even in her own mind.

"Well, we can't have that." Diana rose and smoothed out her skirts. "Come to my room at the other end of the hall. I have a tin of bonbons, and you must have a few until a tray is brought up."

Charlie stood too and offered her new friend a grateful smile. "Thank you so much. I hope I'm not keeping you from anything important, though. I know how busy Cressida must be. And you. A house party is such a huge undertaking."

"Busy? Oh pfft," said Diana as they exited the room arm in arm. "Cressida's busy lounging about the terrace at the moment. The staff here at Heathcote Hall are so well-trained, she barely has to lift a finger. And I'm not busy either. After you've eaten, if you're not too tired, what say I show you about the gardens? I'd like your opinion on where we should set up certain activities. Then we should stop by the kitchen to see what pastries Cook and her staff are preparing. We must sample a few to make sure they are of the highest quality."

"I would love that," said Charlie. She'd never been more sincere.

CHAPTER 14

Let's hope your wardrobe is up to snuff, ladies, for
the Season proper has begun!
The Beau Monde Mirror: The Essential Style &
Etiquette Guide

Heathcote Hall, Hampstead Heath
April 17, 1819

The next two days passed in a wild flurry of activity.
Guests began to arrive at the Hall, and once the rev-
elries began in earnest, Charlie barely had time to catch
her breath, let alone spend much time with Max. Much to
her chagrin.

There were seemingly countless rounds of tea and
cake on the terrace and in the drawing room, and innumerable games of cards and charades and bouts of billiards, shuttlecock, and pall-mall. And then there was an
excursion across the heath on horseback and an archery
tournament followed by a picnic beside Heathcote's lake.
Each night there were elegant dinners with endless courses, followed by more cards and charades and impromptu
concerts. There was always something to do, someone to
make small talk with, and some new gown to change into.
And Max seemed to be caught up in the same whirlwind.

The pace Cressida set was nothing less than breakneck, and Charlie suspected this had been the dowager

duchess's aim from the very beginning: she clearly wanted to keep Charlie and Max occupied and away from each other. It didn't help matters that Cressida kept thrusting eligible young women like Lady Penelope in her son's direction. It seemed she'd deliberately engineered seating plans or devised small groups and teams in such a way to put the greatest amount of distance between Max and his bride-to-be.

It was enough to make Charlie want to grind her teeth and stomp her very sore feet.

Although, Charlie was relieved that most of the guests were pleasantly polite to her—at least to her face. No one had dared to give her the cut direct or say anything disparaging. It was really only Lady Penelope who continued to give her false smiles and compliments while simultaneously trying to inveigle herself into Max's company whenever she could. If there was a spy lurking about, taking note of how she behaved or what she said, Charlie wasn't aware of anyone paying particular attention to her. All the same, it was unsettling to think someone might be watching her while she was completely oblivious to it.

Of course, Charlie was also ecstatic to have Sophie by her side a good deal of the time. She and Nate had brought baby Thomas with them, and Charlie had made sure that the makeshift nursery that had been set up on the third floor near their bedroom had everything they would need.

When Gabriel and Arabella, the Earl and Countess of Langdale, arrived at Heathcote a few hours before the betrothal ball was due to begin, Charlie was beside herself with happiness. Arabella and Sophie joined Charlie in her dressing room just as Molly was sliding a diadem encrusted with diamonds and pearls into Charlie's beautifully styled hair.

"I still cannot believe that you and Gabriel managed to get here in time," said Charlie, catching Arabella's gaze in the dressing-table mirror when Molly stepped back. "You must be exhausted. How many days did it take you to journey from Edinburgh to London again? Five?"

Arabella pushed her spectacles up her nose. "Four and a half, actually. And yes, I'm a wee bit weary. But that doesn't matter at all because how could Gabriel and I miss such a wonderful and momentous occasion? We are both so happy for you and Max. And I know how long you've dreamed of this, Charlie. When we met in Gunter's Tea Shop—wasn't it just over a year ago now?—and our Society for Enlightened Young Women formulated our list of eligible rakehells, Max's name was at the very top. Indeed, he was the very first gentleman you mentioned. All of us—Sophie, Olivia, and I—knew how you felt about him from that moment. And at long last, your dream is coming true."

"Hmm. About that," said Charlie, wrinkling her nose. "Our engagement is…I'm afraid it's *not* actually all that I'd dreamed of." And then she confessed all to Arabella—the nature of her arrangement with Max and the series of events that had precipitated it all, including Lord Rochfort's villainy.

"Oh my goodness, Charlie. That's…that's…" Arabella crossed the room and enveloped her in a warm hug. "I'm so sorry. I had no idea. And here I am blathering all kinds of congratulatory platitudes—which, of course, are heartfelt—but are not at all helpful given the way things really are." She straightened and her forehead dipped into a frown. "And Max is a colossal clodpole. Why are all of our men so…so stubborn and completely oblivious about how they really feel? Even when it's so obvious to everyone else that they are in love?"

Charlie laughed and reached for one of Arabella's hands, which still rested upon her shoulder. "Yes, they are oblivious at times, aren't they? But you weren't to know that Max is a being a clodpole. Sophie"—she caught her other friend's sympathetic gaze—"had no idea either until I told her. It seems that the course of true love hasn't run smooth for any of us."

"Well, I'm certain Max will come to his senses sooner rather than later," said Sophie. "I mean, look at you, Charlie. How could he not? Aside from being brave and clever and warm and caring, you're beautiful."

Charlie felt a blush warm her cheeks. "It's my new gown," she murmured. "Madame Boucher encouraged me to try something different. I don't usually wear turquoise, but I *think* it suits me."

"Aye, it most certainly does," said Arabella. "It brings out the color of your eyes and your hair."

"And I love the sweeping neckline," added Sophie. "The cut is perfect for your figure. Max won't be able to take his eyes off you."

Charlie rose from the dressing table's stool and smoothed her silk skirts. "Thank you. Both of you. You always know how to make me feel better. The only thing that could make this evening a little more perfect is if Olivia and Hamish could be here."

Arabella pushed a blonde curl behind her ear. "I believe they'll be back in Town by the beginning of May. I received a letter from Olivia the day before we departed Edinburgh."

"Oh, wonderful," said Charlie. Then she frowned at Arabella. "Are you all right? You've gone awfully pale all of a sudden."

"Yes, you have," agreed Sophie. "Would you like to sit down?"

Arabella nodded. "Aye. I would...thank you."

Charlie led her friend to a nearby armchair. "Can I get you anything? A glass of barley water, perhaps? A pot of tea?"

But Arabella shook her head. "No...I'll be fine. I expect the fatigue of the journey has caught up with me, that's all."

"Are you certain? I can ring for anything you'd like. It's no trouble at all."

Arabella smiled weakly. Her cheeks were as pale as the ivory satin of her ball gown. "I...I might go back to my room for a wee bit if that's all right. Perhaps I just need to lie down."

"Of course," said Charlie, concern lacing her tone.

Sophie drew close and offered Arabella her arm. "I'll go with you. And if Gabriel isn't about, I'll send Nate to look for him."

"Thank you," murmured Arabella as she shakily rose to her feet. "I'm sure I will be as right as a trivet before too long. There's no way on earth I'm missing your betrothal ball, Charlie."

Charlie touched her arm. "You must look after yourself first, my sweet friend. Rest as much as you need to. We'll all still be here on the morrow."

After Arabella and Sophie had quit the suite, Charlie crossed to the armoire in the bedchamber and retrieved her mother's diamond and pearl *en tremblant* brooch from her jewelry box. It matched the diadem, which had also once belonged to her mother, perfectly. After Charlie pinned it to the lace overlay on her bodice, tears welled in her eyes and her vision misted. An overwhelming wave of bittersweet emotion flooded her heart. It was times like this that she missed her dearly departed mama, Elizabeth, more than she could say.

A knock at the bedroom door made her jump. After hastily wiping away the tears that had slipped onto her cheeks, she nodded at Molly, who'd emerged from the dressing room. "You may answer it."

When the door opened, Charlie's breath caught. *Max.*

Even though she hadn't seen him as often as she would have liked over the past two days, she certainly hadn't expected him to come knocking on her bedroom door. But now that he was here, she was glad that he had, whatever the reason.

Hoping he wouldn't notice that she'd been crying a moment before, she offered a smile and said in a tone she hoped was playful, "Max, you naughty boy, what are you doing visiting my bedroom? I know we're engaged, but surely that's not allowed. I thought we were trying to keep my name *out* of the gossip columns. Especially given the fact there might be a spy for the *Beau Monde Mirror* in our midst." Charlie had managed to share her suspicions with Max shortly after his arrival at Heathcote.

Max's mouth tilted into a crooked smile as he crossed the threshold. "Heathcote is my home, you are my fiancée, and spy or no, I'll do whatever I like within its walls." Then he winced. "I sound insufferably arrogant again, don't I? Even for a duke."

Behind him, Molly closed the door, then scuttled away into the dressing room again.

Charlie laughed. "Well, if you need to ask... But I'm sure it can be trained out of you by the right woman."

"Good God, you make me sound like a stubborn ass or a recalcitrant pup."

Charlie shrugged a shoulder. "If the cap fits... All teasing aside, though, and at the risk of inflating your ducal arrogance even further, I should mention that you are looking particularly elegant this evening, Your Grace."

Indeed, it wasn't a lie. Max's black evening jacket, midnight-blue satin waistcoat, and gray trousers fit his Corinthian's physique so well, the garments seemed to be painted on, as though Madame de Beauvoir had spilled her paint pots across his wide shoulders and down his muscular thighs. A sapphire pin winked at Charlie from the depths of his elaborately tied cravat. If she were the least bit poetic, she'd compose odes to Max's fine figure and far too handsome face.

Max tilted his head in acknowledgement of her compliment. "Thank you, my lady." His deep blue gaze raked over her slowly, lingering on her face, her bust, and her hips before returning at a leisurely pace to her eyes. "And I must say that you are looking exceptionally lovely too. I like that color on you. I don't think I've ever seen you wear it before. Turquoise, is it?" His mouth twitched. "Or has your modiste given it some other exotic name like Adriatic aquamarine or peacock blue or duckpond teal? I can never keep up with feminine fashions."

Max had been paying attention to her attire? For goodness knew how long?

What a bemusing thought. Charlie felt her cheeks grow warm and her pulse capered about as though she'd begun to dance a lively quadrille. How was she supposed to be circumspect about this faux engagement when he subjected her to such heated looks or remembered such seemingly inconsequential details? It was as though she'd always mattered to him and he'd kept a catalogue in his mind of what she'd worn or hadn't worn on various occasions. It was rapidly becoming an impossible feat to remain unaffected under the circumstances. "Turquoise will do. And thank you," she returned, her voice noticeably husky. She raised a hand to her mother's brooch. "I think the diamonds and pearls help too."

"Yes, they're stunning," agreed Max. "And to that end…" He reached into his jacket and withdrew a long, slender, velvet-covered box. "I have something for you. Another betrothal gift. I hope it will match your diadem and brooch."

"Oh…" Her curiosity piqued, Charlie took it from him and lifted the lid, then gasped with pleasure. Inside lay an exquisite diamond and pearl necklace. The tear-shaped gemstones glimmered in the fire and candlelight. "Oh, Max. It's utterly beautiful. You shouldn't have."

"Of course I should." Taking the necklace from the box, he raised a brow. "May I help you put it on?"

"Yes…thank you." Charlie moved to stand in front of a nearby gilt-edged looking glass and Max followed. After he draped the necklace about her throat and fastened the clasp, he stilled. His gaze locked with hers in the mirror. His hands, large and warm, rested lightly upon her shoulders.

"Gorgeous," he murmured. His breath fanned the curls at her temple. The scent of his spicy cologne or whatever soap he used enveloped her.

For the space of a heartbeat and a quickly drawn breath, Charlie wondered if Max was going to kiss her.

≈

Dear God, she was beautiful.

As soon as Max had entered Charlie's bedroom and laid eyes upon her in her evening finery, he was transfixed. His tongue had been uncharacteristically tied in knots, and not just because her turquoise silk gown was molded to her luscious figure in all the right places, or the fact her chestnut curls were elegantly arranged at the back of her shapely head bar a few thick, glossy spirals that cascaded over one shoulder.

It was because *her* warm-as-brandy eyes had shone with admiration and desire too. They'd been riveted to him. He could have sworn she was holding her breath. Waiting for his next move in this strange dance they both found themselves in. One in which she approached and he habitually ducked away, fearing what would happen if they got too close. That they'd go too far and Charlie's choice to end things would be taken away.

Yet here he was in her room, unable to do anything but stare at her divine reflection as lust surged, hot and potent, pounding through his veins...

Up until recently, Max had never really allowed himself to indulge in the glorious sight of Charlie. To let his gaze linger, let alone his hands. But now...now Max's resolve to keep his promise to Nate to stay away, to keep his distance, was rapidly disintegrating in the face of Charlie's breathtaking loveliness. Her innate sensuality. His self-serving, covetous streak was in danger of taking over. Of seizing the reins.

He wanted to hold her. Kiss her. And more. So much more...

It would be so easy to take what he wanted. He could see Charlie desired him as much as he desired her. The way her breath had quickened as he'd brushed aside her curls to place his gift around her neck. How her pupils had dilated. How she watched him, even now. How her gaze kept straying to his mouth...

Sweet Jesus. Max had to thrust down the sudden urge to remove his hands from Charlie's shoulders and span her waist instead. To skate his palms upward, caressing her ribcage before brushing the underside of her full breasts with his thumbs. He'd watch her nipples pebble beneath her bodice, and her breath would catch again. And then maybe she would moan and arch back against him, pressing her derriere against his rapidly hardening groin. She'd turn in his arms, and then he'd make use of that massive tester bed behind them...

Bloody hell. They had a betrothal ball to attend with

upwards of two hundred guests in attendance. It was due to start shortly, and he and Charlie were expected downstairs to stand alongside his mother to receive everyone.

At least his mother had been behaving herself since their heated discussion at Devereux House nearly a fortnight before. As far as he knew, she hadn't insulted Charlie about her figure again. And according to Mr. Hunt, the inquiry agent, the dowager duchess had stayed away from Rochfort. Because she appeared to be keeping her word, their relationship had returned to its usual level of "distantly polite" rather than "testy", which was fortunate during a house party when so many eyes were upon them.

The ormolu clock on the mantel chimed the three-quarter hour, and he dropped his hands. "Are you ready, my lady?" he asked in a voice that was more than a little husky. "It's time I escorted you to the ball."

Charlie blinked as though waking from a dream, then nodded. "Ah yes. Let me get my gloves and my fan. I'll only be a moment."

She disappeared into the dressing room, and when she returned, a sliver of guilt pierced Max's chest. Since he'd arrived at Heathcote, he'd been deliberately avoiding Charlie. Giving her only crumbs of his attention because it made it *easier* for him to do the right thing. Of course, he'd reasoned a thousand times over that she wouldn't be lonely. Aside from her father and his new love interest, Lady Tilbury, she had Nate's wife, Sophie, to keep her company. She seemed to be getting on well with Diana, and now another one of her close friends, Arabella, was here.

But this was their betrothal ball and Charlie's moment to shine. For the upper echelons of the *haute ton* to accept her as one of their own again. And he, the Duke of Exmoor, really should be by her side as much as possible to demonstrate his belief in her. To show that she belonged and should be treated with due deference. She deserved nothing less.

Max pulled on his own evening gloves, then offered

Charlie his arm. He noticed how forced her smile was as she looked up at him through her lashes.

"You're nervous," he observed quietly as he escorted her into the hall.

Charlie's nose wrinkled. "A little. I pray no one openly snubs me tonight. Now, that would be too humiliating for words."

The idea that anyone would do that beneath his roof made Max bristle with anger. "I'm certain they won't. But if they do, they'll have me to answer to."

"Goodness, you sound as fierce as can be," murmured Charlie. "But I appreciate your support. Truly, I do."

"It's the least I can do." They reached the stairs and began to descend. The hum of excited voices from the entry hall below reached their ears.

"Considering the number of guests my mother has invited this evening, it's sure to be a huge crush, and we'll inevitably be pulled in different directions on occasion." Max paused on the landing and turned to face Charlie. "But if anything untoward should happen when I'm not with you, you must seek me out immediately. I won't have anyone showing you disrespect." Lord Mowbray's less-than-gentlemanly perusal of Charlie on Easter Sunday sprang to mind, and his gloved hands curled into fists. In hindsight, he should have paid more attention to the guest list rather than letting his mother have free rein.

Charlie offered him a smile. "I will. And I know how busy it will get. But I won't mind if you mingle as long as you promise to dance with me at least once."

"I promise to dance with you at least twice, if not three times," said Max as they resumed their descent. "And any waltz *is* mine."

Charlie laughed then. "I never took you for the possessive type, Max."

Possessive? Had he begun to think of Charlie as his? His alone to cherish and protect? Why else would such fierce emotion burn through Max's chest and twist his gut whenever he imagined someone like Mowbray dancing intimately with Charlie or subjecting her to lascivious glances?

What a sobering thought. But he didn't have time to examine his feelings further as they'd reached the entry hall and a throng of assembled guests began to greet both him and Charlie.

The madness was about to begin.

CHAPTER 15

Were you one of the lucky members of the ton
who received an invitation to the betrothal ball of
a certain devilish duke and a thoroughly
disreputable young lady?
It's sure to be the event of the Season with
entertainment galore.
The Beau Monde Mirror: The Society Page

As Max had predicted, it was a crush. And as he'd promised her, they'd danced three dances, including two waltzes. Charlie was on cloud nine as he effortlessly spun her about the ballroom, his eyes locked with hers as though she were the only woman in the room. For a man who professed he was incapable of love, he certainly knew how to put on a convincing act, and Charlie had to keep reminding herself that's exactly what it was—just an act.

As for the guests who weren't close friends or family, all of them were suitably polite—some were even effusive in their greetings and congratulations—and after two whirlwind hours of chatting and laughing and dancing and drinking champagne, Charlie had decided the betrothal ball could be declared a raging success—in her mind, anyway.

She was no longer an outcast. She was a disreputable debutante no more.

But then everything went horribly wrong.

In hindsight, Charlie couldn't quite pinpoint the exact moment when things began to unravel and turn into a complete mess. Perhaps it was when Max retreated to the terrace to share a brandy and a quiet chat with Nate and Gabriel; Charlie hadn't begrudged the fact that he'd left her side because she'd also drifted away from her fiancé on a number of occasions to speak with Sophie and Arabella and even Diana.

Or maybe it had been when her father and Lady Tilbury had disappeared outside for some "fresh air" in the gardens. Then Arabella had given Charlie her apologies—her dear friend had been looking decidedly green about the gills when Sophie had escorted her from the ballroom to rest upstairs in her room. Arabella had entreated Charlie not to tell Gabriel, though, because she hadn't wanted to spoil his fun. Sophie soon sent her apologies that she would also be absent for a while—apparently little Thomas was terribly unsettled, so she'd retreated to the nursery to try to help his nurse and the wet nurse sort out the problem. And as for Diana, Charlie was unsure where she'd got to.

In any event, Charlie suddenly found herself quite alone in a crowded ballroom. And that's when the mood around her began to shift. It was gradual at first, like a dark mist penetrating the room. Polite smiles and nods were replaced with knowing looks and smirks and whispers behind fans. With growing horror, Charlie realized everything that had been said to her by everyone who wasn't close to her must have been a complete lie.

Most of these people didn't know her, nor she them. Not at all. The only reason they were here paying lip service to Lady Charlotte Hastings was because the Duke of Exmoor's mother and sister-in-law had invited them. Perhaps they merely wished to satisfy their morbid curiosity about the disreputable Lady C.: Was she really as bad as the *Beau Monde Mirror* made her out to be?

Her cheeks stinging with a burning blush of embarrassment, Charlie was about to seek out Max as she'd promised earlier, when out of the corner of her eye, she spied Lady Penelope approaching.

Wonderful.

A vision in pale pink satin, the young woman seemed to drift between the knots of chatting guests like a graceful swan. For the past two days, she'd been wearing a mask of careful civility whenever she'd conversed with Charlie. But the woman had clearly decided to discard her disguise now that Charlie was alone; the look of cool disdain in her blue eyes clearly marked her as a combatant, not an ally.

"What are you doing over here all by yourself, my dear Lady Charlotte?" she said in a silky tone. "Don't tell me the 'duke of your dreams' has deserted you already?"

Oh, so the gloves really were off.

Unable to ignore such a barb, Charlie plastered a false smile on her face and prepared to do battle. "Actually, I was about to join him for a turn about the terrace. It's suddenly become unpleasantly stuffy in here."

The duke's daughter gave a little laugh. "Yes, of course you were." She leaned closer and murmured by Charlie's ear. "Don't think your current elevation in circumstances will last. If you haven't worked it out by now, Max's mother is on *my* side. And see everyone here?" She turned and gestured at the room with her closed fan. "Did you know that we're all taking bets on how long this ridiculous engagement will actually last? Personally, I think it will end before this farcical house party is over."

Horror and humiliation coiled through Charlie, tightening her chest. Surely not... But everyone was staring at her and Penelope. Smirking and snickering. The mood in the room *had* changed. It had grown ugly, and she was the outsider. The object of everyone's derision. The butt of all their jokes.

Oh, dear Lord, how had she not seen it before?

Before she could think to summon a quelling setdown or stalk away, Lady Penelope turned on her slippered heel and glided across the room to where her parents conversed with Cressida. The Staffords did not spare Charlie a glance, but Cressida did. She arched an eyebrow at her, then turned her attention to Lady Penelope as she approached, smiling warmly at the young woman, holding out a gloved hand to her in greeting.

The dowager duchess's message had never been clearer. *You are not wanted, Lady Charlotte Hastings, but Lady Penelope Purcell is.*

Tears stung Charlie's eyes, and for a brief moment she contemplated giving into the overwhelming urge to flee the ballroom. But stubbornness and the knowledge that she had friends here that *were* on her side made her stay. Max wanted her here, and unless he broke things off with her, she wasn't going to give in without a fight.

Burying her mortification and fanning the flames of her indignance, she armed herself with another glass of champagne and retreated to a shadowy corner where the light of the enormous chandeliers didn't quite reach. She just needed a few minutes to regroup before she sought out Max. She didn't want him to notice how upset she really was. The last thing she wanted to do was make a fuss or cause a scene. This ball would end, and a good deal of these horrid people would depart—assuming Penelope's malicious claim was even true—and she would still be Max's fiancée, even if it was in name only.

She sipped her champagne and watched the swirling throng before her—a lively country dance had started up. No one seemed to be watching her or smirking anymore, so perhaps she had imagined the whole change in mood. Yes, her mind had simply been playing tricks on her. For so long she'd seen herself as a social pariah, it was only natural that she'd jump to the wrong conclusion.

She sensed someone by her side—a tall male presence —and when she slid a sideways glance in the man's direction, she had to bite her tongue to stop herself from uttering a string of very unladylike curses.

It was Lord Mowbray.

Ugh. The odious man made her skin crawl. Ever since last year, when he'd propositioned her at a soiree —he'd cornered her, much like this, and had whispered in her ear, "Rumor has it that everyone has had a piece of you, so why not me?"—she'd been wary of him. She'd never told anyone about that incident or the fact Lord Mowbray had called her a prick-teaser after she'd told him to sod off because she'd been too ashamed. But now... Now she wasn't going to let him have the last word.

She raised an eyebrow, determined not to be cowed by him. "What, are you and your sister taking it in turns to harass Lady Charlotte Hastings, hoping that you'll drive her from the ballroom?" she asked. "Are your parents in on the plan too? Can I expect them to join in on the fun?"

He grinned and leaned in so close, his claret-laced breath gusted across her face. "Come now, Lady Charlotte. There's no need to be rude."

"Ha! That's rich coming from you. I've sometimes wondered if 'rude' is your middle name."

"Ah, so you think about me sometimes, do you?" His shoulder brushed hers. "I certainly think about you and what you and I might get up to. You're not wed yet. What do you say you and I go somewhere a bit quieter to explore the matter further?"

Charlie rolled her eyes. "You really are that conceited that you think I would even consider betraying my fiancé? And with someone like you? Especially after the way you insulted me in a similar fashion last year."

He sneered at her then. Or perhaps it was more of a leer. A leering sneer. "Now, listen here, you stuck-up little slut—"

Charlie spun to face him, her skirts whipping, then took a step forward so the marquess was forced to take a step back. "Are you hell-bent on getting yourself called out, Lord Mowbray?"

His lip curled. "What? Are you going to go running to your fiancé?"

"Actually, I'm quite a good shot myself. I can shoot the cork out of a champagne bottle at forty paces, did you know? And I can fence. But I'm beginning to think that you're just not worth the effort, *my lord*. In fact, the most appropriate response to your entirely unwelcome, thoroughly despicable proposition, is this." With a flick of her wrist, Charlie tossed the contents of her champagne glass onto Lord Mowbray's crotch. "Oops."

"You bitch," he hissed.

"Yes," she said with an arch smile. "I am. And you'd best remember that, Lord Mowbray. I don't ever wish to have a discussion like this again."

After depositing her empty glass on the tray of a nearby footman who was gawping in open-mouthed shock, Charlie tossed her head, spun around, and tried very hard to elegantly saunter out of the ballroom, even though she was shaking from head to toe.

She'd had enough of this charade, and she was so angry, she didn't trust herself to speak with Max. The last thing she wanted to do was cause a great hullabaloo that resulted in another duel and more bloodshed.

Yes, she needed time to calm down. To let her temper cool to at least the point of simmering rather than boiling over.

Most of all, she needed another drink, and the only thing that would do was brandy. Good brandy. Or even better, cognac.

And she knew exactly where to find it.

~

When Max returned to the ballroom to join Charlie —he rather thought he might like to hold her in his arms and dance with her one last time before the evening was through—he quickly discovered she was nowhere to be found.

Sophie and Arabella, Lady Langdale, had gone too, but a footman approached both Nate and Gabriel with messages from their respective spouses. Both ladies had repaired to their apartments—Arabella was apparently feeling unwell, and Nate's son was unsettled—so perhaps Charlie had accompanied one or both of them upstairs.

His friends had just quit the ballroom to check on their wives when Diana pulled Max aside. The shadow of concern in her eyes set off a frisson of alarm inside his chest.

"I expect you're looking for Charlie," she murmured.

"Yes. What's wrong?"

"It could be nothing," she began, "but about half an hour ago, I saw her leave the room. She'd been talking with Lord Mowbray. He also departed shortly after their exchange but has since returned." She gestured with her chin. "He's presently over there, conversing with his parents and your mother."

Max stiffened. *Bloody hell.* If that dirty dog had done something to upset Charlie...

But he was jumping to conclusions. She simply could have gone upstairs with her friends to make sure they had everything they needed. It was the sort of thing she would do.

Deciding he must find her to see for himself that she was indeed all right, he quit the ballroom and headed for the hall where the ladies' retiring room was located. But the maid on duty claimed she had not seen Lady Charlotte.

Racing up the stairs two at a time, he quickly reached the second floor. Charlie was not in her suite of rooms, and curiously enough, neither was Charlie's lady's maid, Molly, so Max couldn't question her. But perhaps Charlie had given the girl the night off.

Re-entering the corridor, he pushed his hands into his hair and tugged as though the action would pull loose the answer to Charlie's whereabouts.

Where the hell could she be?

Idiot. He hadn't checked with the Langdales if Charlie was with Arabella. Or with Nate and Sophie in the nursery upstairs.

When Max knocked on the door to Gabriel and Arabella's suite, Gabriel answered. "No, Charlie's not here," he said. "Can I do anything? You seem worried."

"No, but thank you. I suspect she's upstairs lending Nate's wife moral support. How is Arabella?"

Gabriel ran a hand through his already tousled hair. "Sleeping." He glanced back into the shadowed bedroom before addressing Max again. "If you don't mind, old chap, I think I'll call it a night too. It's been a hectic few days, and if Arabella needs anything…"

Max clapped him on the shoulder. "Of course, my friend. I understand. It goes without saying that your wife's well-being takes priority."

"Although if *you* need any assistance, don't hesitate to rouse me," added Gabriel. "You know I'm always here for you, just as you've always been there for me."

Max was tempted to quip, "Oh, how the mighty have fallen," considering Gabriel had always seemed the *least* likely of any of their friendship group to wed, let alone fall deeply in love, but he didn't. Instead, he thanked his friend and bid him goodnight.

Charlie wasn't with Nate or Sophie either. As Max stood in the hall outside the makeshift nursery, the sound of a grizzling baby reached his ears. "How is Thomas?" he asked.

Nate scratched his jaw. "The poor lad is having a bad night, I'm afraid. The nurse thinks it's wind. The wet nurse thinks he's cutting a tooth. And Sophie is beside herself with worry. I hate to bail on you and Charlie, but I'm about to pack them all up and take them back to Westhampton House, then call a physician, even if it's just to ease Sophie's mind."

"You do what you need to," said Max. "And I'm sure Charlie is fine. I'll find her. She's probably sick of the hubbub in the ballroom and is curled up with a book somewhere."

"Yes, I'm sure she is too," said Nate. "You know what she's like. She knows her own mind, and she's more than capable of looking after herself."

But Charlie wasn't in the library either. Or the terrace. Or the conservatory.

His frustration and anxiety mounting, Max returned to Charlie's rooms again. With all his to-ing and fro-ing, it was quite likely that he'd missed her along the way.

Her dressing room, bedroom, and sitting room were all shadowed and silent save for the ticking of the mantel clocks and his own rough breathing.

And then an altogether terrifying thought ran through

Max's mind. What if Rochfort had something to do with Charlie's sudden disappearance? He seemed like the sort of man who held grudges. Kept score. Waged personal *vendettas* against those who crossed him. The house party and betrothal ball were by no means a secret. According to Mr. Hunt, the inquiry agent, the baron had been recently spotted out and about Town with his partially paralyzed arm in a sling. What if Rochfort had decided to punish Max for causing such a grievous injury by hurting Charlie? And what better time to strike than during a ball when everyone was making merry and distracted…

Max drew a deep breath and attempted to control his riotous, panicked thoughts. There was no evidence Charlie was in trouble. He needed to stop letting his imagination run down all sorts of dark, illogical corridors. She was seen exiting the ballroom less than an hour before. Mowbray had been accounted for. There was an entire army of dependable footmen stationed at all the doors. Charlie was fine. She was here somewhere. He just had to calm down and think.

And then he heard it, the faint melodious sound of singing. A woman singing.

Charlie?

Relief surged inside Max's chest as he followed the voice. At first he thought it was coming from his room, then he realized it was actually emanating from his private study, a little farther along the corridor.

> *"Should auld acquaintance be forgot,*
> *And never brought to mind.*
> *Should auld acquaintance be forgot,*
> *And days of auld lang syne?"*

Good God. Was Charlie really singing *Auld Lang Syne?*

Max pushed through the study door and blinked in confusion. The room was virtually shrouded in velvet darkness and appeared empty at first glance. The only light emanated from the glowing coals in the fire and a silvery shaft of moonlight that penetrated a gap in the heavy damask curtains and illuminated a path across his desk.

"Charlie?" he called.

She clearly hadn't heard him as her disembodied voice continued to float about the room.

> *"For auld lang syne, my dear,*
> *For auld lang syne.*
> *We'll take a cup o' kindness yet,*
> *For auld lang syne."*

Max's gaze searched the darkened room, but he could see neither hide nor hair of his fiancée. Where the blazing hell was she?

But she *was* here. And he was beginning to suspect she was inebriated, given the slight slurring of her words and the discordant quality of the tune. Was she hiding in the stationery cupboard or behind the settee?

Or beneath his desk? The heavy Jacobean chair that he used had been pushed back toward the window and sat at an odd angle.

He swiftly lit a candle and rounded the carved mahogany monstrosity that used to be his father's desk. And there she was, sequestered in the alcove where his legs would go. Her silk skirts and petticoats were bunched up around her bended knees. She'd kicked off her slippers, and her diamond diadem sat at a crooked angle.

When Charlie saw him, her mouth lifted in a bright smile and she raised a bottle—it looked to be his favorite cognac—in the air as though she were about to toast him. "Oh, hullo, Max," she crowed. "You've come to join me." She frowned. "Oh, but there's two of you..."

Before Max could respond, a giggle burst forth and she waggled her eyebrows. "Two Maxes. Now, that might be fun..." She took a swig from the bottle, then pouted. "Well, I hope at least one of you will try to ravish me. We're engaged, after all."

Even though concern clamored around inside Max's gut—Charlie was clearly soused—he couldn't help but smile. After he placed the candle upon the desk, he lowered himself to the floor. "Charlie, I've been looking everywhere for you," he said gently. "Is everything all right?"

Another frown creased her brow. "Lady Penelope is a cow. And Lord Mowbray is a right royal ass," she said crossly. "As if I'd ever want to have a...have a tryst with someone as beastly as him." A snort of laughter escaped her. "You should have seen his face when I tossed my champagne onto the fall of his evening breeches. But he deserved it. Oh, no." She clapped a hand over her mouth, and her eyes widened in horror. "I wasn't supposed to say that," she said through her fingers, then she reached for his arm. "Please don't tell Max," she entreated. "I couldn't bear it if he called out that conceited coxcomb."

Anger thundered through Max at the thought that Mowbray had made a lewd proposal to Charlie. Nevertheless, he tamped down his roiling fury and said, "It sounds like you handled the situation admirably."

"I did," she said with a decided nod, then poked him in the chest. "Mark my words, no one gets away with being rude to Lady Charlotte Hastings."

Another sip and another sigh, then she dragged the diadem off her head, scattering hairpins before casting it onto the rug near his feet. A few dislodged curls tumbled around her cheeks, and she huffed out a breath to blow one away from the corner of her mouth. "Don't tell Max that I drank nearly all of his cognac," she said in a loud whisper, then gave him an exaggerated wink. "Don't you know I'm a bad, bad girl? A dish..." She emitted a hiccup. "A dish..." Another hiccup. "I mean, a *dishreputable* debutante?"

And Max was a bad, bad boy. He really should have taken the bottle of cognac off her by now. It was clear she'd had far too much. He clasped it around the neck and gently prized it from her fingers. "Do you mind if I have some too, before it's all gone?"

She waved a clumsy hand in the air. "Help yourself. Max won't mind. He's very sweet although he'll tell you differently. Oh, dear"—she giggled again, then slumped back against the desk—"I might be a *teensy* bit foxed...or bosky…or tipsy." She gave another snort of laughter. "Only, I can't really be drunk because young ladies like me don't get drunk…" She hiccuped again. "And I can say Epish…Epis…Episcopalian. See?" She grinned. "I can't be drunk. When you're drunk, you can't say that."

Max couldn't help but laugh. "I don't think that I can say that word even when I'm sober," he said. "All right, Lady Charlotte. The party is ov—"

"Wait." She reached out and grasped his arm again. Her remarkable brown eyes locked with his. "We can't go yet. Because I have to tell you a secret."

Interest stirred, then Max inwardly admonished himself. He really should curtail this conversation because he might hear something he wasn't supposed to. "The thing about secrets," he said, "is that they are supposed to stay just that. Secret."

But Charlie wasn't listening. "Actually, I have three secrets," she said with a sly wink. "But you must promise not to tell Max a single one."

"Charlie—"

She pressed a finger to his lips. "Shhhhh. You must not tell him about the painting. The naughty one on my list. Or what I did when I was seventeen. Or the fact that I'm in—" Her breath hitched, and she rose to her knees. "Oops. I nearly said it. Silly me." She bit her lip and leaned closer, framing his face with her hands. "Oh, I'm in deep trouble, Max. So, so deep…" Her mouth tilted into a wistful smile. "Just look at you, my impossibly handsome fiancé. If only…"

Max was going to go to straight to hell for this. "If only what?" he prompted.

Sadness clouded Charlie's gaze. "If only all of the things on my list would come true. Not just one or two…" A frown creased her brow and she swayed. "Oh, look. Now there's three of you." As she toppled over, Max only just caught her before her head hit the floor.

CHAPTER 16

"Oh, sleep! It is a gentle thing beloved from pole to pole…"
Mr. Samuel Taylor Coleridge's epic poem,
The Rime of the Ancient Mariner, has been serialized
just for our readers.
Part the Fifth is featured today…
The Beau Monde Mirror: The Literary Arts

When Max gently lay an-all-but-unconscious Charlie upon the tester bed in her bedroom, he was relieved to see she was beginning to stir. On his return from her dressing room with a few items he thought she might need, a few mumbled words tumbled forth from her lips and her eyelids fluttered open.

"Oh, Max," she moaned, reaching for him. "I think I had far too much cognac. The room is spinning around and around. Please make it stop."

"I wish I could." He sat carefully upon the edge of the bed and smoothed a few tangled curls away from her flushed face. "Do you know where your maid, Molly, is?"

She frowned, then smiled sleepily up at him. "No. I gave her the evening off. I expect she's snuck off somewhere with Edwards the footman. They've been making eyes at each other for weeks and weeks."

All of a sudden, her expression changed. Her smile turned into a scowl, and she plucked at the bodice of her gown. "I'm hot and uncomfortable. The lace itches, and my corset is far too tight. I want to take it all off."

Devil take him. Max ran a hand down his face.

He supposed he *could* summon another maid, but that might spur a lot of inconvenient questions and potential belowstairs gossip about how Lady Charlotte Hastings had ended up so intoxicated. Arabella, Lady Langdale, was indisposed, and Sophie was probably on her way back to Mayfair by now. Of course, there was Diana, however he wasn't sure where her allegiance lay. She *seemed* to like Charlie, although she also might disclose something of Charlie's inebriated condition to his mother, and that was the last thing Charlie needed.

So, it looked like Charlie might be stuck with him to help her out.

Bloody hell.

Max blew out a sigh and silently vowed he wouldn't look as he helped her to disrobe. He'd undressed countless women. He could do it with his eyes closed, blindfolded, in the darkest corner of a pitch-black coalpit on a moonless night.

"Very well," he said. "I'll help. Although the process might be easier if you sit up."

At that, Charlie shot bolt upright. "Oh, no…I think—" One of her hands flew to her mouth, and Max could see the panic flaring in her eyes. The beads of perspiration upon her brow and the pallor of her cheeks.

In the blink of an eye, he grabbed the washbasin off the bedside table where he'd deposited it a short time before and thrust it in front of Charlie.

As she cast up her accounts in the china bowl, he held her tumbling hair out of the way. When the bout of vomiting appeared to be over, he removed the bowl, then returned with a tumbler of fresh water and a damp washcloth.

"Thank you," she murmured weakly and offered him a tremulous smile. "I'm so sorry…"

"There's no need to apologize." Max sat on the side of the bed again. He was pleased Charlie seemed more like herself. "It's not as though I haven't done anything like this. Too many times to count, actually."

"You're just trying to make me feel better before I drown beneath a wave of hideous embarrassment," said Charlie. "But I appreciate your efforts all the same." She sipped the water and wiped her face. "Good Lord, what a mess I am. I think I might like to repair to the dressing room. I need to get these blasted pins out of my hair." She tugged at the collapsing, Grecian-style coiffure. "I feel like a hedgehog has taken up residence on my head, and heaven knows I could use some tooth powder and a comfit or two."

"If you feel up to it. And if you still need a hand with your gown and necklace etcetera, I promise to be the perfect gentleman and loosen or remove anything you want. Without looking, of course."

"Of course. Not that I'd mind if you sneaked a peek. But I know what a stickler you are for the proprieties, Max. At least around me." She sighed. "It's really just the pearl buttons at the back of my bodice that are a darned nuisance. There are far too many, and they're all annoyingly tiny. And perhaps you could loosen the knot at the top of my corset. Molly always ties it far too tightly."

"Your wish is my command, my lady," Max said. "I'm here to help."

And help he did, although by the time he'd undone the row of damnably small pearl buttons, he was a lather of frustrated lust, despite his best efforts not to be. The more he tried to focus on the task at hand and ignore the fact he was revealing inch by delicious inch of Charlie's bare shoulders and her undergarments, the worse things got. It also didn't help matters when he was working at the ruthlessly knotted ties of her pretty silk corset—one that was strikingly similar to the one she'd been wearing at the Rouge et Noir Club—that he suddenly recalled that Charlie had mentioned something to him about a naughty painting. Because if she *had* posed for a *risqué* portrait... No, he would *not* think about his friend's sister in an even greater state of undress than she was right at this very moment.

He would *not* get a cockstand.

He began to count in Latin in his head to take his mind off what he was doing *and* the fact that Charlie's chemise had slipped perilously low; in the dressing-room mirror, he could clearly see her plump, creamy breasts practically spilling over the top of her cursed corset. And was that a hint of an apricot-hued nipple?

Oh, hell. He began to count again. *Unus, duo, tres, quattuor, quinque, sex...sexual congress. Damn!* He should have recited pi or Newton's Laws of Motion. There was nothing remotely licentious about any of that. Thankfully, the knot soon gave way and after muttering, "There you go," Max beat a hasty retreat to Charlie's bedroom, where he found a decanter of sweet sherry on a side table. Even though it was not to his taste, if he downed a glass or two, perhaps it would put out the fire in his loins.

By the time he was feeling a little calmer and contemplating pouring a third glass just for good measure, Charlie emerged from her dressing room. She'd changed into a perfectly sedate, perhaps even matronly cotton night rail and a woolen shawl. But there was nothing the least bit matronly about her chestnut hair. Now that it was loose, it cascaded about her shoulders in thick undulating waves of coppery gold fire. It was like autumn come to life, and he had to suppress the urge to seize it and press his face into the silken mass.

But the worst part was that her feet were bare. He'd never seen her naked toes before; they were all kinds of dainty, and her ankles were neat, and oh, dear God, he needed to *stop* staring and imagining all kinds of wicked things he could do with Charlie from her toes up.

Max swallowed. He'd best go. Charlie wasn't well, and of course he couldn't break his dashed promise to Nate. "If you're feeling better, I'll bid you goodnight…"

Charlie sat upon the bed, and as she lounged back against the pillows, she curled her legs up like a cat and drew her naked feet beneath her nightgown. Her eyelids began to droop. "The room's stopped spinning," she said as though she hadn't heard him.

"Well, that's good. As I said, I should—"

"Oh…" She placed a hand to her forehead. "But now I feel a frightful megrim coming on. It's as if someone decided to place a nail right here and strike it with a hammer, over and over again."

Max winced in sympathy. "Can I get you anything? A cold compress or some tea?"

Charlie closed her eyes and sank farther into the pillows. "No. It's all right. Maybe it will go away while I sleep."

Perhaps he should stay. At least until Charlie was comfortable and settled. And then he could sneak back to his room unobserved via the jib door connecting their suites; he didn't have the key on him, but he could pick the lock easily enough.

He approached the bed. "Here, let me tuck you in," he said, drawing the covers back and Charlie stirred enough to climb beneath them. Max gently drew the sheets and counterpane up to her chin, then dropped a kiss on her forehead. "Good night, Charlie," he murmured, then he crossed his arms over his chest so he wouldn't stroke an errant curl away from her forehead.

She mumbled something, and as she burrowed into the pillows, he thought he saw her mouth curving into a contented, almost feline smile.

Settling into a bedside armchair, he watched her fall deeper into sleep. How beautiful she was. Indeed, he'd always thought so. He recalled a day just under a year ago —Nate's wedding day, in fact—when his friend had caught him casting an admiring look Charlie's way. Of course, Nate had warned him off, and Max had readily acquiesced. How could he not? Nate had been one of the few people he'd formed any kind of bond with. But as he'd said to Charlie, just because he was friends with her brother and Gabriel and Hamish, that didn't mean he was capable of falling in love with a woman.

Now, falling in lust with a woman, especially someone as gorgeous as Charlie…he could readily acknowledge that.

Max yawned and scrubbed a hand down his face. It was far too late, and he was far too tired to continue with such circuitous thinking that led nowhere. But as much as he wanted to retire for the night, he was also worried Charlie might wake and need something. She wasn't entirely out of the woods yet.

She was beneath the covers. What if he stretched out beside her for a little while? Surely that was permitted. After checking all the doors to Charlie's suite to make sure they were locked—it was better to be safe than sorry —he shrugged off his coat, removed his neckcloth, and kicked off his shoes. There was no point in being uncomfortable. He carefully lay down beside Charlie, and to his astonishment, she immediately rolled toward him and nuzzled his neck. Her warm breath tickled his ear. "You smell nice," she murmured. "Like expensive shaving soap and Max."

Oh, hell. Max released a sigh. Despite his best efforts, his ever-present desire for her stirred and sparked.

His mind returned to the secrets she wasn't supposed to tell him. The painting. Well, if she'd sat for some kind of revealing portrait, it was really none of his business, no matter how much his curiosity flickered and burned inside him.

As for what she'd done when she was seventeen, it wasn't his business either. When he thought back to all the things he'd done at that age... Good Lord, despite the fact his diabolical tyrant of a father had still been alive, he'd managed to get up to all types of mischief at Eton and during the holidays when his father hadn't been around, ruling the roost with his iron fist, a horsewhip, and even worse, his acerbic tongue lashings.

But he didn't want to think about his father, the man who'd made his life miserable for so long when he hadn't measured up to his exacting standards. The man who'd taught him—no, drummed into him—that it was far easier and safer *not* to feel anything soft or warm or tender for anyone at all. That to do so was a sign of weakness, and weakness must be rooted out and crushed at all costs.

While a part of Max truly did want to be the kind of man Charlie wanted for a husband, he knew he could never be. His heart was damaged beyond repair. Frost-bitten and stunted like a ruthlessly pruned and blighted shrub that would never grow again. He couldn't be the duke of any woman's dreams, let alone hers.

Charlie curled herself around him, snuggling closer, and all at once, an intense, all-consuming longing seared through Max's chest, stealing his breath. His throat burned and felt far too tight as though he'd contracted some sort of ague and it was too painful to swallow. And then the shivering started. A bone-deep chill that began in his heart and radiated outward, encasing every fiber of his body in ice, freezing his blood. Numbing his nerves, deadening every feeling except for an overwhelming, smothering sense of impending doom. Darkness gathered at the corners of his vision.

Oh, God. Somehow, he clambered out of the bed without waking Charlie and staggered to the nearest window. The curtains were open, and he gripped the sill and pressed his forehead against the cold pane. His breath sawed in and out in harsh, ragged pants, fogging the glass. His heart pounded unsteadily in a petrified, drunken gallop. It felt as though he was a hobbled horse who'd just run a mile with the hounds of hell snapping and snarling at his heels.

From the shadows in the corner of the room, the shade of his father watched and smirked.

It had been years and years since Max had suffered a debilitating attack of nerves like this. From experience, he knew the best he could do was hold on and wait for the violent, wracking tremors to ease. For the panic to subside and his breathing and heart rate to slow. To reassure himself that his father wasn't here, waiting to punish him for being a pathetic milksop. A good-for-nothing failure. A weakling.

Max looked up and caught his reflection in the window-pane. He looked haggard. A mess. God, he hated this house. No matter how much he tried to ignore the bad memories, there were too many of them at Heath-cote. He'd readily agreed to his mother's plans to hold the house party here because it had been expedient for him to just say yes. It didn't seem like such a good idea now.

Beyond the darkness of Heathcote's grounds was the place Anthony had fallen from his horse. And to the right, near the wooded grove one passed on the way to the heath itself, was the site where Max's first horse had died. Max had only been twelve years old, but the nightmare of that long ago day was a permanent scar carved deep inside him. It was a memory he tried very hard to avoid. Clearly, to no avail tonight…

Behind him, Charlie murmured, but in the window's reflection, Max could see she still slept peacefully.

He turned around and pushed his sweat-drenched hair out of his eyes with an impatient shove of his shaking hand.

Charlie had set about getting drunk after that dog Mowbray had propositioned her. But Max didn't think that was the only reason she'd fled to his study and had downed half a bottle of cognac. For some time now, he'd sensed Charlie was unhappy. And even though they were engaged and her social standing appeared to be improving, it hadn't helped improve her mood. Not one bit.

And deep down, Max suspected he was largely to blame for that. He knew she cared for him—he'd seen it in the warmth of her gaze and her touch and her smile. She'd also admitted numerous times that she desired him too. And yet, he kept pushing her away and turning his back. Denying her over and over again.

If he were honest with himself, he would admit that he was miserable with the situation too. Being so close to Charlie, wanting her all the time but not being able to touch her the way he wanted to, it was slowly driving him mad. It was unhealthy.

It was self-destructive.

And this impossible situation had all come about because of his damned promise to Nate. A promise born out of obligation that he now regretted with every fiber of his being. His loyalty was divided, and he was being pulled in different directions. The tension was excruciating. No wonder he'd snapped and come undone tonight.

One thing was clear—he and Charlie couldn't go on this way, or they were both bound to unravel.

He began to weigh up the arguments for continuing to keep Charlie at arm's length versus giving in to his overwhelming need to have her. Perhaps Charlie had a point. It wasn't any of Nate's business what the two of them did together when they were alone. And as Charlie had also said, what Nate didn't know wouldn't hurt him.

She was twenty-two—a woman, not a girl—and she definitely knew her own mind. She was also a passionate creature by nature. His mind strayed to her now not-so-secret list of wishes and desires. While Max couldn't give her everything she wanted, what if he could make her happy by helping her to fulfill at least *some* of the other things on her list?

Of course, it was also self-serving on his part because why wouldn't he want to kiss Charlie in the rain or in the moonlight or ravish her in a carriage? He certainly wanted to do all of those things.

Yes, as long as they were careful and took precautions and Charlie understood that he was motivated by lust, nothing more, perhaps they could explore the physical side of their relationship. They could be friends who indulged in an amorous tryst or two every now and again. It wouldn't be about love or romance or having a happily ever after together. It would be about having fun and alleviating some of this damned pent-up tension.

Satisfied that he'd come up with a temporary solution to both of their problems, Max picked up a blanket at the end of the bed and took up residence in the bedside armchair again. His mouth curved into a smile as his own eyelids began to droop. If Charlie agreed to his plan, the coming weeks would be interesting indeed.

CHAPTER 17

If you are suffering from a loss of appetite,
dyspepsia, megrims, anxiety, or any other type of
nervous complaint including melancholia,
hysterics, or perhaps you're simply heartsore,
Dr. Brompton's *Restorative Nervous Tonic* might be
just the elixir you need to restore your equilibrium
this Season.
*The Beau Monde Mirror: General Health & Medical
Miscellany*

Heathcote Hall, Hampstead Heath
April 18, 1819

When Charlie awoke the next morning, she was
aware of several things. Her head ached horribly.
Her stomach roiled uneasily. But worst of all was the
overwhelming sense of mortification that washed over
her when she recalled what had happened after she'd fled
the ballroom the night before.

Her memory was somewhat hazy right up until the
point she'd been violently ill in front of Max. From what
she could recall, he'd been nothing but patience personi-
fied, but even so, it was wince-inducing to think he'd
seen her at her very worst. And the fact that she couldn't
quite recall what she'd said and done before that… It was

unnerving in the extreme. Getting so completely drunk was an experience she *never* wished to repeat.

Even though she felt hideous, she forced her protesting body out of bed. The morning sunlight streaming in through her bedroom window made her head throb even more, but she wouldn't be deterred from fulfilling her duty. As much as she wanted to stay in bed and hide beneath the covers until she felt better, at least in a physical sense, she also owed it to Max, her father, her brother, and her friends to put in an appearance at breakfast.

She padded to the bellpull and rang for Molly, who appeared within minutes with hot water, a bright smile, and a bottle of some nasty smelling concoction called Dr. Brompton's Restorative Nervous Tonic; she must have noted her mistress had been unwell last night.

After Charlie had washed and had her hair tamed into a suitably sedate style, she donned a fresh gown of pale peach muslin. Pinching some color into her wan cheeks, she hoped she might pass for well-enough if one didn't look too closely.

On entering the morning room, where breakfast was served, she discovered Arabella already ensconced at one end of the massive mahogany dining table with a pot of tea, toast, and a coddled egg before her. There was no sign of Father, Lady Tilbury, Gabriel, Nate, or Sophie. Much to Charlie's relief, Max was also absent. Indeed, the room was surprisingly empty. Also missing was Cressida, Diana, the Duke and Duchess of Stafford, Lord Mowbray, and Lady Penelope. Thank the Lord.

Arabella greeted Charlie with a warm smile. "Good morning, my friend. It looks like quite a few guests have opted to sleep late or have breakfast in bed." Her brow knitted into a frown as Charlie drew closer. "Is it a good morning? You look…"

"Peaked? Pasty?" After a footman stepped forward to pull out a chair for her, Charlie gingerly lowered herself onto the silk-upholstered seat. "I'm ashamed to say that I'm a little worse for wear this morning."

"Oh, dear. Well, let's furnish you with a cup of tea

straightaway. And something plain to eat?" Arabella caught the footman's eye and requested another teacup and fresh toast. "Now tell me what's ailing you, dear Charlie. I sense it's more than a physical affliction."

When Charlie had filled her friend in on everything that had transpired the night before and how embarrassed she felt about Max witnessing her drunken state, Arabella patted Charlie's hand. "I wouldn't worry that Max's regard for you has changed. He clearly went out of his way to look after you last night. It's more than evident that he cares for you."

"Do you think so?"

"Aye, I do. He could have rung for a maid or approached his sister-in-law, Diana. But he didn't. And earlier this morning, before Gabriel went riding, he told me that Max had been looking for you after you quit the ballroom last night." Her mouth curved into a smile. "I wish I could have witnessed Lord Mowbray receiving his comeuppance, by the way. But I digress. Apparently, Max came to our suite, hoping on the off chance you'd paid me a visit to see how I was faring. Because you weren't with me, Max then intended to check if you were lending Sophie your support in the nursery."

"Really?"

"Yes, really. According to Gabriel, your fiancé was quite frantic with worry and determined to find you. Even he suspects that Max is smitten but in denial."

Frantic with worry? Smitten? Charlie picked up her cup of tea and took a sip. How…interesting. It was nice to know that others could see that Max might be harboring unacknowledged feelings for her and that she wasn't imagining things.

Charlie selected a piece of toast. "Have you seen Sophie this morning, by any chance? I hope Thomas is better."

"Oh, I heard that your brother whisked Sophie and Thomas back to Westhampton House last night, just in case they needed a physician. I suspect baby Thomas was just teething, the poor wee mite. If I'd been well enough, I would have lent a hand."

"I must say, I'm very pleased to see you looking well now."

"Oh yes. I am, thank you. That horrid nausea has passed. It's strange, though." Arabella replenished her cup of tea. "I started to feel so afflicted just before our journey back to London. Every evening, I've felt as ill as can be. But then, in the morning, I'm perfectly fine again. I hope whatever it is passes soon."

Charlie gave Arabella a quizzical look over the rim of her teacup. "How long has this been going on?"

"A week, I suppose…" Arabella put down her own teacup with a clatter. Behind her gold-framed spectacles, her eyes widened. "I've missed my courses too," she murmured. "They're two weeks—no, nearly three weeks late. Oh, my goodness." Her clear hazel gaze connected with Charlie's. "Do you think that I could be…?"

Charlie couldn't help but smile. "You're the one who is clever enough to be a doctor, Arabella. What do *you* think?"

"Oh…" Her eyes were shining with tears now. Her cheeks glowed. "I just…I've been so busy of late, I didn't even think that I might be… I must share the wonderful news with Gabriel as soon as he gets back from his ride."

"Yes, you must. And congratulations, Arabella." Charlie reached out and squeezed her friend's hand. "I'm so happy for you and Gabriel."

"Thank you."

Charlie's gaze wandered over to the French doors that afforded one with a view of the flagged terrace and Heathcote's pristine lawns and the lake beyond. "I haven't seen Max this morning. Do you happen to know if he went riding with your husband?"

"Oh. To be perfectly honest, I have no idea," said Arabella. Her gaze shifted to the doorway of the morning room. "Speak of the devil…"

Max. Without even turning her head, Charlie was aware of his approach. It was as though she could feel his magnetic presence. His dynamic energy. The way his gaze focused on her and her alone. If it were the least bit socially acceptable, she would have slithered beneath the table or thrown a linen napkin over her face to hide her acute mortification. She might not be able to recall most of what she'd said to this man in her foxed state, but she did have a hazy memory of him holding her hair while she cast up her accounts. And he'd also helped her to undress…

The burning blush already heating Charlie's cheeks seemed to engulf her entire neck and face as Max greeted Arabella and then her. "My lady," he said with a bow. "I'm pleased to see you here at breakfast. And looking so well."

"I… Yes. Thank you, Your Grace," mumbled Charlie. Max looked… Well, like he always did. Too handsome for words. She was about to invite him to take breakfast with them, but then she caught sight of Lord Langdale striding across the lawn toward the morning room. "Arabella," she murmured. "Gabriel's returned."

"Oh…" Arabella put down her napkin and rose to her feet. "If you'll both excuse me…"

"Of course." Max, ever the gentleman, gave another bow.

As soon as Arabella reached the terrace, she picked up her skirts and dashed down the stairs and across the grass to meet her husband. There were tears in Charlie's eyes as she watched Arabella whisper in her husband's ear. He gave a whoop of sheer joy, picked her up, spun her around, and kissed her soundly. All the while, Max looked on, bemused.

"I take it you know what that's all about," he said as he claimed the seat beside Charlie.

"Yes." She dabbed at her eyes with a napkin. "But it's not my confidence to share."

Max's lips quirked. "I think I could hazard a guess. It wouldn't have something to do with the fact Lady Langdale was indisposed last night, would it?"

Charlie smiled. "It might."

Max nodded. "Well, I'm very happy for both of them." His eyes narrowed, his look growing speculative as it settled on Charlie's face. "Judging by your reaction, I take it that you are not averse to the idea of having children one day?"

Charlie dropped her gaze to the table lest Max see the yearning in her eyes. "I would love to have children one day. With—" *With you.* "With whomever I marry." She shrugged a shoulder and tried to sound nonchalant as she added, "It is a wife's duty, after all." She picked up her tea. "And what about you? How do you feel about becoming a father one day, Your Grace?"

"As a duke, it is my duty to sire an heir and probably a few spares, at the very least."

"Yes, but how do you *feel* about it, Max?"

"To be honest, I've never really examined my feelings in relation to starting a family before. Although…" His attention shifted to the open French doors and the now deserted lawn. "I hope that I would react in a similar way to Gabriel upon hearing such news."

"I hope you would too."

Max's throat worked in a swallow. And then his gaze touched Charlie's face. "About last night…"

Charlie closed her eyes as she was swamped by yet another wave of embarrassment. "I'm so, so sorry for acting like a complete sot. What you must think of me…"

"I don't think any less of you, Charlie, if that's what you're worried about. And there's certainly no need to apologize. Actually, I should be apologizing to you because I wasn't there by your side, protecting you from Mowbray. No wonder you were upset."

Charlie winced. "I told you about that? My memory is a little fuzzy up until a certain point."

Max smiled. "You did. And I'm suitably impressed with how you dealt with the situation. Mowbray deserved it. You'll be pleased to know that as of this morning, he's gone. Lady Penelope and her parents are in the process of leaving too. They are no longer welcome at Heathcote. Or any of my properties, for that matter."

"Oh…I…" Charlie frowned. "Not solely on my account, I hope. I didn't mean to cause a fuss that would result in the whole family being evicted."

"It wasn't just the incident with Mowbray. You see, it seems his sister is just as devoid of a moral compass."

While that didn't surprise Charlie as much as it

should, she felt compelled to ask, "Whatever do you mean?"

Max helped himself to a piece of toast. "Last night, after you'd fallen asleep and I was certain you were resting comfortably, I returned to my room. Smedley, my valet, informed me that in my absence, I'd had a visitor to my bedchamber."

Charlie almost dropped the knife she'd been using to spread marmalade on her own toast. "Max, don't tell me that"—she dropped her voice to a whisper—"that Lady Penelope was lying in wait for you."

Max's mouth flattened into a grim line. "She was. But thank God for Smedley. If he wasn't so dedicated to his duty…" He shook his head. "I hate to think what might have happened."

"I do too. The audacity of that woman, trying to ruin our betrothal and entrap you in a compromising situation." Charlie shivered.

"I'm glad you agree," said Max. "In any event, I had a word with the Duke of Stafford first thing this morning when he was on his way to the stables, and I let him know in no uncertain terms that I was not impressed with the behavior of his offspring and that I would like them all to leave. Of course, he was suitably affronted and doubted my version of events, but I don't particularly care what he thinks at this point." His mouth twitched with a smile. "As I stated last night, this is my home, and I'll do whatever I like within its walls. Sometimes it's gratifying to be the arrogant duke."

Charlie laughed. "I'm sure it is. But you've done the right thing, considering the circumstances. If Lord Mowbray and Lady Penelope were to stay on, it would be too awkward for words."

Max sighed. "Yes. But I still have to deal with my mother. No doubt she'll have something to say about it when she hears that I've all but thrown them out. Especially Lady Penelope."

Charlie reached out and touched his forearm. In the morning light, the diamond on her betrothal ring sparkled. "I have every confidence that you'll be able to handle it with aplomb, Your Grace."

Max covered her hand with his and kept it there as though he didn't wish to let her go. Beneath his sleeve, Charlie felt the muscles of his forearm shift, then settle. His dark blue gaze met hers. "Charlie…I want to make it very clear that I have eyes for no one but you. No other woman commands my interest or occupies my thoughts like you do. And when we return to London…" His thumb caressed her wrist. "When things are quieter and we're both under less scrutiny, I'd like to pursue you in the way that I really want to. In the way you've hinted that you'd like me to. If you are still agreeable…"

Charlie's breath caught. Her skin tingled. Her heart capered. Heat bloomed in her cheeks and shimmered through her, all the way to her toes and everywhere in between. "Yes, I'm still agreeable, Max. More than agreeable. I…I'm not ashamed to admit that I want you too. Quite desperately."

"The feeling is mutual." Max raised her hand, turned it, and placed a whisper-soft kiss on the inside of her wrist. His eyes held hers as he murmured in a low velvet voice, "I look forward to our next not-quite-so-proper liaison, my lady. I'll send word to you tomorrow when you're back at Hastings House."

And then he rose and quit the morning room. Charlie dazedly watched him walk away, and as desire flowed through her veins like sun-warmed honey, she wondered for a moment if she were still abed and dreaming. But no, her father and Lady Tilbury had just entered the room and were headed her way.

If they wondered why she was grinning like a besotted ninnyhammer when they joined her, she didn't really care.

At long last, Max had admitted that he wanted her and that he was willing to do something about it. Even though she had no idea why he'd changed his mind, questioning the reason for his complete turnabout was certainly the last thing on hers.

She'd roused the rake and couldn't be happier.

CHAPTER 18

Even though she's engaged to a duke, it appears
that the disreputable Lady C. cannot seem to avoid
scandal. What did she get up to with the very
eligible Lord M.
during her betrothal ball? Read on to find out what
transpired that night in the ballroom
right in front of the who's who of the ton.…
The Beau Monde Mirror: The Society Page

Exmoor House, Grosvenor Square
April 20, 1819

Charlie was right. There was a spy who worked for the *Beau Monde Mirror* in their midst.

A servant from his mother's household. Or, perish the thought, Diana or even his mother. Of course, there'd been a multitude of other tonnish guests present who might've witnessed Charlie's altercation with Mowbray. Max doubted Mowbray himself would've gone to the papers. The *Beau Monde Mirror's* story did not paint him in a favorable light either. Although, as far as Max was concerned, the scoundrel hadn't been castigated nearly enough for his despicable behavior.

He would have to tackle his mother later in the day because he had more pressing matters to attend to. Matters that involved his fiancée and her happiness.

With a disgruntled sigh, Max tossed the copy of the scandal rag onto his bed, then turned around to submit to the fussing of Smedley. Ordinarily, Max would dress himself before he went for his early morning ride in Hyde Park, but today he wanted to look his best for Charlie. He'd sent word to her the day before that he'd meet her at Hastings House at seven o'clock, and he'd suggested that she wear a riding habit for the occasion. With any luck, her mare, Aurora, would be saddled and waiting when he arrived as well.

When his cravat was tied to his valet's satisfaction and he was vested, coated, booted, and armed with his beaver hat, riding gloves, and riding crop, Max quit Exmoor House and headed to the nearby mews where his mounts were kept. The sky was a dark leaden gray and the air chill and mist-laden as he rode the short distance to Hastings House upon his Thoroughbred stallion, Ghost. Even though it looked like rain, Max wouldn't be deterred from accomplishing his mission.

When Charlie appeared on the front steps of Hastings House, the cheerful smile that bloomed across her lovely face immediately brightened the cold, drear morning. Suitably attired in a beautifully cut riding habit in eye-catching scarlet, she'd completed her ensemble with a black riding hat adorned with an elegant sweep of pheasant feathers; it sat at a jaunty angle atop her barely tamed bronze curls.

"Good morning, Your Grace," she said, taking Max's proffered arm so he could escort her down the stairs to where Charlie's groom waited with Ghost, Aurora, and a third mount, presumably another horse from Lord Westhampton's stables that required exercise.

As they descended, she leaned closer to him and added in a soft voice the groom couldn't hear, "I must confess that when your note arrived, I was more than a little bit excited to see what you had planned for today. Can I expect that we'll ignore the dictates of decorum and ride hell-for-leather down Rotten Row?"

"Lady Charlotte, I'm more than a little shocked that you would think I would lead you so wildly astray," replied Max with mock horror. "I mean, I know it's been reported in the *Beau Monde Mirror* that your alter ego might have expressed an interest in doing such a thing, but it would be remiss of me, your fiancé, to encourage such hoydenish behavior."

At the bottom of the stairs, Charlie laughed. "Considering all of London will be reading about disreputable Lady C.'s outrageous antics at her betrothal ball, I hardly think what I get up to this morning in Hyde Park will signify."

Max had to suppress a smirk. Charlie would not make such a pronouncement if she had any inkling about what he had in store. "You saw the latest article in the *Beau Monde Mirror's* Society Page, then?"

"I did. But nothing shall dampen my spirits this morning. Not a horrid piece of inaccurate gossip that's been leaked to the press by some unscrupulous, eavesdropping, scandalmongering spy." She turned her gaze to the ever-darkening sky. "Or even gathering clouds and a spot of rain."

"I'm pleased to hear it." Indeed, based on his knowledge of Lady C.'s scandalous list of "Secret Wishes and Dreams", he was rather hoping it did rain.

When the groom stepped forward to assist his mistress into the sidesaddle, Max held up a hand. "I'll take it from here. Indeed, once Lady Charlotte and I are away, I'd appreciate it if you made yourself scarce."

The young man glanced his mistress's way for her direction, and she smiled. "It will be all right, John. His Grace will take good care of me."

The groom bowed and moved back to wait at a discreet distance. "Of course, my lady. Your Grace."

Charlie gave Max a coquettish smile from beneath her lashes as he slid his hands about her waist to help her mount her bay mare. "So high-handed this morning, Your Grace. I like it."

Max lifted her onto the saddle, enjoying Charlie's gasp of surprise as he did so. "I didn't think you liked it when I was too domineering, my lady," he said, flipping up the hem of her skirts to ensure her left foot was set securely in the slipper stirrup.

"Well, it depends on what you're being high-handed about," murmured Charlie as she watched him make a slight adjustment to the leather strap. "But being alone with you suits me, so I don't mind at all in this instance."

"Good," said Max. He couldn't resist sliding his hand up her shapely stocking-clad calf and brushing his gloved thumb against the soft bare flesh just above her garter. Her sharp intake of breath and the way her brandywine eyes widened and darkened made him smile. "I can be as high-handed as you like today."

"Your Grace, if your hand goes any higher, I might burst into flames right in the middle of Berkeley Square," Charlie murmured huskily.

Max chuckled softly. "Well, it's a very good thing that it's just started to rain." And indeed it had. A light mizzling shower misted around them. Tiny droplets settled on the velvet brim of Charlie's hat and her curls like a veil of soft silver gossamer. "But of course, we can always do this another time…"

A fierce light flared in Charlie's eyes. "There's no way in Hades I'm postponing this ride with you, Max. It could start to hail or even snow, and I wouldn't care."

"This morning, your every wish is my command, my lady," said Max, withdrawing his hand, then gently squeezing one of hers where it rested upon the pommel.

"It is?" whispered Charlie.

"Yes," said Max, holding her gaze. "It is."

Anticipation for what was to come coursing through his veins, Max all but vaulted into his own saddle. Then they were off, wending their way through the early morning traffic toward Hyde Park.

Within fifteen minutes, they'd entered the park via Grosvenor Gate and were trotting down a broad avenue of walnut trees in the direction of Rotten Row. There weren't many riders about; Max surmised the inclement weather had kept them away. He didn't mind at all. By the time they reached the eastern end of London's most famous and popular bridle path, the rain had grown heavier, and the riders had grown even sparser.

"Are you certain you want to do this, Charlie?" asked Max as they reined in their horses. "It will be a wet, muddy ride." Ghost must have sensed the excitement humming through Max as the horse began to snort and stamp the ground impatiently.

"I don't mind getting a bit dirty if you don't, Your Grace," rejoined Charlie, her eyes sparkling with mischief. Even though her pheasant feathers were drooping and dripping, and her cheeks and even the tip of her nose had turned pink with cold, she looked nothing but radiant. "Actually, I propose we up the stakes. If we *are* going to hurtle pell-mell down Rotten Row in the pouring rain, we should make this worth both of our whiles. Let's make it a race to the end."

"What a capital idea, Lady Charlotte. And what prize can the winner claim?"

Charlie slid him a sly smile. "A kiss, of course. The nature of said kiss, and the timing and place in which it occurs, shall be the winner's choice."

Max flashed her a wolfish grin in return. "Done."

They lined up their horses by a towering oak, then Max raised his crop in the air like a sword-wielding cavalry officer and called, "Charge!"

Ghost and Aurora leapt forward. Rain lashed, hooves thudded, and mud flew as they dashed headlong down the track. Max kept pace with Charlie until the halfway mark, then he let Ghost have his head. Aurora might be fleet of foot, but she was no match for his Thoroughbred racehorse. And Max wanted to win. There was no way he was going to let this opportunity to fulfill Charlie's dream of being kissed in the rain slip through his fingers.

When Charlie caught up to him at the end of the row, she was laughing and breathless. Somewhere along the way, her hat had fallen off, but she didn't seem bothered as she reined in alongside him. "Congratulations, Your Grace."

"Thank you, my lady." Max slid from his saddle. After he'd tethered Ghost to the low-hanging branch of a nearby beech tree, he approached Charlie. "And now I'd like to claim my prize."

"Here? Now?" Charlie pushed a sodden curl away from her cheek. "In the middle of Hyde Park?"

"Yes, right here. Right now. The park is practically deserted, after all. And the downpour is beginning to ease, so we're not in any imminent danger of drowning." Max cocked a brow as he gently grasped Charlie's waist. "Unless of course you've changed your mind about wanting to be kissed passionately in the rain..."

"Ah, your thoroughly wicked master plan is revealed at last." Charlie placed her hands on his shoulders.

"If my memory serves me correctly, it was you, my dear Lady Charlotte, who suggested the precise nature of the prize the winner could claim." Max lifted her down but didn't release her from his hold. "But if you're having second thoughts, our kiss doesn't have to be remotely passionate at all. It can be quite proper and chaste. In fact, I can always just kiss your gloved hand like a perfect gentleman."

Charlie arched a brow. "Well, if that's enough to satisfy you..." She took a step back, out of his arms, and raised her hand, calling his bluff. "Kiss away, Your Grace."

"Minx." Max backed Charlie up against the trunk of the beech tree, crowding her in with his body. The leafy canopy above their heads protected them from the worst of the drizzling rain. Planting both of his hands beside her head, he leaned in. His breath misted and mingled with hers in the cold, damp air between them. "You know that's not what I really want, nor what you want either."

Her luscious mouth curved with a siren's smile as she looked up at him. Her long lashes were spiky and shimmering with raindrops as she slid her hands up to his neck. Pressed her magnificent breasts against his chest and curled her fingers into the wet hair at his nape, pulling it ever so gently. The heady scent of her floral perfume teased him, making his mouth water. "Well, what are you going to do about it, Max?"

"This." Max tugged off one of his gloves with his teeth, then cupped Charlie's smooth-as-alabaster cheek with his bare hand. Dragged his thumb across her lower lip. As much as he wanted to kiss her with fervent abandon, he also wanted to savor this moment. Extend the delicious, breath-stealing anticipation of claiming this gorgeous young woman in his arms. A woman he'd wanted forever but had steadfastly stayed away from because of an obligation to his best friend. Until now…

As Charlie's gaze dipped to his mouth, he didn't want to think about the fact he was about to break his promise to Nate. Or that they were in a public place where anyone might stumble upon them.

All that mattered was Charlie and the tendrils of desire wrapping around them, binding them closer together. The heat surging through his veins. The sharp, searing ache of some emotion akin to longing deep within his chest. The heavy throb of lust in his groin.

The quickening of her breath when he pushed his hips against hers and she felt how badly he burned for her.

"Max…" Charlie arched into him. "Please."

Her whispered plea was like a spark set to tinder. Max's mouth crashed down on Charlie's. Plundering. Ravaging. He lashed her plush, pliant body to his. Gripped her shapely head and tipped it back so he could devour her thoroughly. She tasted heavenly—like spring rain and warm honey but most of all, just Charlie. The most intoxicating manna that he could easily feast upon forever.

Yet for all its unbridled savagery—the rough, desperate slide of lips and wild tangling of tongues—their kiss was agonizingly sweet. Charlie opened for him, accepted every shameless thing that he did and returned it in kind. Stroked her tongue inside his mouth just as deeply. When he blatantly palmed her breast, she pushed a hand beneath his waistcoat, her fingers twisting in the damp linen of his shirt as though she wanted to rip it away. And when he drew back to suck in a ragged, much-needed breath, she moaned his name as if she couldn't bear his absence for even a second. Almost immediately, she speared her fingers into his hair, knocking off his hat as she dragged him down for another mind-spinning, bone-melting, blazing-hot kiss.

Everything about Charlie's kiss was sublime. It was everything a kiss should be and more.

As Charlie had so accurately declared beneath her spring kissing bough, just one kiss wouldn't be enough. Between them they'd started a raging fire that would be practically impossible to contain, let alone put out.

When they at last drew apart, Charlie's lips were swollen and glistening. And she was smiling. "Now, that is precisely the sort of kiss I wanted from you on Easter Sunday, Maximilian Devereux." She poked his chest with a finger and pouted. "And yet you've kept me waiting so long. Foolish man."

Max felt himself grinning like a moonstruck youth. "I am. The king of fools. Can you ever forgive me?"

"Perhaps. As much as I adored the fact that you kissed me in the rain just like I've always dreamed of, if *I'd* won the race, I think I might have chosen to kiss you somewhere a little warmer and a little more private. And while your mouth tastes divine"—she trailed a gloved finger down his torso toward the waistband of his buckskin breeches, where his cock still strained against the tight confines of leather and laces—"I can think of other places I'd like to kiss you as well. If you'd let me…"

What? Did Charlie really mean that? Did she understand the full import of her words? Max swallowed hard as the wonderfully lewd image of Charlie on her knees before him filled his head and made his blood pound anew. Dear God, he couldn't think about Charlie doing *that* to him. Could he?

He caught her tormenting hand with his. When he spoke, his voice was rough and thick with lust. "Now I'm intrigued. How much *do* you actually know about bed sport, Lady Charlotte Hastings?"

She lifted her chin, her gaze bright with challenge. "I'll put it this way—somewhere between much more than a proper young lady should know, and nowhere near as much as I'd like to. Are you shocked?"

"No. I mean yes. Perhaps a little. But not in a bad way.

Rather, in a pleasant way. And I shouldn't be shocked at all, considering you admitted you knew more than the average tonnish miss when we were at the Rouge et Noir Club."

She laughed at that. "Pleasantly shocked. I suppose your reaction could be worse. At least you're not condemning me for being a wicked, brazen hussy."

"I would never do that. I adore how bold and fearless you are. How much you embrace life with both hands. I wish that I could give you more than—"

She pressed a finger to his lips. "It's all right, Max. I don't expect more than you've already given me. Moments like this are enough."

Oh, God. The tenderness and understanding in her eyes and her touch, it was almost too much. He brought her hand to his lips and kissed it. He couldn't put into words what he wished for. He couldn't even think it because if he did, he'd come undone, just like he did a few nights before at Heathcote Hall. Even now, the cold was creeping into his bones. Freezing the air in his lungs. Making his heart thump uncomfortably against his ribs.

They really needed to head back to Berkeley Square.

Passion. This is just about passion and attraction, he reminded himself. *Brazen, wicked lust. Fulfilling the physical needs Charlie and I both have. That's all.*

Drawing a deep breath, he said, "Thank you for understanding. And I do want to give you more moments like this. I have some parliamentary legislation I need to go over today—a draft bill that Prinny wants my opinion on—so I apologize in advance if it seems like I'm neglecting you yet again. But tomorrow evening, if you are not otherwise engaged, I'd like to take you somewhere. Some place that's special. When it's all arranged, I'll send word about the specific details."

Charlie's eyes glowed. "Of course I'll be available. I can't wait."

"Excellent. Now let's get you home. I don't want you to catch cold."

As for himself, after that incendiary kiss, Max doubted he'd ever feel cold again. Not unless he dwelled on the emotions threatening to unfurl inside his chest. Emotions that terrified him. Feelings that once upon a time, he would have immediately ripped out and stomped upon. But not today. Today he would let them linger for a little while. For Charlie, he would bear the bittersweet agony of tenderness taking root in his blight-ridden heart.

Because she was worth it.

CHAPTER 19

Today's article on 'Essential Style' features general
reflections on the fashions recommended for well-
bred young ladies for all daily occasions—from
indoor morning dress to walking dress styles
suitable for wearing about Town, we will ensure
you look nothing less than your best…
*The Beau Monde Mirror: The Essential Style &
Etiquette Guide*

Gunter's Tea Shop, Berkeley Square
April 21, 1819

"He…he kissed you? In the m-middle of Hyde Park in
the rain?" Olivia MacQueen, the Marchioness of
Sleat—formerly Olivia de Vere and a fellow disreputable
debutante—looked at Charlie with wide brown eyes
across the linen-draped tea table. "That's so wonderfully
romantic."

When Charlie received word that Olivia and her husband, Hamish, had returned to London the day before,
she'd immediately suggested that all four members of the
Society for Enlightened Young Women gather for a re-
union at their favorite tea shop. Charlie was thrilled that
Olivia, Arabella, and Sophie had all readily agreed.

"Yes, it is wonderfully romantic," said Sophie, placing
her silver spoon beside her now empty ice-cream bowl.

"It's about time Max stopped treating you like his best friend's bothersome little sister."

"Aye." Arabella smiled her approval over her cup of tea. "I'm so happy for you, Charlie. The fact that he chose to help you fulfill some of your dreams speaks volumes."

"Thank you. And I think you're right." Charlie felt herself flushing with pleasure. "My only concern is that Nate will find out, so all of you must promise not to breathe a word about our Hyde Park tryst. Thank heavens *that* hasn't appeared in the papers. My meddlesome brother will be sure to do something completely ridiculous if he suspects Max and I are..." The heat in her cheeks spread across her entire face. "Well, you know."

Olivia frowned. "You don't really believe that Nate would c-call Max out, do you?"

"I'm not sure," said Charlie. "My brother means well—he doesn't want to see me heartbroken. I'd certainly hate to think their friendship might be ruined if Nate learns that Max hasn't kept his word about keeping his distance."

Sophie reached out and touched Charlie's arm. "You know my thoughts on the subject. My husband has no business insisting your engagement to Max is in name only. Especially when all of us can see that Max cares for you. Deeply. And he always has."

Charlie sighed. "I wish Max would recognize how he feels about me. He's such a dunderhead. Why do men have to be so daft when it comes to matters of the heart?"

"I agree. They are daft," said Arabella. "But he'll come to his senses soon enough. Gabriel certainly did."

"Yes, and so did Hamish," added Olivia. "Despite the fact he's as stubborn as a Highland bullock on occasion."

"And Nate too," said Sophie. "As we all now know from experience, some men find it easier to express their feelings in other ways—through thoughtful acts and in a physical sense—before they can give voice to them."

"I wish there was a guidebook for women on how to manage men," said Charlie.

Arabella laughed. "I'm sure most men wish they had a guidebook that gave them advice on how to manage us."

Talk turned to baby-related matters—Thomas, whose bout of teething had passed, and Arabella's due date, which she estimated to be in early December—and then onto Arabella's charity work. Her mother-in-law, Caroline, had offered to take on a greater role in managing Arabella's newly established orphanage in Edinburgh, and Arabella was most grateful. "It will leave me more time to focus on the setting up of more dispensaries for the poor here in London. And of course, this wee project in here." She rested a hand upon her still-flat belly and smiled. "I'm pleased to report that Gabriel couldn't be more supportive. Once upon a time, he would've wanted to coddle me just like a defenseless bairn who needed protecting from the world, but he's quickly come to realize this Scottish lass is made of sterner stuff."

"That's wonderful, Arabella," remarked Charlie. "You know, lately I've been thinking about my lot in life as an earl's daughter, and how I really should make myself more useful. Thanks to Max's intervention, my reputation is beginning to lose its tarnished edge, so I've been wondering about charitable concerns that I could make a significant contribution to. Olivia, you mentioned before that you've been helping Hamish's sister, Lady Isobel, and the local minister's wife with establishing a village parish school on the Isle of Skye. And Arabella, I recall how you once told me about the plight of poor, unwed mothers here in London and elsewhere and how that, in part, drives you to do what you do. There are so many things I could be doing with my time instead of fretting about Max or worrying about being spied upon by his mother or someone in her employ." Charlie had already told Sophie, Arabella, and Olivia about how the *Beau Monde Mirror* had reported on her set-to with Lord Mowbray at the betrothal ball and how the Mayfair Bluestocking Society had been disparaged after she'd chatted about the group's activities with Cressida and Diana. "I need a greater purpose. I want to make a difference in someone else's life."

"Well, what do you feel passionate about, dear Charlie?" asked Sophie. "That should answer your question."

Charlie tapped her cup of tea with a fingernail. "You know, I often think about society's hypocrisy when it comes to the sexes and how we're treated differently. How men can do as they please, yet we are bound by strict rules controlling every aspect of our behavior. When I suggested we formulate the Society for Enlightened Young Women, I wanted all of us to gain knowledge of the opposite sex and sexual congress, because knowledge is power. Young women, debutantes, should know what they can expect when they wed. Being kept in the dark about such matters is entirely unfair and indeed, dangerous. For instance, if one encounters an unscrupulous rakehell set on seduction and one hasn't the slightest idea about what's going on, let alone how to prevent conception..." She shuddered. "Of course, there's no way I can possibly launch a public campaign to educate women about sexual congress. I'd probably be locked up in Bedlam for doing something that would undoubtedly be deemed outrageous. But I also keep thinking about women who find themselves in situations they don't wish to be in as a result of sexual intercourse. The women society unfairly labels as fallen." Her mind drifted back to the courtesans she saw at the Rouge et Noir Club. Max asserted they were all well-paid and wished to be there, but what if some of them didn't? What happened when they fell pregnant or contracted some awful venereal disease? Or some horrible man like Lord Rochfort treated them badly? "I wish I could help those women in some way."

"Your idea has some merit, Charlie," said Arabella. "Perhaps when the Mayfair Bluestocking Society next meets, we can discuss establishing a charity that would provide support for unwed mothers, or any woman in need. Though, I imagine overtly promoting such a cause will create a good deal of controversy among the politer members of society."

Charlie grinned. "But when has that ever stopped us from doing anything?"

"Exactly," said Olivia.

"I, for one, think it sounds like a wonderful idea,"

added Sophie. "It's exactly the sort of charity enlightened women like us should be involved with. You can count on my unqualified support too."

"Let's drink to that," proposed Charlie, and they all raised their teacups and clinked them together. "Here's to friendship and supporting fellow women."

After placing an order for a fresh pot of tea, Charlie's gaze wandered out of the bow window beside their table. The day was fine, the sky a glorious azure blue, and a fresh wind tossed the branches of the plane trees in the private park in the center of Berkeley Square. A sense of contentment settled over her like a soft cashmere rug. She was with all her best friends. She and Max were growing closer. For the first time in a long time, she had so many things to look forward to. The fire in her soul had been revived.

Then her heart stuttered, and her breath caught in her throat. A shiver raced over her skin, raising gooseflesh. She gripped her almost empty teacup so hard, it was a miracle she didn't snap off the porcelain handle.

Lord Rochfort was right outside Gunter's. Clothed all in black—even the sling that supported his injured shoulder was fashioned from black silk—he was conversing with another bespectacled gentleman, a man who also seemed vaguely familiar. Charlie searched her memory, trying to place him, but her mind drew a complete blank.

And then to her horror, Rochfort caught sight of her staring at him. He bared his teeth in a grin, tipped his top hat in a mocking salute, and then after farewelling the other gentleman, turned on his heel and strode away.

"Charlie, are you all right? You've gone as white as the tablecloth."

Charlie tore her attention away from the window and met Sophie's concerned gaze. "I... Lord Rochfort is outside. In the square," she whispered. "It... Seeing him here, so close to Hastings House, it took me by surprise."

"You don't think he's spying on you, do you?" asked Arabella. Her finely drawn brows had arrowed into a frown.

Charlie swallowed. Her mouth was so dry, it felt like it was filled with ashes. "I shouldn't think so. But he's such a horrible, devious man. Who knows what motivates him?"

"From what you've t-told me about him, Charlie, it's only natural that you'd be shaken by the mere sight of him," said Olivia. "But if you're worried, you should tell Max. You said he was keeping an eye on the blackguard."

"Yes…" Charlie forced herself to smile. "Don't mind me. Another cup of tea and the company of my dearest friends will quickly restore my equilibrium. Ah, and here comes the waiter with our pot now."

As Olivia began to dispense fresh tea for everyone, Charlie's attention was drawn to the teashop's doorway. The gentleman who'd been talking with Lord Rochfort had just entered. He was well-dressed, and a large leather folio was tucked beneath one arm. Upon removing his beaver hat, he revealed a balding pate. That's when she remembered where she'd seen him before. The hair at her nape stood on end.

He was the male visitor Cressida had received at Devereux House when Charlie had been taking tea with the dowager duchess and Diana. Charlie's gaze narrowed on him as he crossed the bustling teashop to one of the cake displays near the counter.

The fact that this man knew both Cressida and Lord Rochfort might be inconsequential. But what if it did mean something?

"What is it?" asked Olivia as she passed Charlie her replenished cup of tea. "You seem distracted."

"Lord Rochfort hasn't come in, has he?" asked Sophie, her worried gaze darting to the door.

"No," murmured Charlie. "But the gentleman the baron was speaking to outside has. And I think I recognize him." She quickly explained how she'd glimpsed him through the drawing room doorway at Devereux House.

"That does seem a wee bit odd," observed Arabella, peering over her glasses at the man who'd now taken a seat at another table on the opposite side of the teashop. "He has the look of a man of affairs about him. Someone professional rather than a member of the ton. But maybe that's just because he has that folio with him. It lends him a business-like air."

"Yes…" Charlie beckoned over the waiter who'd brought their tea. She was such a frequent visitor to Gunter's, she knew most of the staff, and they knew her. "Jacques, I know this may seem like a peculiar question, but that bespectacled gentleman who just came in and is now sitting over there"—she gestured discreetly in the stranger's direction—"do you by any chance know his name? Or what he does for a living?"

The young man frowned for a moment, then nodded. "*Bien sûr*, my lady. It's Monsieur Erasmus Silver. I believe he's a…" He rubbed his chin. "How you say, *éditeur de journal?* A newspaper editor. *Oui.*"

"Newspaper editor?" Charlie's pulse quickened. "Have you any idea which particular paper he works for?"

Jacques's brow furrowed in concentration again. "Perhaps it is the *Beau Monde Mirror?* I'm sorry I cannot be more certain."

A wave of white-hot anger surged inside Charlie at the knowledge that the man blithely sipping his coffee on the other side of the room worked for the publication that had done nothing but belittle her and besmirch her reputation for the last four years. She suddenly felt like she'd been thrust into a furnace. Indeed, her skin prickled and her cheeks blazed with heat. And then her fury hardened and cooled like newly forged steel. Fierce determination settled in the pit of her stomach, and a plan began to take shape in her mind.

Aware that Jacques was awaiting further direction, Charlie managed to bury her ire and summoned a smile. "Thank you so much. You've been wonderfully helpful." When she took care of the bill, she would make sure the young man was rewarded with a sizable tip.

"Well," said Sophie once the waiter had moved on to another table. "It looks as though you've discovered who the tattler in the Dowager Duchess of Exmoor's household is."

"Perhaps," said Charlie. "But I think I'd like to test that

theory before I denounce Max's mother as a two-faced, backstabbing witch."

"How will you do that?" asked Olivia.

Charlie smiled. "I have an idea, but I'll have to ask one of my respectable married friends to assist me."

"Oh, I will," declared Sophie, her blue eyes dancing with excitement. "What do I have to do?"

Charlie placed her linen napkin on the table and smoothed down the skirts of her walking gown as she stood. "Just play the part of 'respectable chaperone' while I join Mr. Silver. This won't take long."

"Good luck," offered Olivia.

"And we want to hear all the details when you return," added Arabella.

Charlie grinned. *"Bien sûr."*

Erasmus Silver's bushy eyebrows plunged into a frown when Charlie stopped by his table and offered a greeting that encompassed a bald-faced lie. "Mr. Silver, fancy meeting you here," she said brightly. "It's so lovely to see you again. Would you mind if we joined you?"

His tone was frost-laden as he peered over his wire-rimmed spectacles at her and then Sophie, who waited close by. "I'm sorry, but I don't know you, Miss…"

Charlie placed a hand over the fichu at her throat. "My goodness, how embarrassing," she replied. "It's Lady Charlotte Hastings, Mr. Silver. We have a mutual acquaintance—Cressida, the Dowager Duchess of Exmoor. You recently visited Devereux House while the dowager duchess and I were taking tea."

"Oh…I…" Now Erasmus Silver had to decide whether to call Charlie out for lying about their non-existent prior relationship or to go along with her ruse. Behind his spectacles, his pale gray eyes narrowed to slits. "Of course, Lady Charlotte. I remember now." At last, he stood as etiquette decreed. "Why don't you and…" His gaze skipped to Sophie.

"Lady Malverne, my sister-in-law," Charlie supplied by way of introduction.

"Why don't you and Lady Malverne take a seat?"

"We'd love to," declared Charlie with false sweetness.

Once she and Sophie were settled—and after Mr. Silver had taken a moment to push a notebook and pencil back into his folio—he pinned Charlie with an expectant look. "Now, what can I do for you, my lady?"

He was astute enough to realize that Charlie didn't wish to linger about making small talk over cups of tea or coffee and plates of cake, and that was fine with her too. If he'd said, "I'm a busy man, now get on with it," she wouldn't have minded in the least. Only just resisting the urge to upend his hot cup of coffee in his lap, she placed her forearms on the table and leaned forward in a conspiratorial fashion. "I understand you're the editor for a certain publication of some renown, the very popular *Beau Monde Mirror…*"

Mr. Silver sat up ramrod straight and squared his shoulders, almost as though he were preparing for an attack. Given the fact the paper had been waging war against the Earl of Westhampton's daughter and her friends for several years, Charlie couldn't blame him. "You are correct, Lady Charlotte," he said stiffly. "But I would've thought you would know that, considering we've apparently already met."

Charlie didn't flinch at his little dig. Instead, she leaned even closer and lowered her voice. "Well"—she glanced about their table as though checking who was in their immediate vicinity and might be eavesdropping —"I'm sure you're always on the lookout for the latest on-dits for your newspaper's society page. And I happen to have an especially juicy tidbit just for you. If you'd like to hear it…"

Mr. Silver grew very still. "Go on. I'm listening."

Charlie really hoped her gambit would pay off. "Before I share my intelligence with you, Mr. Silver, I need your assurance that you won't divulge the name of your source. Because the subject of the on-dit would be most upset if she were to find out who broke her confidence. It could prove rather awkward for me."

Mr. Silver's eyes gleamed. "So, you know this person well? You're certain your intelligence is sound and not just an unsubstantiated rumor?"

"Oh yes," Charlie lied. "And if my word isn't enough, Lady Malverne here"—she nodded at Sophie—"can corroborate my scandalous story."

Sophie inclined her head. Apart from a certain telltale twinkle in her eyes, she maintained a serious expression. "Yes, indeed. I certainly can."

"Well, then," said Mr. Silver, this man who'd created untold havoc in her life and that of her dearest friends. "I'm all ears, Lady Charlotte."

Charlie looked the gossip-hungry editor in the eye. "It involves none other than the Dowager Duchess of Exmoor herself," she said. "It seems my mother-in-law-to-be is not the model of decorum that everyone thinks she is. You see, she's been having an affair with one of London's most notorious rakehells..." She paused for effect before adding in a melodramatic whisper, "Baron Rochfort."

Mr. Silver snorted. "Surely you jest."

"I do not," said Charlie. "While visiting Devereux House, I stumbled across several love letters penned by the dowager. She spoke at length about their trysts. And I hope you can forgive me for being so indelicate, Mr. Silver, but she also mentioned Lord Rochfort's particular proclivities when it comes to bed sport." She dropped her volume to a dramatic whisper again. "I could elaborate further about the baron's penchant for riding crops and birch rods—and goodness, just imagine the fun you could have with the title of the article: 'Birching the Baron', or even 'Disciplining the Duchess'—but I feel Gunter's Tea Shop is not the place for a young lady such as myself to divulge such vulgar details."

Above his starched neckcloth, Mr. Silver's face had turned a deep ruddy shade that bordered upon puce. "Yes. Quite," he said in a strangled voice. "But I think you've provided me with sufficient information, Lady Charlotte."

Charlie blinked. "I have?" Out of the corner of her eye, she spied Sophie pressing a lawn kerchief to her mouth to suppress a fit of laughter. "But you haven't heard about the time—"

The editor of the *Beau Monde Mirror* held up a hand. "That's quite enough, my lady. I shall make a note of all you've shared with me, but I cannot promise that this story will end up in the paper."

"Whyever not?" asked Charlie. "I mean, you'd make a fortune in sales. And you never use anyone's full name in your gossip column—pardon me, I mean 'Society Page'—so you cannot be sued for libel. And as you said, you don't divulge your sources, so how can there be a problem?"

"I'm afraid there are some things that even the *Beau Monde Mirror* cannot publish."

Charlie's tone hardened. "Oh, I see. Or is it more the case that you're quite happy to slander and humiliate particular members of the ton that you see as easy prey, but there are other individuals that you won't touch with a ten-foot barge pole? That hardly seems fair."

"Life in general isn't fair, my lady," replied the editor coldly.

"Oh, believe me, I learned that lesson four years ago, Mr. Silver. Thanks to you." Charlie stood abruptly. She'd had enough of conversing with this "gentleman", and she was now quite certain where the loyalties of the *Beau Monde Mirror's* editor lay, given he had all but refused to print anything that cast aspersions on the dowager duchess's uprightness of character. He was protecting her and possibly Lord Rochfort as well. But why?

More importantly, now that she'd kicked the hornet's nest, would she get stung?

By the time Charlie got back to the table where Arabella and Olivia still sat, her trembling legs felt like blancmange. What on earth had she been thinking? The ramifications of what she'd just done could be catastrophic.

With Sophie's support, she recounted her conversation with the editor and her fears for the future. "What if Erasmus Silver goes to Cressida—or even Lord Rochfort—and tells them what I attempted to do? To say they won't be happy would be an understatement. And should I tell Max?" She caught the gazes of each of her friends. "How will he feel when he learns I said terrible, horrible, untrue things about his own mother? I don't wish to upset or anger him, not when things between us have been going so well. Indeed, tonight he's taking me somewhere special. A surprise he's been planning since the beginning of the week." She buried her face in her hands as anxiety twisted her insides into tight knots. "Oh, what have I done? I'm such an impulsive fool."

Olivia patted her shoulder. "You've collected evidence to support your theory that Cressida is the one who's been feeding damaging stories about you to the *Beau Monde Mirror*."

"But that's just it," sighed Charlie as she dropped her hands. "It's only a theory. I haven't proved it at all. Not really. Yes, Cressida knows Mr. Silver and he appears to want to protect the dowager duchess's reputation, but as for anything else…" She shrugged. "It's still nothing but speculation on my part."

"In any event, I think you should tell Max what you've learned," said practical-as-ever Arabella. "I truly believe it won't affect how he feels about you. He's defended you against his mother's insults and machinations at every turn."

"Yes," said Sophie. "You must be honest with him. It might just be the ammunition he needs to call out his mother for her duplicity. I, for one, am certain she's guilty. And Max might also find it interesting to know that Lord Rochfort is on friendly terms with Mr. Silver."

"Considering Lord Rochfort gave my stolen diary to someone at the *Beau Monde Mirror*, I suppose it's not all that surprising," Charlie said dully. "But you're right, my dear friends. I can't keep this from Max. The sooner I tell him about all of this, the better. I just pray that he'll understand why I did what I did."

CHAPTER 20

Many of our dedicated readers no doubt believe 'cleanliness is, indeed, next to godliness'. But for anyone who is a doubting Thomas or Thomasina, you might find the following essay, *On the Efficacy of Baths in Preserving Health and Restoring Beauty* by Dr. Brompton, a Physician, to be most informative.
The Beau Monde Mirror: General Health & Medical Miscellany

Exmoor House, Grosvenor Square

"His Grace is not in the library, my lady," said Chiffley as soon as the door to Exmoor House opened. "He's in his private chambers. With his valet."

"Oh." Charlie frowned. "Oh, I…" She twisted the handle of her reticule with gloved hands. "The matter I need to speak to him about is quite urgent. Is there any chance—"

Chiffley sighed and Charlie felt a pinch of guilt. Her indecorous intrusions undoubtedly vexed the man no end.

"I shall have Harvey here"—he nodded toward one of the nearby footmen—"escort you upstairs to His Grace's sitting room. His Grace has just returned from Angelo's Fencing Academy, so I'm not sure what state you'll find him in." He peered past her, out to the square. "You haven't a maid with you?"

Charlie lifted her chin. "No."

Another long-suffering sigh. "Would you like me to send up one of His Grace's maids with a tray of refreshments?"

Charlie narrowed her gaze. "No. Thank you." While the butler seemed determined to preserve her reputation yet again by arranging some sort of chaperonage, she didn't have time for this. The longer she waited about on the doorstep, the greater the chance there was of someone noticing that Lady Charlotte Hastings was paying an unaccompanied visit to the Duke of Exmoor's townhouse in broad daylight. Even though they were engaged, it still wasn't the "done thing" and would no doubt raise an eyebrow or two. "I won't be staying long," she added for good measure.

The butler stepped back, his expression resigned. "Very well, my lady."

"Thank you."

The moment the suitably expressionless footman showed her into Max's sitting room, Smedley, his valet, emerged from a connecting room—presumably Max's bedchamber. The man's eyes turned as round as saucers as soon as he saw her. "Lady Charlotte. My goodness," he exclaimed. "His Grace is—"

"What the devil is going on, Smedley? Can't a man have a bath in…" Max's words died on his lips when he appeared in the open doorway. Dressed in nothing but a thin linen towel that was slung low about his lean hips, his eyebrows shot up while Charlie's mouth dropped open.

Good God! Max's muscular physique was…

She literally had no words for such chiseled perfection. The dusting of hair in tantalizing places including the thin trail which arrowed down his taut lower belly straight toward his… Charlie swallowed and heat scorched her entire face. To think she'd been pressed up against that breathtakingly beautiful body only yesterday when Max had kissed her in the rain in Hyde Park… She clutched at the doorframe with one hand. No wonder her own body had suddenly turned liquid with longing.

While she continued to gape like a featherbrained peagoose, Max disappeared, but a moment later he was back, cinching a royal blue satin robe around his waist. "Leave us," he said to the room, and Smedley, Harvey, and another footman who'd been lingering all goggle-eyed by the sitting room door immediately scurried away.

Charlie drew a bracing breath and somehow found her voice. "Max, I... My apologies for interrupting your..." She had to drag her eyes away from the captivating sight of his partially exposed pectoral muscles and back to his face. "I...I had to see you. Of course, I didn't mean to see *this* much of you..." Oh, bother. She was rambling. She dropped her gaze, but then she couldn't seem to stop staring at Max's lower legs—his muscular calves and his shapely bare feet. Good heavens. Even his *feet* were gorgeous...

And that's when she noticed something odd. The little toe on Max's left foot was missing. It simply wasn't there. But there was a pale scar. Had he been injured at Waterloo? Nate had never mentioned it. Compassion welled in her heart. To think of Max suffering, even if it was just the loss of a pinkie toe, made her unaccountably sad.

When she dared to look up again, Max's mouth was twitching with a smile. It was clear he didn't seem to mind the fact that she was blatantly staring at his bare legs and feet as he said, "No harm done, Charlie." Crossing his arms over his chest, he leaned with studied nonchalance against the doorjamb. "Although, given the fact you've managed to persuade Chiffley to let you in, I suspect it's something important."

"Well, yes." She grimaced and twisted her hands again, willing herself to confess all. "Actually, I think I've just done something beyond foolish. Something that you might hate me for."

"I seriously doubt that," he said, concern creasing his brow. "But come, let's sit by the fire, and you can tell me all about it."

By the time Charlie finished recounting what had

happened at Gunter's Tea Shop, Max's frown had descended into ferocious territory. "I can't believe Erasmus
Silver was at my mother's house," he said, his voice hard
with anger. "If she's had anything at all to do with this
concerted campaign to discredit you since our engagement, by God…" He thumped his curled fist on the arm
of his wingback chair and shook his head. "As for
Rochfort, it doesn't surprise me at all that he and Silver
are on friendly terms. But my mother?" He shook his
head, his expression grim. "I agree with you. That slippery, soulless eel Silver appears to be protecting her. The
pertinent question is *why?* Why is the Dowager Duchess
of Exmoor so special? You'd think a salacious story about
a high-ranking member of the ton would be impossible
for him to ignore."

"You're…you're not angry at me for attempting to
spread false gossip about your mother?" Charlie asked. "If
Erasmus Silver does take the bait after all…"

Max met her eyes. "Nothing ventured, nothing gained.
Your reasoning and method for testing your hypothesis
were sound. And to put your mind at ease, I'm certain
Silver won't do a thing. If he really did want to publish
the story, he would have jumped at the chance to gather
every last little detail from you. But he didn't, and that is
decidedly odd. Of course, Silver could just be protecting
Rochfort, the other subject of your story…" Max sighed
heavily. "Damn it. I wish I knew more about the company
that owns the *Beau Monde Mirror.* My man of affairs and
an inquiry agent have been trying to dig up information
on them, but to date, their inquiries have yielded nothing
helpful."

"I'm also worried about the fact that I've just poked a
dangerous bear with a terribly big stick," said Charlie. "If
Erasmus Silver goes to your mother or Rochfort and tells
them what I tried to do…" A shiver raced down her spine.
"I can't imagine either of them shrugging it off."

Max reached out and clasped her hand. "You've
nothing to fear, Charlie. I'll protect you."

Alarm flared inside Charlie. "Please promise me you

won't do anything rash. I've caused enough trouble as it is."

"I won't. And you haven't done anything wrong. Well"—Max's mouth quirked with a smile—"that's not entirely true. You did walk in on me as I was about to take a bath. Imagine the field day the *Beau Monde Mirror* would have with a story like that if it ever got out."

Charlie clutched her throat in mock horror. "Perish the thought. But in all seriousness, Max, I'm so sorry for barging in. *Again.* And your bathwater is probably cold by now, so I should go. I have to get ready for this evening too." She stood. "I don't want to be late for whatever it is you have planned. Actually"—she gave him a reproving look—"you said you were going to send word to me about all of the details, but you haven't."

Max rose too. Cocking a brow, he said, "Actually, I have. However, you came barging into my private rooms —your words, not mine—rather than returning home to Hastings House, didn't you? But I agree. You should go before I decide to drag you into the bath with me."

Charlie laughed. "Silly man. And you think that sort of threat will scare me away? You know I'm not a shrinking violet."

"No, you're not." Catching her hand against his chest, Max swooped down and gave her a swift, hard kiss. "I'm serious, though. If you don't leave now, I will have my wicked way with you, and then we'll both be very late…" His mouth kicked into a grin. "For Almack's."

"Almack's?" Charlie gasped. "How on earth did you manage to procure vouchers?"

"I'm a duke." He winked. "I can have whatever I want, whenever I want it, don't you know?"

I wish you truly wanted me. For your wife. Charlie swallowed a sigh. Even if Max never professed his undying love for her, she would take what she could get from this new, oh-so-devilish, willing-to-take-chances Max rather than the keep-you-at-a-distance Max of old. "I'm beginning to suspect that you're working your way through my not-so-secret list, Maximilian Devereux."

His wicked grin was back. "I might be. You deserve to be happy, Charlie. I might not be able to give you everything you want, but I'm going to try my damnedest to make you smile."

"Well, how can I take issue with that?" she returned. "And thank you. Not only for the Almack's voucher, but for believing in me." Standing on tiptoe, she reached up and kissed him on the cheek. Stubble prickled her lips, and she smiled. "I'll see you tonight, Your Grace," she whispered against his ear while she trailed her fingers down his bare chest.

As she turned to go, she swore that she heard Max mutter, "Minx." But she didn't mind at all because she knew without a doubt that he liked her just the way she was.

~

As soon as the door shut, Max uttered a string of the worst curse words he knew.

What the bloody, blazing hell was his mother up to? He had to find out.

After washing and dressing rapidly, he marched over to Devereux House. He found his mother in her private study, dictating a letter to her secretary. Diana sat by the fire, reading a novel. Everyone looked up the moment he walked in.

"Maximilian." His mother's smile quickly disappeared when she noted the thunderous expression on his face. Her private secretary and Diana quickly disappeared too.

"Now, what can I do for you?" she asked when they were alone. Leaning back in the elegant shepherdess chair behind her desk, she didn't look the least bit perturbed. It was almost as though she'd been anticipating both his arrival and his foul mood.

"I think you know why I'm here," he growled.

"My secretary tells me you picked up your Almack's vouchers this morning, so I haven't the slightest idea why you've come back again so soon, my son," she said smoothly. "However, judging by the look on your face, you clearly don't wish to take tea with me and chat about the weather. So why don't you enlighten me?"

By God, she was cold-blooded. But then she always had been. Max fought to rein in his anger and modulate his voice. "Why are you consorting with the likes of Erasmus Silver? And to what end?"

His mother's brow descended into a puzzled frown. "Erasmus Silver? I'm not sure if I've heard—"

Max raised an admonitory finger. "Don't. Don't you dare tell me that you don't know exactly who Erasmus Silver is, or that he's the head editor of the *Beau Monde Mirror*, the most scurrilous scandalmongering rag in the country that has published harmful gossip, not just about me and my closest friends, but all but ruined my fiancée on multiple occasions."

His mother's already pale complexion blanched to the shade of the parchment paper on the blotter before her. "You're right," she said. "I do know who he is."

"And would you care to explain *how* you came to know him?"

His mother seemed to rally. Leaning forward, she placed her hands carefully on the blotter and met his gaze. "In keeping with my station as the Dowager Duchess of Exmoor, I support a number of prominent charities and societies by serving as a patroness or a trustee. One of these groups is the London Royal Academy of Art, and in less than two weeks, their annual exhibition opens. I recently met with Mr. Erasmus to discuss promoting the exhibition's opening in the newspaper's society pages. That's all. You may not like it, but the *Beau Monde Mirror* does have a significant readership."

Max gave a derisive snort. "Not good enough, Mother. Why couldn't your personal secretary undertake such a task for you? Have you never heard of writing a letter? I've also been informed that Mr. Silver visited Devereux House several weeks ago. Was that to discuss the Royal Academy of Art Exhibition or another matter entirely?"

His mother's eyes glittered. "Are you spying on my

movements again, Max? Like I'm some common sneak-thief? How dare you!"

"And how dare you consort with gutter-dwelling creatures like Erasmus Silver and Lord Rochfort. You're the Dowager Duchess of Exmoor, for God's sake. And you accuse my fiancée of having a disreputable reputation."

"Your busybody of a fiancée should keep her pesky nose—" She broke off and clamped her lips together.

"Out of your business? Is that what you were going to say? Did your friend Mr. Silver come by to tell you about a certain conversation he had with Lady Charlotte this afternoon?" Max planted his hands on the blotter and leaned forward. "I thought you barely knew Silver, so why would he do such a thing?"

"You are making a gross assumption with no evidence to support—"

"But it's a logical assumption, no? For some reason I can't fathom, Erasmus Silver is protecting you. Why else would he refuse to publish a juicy piece of gossip about you? The man thrives on it."

"Erasmus Silver is a gentleman."

"Good God, now I know you're lying. Next you'll be telling me that Lord Rochfort is a gentleman too." Max straightened. "This is my final warning, Mother dearest. Stay away from Silver. But most of all, stop feeding him damaging gossip about Lady Charlotte. You'll deny it, of course, but I *know* it's you who's been slandering her."

"Slandering?" His mother sniffed. "As if I'd ever engage in such vulgar behavior. Besides, I barely think about the girl."

"That young woman is going to be my wife whether you like it or not. And all of London will see that tonight when I waltz around Almack's Assembly Rooms with her and no one else."

With that, Max turned on his booted heel and headed for the door. "Oh, and by the way, if we *ever* have to have a conversation like this again, you'll be packing your trunks and departing for the dower house in Devonshire within the hour."

Max didn't stay to observe his mother's expression, but he did hear something smash after he shut the door behind him.

Good.

At long bloody last, she was taking him seriously.

CHAPTER 21

Do you have your voucher permitting you entry to
Almack's Assembly Rooms?
We all know how exacting the vaunted Lady
Patronesses of Almack's can be. Read on for
essential advice that will not only help you gain
access to London's most exclusive marriage-
hunting ground, you'll learn how to avoid being a
wallflower.
*The Beau Monde Mirror: The Essential Style &
Etiquette Guide*

Hastings House, Berkeley Square

Charlie waited in the vestibule of Hastings House,
checking her reflection one last time in the gilt-
edged mirror. Her eyes glowed and her cheeks were so
pink with excitement, she didn't need to pinch them. But
she might need to pinch herself elsewhere to make sure
she was awake. She was going to Almack's! With Max!

How long had she dreamed of such a thing? If she
were perfectly honest with herself, it would have been
from the moment she'd met Max when she was only sixteen and he was twenty-two. She could recall the exact
moment that long ago summer when Nate had showed
his handsome-as-sin university chum into the grand
entry hall of Elmstone Hall, their country manor in

Gloucestershire. She'd been smitten instantly. With his dark golden hair, sparkling eyes of sapphire blue, and his square-jawed beauty, Maximilian Devereux was the epitome of the hero she'd always pictured in her fantasies.

Indeed, tonight she at long last felt like a princess in a fairy tale waiting for the arrival of her very own prince charming. She'd certainly dressed for the occasion. With her curls piled high on her head, pearls at her throat, ears, and threaded through her hair, and a ballgown of soft shell-pink silk falling in graceful folds about her figure, she was certain the patronesses of London's most exclusive venue would not take issue with her appearance and refuse her entry. And of course, she'd be on the arm of a powerful duke.

Molly waited nearby with her gloves, fan, and matching reticule. "You look as fine as can be, my lady," she sighed as she handed Charlie her gloves. "I'd be happy to accompany you in the carriage."

"No, you have the night off. You deserve it," said Charlie as she tugged on her white satin gloves. No doubt Molly wished to gawk at all the other fine ladies as they arrived at the assembly rooms, but she didn't want her maid shadowing her tonight. Max was sending one of his carriages around, and she was certain he'd ask Diana to accompany them for the sake of appearances. He wouldn't ask his mother. Not after the goings-on at Gunter's.

As for her father, he was, as usual, elsewhere. In fact, Charlie had barely seen him of late, but she didn't mind because he seemed so content and happy. The mantle of sadness he'd worn for so long was gone. If he wasn't at one of his clubs, he was usually out and about with Lady Tilbury. Charlie strongly suspected it was only a matter of time before he announced that he'd proposed to the lovely widow. It was a day she looked forward to.

Charlie had just finished fastening the pearl buttons at the tops of her gloves when there was a knock at the front door. The footman opened it to reveal her fiancé in all of his evening finery. But nothing was as fine as the smile that broke across his face as his warm gaze wandered over her with frank appreciation.

"Lady Charlotte, I've never seen you looking so beautiful," he said in such a smooth dark voice, Charlie's toes curled in her pink satin slippers.

"Why, thank you, Your Grace. And I could say the same about you," she returned. "I mean, you look very handsome."

He bowed and offered his arm. "Your chariot awaits, my lady," he said. "Let us away to Almack's, where we'll dazzle the ton with our waltzing."

Charlie tucked her gloved hand into the crook of Max's elbow. "I can hardly wait."

As Max handed her into his carriage, Charlie was astonished to discover that she was the cab's only occupant. "I thought Diana would be joining us," she said when Max climbed in and took the seat beside her.

"I'm afraid I want you all to myself," Max said with a rakish grin as the door shut and the carriage moved off. "Do you mind terribly? We are engaged, and so I thought that might give us a little bit of leeway when it comes to observing or not observing the rules, as the case may be."

"Ordinarily I would agree with you, but we are going to Almack's. People are bound to talk if we arrive together in a closed carriage without a chaperone."

"They will regardless, Charlie."

"True," she said with a sigh.

"However, if you would prefer it, would you like to bring someone along? I saw your maid hovering about the vestibule. One word from you, and I'll stop the carriage. We could even travel separately. I can hail a hackney coach easily enough."

"Now that would be beyond silly," said Charlie. "No, you're right. Let the ton talk if they want to. Besides, it's a short drive, so even if Nate hears about our unchaperoned journey, he can hardly complain. It's not as though we can get up to too much mischief in the space of ten minutes."

"Speak for yourself," said Max with a devilish smile. He rested his large hand on her knee.

Charlie rapped him lightly on the knuckles with her closed fan. "You must promise to behave, Your Grace. I won't have you rumpling my gown or messing up my hair before we arrive."

He laughed. "I promise," he said. "But your decree also begs the question: can I rumple your gown and mess up your hair afterward?"

Charlie's pulse raced faster than a Scotch reel. Did Max really mean that? Judging by the wicked gleam in his eyes, she suspected he might. "Perhaps," she said with an arch smile. "If you sweep me off my feet tonight, who knows what might happen after the assembly."

In the shadowy cabin, Max's heated gaze captured hers. "Well, now I'm the one who can hardly wait," he murmured, and Charlie swore she blushed all over.

It didn't take long for them to reach King Street, where Almack's was located. However, the thoroughfare was completely congested with traffic; Max's carriage began to crawl toward their destination at a frustratingly slow snail's pace.

"I'm quite happy to walk the remaining distance," said Charlie. "It's not far."

"No, you shall arrive in style." Max's voice was firm. "I want everyone to know that you're arriving with me, the Duke of Exmoor, and as my fiancée, you are not to be trifled with."

"Hmm." Charlie looked out of the carriage window. She could see the gas lamps illuminating the rather plain façade of the much-vaunted assembly rooms. A small crowd of elegantly dressed attendees was milling out the front, waiting to be admitted. It wouldn't do at all to arrive late. Indeed, the patronesses had been known to turn guests away for breaching their strict rules.

And that was when Charlie was struck by the most novel thought. It was as though someone had just lit all the gas lamps in her own mind, bringing blazing clarity into her world.

Her heart hammering, she turned to the man beside her, the duke of her dreams. "Max…" She bit her lip, suddenly beset with nerves.

He reached for her hand and squeezed it. "It's all right, we won't be late."

"No, that's not..." She swallowed. "I..." She inhaled a bracing breath. "I don't want to go. I've suddenly realized something about myself. This girlish dream of mine —to waltz at Almack's—it's not actually about the dancing at all. It's really about my need—and I suspect the need of most young women—to be accepted by the doyens of Society. To gain their hard-to-win approval. But now, as I sit here with you, I've decided I don't give a fat flying fig about the patronesses of Almack's or what they think of me. I don't want to adhere to their ridiculously strict rules or narrow views of what constitutes acceptable behavior. They don't matter to me. At least, not anymore. Of course"—she cast him a smile —"waltzing about the assembly rooms in your arms would be lovely. But that's only because I'd be sharing the experience with you. You, Maximilian Devereux, it's *your* opinion of me that matters. And that of my own friends and family. All the rest is just...mindless noise. It means nothing."

Max's eyes searched hers for the space of several heartbeats. He nodded. "I understand," he said solemnly. "And you're right. I certainly don't give a jot about what any of those conceited, judgmental women think. Ultimately, I just want you to be happy. So, if you don't wish to go, we won't."

He reached into the inner pocket of his evening jacket and withdrew the Almack's vouchers. He flashed a wicked smile. "Would you like to do the honors, or shall I?"

Charlie looked at the cream tickets with their official red seal and the signature of one of the patronesses scrawled across it. "Are you certain you are all right with this, Max? You did go to a lot of trouble to procure them for me. And aren't they ten guineas apiece?"

"Never put a price on your happiness, Charlie. Life is too short."

"You're right." She took the vouchers from Max and ripped them in two. "There." With a grin, she tossed the pieces into the air and watched them flutter to the carriage floor. "That was most satisfying."

Max reached up and rapped three times on the carriage roof.

"You're taking me home?" Charlie asked as the coachman deftly maneuvered Max's carriage out of the line of traffic and proceeded down the wrong side of King Street until they were clear of the snarl.

Max turned to her, and his mouth curved into a slow, lazy smile. "Eventually. I believe there's another item on your secret list of wishes and dreams we can mark off."

Oh... Charlie's breath quickened. "I gather you're not taking me all the way to the coast so I can sea-bathe?"

"As tempting as that proposition sounds, not tonight." Max removed his top hat and gloves and placed them with deliberate care on the seat across from them. "No. Tonight I think a carriage ravishment is in order." He reclaimed the spot beside her, his arm resting behind her head, then cocked a brow. "That is, if you are still amenable to the idea, Lady Charlotte."

"I've never been more so," she whispered. Acute longing seemed to have stolen her breath as she took in the sight of Max looking back at her with lust in his gaze. "Right at this very moment, if you consulted any dictionary, the definition of 'amenable' would be *Lady Charlotte Hastings.*"

That devilish grin appeared again. "I think that same dictionary would define the term 'utterly captivated' with the words *Maximilian Devereux, the Duke of Exmoor.*" He leaned in close and caught one of her trailing curls with gentle fingers. "So, my lady"—his warm breath brushed against her lips as he whispered in a dark velvet voice full of wicked promise—"are you ready to be ravished and rumpled to the point of complete dishevelment?"

Charlie's heart somersaulted with sheer delight. "My answer to that is a resounding 'yes', Your Grace. Ravish and rumple away."

Max reached for one of her hands. Holding her gaze, he slid the pearl buttons at the top of her glove undone, then slowly peeled the satin away. "I'm firmly of the opinion that a ravishment done the right way should never be a hurried affair," he murmured, then repeated the process with her other glove. Wherever his teasing fingertips brushed, he left a trail of gooseflesh. "A ravishment should be slow." He placed a kiss upon the tender skin on the inside of her wrist. "Deliberate." He kissed the crook of her elbow. "And thorough."

He pushed the curls grazing her neck to one side and feathered a kiss across her jawline. "No part of you should be left untouched or wanting. But tell me, Charlie…" His mouth slid to her neck, and she felt his tongue taste an exquisitely sensitive spot just below her ear. "What did you imagine when you put this particular item on your list? Was this what you had in mind?"

"This is far better," she admitted on a breathless whisper. Her fingers curled into Max's lapels. "I'm quite content to follow your lead."

"Good." All at once, Max dragged Charlie across his lap. One strong arm lashed her body to his while his other hand cradled her face. His thumb stroked across her lower lip. "Do you know how lusciously beautiful you are, Lady Charlotte Hastings? Or how much I want you?"

Judging by the steel-hard shaft jutting against her thigh, Charlie could indeed feel how much Max desired her. The thought of his arousal made her whole body liquid with longing. The blood flowing within her veins had turned to molten honey, and her very bones were as soft as sun-warmed butter. "I…I have an idea," she murmured, sliding one of her hands between them. With gentle fingers, she caressed his long hard length through the fall of his evening breeches.

Max groaned and buried his face in the crook of her neck. "Sweet Jesus," he whispered hoarsely, then stilled her hand with his. "This is supposed to be about your pleasure, not mine."

"Pleasing you will please me," she returned. The knowledge that she could bring Max undone with just her touch was heady indeed.

"All in good time, sweetheart. All in good time." Max

speared his fingers into her hair and brought his mouth down on hers in a searing, breath-stealing kiss.

Max's tongue boldly slid between her lips, and Charlie opened for him without hesitation. He delved deeply, each hot, slick stroke a languorous caress that she eagerly returned in kind. As each delicious, drugging kiss slid seamlessly into another, then another, Charlie soon found that her head was spinning and her body was aflame. However, all too soon, kisses weren't enough to appease the fire that Max had ignited inside her. And he knew. Whether it was the way she squirmed upon his lap, or when he pulled a ragged moan from her throat, it hardly mattered. All that mattered was she needed more.

And Max gave it to her. His clever fingers deftly loosened her buttons and laces, and before she knew it, he'd freed her breasts from the confines of bodice and stays. In the cool night air, her nipples hardened to tight, aching points.

"Dear God," he murmured, his voice filled with reverence. The ambient glow of passing gas lights intermittently illuminated her body and his rapt expression as he studied her nudity through half-mast lids. His hands cupped her gently, lifting and squeezing as though learning the shape and feel of her. "Charlie…I…"

Unashamed, she smiled and let her fingers drift through his thick, ruffled locks. "You're speechless?"

"Yes. For such a long time, I've envisioned you just like this in my arms—" He broke off. Swallowed. His gaze met hers briefly before dropping again. "I hope you'll forgive me for being so crude, but there's no other way to say it. Lady Charlotte Hastings, your tits are utterly magnificent. If I were the least bit artistic, I'd capture their likeness on canvas. Or in marble. At the very least, I'd write a sonnet about them."

"We have something in common, then."

"How so?"

"I've also had thoughts about composing odes to your fine physique and handsome face."

He smiled as though genuinely pleased by her confession. "While we're exchanging confidences, my lady, I have another one I'd like to share."

"Oh, yes?"

Max's thumbs brushed in teasing circles over and around her tightly furled nipples. "Not only have I long imagined what your delectable breasts would look like, their size and shape, and the precise color of your nipples —and I was right, they're apricot-pink—I've also wondered how they would taste. And if I don't bury my face between them at least once, I think I might die."

A breathy laugh escaped Charlie, and she clutched at Max's head. "Well, we can't have that, Your Grace. Do what you must."

"Thank God," he groaned. He gave her a swift, hard kiss, then his mouth slid downward. He pressed his face into her cleavage, inhaled a deep breath as though memorizing her scent, then turned his head and seized one of her nipples between his lips. The sensation of his hot mouth gently but insistently suckling her was divine. At the same time, he continued to torment her other nipple, plucking and circling the taut, sensitized peak with his fingers.

"Max," she gasped, clutching at his head. His ministrations were exquisite torture. She wasn't sure if she wanted him to stop or go on forever. Max was relentless, giving her no quarter. He transferred his mouth to her other nipple, tugging on it gently with his teeth before laving it with his tongue, driving her wild.

Desire pulsed between Charlie's thighs, and she shifted restlessly on his lap.

"Do you want more, sweet Charlotte?" he whispered into the darkness. One of his hands slid beneath the hem of her ballgown and skated up her leg to her knee. His fingers danced circles over the sensitive flesh just above her silk stocking.

"Oh God, yes." And she meant it. With Max, she wanted everything.

He caught her mouth in another blazing-hot kiss, and his fingers continued their wicked march up her thigh until they reached the curls hiding her sex. When he paused, Charlie whimpered in frustration.

"Are you wet for me, Charlie?" he murmured against her lips.

In response, she slid a leg to the side in shameless invitation. "Why don't you find out, Your Grace?"

Max didn't hesitate to act. One long finger traced a teasing path between her slick, swollen folds before settling on her core. At the exquisite contact, Charlie shuddered and clutched at his shoulders. While she'd pleasured herself on many occasions, it had never, ever felt as wonderful as this. "Max," she breathed as he began to mercilessly torment her oh-so-sensitive bud, rubbing and flicking and gently pinching. "Oh, that feels so good. Oh, don't stop."

"I won't." When Max set his mouth to her breast, working her into a frenzy with tongue and lips, Charlie couldn't contain a moan. The tension inside her was building, coiling tighter. Her release was so close. Perhaps sensing she was on the edge of bliss, Max slid a finger inside her. As he worked in and out of her quivering sex, he continued to tease her core with the pad of this thumb, circling and circling. Increasing the pace. Driving her higher.

The moment he buried his face in her neck and lightly nipped the taut tendon at the juncture of her shoulder, she cried out in ecstasy. A wave of pleasure engulfed her, and she shuddered and shivered in Max's arms as she rode the crest to completion. Drifting in a haze of delicious delirium, she clung to Max, her face pressed into his shoulder until he withdrew his hand and roused her with a gentle kiss at her temple.

"I take it you found satisfaction, my lady?"

She laughed and lifted her head. "I think it's rather obvious that I did. I've never experienced such a powerful release before. It's never been quite so…intense when I've —" She broke off and felt herself blushing, which was quite ridiculous, given the circumstances. She drew a breath and completed the thought. "When I've pleasured myself. Thinking about you."

He brushed a lock of hair from her cheek. "You think of me when you touch yourself? I'm sincerely flattered."

She studied his face, and even in the uncertain light, she detected a smile in his eyes. "You're not shocked?"

A ghost of a smile hovered on his lips. "About which part? The fact that you pleasure yourself on occasion, or that when you do so, I'm the man you're picturing in your mind."

"Both."

"Both admissions please me. More than I can say. Because when I come by my own hand, I'm usually thinking about you too."

"Oh… You are?" His confession filled Charlie with a warm glow.

"Of course," he said. "Keeping my hands off you has been such a struggle for me. You have no idea. Up until now, I've had to make do with libidinous fantasies in the night in my private chambers."

A hot thrill coursed through Charlie. She couldn't resist asking, "And what do I do in these libidinous fantasies, Your Grace? Were there any carriage trysts?"

He laughed. "There might have been."

"And is this where your fantasy ends? With me achieving satisfaction, whereas you are left wanting?"

Max's expression sobered then. "As I said earlier, tonight is about fulfilling your dreams, not mine."

"But what if one of my dreams is to ravish you, Max? In a carriage when we're all alone? You can't deny that you want me. I'm sure that cockstand of yours could drive a nail through wood."

Max let out a snort of laughter. "Lady Charlotte Hastings. I can't believe that you just said that."

"If I have my way, you'll soon be saying, 'Lady Charlotte Hastings, I can't believe that you're actually *doing* that'. But I am going to do it, Max. I'm not going home until you've come, too."

∾

Devil take him. Charlie had that determined glint in her eye and stubborn set to her jaw that Max knew so well.

He should say no to her salacious proposition. He really didn't expect her to return the favor. But as she continued to sit on his lap with her chestnut hair in complete disarray, her rumpled skirts pushed up around her thighs, and her bountiful breasts still on full display, his will was quavering. His throbbing cock and aching ballocks certainly had no objections.

He blew out a frustrated sigh and prayed for the strength to resist temptation. But all of his good intentions went up in a puff of smoke as soon as her wicked fingers stroked his shaft and she pressed her mouth to his ear and whispered exactly what she was going to do to him.

Dear God above. Holding back the tide or stopping the world from turning would be a far easier task than saying no to his bold and beautiful fiancée. Especially when she began to undo the fall of his breeches and her bare fingers encircled his hot, rigid length. If he hadn't gritted his teeth, he might have exploded like an untried youth at that very moment.

However, when Charlie hopped off his lap and slid to her knees between his legs, the gentleman in him tried one last time to stop her.

"Charlie," he murmured, cupping her face between his hands. "Are you sure you want to do this? Do you really know what to expect?"

She bit her lip, and for a moment, uncertainty flickered in her gaze. "I will confess that I've never done this before. But I have a thorough understanding of what to do and what will happen when you come. You seem to forget that all of my friends are married to former rakehells and, well, we talk. I'm more than ready to try this if you are." She gave his cock another gentle squeeze, and when an involuntary hiss escaped him, her mouth curved into a provocative smile. "I promise I won't bite. Well, not unless you want me to…"

Minx. Max shook his head. "Very well. You've convinced me. I'll let you have your wicked way with me. Only, I reserve the right to stop you at any time."

"Of course." She lifted her tumble-down curls and pushed them over one shoulder. "Now, hold on tight, Max, because you're about to lose all control."

Sweet Charlie, for all her inexperience, wasn't wrong at all.

As soon as her hot, wet mouth surrounded him, Max was done for. Lust pounded hot and hard through his veins, straight to his groin, and all rational thought fled.

What Charlie lacked in finesse, she more than made up for with enthusiasm, and in no time at all, Max was cursing and shaking and groaning, and dear God… What she was doing with her tongue… She'd said she was a novice but… *Holy blazing hell.*

Max's thoughts began to fracture. He clutched at her head, and just as he realized he should warn her that he was going to orgasm, his ballocks contracted…and, oh sweet Jesus, he was there. A deep groan erupted from his throat as pleasure surged and he shuddered and jerked before sinking into mind-numbing ecstasy. Replete and spent, satisfaction radiated through him, flooding every part of him, penetrating deeply, right down to his very bones.

When Charlie joined him on the seat again, he roused himself enough to gather her into his arms. "You are magnificent," he murmured into her hair. "I really did lose control. For a moment, I think I even forgot who I was."

She kissed his throat, then he felt her lips curve in a smile against his skin. "Good. I'm glad. Now we're both thoroughly rumpled and satisfied. It's a night I will never forget."

Max captured her chin and gently turned her face to his. "Thank you, Charlie. I mean that sincerely. This is a night I will never forget either. I wish…"

I wish that I could be the man you deserve. A man who could love you… He swallowed the words. He didn't want to make her sad, not when he could see the glow of satisfaction and triumph in her brandywine eyes.

But somehow, ever-perceptive Charlie knew exactly what to say to ease the guilt shredding his soul. "You wish that we could do this again sometime?" She brushed a kiss across his lips. "Well, so do I. It's been far more enjoyable than waltzing around a stuffy ballroom."

Max laced his fingers through hers and brought her hand to his lips. "That, my dear, is something we can agree on."

CHAPTER 22

My List of Secret Wishes and Dreams:

1) ~~Sneak into a 'Gentlemen's Club' to see what all the fuss is about;~~

2) ~~To be kissed, with passion, in the moonlight by a rake;~~

3) ~~Or in the rain (either will do);~~

4) ~~Ride hell-for-leather down Rotten Row at least once (Preferably not in the rain unless there's any chance said passionate kiss happens straight afterwards.);~~

5) Sea bathe, naked;

6) ~~Sit for a licentious portrait à la Lady Hamilton;~~

7) ~~To be thoroughly ravished in a carriage;~~

8) ~~Waltz the night away at Almack's;~~

9) To experience a Grand Passion that I will remember long into my dotage;

10) The man (or should I say duke?) of my dreams falls in love with me.

Hastings House, Berkeley Square
April 28, 1819

Charlie's quill hovered over the ninth item on her "not-so-secret list of wishes and dreams" and she frowned. Was she ready to say that she'd had her Grand Passion? Could she put a line through it because she'd achieved her goal?

No, not yet...

She smiled to herself and let her gaze wander out of her sitting-room window to the light rain falling on the plane trees in Berkeley Square. Her Grand Passion with Max was still very much ongoing. In the week since he'd first "ravished" her in his carriage, he'd also ravished her just as thoroughly on the way home from the theater a few nights later. And following an intimate dinner party hosted by Olivia and Hamish at Sleat House in Grosvenor Square the night before, she and Max had managed to slip away to share a passionate kiss in the back garden.

A knock at the door roused Charlie from her musings, and she closed her notebook just as Molly admitted Sophie. Charlie had been expecting her, and a tea service along with a plate of cakes, sandwiches, and savory pastries were already set out on the low table by the fire.

Once they were armed with cups of tea and settled upon one of the settees—Peridot had claimed the other chair—Sophie began to unabashedly quiz Charlie. "So, what happened?" she asked, her blue eyes sparkling with curiosity. "Did your moonlit tryst go according to plan after Nate and I left?"

Even though Charlie felt herself blushing, she didn't mind her sister-in-law's good-natured interrogation. "It did," she said. "And I'm grateful you convinced Nate to go home a little early, otherwise I wouldn't have been game enough to suggest taking a turn about the terrace with Max. I'm sure Arabella and Olivia noticed how flushed and disheveled I was when we returned to the drawing room. If their husbands had any inkling, I trust they didn't go tattling to Nate about what we got up to."

"As far as I know, they haven't," said Sophie, helping herself to a cucumber sandwich. "Indeed, I'm absolutely certain that Hamish and Gabriel wouldn't want to see Max and Nate come to blows. Or worse. No, I'm sure Hamish and Gabriel will bury their heads in the sand to keep the peace."

Charlie winced and crumbled a discarded edge of her pastry onto her plate. "I feel dreadful going behind Nate's back. But now Max and I are getting closer—at least in a physical sense—I need to be a little mercenary and make use of every opportunity I can to be intimate with him. Before I know it, the end of the Season will be upon us, and if Max isn't able to acknowledge that he's in love with me…" She shook her head. "I won't settle for anything less than a love match, Sophie. I want all of him or nothing at all."

"And nor should you settle," said her friend. "I'm sure Max is heading in the right direction. Last night, he couldn't stop sneaking glances at you when Nate wasn't looking. And don't think I didn't notice how he held your hand below the card table when you were playing piquet with Gabriel and Arabella."

A jolt of panic shot through Charlie. "Do you think Nate noticed as well?"

"I'm sure he didn't," said Sophie. "He was playing billiards with Hamish in the next room at that point. No"— she grinned—"it was only Olivia and I who observed what was really going on."

Charlie's smile returned. "Max *has* been very attentive of late. And I'm thrilled he's willing to take chances. He kissed me in the shadows of his private box at the Theatre Royal the other night. And when he took me out in his high-perch phaeton in Hyde Park two days ago, he found a secluded grove that we made good use of for several minutes. I must say, while this skulking about adds an element of excitement to our romantic trysts, I would give anything to be able to spend a whole uninterrupted night with Max."

Sophie patted her arm. "It will happen. In time."

Charlie sighed and offered a corner of her Welsh rarebit to Peridot, who'd woken up and was batting at her mistress's knee with her paw. "If only Max would throw another house party at Hampstead Heath. The greatest challenge for me right now is watching my tongue during the heat of the moment, so to speak. When Max and I are alone, I'm terrified I'm going to blurt out how I really feel about him and scare him away." She slipped Peridot another morsel. "I swear he's as skittish as a horse."

"He is. But it seems to be the case with our men,

doesn't it? When they're in the process of falling in love, they're liable to bolt at the slightest provocation. I hope you take heart, though. Even though your engagement is supposed to be one of convenience only, you and Max have been firm friends for years, and now you're well on the way to becoming fully-fledged lovers. You still have time on your side. I'm sure that Max will come to his senses and realize he's actually head-over-heels in love with you before the end of the Season."

"Oh, I hope so, Sophie. And I suppose, as they say, slow and steady wins the race. Max and I have come so far. I won't give up on him just yet."

Sophie smiled. "Good. Speaking of races, when will Max return to London?"

"The day after tomorrow." Max had quit London at first light to attend a race meeting in Suffolk the following day—the 1000 Guineas over the Ditch Mile in Newmarket. "He promised his mother that he'd be back in time for the opening of the Royal Academy Art Exhibition at Somerset House, so I trust he'll keep his word. Cressida is a trustee and expects both of us to attend." Charlie grimaced into her tea. "Lord knows why she wants me to go."

"Perhaps it's her way of making amends for leaking stories about you to the *Beau Monde Mirror*," suggested Sophie. "You mentioned Max had confronted her about that and she'd all but admitted that was the case."

"Perhaps…" Charlie wasn't convinced. She had an uneasy feeling that Cressida would still retaliate in some way, shape, or form. Donning a smile to hide her misgivings, she added, "In any case, I'm happy that Max was able to organize tickets for you, Nate, my father, and indeed, all of our friends to attend as well. It could prove to be quite an enjoyable event."

Sophie put down her cup of tea. "I, for one, am looking forward to it. I might not be able to paint to save myself, but I do appreciate a good work of art."

"That reminds me"—Charlie glanced up at the mantel clock—"we must be on our way, otherwise we'll be late for my appointment with Madame de Beauvoir."

"Oh, yes." Sophie dabbed at the corners of her mouth with her linen napkin, then rose to her feet. "I can't wait to see your finished portrait. I'm sure you look divine."

When the French artist unveiled Charlie's painting in her Half Moon Street studio a short time later, Charlie was genuinely pleased with the result. "You've made me look quite lovely, Madame de Beauvoir. As we agreed, it's tastefully licentious, yet there's still an element of mystery about it; the subject could be me, or it might be someone else entirely. It's perfect."

A bright smile broke across Madame de Beauvoir's face. "Oh, my lady. I am so happy to hear you approve. An unveiling is always so nerve-wracking."

"Lovely?" exclaimed Sophie. "It's more than lovely, Charlie. Your portrait is breathtaking. You could be Aphrodite."

"*Exactement.* The goddess of beauty, love, and passion. That is you, Lady Charlotte, with all of your exquisite curves and chestnut locks. All of the gentlemen of the ton should be falling at your feet, *mais non?*"

Charlie laughed. "Well, if I go out and about in a barely-there gown just like that, there's no doubt I'd be noticed."

Sophie nudged her and murmured, "Perhaps you should model a gown like that for Max."

"Hmm, now that's an idea," said Charlie.

Madame de Beauvoir clapped her paint-speckled hands together. "*Maintenant*, my lady, once the paint has finished drying—it will be ready in a few days—and after you've chosen a frame, I will have your completed portrait delivered to Hastings House, *oui?* Will that suit?"

"Yes, that would be wonderful," said Charlie. She had the perfect place to hang it in her bedchamber. No one but her closest confidantes would know that the "goddess" lifting the hem of her gown to dip her toes into the water was Lady Charlotte Hastings.

And as soon as her aunt Tabitha returned to Town, Charlie would give her the biggest hug for making her feel beautiful again. Although, truth to tell, it wasn't only the portrait that had helped to restore her flagging self-confidence.

Mostly, it was Max and the way he looked at her with desire in his eyes.

Hopefully, before too long, his gaze would also be filled with love.

After Charlie had chosen a delicately carved wooden frame covered in gold leaf, Madame de Beauvoir asked her and Sophie if they would be attending the Royal Academy's Art Exhibition.

"Why yes, we are," said Charlie. "And are you, Madame de Beauvoir?"

A delicate pink blush stained the French woman's cheeks. *"Mais oui,* I am, my lady. In fact, I submitted two paintings—a portrait of a young lady and a still life—and the Academy's council accepted both. It is the first time my work has ever been featured in such a prestigious exhibition, and I consider it a great honor."

"Oh, that's simply marvelous," declared Charlie. "I shall look out for them as soon as I arrive, then shamelessly boast to everyone within hearing distance that I know the extremely talented artist. And at the end of the event, we shall toast you with fine champagne."

Madame de Beauvoir's blush deepened. "You are too kind, my lady."

When Charlie and Sophie emerged onto Half Moon Street a short time later and began wending their way back to Berkeley Square, it began to rain. Edwards, who was trailing them, furnished them with umbrellas.

"Perhaps we should have taken my carriage," said Sophie as she side-stepped a puddle. The shower was growing heavier by the moment.

They'd just turned into Curzon Street. "If we pick up our pace, we'll be back at Hastings House within a few minutes," said Charlie. They paused on the pavement to wait for a hackney coach to splash by, and that's when Charlie felt a strange prickle at the back of her neck that had nothing to do with the cold rain. A few feet away, also pausing at the curb, was a man dressed all in black. His face was shielded by his beaver hat and his umbrella, but there was something about his manner that struck her as odd. Was he watching them? Or even worse, following them?

Another shiver slid down her spine. She was grateful she'd brought Edwards along. He might be young, but his height and the breadth of his shoulders were impressive. If the stranger *did* have a nefarious agenda, he'd keep his distance if he had any sense.

But then again, perhaps she was just being fanciful. Any man dressed all in black tended to remind her of Lord Rochfort. This man was definitely the wrong build —he was too short and narrow-shouldered to be the baron. And from what she'd glimpsed of his profile, he had a weak chin, so not like Rochfort at all, who was almost as square-jawed as Max.

Yes, this fellow was probably just a stranger going about his business, and there was nothing sinister going on at all.

Telling herself to stop being such a nervous ninny, Charlie crossed the street with Sophie, and in next to no time, they were back in Berkeley Square. As she gained the shelter of the portico of Hastings House, Charlie couldn't resist looking back over her shoulder.

There were several gentlemen in dark clothes with black umbrellas in the square, but through the veil of falling rain, it was impossible to tell if any of them might be the stranger that had made her feel uneasy. Curse Lord Rochfort—and yes, Cressida too—for making her as jumpy as a hunted hare. How horrible that she was so distrustful these days.

With a sigh, she entered Hastings House. One thing was certain, she wouldn't be going anywhere on her own for the foreseeable future. And the sooner Max returned to Town, the better. Whenever she was with him, she felt completely safe and at peace. In his arms, she'd found the home she never wished to leave.

Would that Max felt the same way about her.

∾

White's, St James's Street, London
May 1, 1819

The longcase clock in the corner of White's chimed the hour, ten o-clock, and Max had to stifle a yawn. Good God, he was tired. He'd only just arrived back in Town a few short hours ago, but when Hamish, who also lived in Grosvenor Square, had come knocking on his door, he'd decided to take the Scot up on his invitation to share a late evening supper with him and the rest of their friends at their favorite gentlemen's haunt.

"So, how did your horse go at Newmarket, Max?" Nate, lounging in a leather wingback chair in a quiet corner of the club, eyed him with interest over the rim of his coffee cup. "I haven't seen any of the results in the newspapers yet."

Max grimaced. "She came in fourth. The Duke of Grafton's filly, Catgut, came in first."

"Better luck next time," offered Gabriel as he plucked an oyster patty off the silver platter on the low oak table between them. "Actually, whenever you next head off to the races, whether it's Epsom Downs or Ascot—I can never recall what's next on the racing calendar—we should all make an occasion of it."

"That sounds like a braw idea. Count me in," agreed Hamish as he picked up his coffee.

"Excellent," said Max. It was only after he'd taken a sip of his brandy that he realized he was the only one who was imbibing alcohol. Good Lord, how times had changed. "I'll let you know my plans once I've consulted my head trainer," he added. "To be honest, I've been a bit distracted of late…"

Damn, why did he have to say that? Now Nate was pinning him with a gimlet-eyed stare. Guilt pinched inside Max's chest, and he took another sip of brandy. While he hated the fact that he'd broken his promise to Nate and hadn't stayed away from Charlie, he also didn't regret any of the things he and Charlie had done together over the last little while. A man would have to be a bloody monk or pushing up daisies to not act on his desire for a woman like her. Lady Charlotte Hastings was, in a word, stupendous. And if he wasn't so damaged inside, they'd probably be married already.

To cover his verbal blunder—Nate's glower was growing darker by the second—he ventured, "Before I came here, I had a meeting with Hunt, my inquiry agent. As you know, he's been looking into Juno Press—the publisher that prints the *Beau Monde Mirror*—and its parent company, Fortuna Trading. And he discovered something that really shouldn't have come as any surprise to me..." He caught the gazes of each of his friends. "It appears that one of Rochfort's close business associates has shares in the company."

"What? Rotten Rochfort's friend owns the *Beau Monde Mirror*?" said Gabriel.

"Well, technically he's only a part-owner. But yes, it would seem so."

"That explains a lot, then," said Nate. "Part of me wishes you'd put down the dog on Hampstead Heath when you had the chance. If the case had been tried in the House of Lords, your peers would've let you off."

"No doubt," said Hamish. The light in his one good eye was as hard as flint. "If I'd been in Town when you'd challenged the cur to a duel, I would have gladly gone in your stead. Rochfort still hasn't paid enough for all of the pain he put Euphemia Harrington through. The way he extorted her jewels and townhouse from her and forced her into penury..." He shook his head, his expression grim. No doubt he was imagining how he would end the baron by cleaving him in two with a broadsword, or better yet, gutting him with a blunt dirk.

"That reminds me," said Max. "My man of affairs has been working behind the scenes too. Using a third party, he's managed to purchase Euphemia's townhouse on my behalf. I have the deed and intend on returning it to her. I'm not sure if she'll want to come back to London while Rochfort is still about, but at least her property is hers again to do with as she pleases."

"That's very generous of you," said Hamish. "She was

my mistress, and her wee daughter, Tilda, was my ward for a while, so I'd be happy to share the cost."

Max waved a hand. "Think nothing of it, my friend. I'm happy to right an egregious wrong. We'll consider it a case of *noblesse oblige*. Mia Harrington is a housekeeper at one of my Devonshire properties, after all."

Talk turned to parliamentary and business matters, and while Max enjoyed his friends' company, his gaze kept straying to the longcase clock across the room every now and again. While he was genuinely exhausted from the events of the last few days—the traveling to and from Suffolk and the race meeting itself—he couldn't deny he was chafing at the bit to see Charlie. But he couldn't very well turn up at Hastings House at half past ten in the evening, demanding to see his fiancée. Not without creating a stir.

When Nate, Hamish, and Gabriel all decided to call an end to the evening a short time later, Max was green with envy. They were all returning home to their beds, which were no doubt being kept warm by their respective wives, whereas he was going home alone. Before he and Charlie had entered into their faux engagement, it was likely that he would have ended up visiting another gentlemen's establishment like the Pandora Club or the Rouge et Noir Club, or some other back-alley gaming hell. But now, such places held little appeal.

After farewelling Gabriel—he lived close by in St James's Square—Hamish hailed a hackney coach, and Max, still unaccountably disgruntled, climbed inside with Nate and the Scotsman.

He wanted… Damn it, he wanted to be with Charlie. Although he'd only been absent from London a few days, he'd be lying to himself if he didn't admit that he'd missed her. Her smile, her conversation, her lovely face. Her kisses…

But he had no right to call upon her at this hour. Lord Westhampton would no doubt send him away with a flea in his ear, and if Nate found out that he'd paid a late-night visit to Berkeley Square, he'd be a dead man—so he'd best go home and get a good night's sleep.

Perhaps tomorrow he'd take Charlie for a jaunt about Hyde Park. But snatched kisses behind hedges wouldn't be satisfying for either of them, and he couldn't very well throw another house party in the middle of the Season.

At least he'd be spending an inordinate amount of time in Charlie's company the following day, when he was due to escort her to the opening of the Royal Academy's Annual Art Exhibition. But they wouldn't be alone. Half of the ton would be there.

Bloody blazing hell. No wonder couples eloped to Gretna Green with such frequency.

But unless he could tell Charlie that he loved her, she wouldn't marry him. Whether it was over the anvil or in St. George's in Hanover Square, it wouldn't make a difference—her answer to the question, "Will you take this man to be your lawfully wedded husband?" would be a resounding "No."

And Max couldn't say that he blamed her.

CHAPTER 23

Have you secured your tickets to the opening of
the Royal Academy of Art's Annual Exhibition at
Somerset House?
As Sir Francis Bacon proclaimed, *"Painting raises
the Mind, by accommodating the images of things to
our desires..."*
The Beau Monde Mirror: The Fine Arts

**The Royal Academy of Art, Somerset House, The Strand
May 3, 1819**

"Good gracious, it's quite a crush, isn't it?" remarked
Sophie to Charlie as they waited in the grand hall
of Somerset House. Marble arches, colonnades, and several well-rendered sculptures dominated the space. From
a niche in a nearby wall, a Callipygian Venus stared over
her shoulder at them.

Charlie couldn't disagree. "Climbing the stairs will be
an interesting exercise." The magnificent, dizzying spiral
staircase led to the Great Room, the Royal Academy's
main exhibition gallery, in the palace's north wing. "I
hope we don't all end up tumbling back down like in
Thomas Rowlandson's naughty print, *The Stare-Case*. I
came here to see paintings, not tonnish derrieres."

Beside her, Max chuckled. "Well, that would certainly
be a sight. But don't worry, my lady. I'll catch you if you

fall." And then he whispered, "I'd much prefer it if I was the only one permitted to see your delightful derriere."

Charlie bit her lip as warmth flooded her face. Thank goodness no one near them—especially Nate—heard that particular remark. As much as she wanted to respond in kind, she thought it best to remain on her best behavior. For the first time in a long time, it seemed no one was looking askance at her as though she didn't belong. On arrival at Somerset House with Nate and Sophie, several matrons of the ton had even greeted her with genuine smiles.

In an effort to steer the conversation in a different direction, she said, "I take it your mother is already here?"

"I believe so," said Max. "Diana is with her. Knowing my mother, I imagine she arrived early and is upstairs in the Great Room making sure everything is 'just so'. If she hadn't contributed such a sizable donation to the Academy, I'm sure the porters and the Academy council members would have ejected her by now."

"My father and Lady Tilbury could be somewhere here too, but who would know?" remarked Charlie. She stood on tiptoe and craned her neck but could discern nothing but a sea of anonymous heads. "And Madame de Beauvoir. I cannot wait to get my hands on a catalogue so I can find out where her paintings are being exhibited."

Max cocked an eyebrow. "Madame de Beauvoir?"

"Oh, yes…" Charlie hesitated as the crowd of tonnish members moved forward, and she lifted her blue silk muslin skirts to negotiate the stairs. "Louise de Beauvoir is an accomplished French artist I met at the Mayfair Bluestocking Society some time ago. My aunt Tabitha…" She paused again. Should she tell Max about her own licentious portrait? The whole of London already knew the 'disreputable Lady C.' aspired to sit for one *à la* Lady Hamilton. He was bound to find out sooner rather than later that such a painting actually existed. Drawing a fortifying breath, she completed her thought. "My aunt commissioned Madame de Beauvoir to paint a portrait of me. It's only just been completed and will be delivered to Hastings House within the next few days."

Max leaned close and murmured, "I can't wait to see it. I'm sure you look beautiful."

Heat crept into Charlie's cheeks, a heat that had nothing to do with the exertion of climbing the stairs. "I...I like to think so. But the nature of the painting is such that..." She met Max's gaze. "It's a little *risqué*, so I'll be hanging it in my bedchamber."

Mischief danced in Max's blue eyes. "Even better. I take it this is the painting you mention in your list?"

Charlie couldn't help but laugh. "How did you ever guess?"

Max cast her an enigmatic smile. "I wonder."

By the time they reached the top of the stairs, Charlie was hot and alarmingly breathless, whereas Max didn't seem flustered at all. "Look up," he said, pointing to the doorway leading into the high-ceilinged Great Room.

"Is that ancient Greek?" asked Charlie. She couldn't read the inscription carved into the marble archway, but she thought she recognized the script.

"Yes, it is," said Max. "It reads, 'Let no stranger to the muses enter'."

"Well, that's quite apt, if I do say so myself." She gave Max a little nudge in the ribs. "I see that classical education you received at Eton and Oxford is useful for something."

Max laughed. "Yes, indeed. It also comes in handy when one needs to count to ten in Latin or recite pi or Newton's Laws of Motion."

"And you've had occasion to do any of those things of late?" asked Charlie.

Max flashed her a wicked grin. "You'd be surprised, my lady."

They joined the milling throng gathered inside the Great Room, and somehow Max located the rest of their friends in a far corner—Arabella was resting upon a chair that Gabriel had managed to procure for her, and Hamish and Olivia were examining a Highland landscape featuring the distinctive castle of Dunrobin. Sophie already had a catalogue, which she was perusing with Nate.

There was no sign of her own father, Cressida, Diana, or Madame de Beauvoir.

"It looks as though Madame de Beauvoir's paintings are in the adjoining gallery to our right," said Sophie when Charlie drew close. "They're labeled *A Study of Fruit and Flowers* and *Portrait of a Young Lady*."

"I'm glad," said Charlie. "It's almost impossible to view anything at eye level with so many people about. And the way the paintings are all wedged together, cheek by jowl, floor to ceiling…" She tipped her head back and squinted up at a portrait of an officious-looking nobleman hanging high above their heads, just below one of the gallery's distinctive arched windows. "One would need a spyglass to see anything up there."

"I agree," said Max. "I'd hoped to catch a glimpse of Cooper's *The Battle of Marston Moor*, but I suspect that won't happen. Nothing less than a cavalry charge could penetrate this crowd."

"Let's repair to the next room to see if we can find Madame de Beauvoir's work," suggested Charlie. She caught Arabella's eye, and she and Gabriel readily agreed to her proposal. Olivia and Hamish did too.

With Hamish leading the way—the Scotsman was not only tall but as broad-shouldered as a Highland warrior of old—they soon plowed their way into the next gallery, which was far less busy. The artworks had been hung at regular intervals rather than crammed together, and apart from a sizable party gathered in front of a painting at the far end, one didn't need to fight for elbow room. All in all, it was far more civilized.

"Charlie!"

At the sound of her name being called, Charlie turned and came face-to-face with Diana. The young duchess's smile seemed forced, and her gaze darted nervously to Max, then back to Charlie. "I'm so pleased that I've found you both at last. Perhaps you'd like to accompany me into the next exhibition room? There are some wonderful landscapes. One depicts a moonlit bay in Devon, Max, so I'm sure you'd be interested in that."

Charlie frowned, confused by Diana's apparent need

to hurry her and Max along. "That sounds lovely. However, I'd really like to see the work of an acquaintance of mine. According to the Exhibition catalogue, her paintings are on display in here."

Olivia, who was only a few feet away with Arabella and Sophie, called over her shoulder. "I...I think I've found her still life, Charlie. It's lovely."

"Oh, wonderful." Charlie joined her friends and agreed with Olivia's summation. Madame de Beauvoir had depicted an arrangement of pale apricot roses and just-ripe peaches with great skill. There were dewdrops on the velvety, softly tinted petals, and the flesh of one cut peach looked so juicy, Charlie's mouth began to water.

Max drew alongside her. "I have a sudden craving for peaches and cream," he murmured.

Charlie laughed. "Me too."

A sudden burst of tittering laughter on the other side of the room drew Charlie's attention. Several of the women who were clustered around the farthest painting were looking back at her with something akin to scorn in their gazes.

Oh, damn, damn, and damn again. Charlie recognized more than a few of them.

It was Lady Penelope surrounded by a bevy of her equally unpleasant friends. No wonder Diana had been trying to steer Charlie away.

Max, who'd tucked her hand into the crook of his arm, must have sensed the tension vibrating through her body. "What is it—" he began, then uttered a crude curse under his breath. "My apologies," he murmured to Charlie. "I shouldn't have said that."

Charlie couldn't suppress a smile. "I'm glad you did, because it summed up my thoughts exactly."

Sophie tapped a finger on a line in her Exhibition catalogue. "According to this, Madame de Beauvoir's second piece, the portrait, is just over—" Looking up, her gaze settled on Lady Penelope and her snidely giggling cohorts. "Oh..."

Arabella looked over the top of her spectacles, then

lifted her chin. "Come, girls. We are the Society for Enlightened Young Women. We will not be intimidated by the likes of Lady Penelope. We have just as much right to view that painting as anyone else." Squaring her shoulders, she tucked her hand into her husband's arm and sauntered down the room.

"Shall we?" Olivia took Hamish's hand.

The Highlander grinned. "Aye, we shall, my bonnie wife."

"Come, Nate," said Sophie, linking arms with her husband. "Let's not miss out on all the fun."

Max and Charlie followed their friends with a subdued Diana trailing behind.

"The Society for Enlightened Young Women?" murmured Max as they progressed down the gallery, weaving their way through knots of other art-loving attendees. "Why have I not heard of this group before?"

Charlie gave him an arch smile. "A girl must have some secrets, Your Grace. It adds to our allure."

Max bent toward her ear. "Allure is a quality you are *not* lacking in whatsoever, Lady Char—"

He stopped mid-word as he caught sight of the gilt-framed portrait hanging before them.

And then Charlie's heart all but stopped and her stomach tumbled to the floor as her gaze fell on it too. Someone nearby gasped. A man—perhaps it was Nate —swore.

Oh, my God. No.

A hundred thousand times no.

Why on earth was *her* painting—her *privately commissioned* portrait meant for her eyes only—on show at the Royal Academy of Arts Annual Exhibition? Her scantily clad, curvaceous body on display for complete strangers to gawk at and judge and laugh at? Because there *was* laughter all around her. Snickers and outright chortles among the sea of scandalized whispers.

While the face of the nubile Grecian goddess was partially concealed by a curtain of chestnut curls, there was no mistaking the true identity of the woman in the portrait. Because the plaque beneath the painting wasn't inscribed with the words, *Portrait of a Young Lady*.

No, it read, *Portrait of a Disreputable Debutante*.

And *everyone* knew who that was.

It could only be Lady Charlotte Hastings.

Fast. Loose. Hoyden. Slut.

Whore.

The horrible words echoed in Charlie's ears, and she wasn't sure if it was her imagination that had conjured them up or not.

How could this have happened? How could Madame de Beauvoir have betrayed her like this? And it seemed Diana had known too…

The surge of pain, the shame, it was too much.

Hot tears pricked at Charlie's eyes, and her throat constricted with the effort to contain a sob. Suffocating humiliation squeezed her chest and time seemed to freeze. Stuck in a nightmarish moment, all sound bar her own ragged breathing and the erratic, stumbling beat of her heart faded away.

All she could see was her complete and utter ruin. Her reputation smashed beyond repair.

If she could have curled up into a small ball on the floor, she would have.

"Charlie…" Max was in front of her, blocking her view of her own portrait. "It's all right. Hamish has taken it down."

"And Gabriel has thrown his coat over it." That was Arabella. "No one can see it anymore."

"Good," Charlie said through stiff, numb lips. She didn't feel like herself at all. A strange buzzing began in her ears, and the room started spinning. Spots danced in the corners of her vision…

And then Max, just as he'd promised earlier, caught her as she began to fall.

CHAPTER 24

My List of Secret Wishes and Dreams:
1) ~~Sneak into a 'Gentlemen's Club' to see what all the fuss is about;~~
2) ~~To be kissed, with passion, in the moonlight by a rake;~~
3) ~~Or in the rain (either will do);~~
4) ~~Ride hell-for-leather down Rotten Row at least once (Preferably not in the rain unless there's any chance said passionate kiss happens straight afterwards.);~~
5) Sea bathe, naked;
6) ~~Sit for a licentious portrait à la Lady Hamilton;~~
7) ~~To be thoroughly ravished in a carriage;~~
8) ~~Waltz the night away at Almack's;~~
9) ~~To experience a Grand Passion that I will remember long into my dotage;~~
10) The man (or should I say duke?) of my dreams falls in love with me.

Somewhere in London...

It wasn't until they were safely in Max's carriage that Charlie began to stir. Cradled in Max's arms, she made a small sound like a whimper and buried her face deeper into his shoulder. Beneath his coat, one of her hands curled around his waist.

"Charlie?" Max gently brushed a loose curl away from

her cheek and tucked it behind her ear. "Can you hear me, sweetheart?"

"Mmmm…" Her eyelids fluttered, and when she opened her eyes, he saw the moment she recalled what had happened inside the Royal Academy. As horror dawned in her gaze, a shiver passed through her and she snapped her eyes shut again. "Oh God," she moaned against his chest. "I'm so embarrassed I could die."

"I'd rather you didn't." Reaching inside his coat, he located an inner pocket and withdrew a pewter flask. "A sip or two of this might make you feel a little better, though. It's my very best cognac."

"Oh yes, please." Charlie accepted the offered flask, uncapped it, and took a delicate sip. And then another. Handing it back to him, she caught his eye. "Thank you. For everything. I feel so foolish. I'm not normally one to faint."

"I know you're not. And think nothing of it. You had a large shock, and that room was insufferably hot and stuffy on top of everything else."

A ghost of a smile tugged at the corner of her lovely mouth. "You always know what to say to make me feel better," she said softly. Her fingertips absently traced a whorled pattern in his paisley satin waistcoat. Her forehead had pleated into a frown. "Though, I would understand if you need to reconsider our mutually-beneficial-fixed-term arrangement in light of what's happened. I'm afraid my reputation is ruined beyond repair at this point. I'm well and truly a social pariah."

"Good God, Charlie. Of course, I don't want to end our arrangement." He tilted her chin up to meet his gaze. "I'm not going anywhere."

She nodded and her eyes brimmed with tears. "Thank you. That means a lot."

Max gently wiped away an escaped tear with his thumb. "Hey, there. No crying is allowed in my carriage. Not unless you're crying my name."

She laughed at that and accepted a kerchief from him. "I like the sound of that."

"So do I." He nodded toward Charlie's portrait, which was currently leaning against the opposite seat with Gabriel's coat still draped over it. "I also like your portrait. Very much." He cupped her jaw and stroked his thumb over her cheek again. "You're beautiful, Charlie. Don't let what happened back there ever make you doubt yourself or how I—" He'd been about to say, "how I feel about you," but he couldn't say that because he didn't know how he felt.

Or did he?

His chest cramped with an odd combination of regret and acute longing. And a surge of protectiveness so fierce, it chased away the bone-deep fear that he might feel anything remotely tender for the remarkable woman in his arms.

When he didn't continue, Charlie ventured, "I just don't understand how my portrait ended up at the Exhibition. I trusted Madame de Beauvoir implicitly. I can't fathom why she'd betray me like that. It doesn't make sense."

Max scowled out the window. The light was fading in London's streets, and the gas lamps were in the process of being lit. "I suspect my mother is behind it. For some time now, it's been clear that she's determined to drive a wedge between us. Aside from that, she's one of the Academy's trustees, so she had the means and opportunity to engineer the situation. Her absence at the Exhibition is rather telling too."

Charlie shook her head. "I don't know why she hates me so much. I know I'm not perfect—"

Max growled. "Don't you dare say anything disparaging about yourself, Charlotte Hastings. I won't have it. Do you understand me?"

She nodded, and he softened his tone. "I'm sorry. I just don't like seeing you so upset. And all because of my witch of a mother."

Charlie sighed. "I really have no idea how she learned about the painting's existence to begin with. While I'd mentioned my desire to sit for one on my not-so-secret list, that didn't mean I had actually gone through with it."

Even though he didn't want to think his mother would stoop so low, it was clear that she had. "Perhaps she's been having you followed, Charlie. You would have visited the artist's studio on more than one occasion, no? And I suspect she either bribed or coerced Madame de Beauvoir into handing over your portrait. The fact that there was a gilt plaque inscribed with something other than *Portrait of a Young Lady* indicates this abominable scheme to denigrate you was definitely—and quite cold-bloodedly—premeditated."

Charlie's frown was back. "Last time I visited Madame de Beauvoir—five days ago—I did notice a man in Half Moon Street who made me feel odd. He didn't do anything that was overtly sinister. There was just something about him... I thought I was being fanciful, but perhaps I wasn't."

"You should always trust your instincts. In any case, I intend to find out exactly what my mother has done. And there will be a full accounting for her actions. If she is indeed responsible, she will not get away with this. This time, she's gone too far."

They lapsed into silence for a short time with Charlie still snuggled against Max's chest. Indeed, Max had begun to suspect she'd fallen asleep until she suddenly stiffened and sat bolt upright. "Oh, God. My portrait will be talked about in the *Beau Monde Mirror*, won't it?"

"No, it won't."

"How can you be so sure?"

"Because right before I spirited you away in my carriage, your brother, Gabriel, and Hamish decided that they would visit the offices of Juno Press to have a word with Mr. Erasmus Silver. I'm certain the sight of three fuming noblemen and the threat of being sued within an inch of his life will be enough to ensure the editor doesn't print one word about your painting."

"I can't say I feel sorry for Mr. Silver," said Charlie. "And words cannot express how relieved I am, even though I'm still hideously embarrassed. Thank heavens my father wasn't there." Charlie's gaze shifted to the carriage window and the snarls of traffic beyond. "Where are we going, by the way?"

"Exmoor House." Max held his breath as he waited for her reaction.

"Oh…" Charlie's cheeks pinkened, and she bit her lip.

"If you'd rather not, I'm quite happy to take you back to Hastings House, or wherever you want to go, in fact. I presumed… Actually, if I'm being perfectly honest, my first instinct was to take you somewhere safe. My home seemed like the logical choice."

Charlie lifted her gaze. A shy smile lit her eyes. "Of course I want to spend time alone with you at Exmoor House—and I would feel safe there—only…" A small line appeared between her brows. "What will Nate say? And everybody else if they find out?"

"At this point, I don't give a jot about anyone else's views, and that includes your brother's," said Max, perhaps a little too gruffly. With an effort, he gentled his tone. "However, I will send word to your family that you will be staying with me this evening and that my sister-in-law will be chaperoning. They can hardly take issue with that."

"No." Charlie arched a brow. "But Diana won't be chaperoning, will she?"

"No, she won't, but they won't know that. And I'm certain Diana will lie for us if anyone asks. I'm not sure what her role in this whole mess is, but I would be very surprised if she was my mother's co-conspirator. She doesn't strike me as the duplicitous type."

"Yes, I agree. In fact, I've always thought that she quite liked me. And this afternoon, she did try to steer us away from the end of the gallery where my portrait was on display. Perhaps in her mind, she was trying to spare me the pain of being publicly humiliated."

"No doubt we will find out in due course," said Max. "But not tonight." He didn't want to talk about Nate Hastings or his mother or sister-in-law anymore. Not when he had Charlie in his arms and all to himself. Leaning in, he whispered against the delicate shell of her ear, "Tonight I have other plans. Plans that involve discovering just how well all of your delectable curves have been captured on canvas." He brushed his lips over hers in a teasing kiss. "I think a thorough study of both the painting and the subject are in order, don't you?"

Charlie's answering kiss full of heat and fervor was all the confirmation he needed that she was in complete agreement.

∾

Exmoor House, Grosvenor Square

S he *must* be dreaming. Any moment, she'd wake up. Charlie surreptitiously pinched the inside of her wrist as she sank onto the settee before the fire in Max's sumptuous bedchamber. She couldn't believe they were actually alone. And it had been Max's idea to invite her here.

For once, she hadn't had to barge her way in.

The candles and firelight illuminated the room with a soft golden glow, and the gilt frame of her portrait gleamed as Max placed it carefully on the marble mantelpiece between two Ming vases.

"Gorgeous," he murmured before turning back to face her. His smile was warm as he added, "Can I get you anything? A tray from the kitchen if you're hungry, or a brandy, perhaps?"

Charlie donned a smile and smoothed her silk muslin skirts over her lap with damp palms. "A brandy would be lovely." She was too excited to eat. Or was it nervousness that was making her feel so odd?

She watched Max as he removed his coat, then proceeded to pour two sizable nips into crystal tumblers. Could he tell that she was suddenly a little jumpy? Indeed, she felt as flighty as a bride on her wedding night. Her cheeks were hot, and her stomach was awhirl with butterflies. Even her pulse was racing. Thanks to Max and his boundless understanding, she'd managed to temporarily shrug off the cloak of shame this afternoon's horrid events had forced upon her. No, the fact that she'd been publicly torn to shreds again wasn't responsible for her current state of uneasiness.

She had a confession to make, one that she probably should have made weeks ago. One that she could have made in the carriage on the way here, when she'd told Max she would understand if he wanted to end things. But at that particular moment, she hadn't the nerve to go through with it.

Yes, she definitely needed a strong drink to gird her loins and loosen her tongue.

When she had her brandy in hand and Max had stretched out on the seat beside her, she took a large sip, welcoming the sting of the fiery liquor as it burned a trail down her throat.

Max reached out and wrapped one of her curls that had come loose around his finger. "Are you all right, Charlie? Whatever happens this evening is completely up to you. We can simply talk. I can even take you home. I have no agenda other than to make you happy."

Oh, goodness. Why did he have to be so sweet? In some ways, his supportive words made it even harder for her to say what needed to be said. She swallowed a little more brandy, then put down her glass on a nearby side table. "Max..." She took one of his strong hands in hers and absently traced a fingertip over the outline of his long, elegant bones. "I have to tell you something. Something else that's quite shameful. I probably should have mentioned this to you a while ago, but in all honesty, I was never sure that we'd reach the point we are at tonight."

Concern flickered in his deep blue eyes. "I don't think there's anything you could say that would make me think less of you, if that's what you're concerned about."

She blew out a sigh. "You haven't heard it yet. Even though I've admitted to you that I know more than a young lady of my station *should* know about sexual congress, I've never fully explained why that might be the case. You're not a fool, by any means, and you may have had suspicions all along..."

"Go on," he said gently.

There was no judgment in his gaze. No censure. He was simply waiting for her to continue. She inhaled a steadying breath. Ignoring the rapid pounding of her heart, she met his gaze. "I'm…I'm not a virgin."

Max smiled, and she knew everything would be all right. "Neither am I," he said. "Has that ever made you think less of me?"

"No, of course not. But you know it's different for young women. We're supposed to remain chaste until we are wed. We agreed that it would be my decision whether to end our engagement or to wed at the end of the Season. But in light of my confession—now that you know the truth—I would understand completely if you did want to end things sooner rather than later because of my lack of honesty. Not only is my reputation in tatters, my virtue isn't intact. I am thoroughly disreputable to my very bones. So, perhaps your mother is right after all. For many reasons, I'm not the sort of wife a person like you— a duke—needs in his life."

"Charlie, I think it would be entirely hypocritical of me to judge you. What you've just told me doesn't alter my regard for you. My esteem for you isn't diminished."

"Are you certain?"

"Absolutely. And even though I might not be your first lover"—his mouth kicked into a rakish smile—"I hope I'll be your most memorable."

Lover… The word was like a double-edged sword. It thrilled Charlie and made her heart ache at the same time. Of course, she wanted to be *more* than Max's lover. She wanted his love too. But she wouldn't spoil tonight with useless longing. She'd already experienced too much anguish today. Tonight—this opportunity to be with Max, to share his bed—it would be enough.

"What are you thinking?" he asked, his voice low and soft. A beguiling, irresistible nudge.

She gave a little laugh. "To be perfectly honest, I'm thinking how truly awkward my first time was. And it was memorable for all of the *wrong* reasons."

Max's brows plunged into a frown. "The cad didn't force you, did he?"

"Oh, no, nothing like that. It was a mutual attraction, and he had a particularly nice smile. I was seventeen and he…he was the nineteen-year-old son of a local squire whose property adjoins Elmstone Hall. Anyway, my father holds a harvest feast every year to thank Elmstone's farmhands and villagers for all their hard work, and this fellow and I, we both had too much cider. One thing led to another, as things do, and we ended up in one of Elmstone's stables in the loft. There was a lot of straw, and dust got up my nose. And then, while he was undoing my bodice, I sneezed and bumped his head. Even though he got a nosebleed, we were undeterred. But no sooner had he…" She reached for her brandy and took a sip. It was probably best to skip over the mechanics. Max would know what she meant. "I was worried he might lose control," she said. "So, I made him withdraw before he was done. The last thing I wanted to do was get with child. But I think it was his first time too, and he spent all over my legs and skirts. All in all"—she grimaced—"it was sticky and messy and uncomfortable and altogether unsatisfying. In hindsight, I was foolish and reckless and shouldn't have done it. But…" She bit her lip.

But I did it because I was trying not to think about you anymore, Max, the unattainable golden-haired Adonis of my dreams.

She released a sigh and raised her gaze to Max's face. "You're actually the first person I've ever told about this. Sophie, Arabella, and Olivia don't even know. Nor my Aunt Tabitha."

"I shall keep your secret," said Max, his expression solemn. "I'm honored you felt comfortable enough to share it with me. And I can assure you"—he reached for her glass and placed it on the table again—"that you won't be left unsatisfied tonight. Or have to worry about me losing control. This will be all about your pleasure, Charlie. I'll make this night unforgettable for all of the right reasons."

He framed her face in his hands and captured her mouth with his, kissing her with slow, deliberate purpose as though his only agenda *was* to give her pleasure, just as he'd promised. Tipping her head back with one hand, he plundered her mouth with his tongue, licking and tasting. Stroking deep. The fingers of his other hand caressed a teasing path down her neck before roaming across her shoulder, then lower to torment one of her breasts. Her nipple was already a taut peak straining toward his touch through all the layers of her clothes, and he made her harder, circling her with his thumb.

Charlie tangled her fingers in his hair, kissing him back with equal ardor. When he slid his mouth to her neck and pushed her gown away from her shoulder so he could devour her with feverish, open-mouthed kisses, she couldn't contain a moan. Dear God, he was wonderful. She had no doubts that he would make this experience good for her.

But when his mouth skated back to her ear and he whispered, "I think it's time to see what treasures you're hiding beneath that gown, don't you?" Charlie stiffened. Her hands slid to Max's chest as though part of her meant to push him away.

Oh, she was such a contrary ninny. Max was utterly perfect, and she couldn't wait to share all of herself with him. But what would he think of her nude body when she unveiled herself? She knew he would say complimentary things about her curvaceous figure, but would he really mean them?

Perhaps that was why she suddenly felt so skittish again; her lack of self-confidence about her appearance was, and had always been, at the back of her mind. It was the sole reason for her apprehension right now.

When she found her voice, it was obvious that she was more than a little nervous. "I… About that…"

Max pulled back and frowned down at her. "I'm going too fast for you, aren't I?"

She winced. "A little. Which is completely foolish of me, considering everything we've already done together. And of course, this isn't my first time, so I have some idea of what to expect. Although it *was* five years ago and hardly ideal… Oh, Lord. I'm so sorry. I'm babbling and ruining the moment."

"You have nothing to be sorry about, Charlie. Actually, I should apologize to you if you in any way feel like I'm putting pressure on you. I don't want to scare you with the strength of my desire. We can go as slowly as you want. Or we can stop altogether. It's up to you, sweetheart. We won't do anything that you don't feel comfortable with."

"Oh, I want to be with you. That's not the problem." Charlie worried at her lower lip and glanced up at the painting on the mantel shelf. It was time for her to be candid about this issue too. "To be perfectly frank, now that the moment has finally arrived and we can make love without being interrupted, I seem to be suffering from an unaccountable attack of stage fright. I'm…" She met Max's concerned gaze again. "I'm nervous about disrobing in front of you. You see, the reason I sat for that portrait to begin with is that I gained a few pounds over Christmastide and was feeling less than attractive. My aunt Tabitha, God bless her, suggested that I have my portrait painted. She wanted me to see myself in a new light."

Charlie nodded at the painting again. "And I can see that my likeness is appealing to the eye. Only…" She sighed. "I'm not at all slender like all of my gorgeous friends. Or dare I say it, like Lady Penelope. I'm decidedly Rubenesque. And although you've seen 'bits' of me, so to speak, it's always been at night in a darkened carriage. Not in a room like this that's alight with firelight and candles. I'm…I'm worried you'll find the real flesh-and-blood Charlotte Hastings wanting."

Max caressed her cheek, his fingers gentle. "Charlie, I've always found you desirable. And there's no doubt in my mind that I'll find you just as beautiful without clothes. But I want you to set the pace. Make all the rules. We can snuff out all the candles. We can remove every single stitch of our clothing or stay dressed. All I ask is that you tell me what you want or don't want. Will you promise to do that for me?"

She nodded, and a wave of heat and delicious anticipation shimmered over her, washing away the last remnants of her hesitation. "Yes, I will, Max," she murmured huskily. This time her voice was breathless with desire and excitement, nothing more.

≈

E ven though lust hurtled through his veins, making him as randy as a buck at the height of rutting season, Max silently vowed not to rush this experience. For Charlie, he would go slowly and take care. And as much as he wanted to worship her naked body with his eyes as well as his hands and mouth, Max meant every word he'd just said. It was up to Charlie to decide what they would do next. Although he did have one suggestion…

He smoothed an errant curl away from her flushed cheek. "There is one thing *I've* always wanted to do though. If you'll let me."

Her kiss-swollen lips, as ripe and red as summer plums, curved into a smile. "And what's that?"

"I've always dreamed of letting down your glorious hair…watching it fall about your shoulders. Would that be all right with you?"

"Of course." She turned on the settee, presenting her back to him. "Go ahead. Although, my maid uses far too many pins, so it might take you half the night."

"I don't mind at all." Max's fingers were already in her thick chestnut tresses, carefully feeling for hairpins in the intricately coiled mass at the back of her head. Slowly but surely, he loosened her curls until they tumbled down her back, reminding him of a fiery, autumnal waterfall. Leaning forward, he pressed his face against her shoulder, inhaling the sweet floral scent of her. "Beautiful," he murmured. Pushing the silken mass of her hair aside, he lavished the delicate column of her throat with kisses.

Charlie shivered and leaned back against him. His hands skated up her rib cage but paused just below her breasts. "Tell me what you want next," he said in a low, soft voice against her ear. "I'm yours to command, my lady."

"I want…I need to be closer to you, Max," she whispered. To his astonishment, she shifted and turned. Lifting up her skirts, she straddled him, just like she'd done at the Rouge et Noir Club all those weeks ago.

Dear God. Charlie's delightfully deep cleavage was right in front of his face, and her skirts and petticoats were rucked up around her knees, revealing her silk stockings and their delicate blue-ribbon garters. Max already had a fearsome cockstand, but the sight of Charlie positioned upon his lap with her legs spread wide almost had him spending right then and there in his trousers.

He gripped her waist to stop himself from doing anything that she didn't want, like burying his face between her breasts or sliding his fingers up her inner thigh to find the soft curls hiding her sex. With an effort, he strove to keep his voice light as he said, "What next?"

She sank her teeth into her lip and looked up at him through the dark fan of her lashes. "Even though I have qualms about removing my own clothes, would you consider taking off your waistcoat and shirt, Max? You haven't minded going shirtless in front of me before. As far as I can tell."

He grinned. "Gladly." While he loosened his cravat and his collar, Charlie applied herself to the task of undoing his waistcoat buttons. When she pulled his shirt from the waistband of his trousers, her fingertips grazed his hips, and his flesh jumped at the contact.

"Are you ticklish down there, Max?" she asked with a coquettish smile.

"Perhaps…" He tossed his cravat on the floor and undid his cuffs. "You'll have to excuse me while I sit forward to remove the rest."

"I don't mind at all," she said, so he arched his back, shrugged out of his waistcoat, then tugged his shirt over his head. Both garments landed on the floor unheeded.

Leaning back, Max took pleasure in watching Charlie's gaze roam over his nakedness. The way her eyes had darkened and the fact she was biting her lip again was making him harder than an iron rod. "Well, my lady. What do you think?" he asked with a deliberately wicked smile. He was a keen Corinthian, and he knew that he was lean and particularly well-muscled. In the past, other women had always been complimentary about his appearance. But their opinions no longer mattered. Only Charlie's did, and he burned to know if she really did find him attractive too.

"I…" A blush flooded her cheeks. "I think you are the perfect male specimen," she murmured huskily.

He caught her chin lightly and captured her gaze. "Thank you." His voice was gentle yet solemn. "My male pride is definitely appeased, but I assure you that I'm not perfect. You've seen my damaged foot. And I have scars on various parts of my person. My left arm and my lower back." *And then there are the scars on my frostbitten heart…*

Charlie splayed her fingers over his bare chest. "They don't matter to me, Max. You're beautiful."

"And that's how I feel about you," he said softly. "I adore your wild hair and your abundant curves." His hands, curled about her waist, slid to her hips. "How lush and ripe you feel beneath my palms. You're beautiful to me because you're Charlie. You're not like anyone else. And it's you that I want…only you." Plunging his fingers into the silky hair at her nape, he straightened a little until they were chest to chest. Mouth to mouth. "This yearning, this burning and overwhelming need to have you, I've tried to deny it, but I can't. Not any longer. No one else will do."

He wasn't sure who moved first, but in the next instant, he and Charlie were kissing hungrily, like both of them were starving and couldn't get enough of each other. Frantically tasting and licking and devouring.

And Charlie's hands, they were everywhere. In his hair. Kneading his shoulders. Sliding over his biceps and the hard wall of his chest. Across his torso, tracing his ribs, making his heated flesh twitch and leap. And her mouth… Good God, her hot, sweet mouth. She nipped at his ear and grazed her lips across the line of his jaw where his night beard was beginning to form. Dropped a trail of feverish kisses down the tight cords of his neck to his pectoral muscles. She made him hot and breathless and desperate, and as he gripped her luscious arse and bucked his hips, his cock uselessly strained toward the very center of her. He inwardly cursed himself for already breaking his vow to exercise restraint and take things slowly.

But then, he'd also given Charlie free rein to make the rules and set the pace. And really, what could he do when she was using the tip of her tongue to torment one of his nipples, just like he would do to her if her breasts were unbound and free? When she began to lick and suckle his other nipple, pulling a throttled moan from deep within his throat, he wasn't sure how much more he could bear.

He buried one of his hands in her tumbling tresses, and at last, she took pity on him. She raised her head and murmured urgently, "Undo my gown, Max."

"With pleasure," he groaned. He reached behind her, then cursed beneath his breath when he discovered his fingers were trembling. Good God, his fierce desire for this woman was making him as clumsy as an inexperienced youth. Somehow, he managed to release the row of damnably small pearl buttons, then he loosened the laces of her corset and the ribbon tie securing the neckline of her chemise.

At long last, her delightfully plump breasts with their taut apricot tips spilled free. Free for him to gaze at and fondle and taste with tongue and lips until Charlie was moaning and clutching mindlessly at his head and grinding her hips in blatant invitation against his.

"Max." She tugged at his hair, and he reluctantly lifted his head. He stared into her golden-brown eyes, their dilated pupils deep enough to drown in.

"Do you want me to stop?" he asked, his voice hoarse and thick with lust.

"No…I want you to touch me." She reached for one of his hands and guided it between her thighs. "Here."

God in heaven. His fingers brushed her curls, and beneath them, she was hot and oh, so wet. "I can do better than that," he whispered. "I can taste you there…if you want me to."

He held his breath. *Please say yes.*

She smiled. "Well, if you're offering…"

"I am. Wrap your legs around me." Lashing one arm beneath Charlie's buttocks and one about her waist, he surged to his feet and headed across the room.

There was no time like the present to move things to his bed.

CHAPTER 25

"I never knew before, what such a love as you have made me feel, was; I did not believe in it; my Fancy was afraid of it, lest it should burn me up. But if you will fully love me, though there may be some fire, 'twill not be more than we can bear when moistened and bedewed with Pleasures." —An exclusive extract from a *Love Sonnet* by Mr. John Keats
The Beau Monde Mirror: The Literary Arts

As soon as Max settled her upon his wide four-poster bed, Charlie closed her eyes. Not because she was nervous or ashamed, but because she wanted to give herself over to the delicious sensations that Max was about to evoke with his hands and mouth. She'd heard all about this decadent act before—indeed, she'd often imagined it while she'd touched herself in her own bed—and she couldn't wait to experience it with Max.

His mouth ravished hers briefly, the kiss dark and hot and intense. Then he shifted his weight, moving down her body, lifting her skirts and petticoats, exposing her legs and her sex to his gaze.

Even though she'd resolved not to watch, she couldn't resist cracking open an eyelid to sneak a look at Max's face. Would he like what was on display?

She needn't have worried because his expression was

rapt as he studied her. He wedged his broad shoulders between her thighs, pushing her legs even wider. A blush burning her from head to toe, she tried to imagine what she looked like down there, so open and exposed to him, but couldn't.

And then her thoughts all but disintegrated as he parted her throbbing, no doubt slippery folds with his wicked fingers and blew across her swollen bud where her pleasure was centered. *Oh my...*

"Peaches," he murmured against her fevered wet flesh. "I can almost hear your mind working, my darling Charlotte, so I thought you might like to know your pretty pussy reminds me of summer peaches. So slick and sweet and too delicious for words."

And then he set his mouth on her, and Charlie's eyelids slammed shut again.

Oh. Dear. God.

Max's tongue teased her clitoris, circling and flicking and laving and... Oh, it felt so good. So wonderful. So wicked...

Charlie moaned when he slid two long fingers inside her, plunging in and out, in and out while his lips circled her bud, drawing on it with exquisite, delicate suction. The tension that always heralded her release was building, spiraling... She began to gasp and pant, and she speared her fingers into Max's hair, gripping his scalp. With one large hand splayed over her belly, he held her captive, his tongue working her mercilessly, flicking and lapping the pulsing, straining peak of her sex, and oh... she was so close to finding heaven...

And with one last suckle, she was there, tossed skyward into the stars. Her whole body arched, and she let loose an abandoned, pleasure-soaked cry. She clutched at Max's head as sublime satisfaction coursed through her veins, rendering her boneless with contentment.

Max moved alongside her and gathered her into his arms. He rubbed his nose against hers. "Thank you for allowing me to pleasure you that way, Charlie."

"You're thanking *me*?" Charlie caressed his stubbled jaw. "I think it's supposed to be the other way round. In fact…" She slid a hand between their bodies and stroked Max's hard, heavy length through the fall of his trousers. "I can think of the perfect way to say thank you. Do you want me to use my mouth or—"

Max kissed her, and Charlie tasted her own essence on his tongue. "I want to be inside you," he murmured against her lips. "Most desperately. If you'll let me."

He wanted her desperately? Charlie couldn't help but smile. To hear Max make such an admission was both thrilling and heart-melting in equal measure. "I want that too," she whispered. "And of course I'll let you. Only, I don't want any barriers between us. I'm ready to take everything off, Max. I want you to see all of me." And it wasn't a lie. He'd pleasured her so intimately, and she'd reveled in it. There was nothing left to fear or to hide. She trusted Max completely.

He drew back a little and searched her gaze. "Are you sure?"

"I haven't a single doubt in my mind."

Max kissed her again, then set to work, sliding off her loosened gown, corset, and chemise, tugging petticoat tapes undone, and very soon, nothing remained except for her silk stockings.

Max sat back on his haunches, and as his heated gaze wandered over her naked body, she didn't try to cover any part of herself. Not her breasts, nor her softly rounded belly or full hips, nor the chestnut thatch between her thighs. At long last, she felt entirely beautiful. Not just desired but adored. Max might not have made any declarations of love, but the way he was worshipping her with his eyes, she could sense there was more than lust behind his heavy-lidded gaze. And when he whispered, "Charlie, you're a goddess," in a voice that was brimming with awe, she believed him.

∾

Charlie was gloriously naked. Her thick chestnut curls spread around her like a fiery halo upon his cobalt-blue silk counterpane. Her almost translucent skin was as pale and voluptuous as cream. And her nipples, so tight and mouth-wateringly pink...

There were so many things Max wanted to do with her, and none of them involved him wearing trousers. With rough, impatient movements, he dispensed with his remaining clothes and slid over her, covering her body with his, reveling in the contact of his bare flesh against hers.

She wound her arms around his neck. "Make love to me, Max," she whispered, her eyes bright with desire and some other, deeper emotion that went beyond affection.

Max stilled, his breath hitching as a profound realization slammed into him. Not that Charlie loved him. He'd suspected that for some time. No, it was the dawning awareness that *his* feelings for Charlie were far stronger than he'd been willing to acknowledge. No, not willing. That was the wrong word. *Able* to acknowledge.

As tenderness like a soft glowing fire unfurled inside his chest, he closed his eyes and twisted his fingers into the counterpane, waiting for the bone-deep chill that he dreaded to take over and blast through him, turning him into a quaking, useless mess. But nothing happened. Yes, his erection still throbbed, and his pulse continued to race, but the ache in the vicinity of his heart was sweet and warm. So not really an ache, and not terrifying at all.

It was a feeling he could no longer deny. Nor did he want to.

"Max?" Charlie stroked his hair away from his fevered brow. "Are you all right?"

He opened his eyes and smiled. "I'm fine. Never better." He kissed her with lingering fervor laced with gentleness. This, what he and Charlie were doing right now, it wasn't just about satisfying his own lust and hers. This *was* making love, and that was something he'd never, ever done before.

And it was all because of Charlie. She was the woman of *his* dreams.

Nudging her thighs apart with his knees, Max settled his length along the hot damp cleft of her sex.

Oh God, she felt good. So good... His cock was pulsing, ready to explode, but he would take care. She might not be a virgin, but it had been a long time since she'd done this.

He dipped his head and lavished attention on her bountiful breasts, alternately suckling, then swirling his tongue around each sweet, tight peak. He wanted to make sure Charlie was absolutely ready for his entry. He wanted her wet and desperate with desire, just like he was.

When Charlie mewled in frustration and tilted her hips, his erection slid between her dew-slick folds, and he almost lost control. He couldn't delay their joining any longer. Gritting his teeth, he gripped his pulsating shaft in one hand and skimmed the head of his cock through the welling moisture at her entrance before pressing forward, nudging slowly into her.

Charlie's body tensed, and when she sucked in a sharp breath, Max's heart contracted with guilt.

He froze. "I'm sorry if I'm hurting you," he said, staring down into her face. A slight furrow had appeared between her brows, and her eyes were screwed shut.

"It's all right. I'm fine," she whispered. She opened her eyes and offered him a smile. "It burned a little at first, but that's all. I won't break. Don't hold back on my account."

He feathered a light kiss across her lips. "If you're sure…"

She firmed her gaze and gripped his shoulders. "I am. Take me, Max. I'm more than ready. I want this. I want *you*."

"Very well." Max drew a bracing breath, then surged forward in one long, slow glide, burying himself to the hilt.

Oh, God. Charlie was so hot and tight and slick. He nuzzled the delicious curve of her neck, licking the hollow of her throat as her body clasped his. He couldn't get enough of her. Her taste. Her scent. Her everything. "You're so sweet, my darling," he groaned against her satiny skin. "So warm and wet…so lovely."

He felt her body quiver with mirth. "And you're so big.

But not in a bad 'I think I'm going to burst' way. More of a 'I'm so wonderfully full' way." Her hands slid from his shoulders, down the tense muscles of his back until they reached his clenched buttocks and she squeezed. "I can't wait to feel you move inside me."

Her words were all the encouragement Max needed. He began to pulse in and out of Charlie with a smooth, gentle rocking motion. But all too soon, it wasn't enough for either of them.

"I want more...I need...oh yes, that's it," Charlie moaned as Max's thrusts became more urgent. With each sure stroke, he plunged harder and deeper, his rhythm growing faster, more frantic. And Charlie kept up with his pace. She met him thrust for thrust, tilting her hips, welcoming his body as he pounded in and out of her with increasing desperation. Taking everything he had to give.

Her gasps and soft moans were music to his ears, the scrape of her teeth against his shoulder pure delight. He prayed she was almost there because he couldn't hold off for much longer. He was panting and sweating, and his orgasm was gathering force. Passion raced like fire through his veins, tightening his balls... Oh, sweet Jesus...

He took his weight on one arm and lifted one of Charlie's legs, altering the angle of his penetration. All at once, she bucked her hips and cried out his name. Her nails dug into his back, and she spasmed around him, gripping his plunging cock so tightly he saw stars.

The feel of her losing all control was Max's own undoing. On a harsh cry, he withdrew and came in hot, hard spurts between Charlie's trembling thighs before collapsing on the bed beside her. Chest heaving, muscles twitching, he was utterly spent and so goddamned replete, he'd probably be smiling for a year and a day.

If Charlie would have him, maybe for the rest of his life...

∼

S ometime later, when they'd both washed and donned
robes—Charlie's crushed dress had been sent belowstairs with a maid to be pressed—Max ordered a tray, and
they sat together before his sitting-room fire, dining on
an array of cheeses and fruit, all washed down with a fine
claret.

Once sated, Charlie snuggled up to Max on the settee
and watched the play of the dancing firelight in the
depths of the ruby-red wine in her glass. Surrounded by
Max's arms and his velvet robe that smelled exactly like
him, Charlie thought she must be in heaven. Indeed, she
was so drowsy and content, she could have purred like
Peridot.

When Max shifted and stretched his bare lower legs
and toes toward the fire, Charlie couldn't help but notice
his damaged foot. She wanted to ask him about his past
but was too timid to bring up the subject. Of course, she
already knew the story behind the freshly healed scar on
his left bicep. But how he'd come to lose a toe and why
his lower back bore a significant scar—she'd felt the ridge
when they'd made love and had seen the angry welt just
below the dimples at the bottom of his spine when they'd
bathed in his dressing room—was a complete mystery
to her.

Every time she thought about Max suffering, her own
heart contracted with pain.

Whether he'd noticed the direction of her gaze or his
thoughts were simply in concert with hers, Charlie
wasn't sure. In any event, it seemed Max was in the mood
to share his past history with her. She was nothing but
touched as he said quietly, "I suppose you're wondering
about my injuries. What happened to my foot and my
back?"

"Yes." She turned in his arms to look at him. The expression in his dark blue eyes was unfathomable, but his
body remained relaxed as he continued to absently sift
his fingers through her loosened hair. "I'd be lying if I
didn't admit that I am curious. But you don't have to explain if you don't feel comfortable doing so."

"I do want to talk about it. The man I am today—the man I've been for years and years—was shaped during an incident that occurred when I was only twelve years old. My injuries—while they seem relatively minor on the surface—they're not. They go far, far deeper. The damage, it seems, went beyond the physical and never truly healed. My heart, and indeed my very soul, were scarred." His voice was tinged with profound sadness as he added, "It's the reason why I've never been able to love."

Max took a sip of his claret as though fortifying himself to continue, and Charlie simply waited. Even though her heart was already breaking for him, she didn't want to interrupt his train of thought with her own questions. She certainly didn't want to say the wrong thing.

At length he sighed, and his fingers continued to stroke Charlie's hair as if the simple action brought him some measure of solace. "I've never really spoken to anyone about this before, so I hope you'll bear with me if I'm not particularly eloquent."

Charlie touched his cheek. "Of course. I'm here to listen, Max, and to provide a modicum of comfort if I can."

His mouth twitched with the ghost of a smile. "You do. You are." He sighed again, and a deep furrow that was almost a scowl etched itself between his brows. "You know what my mother is like. How cold and manipulative she is. My father…he was even worse. He had what he called 'exacting standards', but in hindsight, it was simply an excuse for him to behave like a cruel tyrant. He maintained that he was training my brother Anthony—and me as well—to be hardheaded aristocrats who'd be capable of making decisions without being hampered by any sort of emotion or sentimentality. Any display of affection was seen as a weakness. We were never hugged by either of our parents, and our nurses were forbidden to do so too. Indeed, our nurses and our pets—father kept dogs at Exmoor Castle—were removed from our sphere on a regular basis to prevent us forming 'unseemly attachments'. Of course, in my case, it didn't work. I still formed emotional connections with others, but I also learned quite quickly that if I hid my feelings—if my father couldn't tell if I liked a particular tutor or hound or horse—they weren't taken away. And even though our father frequently pitted us against each other—he felt competition was important to develop character—Anthony and I still formed a strong filial bond. Our father might have tried to turn us into un-feeling lumps of ice, but he couldn't...at least not for a while."

"Oh, heavens, Max. That's simply awful. My heart weeps for you. It truly does."

"I'm sorry if I'm upsetting you."

"You don't need to apologize. At all. I'm flattered that you feel you can confide in me."

Max nodded. "As I mentioned, I learned to mask my emotions. But everything came unstuck for me when I was twelve. It was late autumn, and we were spending a few days at Heathcote Hall. One of the horses stabled there—his name was Phantom, and he was a handsome gray like Ghost—was one of my favorites. I would ride him whenever I could, although not too much in case Father noticed I had a preference for the gelding above any of the other horses. In any event, even though the weather was quite foul, Father made Anthony and me accompany him on an extended ride about Hampstead Heath one afternoon. It was blowing a gale, and there were intermittent rain squalls." Max's mouth hitched with a sardonic smile. "No doubt he thought braving the elements would 'toughen us up'.

"I recall we'd returned to Heathcote's grounds, and Father decided that Anthony and I must race each other through the woods on the edge of the estate. There was a fallen log on the path that we both needed to clear. I'm not sure how it happened, exactly—I was a skilled rider by that age because Father wouldn't let me be anything less than perfect—but I do know that I was tired, and I suspect Phantom was fatigued too. I mistimed the jump, and Phantom went down."

Max swallowed, and his expression grew haunted. "I'll never forget the sound of his leg snapping and his terrible screams. Father was livid, of course. I'd ruined a perfectly good horse. And so, he thought to teach me a lesson. One I'd never, ever forget…"

Charlie was almost too afraid to ask. "What happened?"

"I'd been thrown clear, but apart from sustaining a few superficial scrapes and being winded, I was relatively all right in a physical sense. Father hauled me to my feet and thrust a loaded pistol into my hand—he'd brought one with him to shoot any foxes or hares he saw on the heath, just for the sport of it—and then he ordered me to shoot Phantom. It was the right thing to do, to put the horse out of his misery. And it *was* my fault. But I couldn't. I just couldn't do it. I loved that goddamned horse, and I hated myself for not having the guts to end Phantom's suffering."

"You were only twelve."

"I know, but in a way, Father was right. In any case, Anthony took pity on me, snatched the gun from my hands, and ended poor Phantom's life. The fact that my brother had been able to do what needed to be done and not me only incensed Father further. He dragged me over to the fallen log and threw me over his lap, yanked my riding breeches down, then proceeded to flay me with his riding crop."

"Oh, my God. That's how you got that terrible scar?" Max nodded, and Charlie couldn't contain her tears. "He was monstrous, Max. An evil, cruel bully."

"I won't disagree. And I wished the story ended there, but it doesn't. You might recall that there is an icehouse in Heathcote's grounds. It's on the edge of the woods near the lake and not far from the bridle path where Phantom fell. As an extra punishment for failing to obey his order and do my duty, my father locked me inside that freezing, dark space. Just before he shut the door, he told me that I needed to stop behaving like a sniveling, puling infant and to grow up. In order to be a man, I needed to be as unfeeling as the blocks of ice contained within the icehouse."

"I can't believe he did that, Max. You could have died."

Max reached for one of her hands and gave it a

gentle squeeze. "Perhaps. I was certainly cold enough. I'm not sure how long I stayed in that hellish hole. It was pitch black, and I lost all track of time, but Anthony eventually crept back and let me out. One thing I do recall clearly, though—I vowed that I must encase my heart in icy armor. Loving hurt far too much, and my emotions had clouded my ability to make rational decisions. I also vowed to myself that I would never, ever find myself in a situation that I couldn't escape from."

"So that's why you learned to pick locks?"

Max nodded. "Yes."

"Well, thank God for Anthony."

"He risked a lot to come back and save me. As it was, my fingers and toes were frostbitten, and that's how I lost my little toe. A physician needed to amputate it, and it took me some time to be able to run with ease again."

Charlie kissed his hand. "And to feel."

"Yes, that's very true. But little by little, my heart did begin to thaw. As you pointed out to me not so long ago, I was able to form friendships at Eton and then at Oxford. But in my mind, male camaraderie was different from forming any sort of romantic attachment. And being in love didn't seem necessary for marriage. My parents certainly didn't love each other.

"And then I met you, Charlie. For so long, I kept telling myself that I felt nothing for you other than a faint regard because you were my best friend's younger sister. And after we became engaged, I convinced myself that I felt nothing for you but desire. But none of that's entirely true. In actual fact, I'm a huge coward, and I've been too terrified to acknowledge how I do truly feel about you."

Charlie's heart leapt, but even so, she couldn't quite believe her ears. She'd suspected for some time that Max desired her. He'd demonstrated that most aptly tonight. But as for anything else... "You really do feel more for me than just a deep and abiding fondness?" she whispered.

"Yes. Tonight everything changed. When we were making love, I realized that I didn't have to be afraid anymore. I didn't have to shy away from the tenderness growing in my heart." He reached out and gently cradled her face with his hands. "That's because I—"

A rap on the door made Charlie jump and Max curse.

"Charlie, I'm sorry—" he began, but the knock came again.

"Your Grace..." Even though the voice was muffled, it sounded like Chiffley. "Your Grace, my apologies for interrupting..."

Max sighed heavily and shook his head. "I'd best deal with this." He strode to the door and jerked it open. "Chiffley, is Exmoor House burning down or being raided by marauding hordes? Because that's about the only reason I'll accept for your intrusion."

Charlie could barely see the butler. Max, ever the gentleman, stood in the doorway, obstructing the servant's view. Nevertheless, she heard Chiffley say, "Again, I offer my sincerest apologies, Your Grace, but Lord Malverne is downstairs asking to see you. He says the matter is quite urgent. I've shown him into the library."

Nate was here? Charlie's heart plummeted. Had her brother discovered Diana wasn't playing chaperone after all? She sincerely prayed he wasn't here to make trouble.

Max must have had the same thought because he glanced back at Charlie, his expression grim, before turning his attention back to the butler. "Tell Lord Malverne I'll be down directly."

"Of course, Your Grace. I also have Smedley here with her ladyship's freshly pressed gown. Would you like him to install it in your dressing room? Or elsewhere?"

"My dressing room will suffice."

The door shut, and Max scrubbed a hand through his hair. "Even though your gown is ready, it's probably best if I deal with your brother." His gaze raked over her. "It will avoid any awkward questions about chaperonage. Or lack thereof."

"I understand," she said. "I'll make myself scarce. There's no point in setting the cat amongst the pigeons."

"Good girl." Max crossed the room and dropped a kiss on her forehead. "Hopefully, I won't be long, my love. You and I have unfinished business."

As he retreated to his dressing room, Charlie sank onto the settee again, a smile playing about her lips. Max had called her "my love" for the very first time, and she was absolutely certain it wasn't a slip of the tongue.

If Nate took up too much of Max's time, she'd march downstairs and dispense with her brother herself, gown or no. It was definitely time to put Nathaniel Hastings in his place.

CHAPTER 26

"In vain I have struggled. It will not do. My feelings will not be repressed. You must allow me to tell you how ardently I admire and love you."—
An extract from Miss Jane Austen's *Pride &*
Prejudice
The Beau Monde Mirror: The Literary Arts

Max found Nate pouring out glasses of his best cognac when he entered the library a short time later.

"What's happened?" he asked without preamble. "I hadn't expected to see you this evening. Apparently, it's something urgent?"

Nate handed him a crystal tumbler. "Aside from wanting to make sure my sister is all right, I have some news about Erasmus Silver and the *Beau Monde Mirror* that I thought you'd like to hear."

Ignoring the twinge of guilt in his gut for continuing to lie about the true nature of his relationship with Charlie, Max claimed the chair behind his desk. "Charlie's well. Well, as well as to be expected given the events of this afternoon. But she was comforted to learn that there probably won't be any scurrilous newspaper articles about her and her portrait."

"No, there won't be," said Nate, grim satisfaction flashing in his smile. "It took Hamish, Gabriel, and me a little while to track down Mr. Silver. He wasn't at the offices of Juno Press when we arrived, but one of the other staff members there—a junior editor who quite conveniently has a personal grudge against Silver—was quite amenable to handing over information for the price of a few guineas. Not only did we learn Silver already had a story about Charlie ready to go to press, but we obtained Silver's home address in Marylebone. He wasn't there either, but the manservant who answered the door was happy to inform us—again, for the price of a few guineas —that his master was paying a visit to a particularly notorious brothel in Soho Square."

Max cocked a brow. "Birchmore House?"

Nate inclined his head. "The very same. It seems Mr. Silver is rather fond of being birched. When we came upon him *in flagrante*, he readily agreed to pull the story about Charlie in exchange for our silence about his sexual inclinations."

Max grinned. "I'm impressed."

"And that's not all," continued Nate. "The best part is, while we were at Juno Press, Gabriel, Hamish, and I spent a bit of time searching Silver's office; the junior editor was happy to turn a blind eye to that as well."

"And what did you find out?"

Nate winced. "I'm afraid you're not going to like what I have to say, my friend. Gabriel unearthed a file on Fortuna Trading, the company that owns Juno Press, and inside there was a record of all of their meetings' minutes. There was also this document which listed all of the partners who have shares in the business." Nate withdrew a folded piece of parchment from his coat pocket and handed it to Max. "Aside from Rotten Rochfort, who appears to be the major shareholder of the company...your mother's name is on that list."

What?

Max scanned the document, and there it was in black and white. Devil take him. It was true. His own mother was a part-owner of the *Beau Monde Mirror.*

His hand shook as he wiped it down his face. "This... this defies belief," he said in a voice faint with shock. "My mother has always portrayed herself as an upstanding pillar of Polite Society. But in actual fact, she's the complete opposite. She's worse than just a gossipmonger. She uses gossip to wage war and destroy her social enemies. And her weapon of choice is a scandal rag. Rochfort's too." Disgust roiling inside him, he tossed the document onto the desk. "I wonder how many unwitting members of the ton he's blackmailed over the years to keep their names out of his vile newspaper."

One thing was certain: his mother and Rochfort would pay dearly for their unrelenting campaign to ruin Charlie's reputation. Such perfidy could not go unpunished.

He met Nate's gaze. "Thank you for going above and beyond and finding all of this out. As you know, I've been using an inquiry agent and my man of affairs to investigate the matter for weeks now, and until tonight, had learned precious little. I'm now kicking myself for playing by the rules when it seems there are none."

Nate shrugged. "It was Gabriel's idea to bribe the junior editor and search Silver's office. But he's always been a rule-breaker."

Max tilted his head. "Yes. I'm truly indebted to you again, Nate. Indeed, all of my friends."

Nate's gaze was as steady and solemn as a judge's as he said, "There's to be no more talk of debts or obligations of any kind. And as for the debt of honor that you think you still owe me, that was settled when you became engaged to Charlie. You know that."

"What debt of honor?"

Hell and damnation. Max's gaze flew to the library doorway where Charlie stood. She'd donned her gown, but her unbound curls fell in wild disarray about her shoulders. God knew what Nate thought. But Charlie clearly didn't care. Her eyes, narrowed in suspicion, darted between him and her brother.

As Max rose to his feet, she advanced across the Turkish rug toward the desk. "Well? I'd like an explanation. I have a right to know if the only reason you entered into this faux engagement with me was to settle a debt."

Her accusing gaze settled on her brother. "And if you were quite happy to go along with it, Nate."

Nate put down his cognac and stood too. His tone was harsh with accusation as he demanded, "Where is your chaperone?"

Charlie snorted. "Oh, don't give me that. If you must know, she's at Devereux House, minding her own business like you should be doing."

He puffed out his chest. "Now see here, Charlie—"

"No, you see here, Nate. I'm a twenty-two-year-old woman, and I'm tired of you interfering in my affairs. And it seems you have been for some time. Despite the fact this engagement appears to be based on some sort of ridiculous gentlemen's agreement that I know nothing about, I happen to love Max Devereux, and there's nothing you can do about it. I know you mean well, but I'd like you to take your misplaced indignation and concern and go home to Sophie and your son. Max and I have some much-needed talking to do."

"Yes, we do," agreed Max. He hadn't missed the fact that Charlie had just openly declared her love for him. He had to set the record straight. He had to make things right.

Nate, for once, had the good grace to look chastened. He inclined his head. "Fair enough, Charlie. I've only ever wanted the very best for you. You know that, don't you?"

She lifted her chin. "I'm a big girl, and I have my eyes wide open. I know what I'm doing. You need to trust me to be able to look after myself and make sound decisions. And your friend too." She turned her attention to Max. "You have a lot of explaining to do, Your Grace."

Max nodded. "I will, and gladly." In some ways, it was a relief that Charlie would know why he'd entered into this agreement with Nate. He didn't want there to be any secrets between them. Not anymore.

Nate took his leave, and as the door shut behind him, Max suggested that they repair to the fireside. "Before we discuss the debt of honor I owed your brother," he said as he took a seat beside Charlie, "I want to share the news that he imparted when he first arrived." He proceeded to tell her how Nate had discovered that both Lord Rochfort and his own mother were both part-owners of the *Beau Monde Mirror*.

Charlie's eyes were like dinner plates. "I'm absolutely flabbergasted," she said. "To think that all this time, your mother has been feigning innocence about her role in defaming me, yet she's intimately involved. I wonder how long this has been going on."

"I'd like to know that too," Max said grimly. "And I intend to find out tomorrow. But rest assured, she will no longer plague you. Now that I know the truth of the matter, both my mother and Lord Rochfort will be called to account for their heinous actions."

Charlie paled. "Promise me you won't call Rochfort out again, Max. I couldn't bear it if something happened to you."

"I promise you that I won't. I have a far better plan that will end his tyranny once and for all."

Charlie seemed satisfied with that, because the next thing she said was, "After you fought the duel with Rochfort and then proposed, you told me that Nate had agreed to the arrangement because it would help to dissipate the scandal surrounding my name. But given the conversation I just overheard, that wasn't the entire truth, was it?" Her eyes glittered with determination, and God help him, were there tears in their golden-brown depths? "I want you to be honest with me about this, Max."

"I will. And you deserve the truth." Max's pulse began to pound as he took one of Charlie's hands in his. The diamond of her engagement ring caught the firelight and winked at him. While he was both grateful and relieved that she didn't pull away from his touch, he was also worried how she would react to his disclosure. But there was no point in putting it off. "Four years ago, your brother helped me to avert a huge scandal that would have brought my own family's name into disrepute."

Charlie's brow dipped into a frown. "Oh. I had no idea."

"It was just after Waterloo. I'd arrived back in London, and my brother, Anthony, threw a house party at Heath-

cote Hall to celebrate my safe return and Old Boney's defeat. Nate was one of the guests, along with quite a few
other members of the ton. Of course, Diana and my
mother were there too."

"Diana told me that your brother had died during a
house party at Heathcote. I hope you can forgive me for
asking such a blunt question, but was this the one, Max?"

"Yes, it was. It was supposed to run over a week but
only lasted a few days because of Anthony's accident."

"I've heard he had a nasty fall while riding."

"Yes. In hindsight, what we did was beyond foolish.
After a long luncheon that involved far too many bottles
of claret, the gentlemen of the party decided to go out on
the heath. During a mad gallop, Anthony lost his seat. He
was knocked out cold for a short time, but when he came
round, he seemed all right. Or so he claimed. I suggested
summoning a physician, but he waved the idea away. It's
a decision I regret to this day."

Charlie's eyes were soft with compassion. "I'm so
sorry, Max. You weren't to know."

He squeezed her hand. "Thank you, but I should have
trusted my gut. As it was, Anthony continued to pretend
there was nothing wrong, even though he had indeed
sustained a significant head injury. Apparently, there was
a slow bleed inside his brain. He drank wine all through
dinner, conversed, and laughed. Later on, we found laudanum in his room, and his valet confirmed he'd imbibed
some before dinner, probably to dull the fearsome
headache he would have had—at least, that's what the
physician who ended up attending him at his bedside
believed."

"That's so tragic, Max. And he was so young too."

"Yes. He was only seven-and-twenty…" He met Charlie's gaze. "You're no doubt wondering what the 'almost'
scandal was and how your brother became involved in all
of this."

"Yes. A little."

Max sighed. "I'll endeavor to explain. Even though
Anthony and Diana seemed to be happily married, it also
turned out that my brother was a philanderer; he was

having an affair with one of the guests at Heathcote behind Diana's back. I certainly didn't know until his lover sought me out."

"Oh. Diana actually did know that, Max. The day I arrived at Heathcote, I discovered her in your sitting room. She was crying, and she confessed that while she loved your brother, she was also angry at him for having an affair."

"I had no idea that she knew. I wonder if she also knew the rest."

"The rest?"

"After dinner, even though Anthony would have been feeling unwell, he arranged to meet his lover for a tryst in her bedchamber…which wasn't such a good idea because he passed out while they were making love, and she was unable to rouse him. The situation was complicated by the fact that this woman was married and obviously quite terrified that her own husband would find the unconscious Duke of Exmoor in their bed."

"Good heavens. What a completely awful situation."

"It was. Although, I am thankful that Max's lover still had the presence of mind to seek me out, despite the fact she was beside herself with distress. She entreated me to help her move Anthony out of her room and back to his own chambers. And of course, I couldn't do it on my own. Not discreetly…"

"So you asked Nate for assistance."

"Yes. And he did so willingly. We moved Anthony—he was completely insensible—and a mere half hour later, he passed away in his own bed. But I've always felt Nate went above and beyond that night. He didn't have to help me cover up Anthony's infidelity to protect Diana and our family name. I've felt indebted to him ever since."

"So that's why you proposed to me?" Charlie's voice was flat with resentment, and her eyes were filled with shadows. "Out of a sense of obligation to my brother, nothing more?"

The thought that he'd hurt Charlie shredded Max's own heart with guilt. It was his fault that she doubted him. It was no one's fault but his that she was in so much pain.

But he also had the power to fix things. To make things right.

It was long overdue.

≈

Confusion and hurt swirled through Charlie. Her throat was tight, and her eyes stung with the effort not to cry. How could she have been so wrong about everything?

Before Chiffley had come knocking on Max's bedroom door, she'd sworn Max had just been about to declare that he loved her. She'd seen it in his eyes. Felt it in his touch.

He'd called her "my love".

But Max had all but confirmed that he'd only proposed to her to settle the debt of honor that he owed her brother. What a lowering, heartrending thought indeed.

Max took her hand in his. "Charlie…" he said. "I won't lie to you. In the beginning, the urge to repay the debt of honor I owed your brother was the reason I gave to justify my actions—for helping you to recover your notebook, for calling out Rochfort, and for proposing that we enter into a fake engagement. But I was lying to Nate and to myself. The moment I first beheld you that long-ago summer at Elmstone Hall, I noticed you. But you were only sixteen, and I was twenty-two. So, I pretended disinterest and was always, always careful around you, out of respect for you and my friend. And of course, I honestly didn't think I *was* capable of forming romantic attachments—at least not a long-lasting one—and neither did your brother, who knew all about my upbringing and history with women. He really did have your best interests at heart by warning me to stay away from you.

"But in the end, I just couldn't, Charlie. I've always been drawn to you. To your laughter, your smile, your intelligence, your wit, your boldness, and your kind heart. And yes, your abundant beauty. And as I told you

earlier tonight, up until now, I've been too terrified to acknowledge my feelings for you. And to acknowledge that
this engagement has never been fake, but very real. But
the lies I've told—to myself and to you—they stop
tonight. The honest to God truth is, Charlotte"—Max
lifted his hands and cradled her face like she was the most
precious thing in the world—"I love you. With every beat
of my heart, with every breath that I take, indeed, with
everything that I am, I love you. I think about you all the
time, and I want you to know that you are the only
woman I want to be with, now and forever. And I pray
that you can forgive me for being such a coward and a
fool for so, so long."

"Oh, Max." Tears misted Charlie's vision. His heartfelt
declaration of love was everything she'd ever dreamed of
and more. "Of course I'll forgive you. And I think you already know that I love you too. With my whole heart and
soul, I love you."

Tears were shimmering in Max's deep blue gaze as he
murmured in a voice thick with emotion, "Say it again,
Charlie."

"Maximilian Devereux"—Charlie reached out to caress his jaw—"I love you. You are, and always will be, the
man of my dreams."

He closed his eyes. Swallowed. And just when Charlie
thought he might kiss her, he shifted to the floor and
took up a position on bended knee.

"I did not do this the right way the first time," he said,
taking one of her hands in his, "so I will endeavor to do
so now. Charlotte Hastings…" His voice was low and soft
and full of promise. "Will you do me the untold honor of
consenting to be my wife?"

"Yes, Max. I will." And before she could even blink,
Max was dragging her into his arms and kissing her with
heart-stopping, breath-stealing ardor. They toppled to
the rug, and Max's hands were everywhere—in her hair,
roaming over her body—setting her aflame.

And it seemed she was rousing his desire too, given
the hard, insistent press of him against her sex. When
Max's mouth slid to her neck and he began to rain soft,

fiery kisses upon her flesh, she managed to whisper, "I have an idea."

"I'm all ears," he said between gentle licks and nuzzles.

"I seem to recall an occasion in which you intimated that you've been naked in your library before. And wicked woman that I am, I must say the idea has always intrigued me."

Max raised his head and gifted her with a smile that was pure sin. "I like the way you think, my love. However, I'll only say yes to your proposal if you agree to strip naked too."

"Well, Your Grace," Charlie said with a grin, "it seems you'd best lock the door. We wouldn't want anyone bursting in unannounced."

Max laughed as he got to his feet. "Charlie, it's you alone who's made a habit of doing that. But nevertheless, I'll comply."

When he returned to the fireside, it wasn't long before Charlie was wearing nothing at all but her engagement ring and a smile. And as Max made slow, sweet love to her before the library fire, she knew without a shadow of a doubt that the duke she'd dreamed of for so long was really, truly hers, body, heart, and soul.

CHAPTER 27

Did you attend the opening of the Royal
Academy's fifty-first annual exhibition yesterday?
Outstanding works abound this year, including
Cooper's magnificent rendition of *The Battle of
Marston Moor*, Gandy's both epic and sublime
Jupiter Pluvius, and the delightfully bucolic *England:
Richmond Hill, on the Prince Regent's Birthday* by
Turner.
The Beau Monde Mirror: The Fine Arts

Exmoor House, Grosvenor Square
May 4, 1819

Max took a sip of his first coffee for the day and
stretched his booted feet toward the rose bushes
bordering Exmoor House's rear terrace. His mouth
tipped into a smile. He didn't think he'd ever felt so blissfully content. And drowsy. With Charlie sharing his bed
the previous night, for the entire night, neither of them
had slept very much.

Everything had been perfect.

She was perfect.

Stifling a yawn, Max took another, larger swig of coffee. On the wrought-iron table beside him sat the morning's broadsheets. A light breeze ruffled the pages of the
Beau Monde Mirror, which, to his immense satisfaction,

contained not one word about Charlie or her portrait. He would happily tell Charlie that as soon as she joined him for breakfast.

His fiancée was presently upstairs in one of the guest bedrooms—for the sake of appearances—with her lady's maid, Molly. Lord Westhampton, to his credit, had sent the maid along to Exmoor House earlier that morning to attend to her mistress's needs. Max was nothing but grateful that his future father-in-law was so accommodating. It seemed he'd taken Max at his word when he'd said that Charlie would be chaperoned.

Max felt only slightly guilty that he'd lied to the earl.

Actually—he grinned as he topped up his coffee from the silver coffee pot—he didn't feel guilty at all.

But the morning wouldn't be all sunshine and roses. After they'd breakfasted, Max would be paying a visit to Devereux House to read his mother the riot act.

As for how he'd end Rotten Rochfort's reign of terror, Max had already decided the best course of action to take. There was a pile of freshly sealed letters on his library desk that he'd already instructed his secretary to hand deliver during the morning. Because Charlie had made him promise not to challenge the baron to another duel, it seemed the only weapon left to him was his quill. And he'd wielded it with alacrity.

Before he met with his friends at White's to celebrate, he'd be visiting Doctor's Common to organize a special license. Now that he and Charlie had professed their love and were truly promised to each other, there was no sense in delaying the inevitable. Indeed, after what they'd done last night—several times—Charlie might already be with child. *His* child. The thought filled him with a warm glow and made him want to puff his chest out with pride. He couldn't wait to make Charlie his wife and his duchess, and he hoped she felt the same way too.

He'd ask for her opinion on the matter as soon as she joined him on the terrace.

The French doors opened, and Max looked up with an expectant smile. But it wasn't Charlie who emerged. It was Chiffley bearing a silver salver with a calling card.

"Your Grace, I know it's quite early, but it seems your sister-in-law is asking to see you."

Even though Max waved the card away, his curiosity was piqued. He was only casually dressed in breeches, boots, an open-necked shirt, and a banyan, but he supposed it didn't really matter. Diana had seen him in similar attire before. "How does she seem?" he asked the butler. He still wasn't sure how deeply Diana had been embroiled in his mother's schemes, but he intended to find out.

Chiffley's beetled brows pulled together in a frown. "A little on edge, perhaps, Your Grace? I've never been a very good judge of ladies and their moods."

You and me both, thought Max. Although, he considered himself fortunate indeed that Charlie tended to wear her heart on her sleeve, leaving him in no doubt about her feelings on any given matter. To Chiffley, he said, "Show Her Grace out to the terrace. And I expect she'd like a spot of tea. Oh, and send along some hot chocolate for Lady Charlotte." Max seemed to recall she'd been drinking that at breakfast at Heathcote one morning.

The butler bowed. "Very good. All shall be arranged at once."

When a footman showed his sister-in-law out to the terrace, Max rose to his feet and sketched a bow. "Diana, what brings you to Exmoor House so early? Is everything all right?"

Despite his own reservations about being able to judge a woman's mood, Chiffley's summation of the young duchess's state of mind had been quite accurate. Diana did indeed have a brittle edge. She offered Max a tight smile. "I... If I'm being perfectly honest, no, I'm not all right. I—"

"Max, I'm sorry I took so long—oh…" Charlie breezed onto the terrace, then stopped short when she saw the duchess. "Oh, Diana. I had no idea you were here."

Charlie's cheeks turned the same blossom-pink hue as her morning gown as her gaze darted to Max. He gave a little shrug. If Diana guessed what they'd been up to last night, he wasn't particularly bothered.

And perhaps Diana did have an inkling, because she blushed too. "Lady Charlotte, Your Grace... My apologies for intruding. I didn't realize...I had no idea that you were otherwise engaged...I mean, of course you are engaged... Oh, drat." She pressed her lips together and shook her head. "I'm so nervous that I'm rambling and making such a hash of everything. That was not my intention at all."

Max gestured to a pair of nearby footmen, and they both stepped forward to pull out chairs for Diana and Charlie. "Why don't we all sit down, and then we can start again?" he said.

As the ladies took their seats, the tea and hot chocolate arrived. Charlie, who seemed to have recovered her equilibrium, played the role of hostess with aplomb.

"Now," said Max when everyone was armed with cups of their preferred brew. "What can I do for you, Diana?"

Diana put down her cup of tea, and her gray gaze shifted between him and Charlie. "As a matter of fact, I'm quite pleased to find Charlie here as well because..." She lifted her chin. "Because I wanted to offer both of you a sincere apology for everything that transpired at the Royal Academy yesterday. Particularly you, dear Charlie. Of course, I had no idea that Cressida had arranged for that purported portrait of you to be part of the Exhibition—"

"As it happens, it *is* actually my portrait," said Charlie quietly. "But the painting was only ever supposed to be displayed in the privacy of my own home. I have no idea how Cressida got her hands on it, nor why she's so intent on ruining me."

"Oh." Diana blushed. "I see. I'm not sure why she's so set against you either, Charlie. In any event, what I wanted to say was, I was so shocked when I saw your painting, my first reaction was to try and steer you away from it to save you from being embarrassed. In point of fact, I should have worked out a way to have it removed, but there were guards all about, and I was worried that I would be accused of stealing. And then I wasn't sure I'd be able to lift it down from the wall. That gilt frame was quite elaborate, and there were guests everywhere—"

"It's quite all right, Diana," said Max. "The blame for this underhanded, despicable act lies entirely with my mother."

Diana winced. "Not entirely…"

Max's gaze narrowed on his sister-in-law. "Do you know how my mother came by the painting? Or if the artist, Madame de Beauvoir, agreed to participate in her scheme?"

"I'm not sure about Madame de Beauvoir's role," Diana said. "All I know is that last night, when I heard your mother and Lord Rochfort discussing what had happened—how your mother's plans to ruin Charlie completely had been thwarted—I didn't know what to think or to do at first. I know one shouldn't eavesdrop, but honestly, it's so hard to avoid overhearing things one shouldn't when there are raised voices. And I was so horrified—"

"Wait a moment." Max held up a hand. "Did I just hear you correctly, Diana? You overheard my mother talking with Rollo Kingsley, Baron Rochfort, last night? At the Royal Academy?"

"Why no. At Devereux House." Diana's brow knitted with a puzzled frown. "I thought you knew that—" She blushed bright red and began to fiddle with the linen napkin in her lap.

"Knew what?"

She swallowed, and her hands fluttered about. "That your mother and Lord Rochfort"—she dropped her voice to a whisper and leaned forward—"are having an affair."

If Diana had suddenly sprouted wings and flown about Exmoor House's back garden, Max would have been less surprised. Charlie's mouth had dropped open, and she looked as flabbergasted as he felt.

He shook his head. It couldn't be true. "But…are you certain, Diana? My inquiry agent organized surveillance of Rochfort House and Devereux House weeks ago. I know you and my mother visited the baron not long after he was injured. But since then, there have been no other reports of her meeting with him."

"Oh…" Diana fidgeted with her napkin again. "Well, I'd say that's because Lord Rochfort enters the house via the back garden gate. He rents a nearby property—another townhouse—that abuts the mews behind Devereux House."

Bloody blazing hell. Why the devil hadn't he—or Hunt his inquiry agent—thought to monitor the rear of Devereux House? His mother must have alerted Rochfort to the fact they were both being watched, so they'd come up with an alternative plan to continue their clandestine affair.

Max felt like the biggest fool in Christendom. And so damned angry he could crush gravel into dust with his back teeth.

With effort, he unclenched his jaw and asked, "How long has this affair been going on?"

Diana shifted uncomfortably on her chair. "I'm not exactly sure…"

A muscle twitched in his cheek. "But if you were to hazard a guess?"

"Since the beginning of the year, when we returned to London after Twelfth Night? But it might have been longer…"

Charlie gasped, and Max met her horrified gaze. If what Diana had just said was indeed accurate, Rochfort had seduced Charlie on Saint Valentine's Day even though he was Cressida's paramour. Not only that, he'd probably consorted with prostitutes like Madame Erato at the same time.

Max wondered if his mother knew about that.

At this point in time, it wouldn't surprise him at all if she did but didn't care.

There was only one way to find out the truth about any of the disgraceful, reprehensible goings-on involving his mother and Rochfort.

Max put down his coffee and pushed to his feet. "Charlie, I think's it's well past time that you and I visited Devereux House and demanded some answers."

Devereux House, Curzon Street, Mayfair

His mother was taking tea in the morning room of Devereux House when Max and Charlie arrived. Diana, perhaps to avoid the storm that was coming, had wisely made herself scarce.

The dowager duchess greeted them both with a tight smile and gestured to the vacant chairs surrounding the satinwood dining table. "When I heard Diana had set out to visit Exmoor House this morning, I suspected I might see you sooner rather than later, Maximilian." Her unsettling, ice-blue gaze settled on Charlie. "But not you, Lady Charlotte. I must say, you're either incredibly brave or incredibly dull-witted showing your face in public, considering what happened—"

Max slammed his hand down on the table. "This. Stops. Now," he barked. "Today. This very minute. You will *not* insult my fiancée ever again. I know everything, Mother. About your affair with bloody Rochfort. The fact you and he own the vast majority of shares in the *Beau Monde Mirror*, and about your concerted efforts to destroy the woman I love. It's all over."

His mother's sangfroid was breath-stealing. There was no shock in her expression, and rather than denying any of the accusations he'd just flung at her, she simply arched an eyebrow. "Love, is it? I very much doubt you know the meaning of the word."

"Between your concerted effort—and Father's—to deny me any sort of warmth or affection during my childhood, it's no wonder you would think that," Max growled savagely. "But don't presume to know anything about me, Mother." He caught Charlie's gaze across the room. She hovered by the door uncertainly, her gloved hands clasped at her waist. He didn't think he'd ever lost his temper in front of her before, and he was suddenly ashamed. "I'm sorry," he said gently. "You don't have to stay to witness this exchange. It's bound to get ugly."

"No, I want to be here." Although she was pale, there

was a militant gleam in his fiancée's eyes. "There are things I wish to know."

Max gave a curt nod and turned back to face his mother. "I only have three questions for you before I banish you from this townhouse forevermore. How long have you been a part-owner of the *Beau Monde Mirror*? How long have you been trying to ruin Charlie? How long have you been screwing Lord Rochfort?"

His mother sniffed. "I won't answer any of your questions if you continue to use that sort of foul language in front of me."

Max let out a short bark of laughter. "The only thing foul in this room is you and your campaign to destroy Lady Charlotte. Why in God's name have you been waging war against her for so long? Good God, I'm beginning to think the sole reason you bought shares in the *Beau Monde Mirror* was just to defame her."

She rolled her eyes. "I'm sure we've been over this a thousand times before, Maximilian. I know it. The whole of the ton knows it. Lady Charlotte Hastings is simply not good enough for you. It's not my fault if she continuously provides ample fodder for the gossip columns. There's not one thing that's been published about her that isn't true, is there?"

"No one is perfect, Mother. No one's conduct is exemplary all the time. Take you as an example, a supposed doyen of Polite Society who's currently fucking the vilest member of the ton. Now, wouldn't that give your friends something to talk about if that salacious fact was reported in the scandal rags?"

At last, a reaction. His mother's eyes flashed blue fire as she hissed, "How dare you speak to me like that?"

"Spare me the righteous indignation. Just tell me why. Why have you devoted so much of your time and money to ruining my fiancée? I swear your campaign has been bloodier and more sustained than Old Boney's campaign against Britain. What has Charlotte ever done to deserve this? It makes no sense. At all."

His mother threw down her napkin and shot to her feet. "How can you be so stupid? It makes perfect sense.

Your fiancée"—she glared at Charlie—"comes from bad breeding stock. Her own mother, Elizabeth—the daughter of an absolute nobody—was nothing but a social-climbing trollop, stealing Lord Westhampton away from—"

Charlie gasped. "You knew my mother?"

"Of course I knew your mother. She made her debut during the same Season I did. But unlike me, she bought her way into the ton. The daughter of a mere shipbuilder in Portsmouth?" The dowager duchess's mouth thinned. "Everyone knew she didn't belong in our ranks. Your father, Lord Westhampton, clearly just wanted her for her money"—her disdainful gaze raked over Charlie—"and her other tawdry assets, which were a lot like yours."

Even though Max's ire was sparking again, he chose to ignore this last dig at Charlie. "So, just to clarify, Mother, you're telling me that the reason you loathe Charlotte so much is that you were jealous of her mother over thirty years ago? Because she caught the eye of the Earl of Westhampton and you didn't?"

His mother made a scoffing noise. "Jealous? Don't make me laugh. Of course I wasn't jealous. I'm the one who married a duke, after all. But of course, that's not the only reason I despise *your Charlie*. You just need to look at her to see she's not—and will never be—duchess material. With her unrefined air, knowing smiles, garish hair, and doughy figure. I remember the first time I ever laid eyes on her in Hyde Park five years ago. You were on horseback, and she was with her brother, Lord Malverne; you'd stopped by their landau to chat. And she was making the most ridiculous calf's eyes at you. Even though I was at a distance, I could see you were attracted to her, Max. That you wanted her too. And it was highly likely that you'd come into contact with her over and over again, given your friendship with her brother. So, that's when I decided that I had to convince you that she was entirely unsuitable."

His mother turned her gaze back to Charlie and smirked. "And you made it so easy for me, my dear. When one of my good friends who was a patroness of Mrs.

Rathbone's Academy for Young Ladies of Quality told me about your deplorable behavior, I was the one who went to the *Beau Monde Mirror* with the story. And when Erasmus Silver mentioned that one of the principal owners was looking for another partner in the business— someone with significant social influence—I thought, why not? Not only would it be a sound business investment, but it meant I could have a direct influence on the newspaper's content. But you, Maximilian…" His mother glared at him. "It didn't matter what I printed about her or her ill-bred friends; it didn't make one jot of difference to you. So, that's when I enlisted the help of Lord Rochfort. *This* Season, I was determined to make you see Lady Charlotte Hastings is no lady at all, but as common as her horrid, social-climbing mama used to be."

"And that's when you took up with Rochfort?" said Max. He clenched and unclenched his fists. Just thinking about the snake, let alone saying his name, made him want to smash his fist through a wall.

His mother tossed her head. "Not that it's any of your business, but yes. Lord Rochfort and I are of a similar disposition—"

Charlie snorted. "So, you're both soulless with no scruples whatsoever. Well, Cressida, your title and precious aristocratic bloodline mean absolutely nothing if you have no character to speak of. And after hearing everything you've just said, your opinion of me also means nothing. The only thing I want to know is how you found out about my portrait. What horrendous thing did you do to poor Madame de Beauvoir to coerce her into giving it to you? Because I don't believe for a minute that she would have surrendered it willingly."

The dowager duchess gave a theatrical sigh. "Well, it certainly wasn't a secret that you wanted to sit for a licentious portrait, now, was it? But to answer your question, Lord Rochfort had you followed, of course. It didn't take long for him to work out that your Madame de Beauvoir had a penchant for painting naked gentlemen, which is not the done thing at all. If word got out, *her* reputation would have been mud. The Royal Academy would have banned her from ever exhibiting again, and her Polite Society commissions would have dried up."

"So Rochfort blackmailed her," said Max.

His mother shrugged. "One must do what one must."

"Yes," said Max. "Which is exactly why you're going to sell your existing shares in Fortuna Trading to me. And then I'm going to banish you to Devonshire with a much-reduced allowance. You can divide your time between the dower house at Exmoor Castle and Lynton Grange. Aside from the change of scenery, you'll enjoy the fresh sea air. I'll even let you maintain a subscription to *The Times* and *Ackermann's Repository*."

His mother paled. "You must be joking."

"Indeed, I am not. You have one hour to pack your things, then I'll be back with my man of affairs and the necessary papers for you to sign, along with my coach that will ferry you to Devon."

Even though his mother raised her chin, her bottom lip quivered. "And if I refuse to go?"

Max shrugged. "Well, I would have no choice but to tell the entire ton that the Dowager Duchess of Exmoor is one of the owners of the *Beau Monde Mirror*. I can only imagine what everyone will think when they learn that one of their own has been spreading filthy gossip about them all, as well as profiting from the practice."

His mother's lips were bloodless, and her eyes glittered. "You wouldn't dare," she breathed.

"What you've done to Charlie is unforgivable, so yes, I would dare. Not only that, but Lord Rochfort is about to experience my wrath too."

His mother's gaze flickered to Charlie, who still waited by the morning room door, then back to Max. "What do you mean?"

He cocked an eyebrow. "As we speak, my personal secretary is delivering letters to the head editors of *The Times, The Morning Post, The Morning Herald, The Sun, The Courier, The Globe, The Star, The Statesman, The London Chronicle, The London Packet, The Evening Mail...* actually, to just about every newspaper that I could think of. So very soon, all of London—indeed, the entire country—

will know that Lord Rochfort is the chief owner of Fortuna Trading, the company that owns Juno Press, the
publisher of London's most notorious scandal rag. He'll
be an outcast. The ton will never forgive him."

"Really, Your Grace?" intoned a dark voice dripping
with sardonic amusement. "I don't think so."

CHAPTER 28

"Till this moment I never knew myself."—An
extract from Jane Austen's *Pride & Prejudice*.
The Beau Monde Mirror: The Literary Arts

In the moments before Lord Rochfort had taken her
hostage, Charlie should have known something was
amiss. First of all, Cressida's gaze had darted to the door.
Secondly, she'd heard the creak of a floorboard just behind her.

And finally, the baron's breath had gusted against her
cheek in the split second before he'd pressed the muzzle
of a pistol against her temple and said, "Really, Your
Grace? I don't think so."

Max spun around, then swore. Holding up his hands
in a placatory gesture, he said in a voice rough with emotion, "Your argument is with me, Rochfort, not Lady
Charlotte. Let her go, and we'll settle this like gentlemen."

Rochfort laughed, and one of his arms—still in a sling
—snaked awkwardly about Charlie's waist. The cold steel
of the pistol's muzzle bit deeper, and her stomach twisted
with terror. "Here's what is actually going to happen, Exmoor. Lady Charlotte and I are going to take a small
journey together, and while we're away, you're going to
visit each and every one of those newspapers you just
mentioned and make sure they don't breathe a word about
my ownership of the *Beau Monde Mirror*. Or Cressida's, for

that matter. And when I'm satisfied that my name and reputation are no longer in danger of being vilified, you can have your fiancée back. You've already caused enough damage in my life. I won't let you destroy me completely."

"Now, let's be reasonable, Rochfort. It's going to take me some time to do all of that," began Max. "Release Lady Charlotte first—"

The baron cocked the pistol's hammer, and at the sharp metallic click, Charlie clamped her eyes shut. Her breath froze in her chest. "I'm not bloody stupid, Exmoor," he bit out. "Now get on your knees and put your hands behind your back. Cressida, use that braid holding back the curtains to tie his hands. And his ankles." He emitted a low chuckle. "For your mother's sake, Exmoor, I won't make you strip."

Max complied, dropping to his haunches. Even though his life was in danger too, he caught Charlie's gaze. "I'm so sorry this is happening, my love." His voice was grave yet infinitely soft. "But I promise you that we'll get through this. Everything will be all right."

Oh, dear God. Charlie's heart cracked a little, and indeed, she felt like it might actually break in two. Max might be adept at masking his emotions, but she just knew that he was blaming himself for not thinking ahead. For neglecting to search Devereux House, and for failing to anticipate Rochfort's actions. For not having at least half a dozen strategies for an exit up his sleeve. But while there was breath in her body, she wouldn't go down without a fight. For Max and for herself, she would find a way out of this.

Swallowing hard against a wave of rising panic, she dredged up her voice. "Lord Rochfort, His Grace is right. I'm sure we can work something—"

The baron jabbed the pistol into the side of her head with such force, tears sprang to her eyes. "Shut it, *my lady*." His breath was hot and harsh against her ear. "Do not say another word." To Cressida, he said, "Are those knots nice and tight?"

The dowager duchess nodded. "Yes. They are. Just the

way you like them." And then she added in a breathless voice, "Be careful, Rollo."

Be careful, Rollo? Charlie's stomach roiled, and she thought she might be ill. Max's grim expression—the flicker of fire in his deep blue eyes and the way a muscle pulsed in his cheek—clearly conveyed his own disgust and anger, but he didn't say anything else. Even so, she was certain his mind was working furiously, just like hers was.

Rochfort began hauling her backward toward the morning room door. He gave a grunt as his injured shoulder collided with the doorjamb, and Charlie's heart lurched with hope. The baron might be holding a pistol to her head, but his shoulder wound clearly still bothered him. If she twisted just the right way, maybe aimed a swift, hard jab at his ribs with her elbow—

All of a sudden, there was a loud smash, and crystalline shards, cut lilies, and a cascade of dirty water rained down around Charlie's head and shoulders. Lord Rochfort's grip on her waist loosened, the pistol fell away, and as the baron toppled to the floor with a heavy thud, Cressida screamed, drowning out the string of profanities that fell from Max's lips.

And then Diana whispered into the crashing silence that followed, "Is he dead?"

Charlie whipped around. The young duchess stood in the corridor just outside the morning room. Her gray eyes were huge in her pale face, and all her attention was riveted to Rochfort's prone form.

"I'm not sure," said Charlie at the same moment that the baron moaned. His fingers flexed in a puddle of water and broken crystal. Quick as a wink, Charlie bent down and picked up the pistol that lay at her feet. She wasn't going to take any chances.

As she straightened and stepped away from Rochfort's body, she pointed the pistol at Cressida, who stood motionless, rooted to the spot. "Untie Max. Now," she ordered. She didn't trust the dowager duchess as far as she could throw her.

Cressida blinked as though emerging from a daze, then scowled at Charlie. "I'll do no such—"

"Oh, spare me." Charlie made sure the pistol was cocked as she took up a duelist's stance. "When I told you that I'd once shot a gun on Putney Heath, I lied, Cressida. I've been shooting many times. In fact, I'd even venture to say that I'm a crack shot. And unless you do what I say"— she narrowed her gaze and took aim at Cressida's chest —"I'm going to give you a complete demonstration of my exceptional marksmanship skills. So, I'll say it once more and once more only: untie my fiancé, or I'll put a bullet in your person. Your choice."

Diana stepped forward. "That's all right. I'll do it," she said. "I don't trust Cressida. You can keep guard."

Cressida shot her daughter-in-law a murderous look as she crossed the room, but Diana didn't seem to notice or care.

When Charlie's gaze connected with Max's, his handsome face split with a devilish grin. "You're simply amazing," he murmured as his sister-in-law freed his hands.

"So are you," she returned with an equally wide smile. "And so is Diana."

"Agreed."

"Oh, please. I think I'm going to be sick," said the dowager duchess.

Max climbed to his feet with the curtain ties in hand. "You don't have time for that," he said as he approached Lord Rochfort, who was moaning again. "Because you have some packing to do." After squatting down, he ruthlessly pulled the baron's arms behind his back and began to bind his wrists. "And if you don't hop to it, I'm going to reconsider where you'll be residing. I think a stint in an asylum might be in order, because I'm seriously questioning the sanity of your choices."

One of Cressida's hands fluttered to her throat. "You wouldn't do such a horrible thing. Not to your own mother."

"Considering you just tied up your own son and were a co-conspirator in the attempted kidnapping of my fiancée, I wouldn't count on that. Now go. By my calculations, you only have fifty minutes left before my carriage arrives to take you to Devon."

Once his uncharacteristically subdued mother had retired to her rooms and a groggy Rochfort had been carted off by a pair of strapping footmen to the coal cellar where he'd be locked up until the Bow Street Runners arrived to deal with him—Diana had offered to send for them— Max turned to Charlie and enveloped her in his arms. He embraced her like he never wanted to let her go.

"Oh God, my love, I'm so, so sorry." His voice was weighted with guilt, and when he drew back to study her face, Charlie could see his dark blue eyes were shadowed with self-recrimination. "I was such an idiot not to have even considered the possibility that Rochfort might have been lurking somewhere within these walls. My arrogance and stupidity put you in danger. I can never forgive myself for that. But there is one good thing I learned about myself today.

"I once feared love more than anything on this earth. As you know, I'd been taught to think it would make me weak. But I was so very wrong. My father was so very wrong. As that dog Rochfort threatened to take you hostage and away from me—" He broke off, shaking his head. "The determination I felt, and yes, my blazing anger, were far more potent because I *do* love you." The sincerity of his conviction, the depth of his feeling shone in his eyes and resonated in his voice. "Your love has made me stronger, Charlie. It fills my heart. It warms my soul. The joy and absolute satisfaction I feel whenever I'm with you, it's indescribable. With you by my side, I am whole and happy."

"Oh, Max." Charlie's eyes brimmed with tears, and her heart swelled with so much love and tenderness, she thought it might burst. "Don't torture yourself with all the if-onlys and might-have-beens. The important thing is we are both safe and whole and together. Nothing can part us now."

"Yes." He brushed her jaw with gentle fingers, then pushed a damp curl behind one of her ears. His voice was soft as a caress as he said, "I'm so very proud of you, do you know that? For your quick thinking and for your bravery…and for your generous, forgiving heart. You, Charlotte Hastings, are the most wonderful woman I've ever met, and I can't wait to spend the rest of my life with you. I know we originally agreed that we'd wed at the end of the Season, but would you reconsider and marry me sooner?"

Max's gaze was so adoring and his words were so sweet, Charlie's own heart and soul were immediately flooded with happiness. "Goodness gracious," she murmured, her voice husky with emotion. "I never thought I'd see the day when you, Maximilian Devereux, would openly declare that you were not just ready and willing, but eager to be caught in the parson's mousetrap. So, I will say yes to your proposal, and gladly, because I love you so much, and I can't wait to begin our new life together too. My only caveat is that we allow enough time for my aunt Tabitha to return to London for the ceremony. I couldn't bear it if she wasn't at our wedding."

"Of course," said Max. "But before I visit Doctor's Common to procure a special license, and before you return to Hastings House, there's one more urgent matter that needs attending to."

"Oh?"

"Yes." Max wiped her cheek, and when he withdrew his hand, something green and slimy was smeared across the pad of his thumb. "You, my dear Charlie, are in serious need of a bath. I don't know what was in that vase, but—"

Charlie clasped Max's face between her hands and silenced him with a resounding kiss. When she drew back, she couldn't help but smile at her handiwork. "Oh, look. Now you're covered in green muck too. I guess you'll have to join me, Your Grace."

"Oh, I intend to, my little minx," he said with a grin. And then he kissed her with such heartfelt passion and love, nothing else mattered but this perfect moment and the bright, shining future awaiting them both.

EPILOGUE

The Enlightened Women's Society of London,
Harrington House, Bloomsbury Square
May 20, 1820

"I declare that the *Enlightened Women's Society of London* is now officially open," Tabitha, Lady Chelmsford, announced in a strident voice to the small crowd gathered in Bloomsbury Square. And then Euphemia Harrington, with the help of her young daughter, Tilda, sliced through the crimson satin ribbon adorning the front door of Harrington House.

Claps and cheers erupted, and after Charlie climbed the short flight of stairs, she embraced her aunt, then Mia and Tilda. When she turned around, her gaze immediately sought and connected with Max's. Her handsome husband stood at the back of the throng—half a head taller than most in the crowd, he was easy to spot—and as he grinned back at her, elation and a feeling of accomplishment suffused Charlie's heart.

This. This was a perfect moment.

With the help of her darling friends, her dear aunt, Mia Harrington, and the Mayfair Bluestocking Society, Charlie had created something special and worthwhile: a charitable society that would endeavor to support women who were in desperate need; women who might be unwed and with child; or women who'd been aban-

doned by their husbands and had nowhere else to go. At
Harrington House, they would find other sympathetic
women who would help them to find a safe place to stay
and decent paid work, and if required, medical care at
one of the innumerable dispensaries that Arabella had established in various locations about London. No one
would be turned away.

Mia did the honors of opening the door, then
everyone trooped into Harrington House to share a celebratory afternoon tea in the drawing room and the
flower-filled back garden.

Olivia, who was round with child, was grateful when
Charlie ushered her over to a vacant shepherdess chair by
the open French doors. Quite a few of the guests had already filtered outside to the terrace and garden to enjoy
the afternoon sunshine. "It's so l-lovely to see Mia and
Tilda back in London," she said as she leaned back and
put her slippered feet upon a padded footstool.

"Yes," agreed Charlie. "I'm still so grateful to Mia. She
didn't have to rent her townhouse to us. And the fact that
she wishes to help manage the day-to-day running of the
Society when we begin to receive clients—Max said she's
an excellent housekeeper—is just wonderful. Her exper-
tise will be invaluable."

"No doubt she feels strongly about supporting other
women, given her own history," remarked Olivia. "And
after Max's generosity—he didn't have to buy back her
townhouse for her—she might feel it is a way to say
thank you to you both."

"Yes, I think you might be right. Most of all, I'm
pleased she doesn't feel like she has to hide from Lord
Rochfort anymore."

Lord Rochfort, the man who'd made Mia's life hell
too, was dead. Charlie couldn't say she was sorry after all
the terrible things he'd done. After the baron had been
incarcerated in the Tower to await a trial by his peers—
he'd been charged with extortion, assault, and attempted
kidnapping—Rochfort had evidently taken his own life.
The coroner had decreed that Rochfort had ingested a
lethal dose of laudanum during his first night behind

bars. The Tower guards had failed to search his person thoroughly, so they'd missed the fact that the baron had a flask of the strong opiate secreted in his coat. Apparently, he'd taken to drinking laudanum regularly to dull the pain of his injured shoulder.

Once Rochfort's ownership of the *Beau Monde Mirror* had been revealed in all the newspapers—and after the baron's demise—the infamous scandal rag that had caused so much grief had been shut down. And Charlie couldn't say she was sorry about that either.

As for Lady Penelope Purcell… Charlie had not seen hide nor hair of the horrid young woman since that terrible afternoon at the Royal Academy of Art's fifty-first exhibition. Although, by all accounts, the duke's daughter had accepted a proposal from a middle-aged but exceedingly wealthy marquis by the end of last Season, and she was now heavy with child and rusticating at his rambling estate, somewhere in the wilds of Northumberland. Rumor also had it that the marquis and his new wife led very separate lives; he was very much a marquis-about-town who believed a wife's place was in the home—or his country home to be more precise. In any event, Charlie doubted she'd be seeing much of Penelope in the future. The same went for her odious brother; Lord Mowbray was reported to be on an extended Grand Tour, exploring the Continent and perhaps even farther afield, and it wasn't known when he'd be back—a most satisfying prospect, all things considered. Or in Max's words, "a good riddance of bad rubbish" at least for the time being.

Hamish wandered over and furnished his wife with a cup of tea and a slice of cake. "You are too sweet to me," Olivia murmured as she smiled up at her burly Scots husband; the adoration in her eyes was clear to see.

Hamish dropped a kiss on her forehead. "Nothing's too good for my bonnie wife and our bairn on the way," he said softly. Looking up, he caught Charlie's gaze and winked with his one good eye. "We'll join you outside shortly."

Charlie nodded and smiled. "I look forward to it."

She found her father and new stepmother, Eleanor, with Aunt Tabitha and her dear friend Lady Kilbride on the terrace by a fragrant rose bower. They were discussing plans to open additional branches of the *Enlightened Women's Society* in other areas of London and other large towns about the country.

In between the knots of guests milling in the garden itself, Charlie also spied Sophie and Arabella chatting with their husbands and Diana, who, now that she'd remarried, styled herself Lady Claremont. Diana had first met Matthew Ellis, Viscount Claremont—an eligible gentleman who'd once courted Sophie—at Charlie and Max's wedding, which had taken place at Heathcote Hall a year before to the day.

On their wedding day—another perfect late spring day just like this one—her father had naturally given her away, and Sophie had been her attendant. But best of all, Nate had been honored to act as Max's groomsman. He'd at last accepted that Max did indeed love her sincerely and deeply, and knowing that warmed Charlie's heart immeasurably.

As Charlie descended the flagged steps to the lawn, she smiled to herself. Sophie and Nate had welcomed another baby boy—Edward, or Ned for short—into the world a month ago, and Arabella and Gabriel were now the proud parents of a five-month-old baby girl named Mary Caroline, after their respective mothers.

The delightful sound of a child's squeal and a giggle drew Charlie's attention. Max, who was talking to Mia, was also pushing little Tilda on a swing. When her husband looked up and saw Charlie, he smiled and beckoned her over.

It amused Charlie no end that her devilish duke of a husband had recently become as broody as a mother hen around babies and young children. Whenever they visited Nate and Sophie or Arabella and Gabriel, he'd invariably demand a trip to the nursery to see how his godchildren were doing. And it seemed procreating was catching. Molly, who'd recently begun to work here at Harrington House assisting Mia, was expecting too. She'd married her dashing footman, Edwards, on Saint Valentine's Day, and even though Charlie was losing her loyal lady's maid, she couldn't be happier for the young woman.

Even Peridot had given birth to a litter of sweet little kittens in early March. Charlie had been gradually finding new homes for them all, but she still had one kitten left.

Charlie joined Max, Mia, and Tilda beneath the shade of the beech tree. Max quite unashamedly slipped an arm about her waist and pulled her in for a kiss.

"You're positively glowing, my love," he murmured against her ear.

"Well, why wouldn't I be?" she said, smiling up at him. "I'm blissfully wed to the most wonderful man, all of my friends are equally as happy, and now we have joined forces to create a worthwhile charitable endeavor that will provide help to fellow sisters in need. Our lives couldn't be more perfect. I feel nothing but blessed."

"Agreed." Max gave her waist a little squeeze. "I take it Hamish and Olivia will join us soon with Tilda's surprise?"

"Yes, they will."

As if her words had summoned them, Hamish and Olivia appeared on the terrace. Hamish was brandishing a small covered basket. As they approached the beech tree, Tilda slid from the swing and raced over to them. She clasped Olivia's hand. "What's in there, Lord Sleat and Lady Livvie?" the child asked in her sweet piping voice. Above the sounds of conversation and laughter, a series of tiny high-pitched mewls could just be heard.

Hamish squatted down and placed the basket upon the grass. He glanced over to Charlie and grinned. "I believe it's a present from Charlotte, the Duchess of Exmoor."

Tilda looked up at Charlie. "It is? For me, Your Grace?"

Charlie knelt on the grass too. "It is. Well, actually, it's a gift from Peridot, my cat. You remember her, don't you?"

Tilda nodded vigorously, her brown curls bouncing.

"Yes, I do. Lady Livvie was looking after her while you were away." Her wide blue gray eyes shifted to her mother. "Can I open the basket, Mama?"

Mia smiled. "Yes, of course, darling."

Tilda very carefully lifted the basket's wicker lid, and a kitten's tiny head immediately popped up. It stopped mewling and blinked at its surroundings.

Tilda squealed. "Are you sure the kitten is *really* for me?" Her gaze skipped between Charlie, Olivia, Hamish, and her mother.

"Yes. She's just for you," said Charlie. "But you must promise to take good care of her. Her mama, Peridot, is counting on you."

"Oh, I will," cried Tilda. She scooped up the tiny bundle of tortoiseshell fur and gave the kitten a gentle hug. "What is her name?"

"You must choose one," said Charlie.

Tilda's forehead dipped into a pensive frown as she stroked the kitten's fluffy head. "I think I would like to call her Marmalade. Because of all her orange patches."

"That sounds just perfect," said Charlie. "I'll tell Peridot when I go home."

She rose to her feet, and Max drew her in for another hug. "I also have a surprise for you when we leave here," he murmured. "Today is special for many reasons, and I have so much to be thankful for and to celebrate...including the fact it's our very first wedding anniversary."

"I haven't forgotten." Charlie looked up into Max's face. The dappled sunlight filtering through the leaves of the beech tree had turned his sapphire eyes to the warmest shade of summer-sky blue. She could quite happily lose herself in those eyes forever. Reaching up, she touched his cheek and inhaled a soft breath. "I have something special to share with you too."

≈

Heathcote Hall, Hampstead Heath

The moment before Max ushered Charlie into their newly refurbished set of private apartments at Heathcote Hall, he felt unaccountably excited. Like a child about to delve into his first-ever Christmas stocking—not that his parents had ever followed such a Yuletide tradition—or a four-year-old about to pull her first pet kitten from a basket. Of course, he already knew what lay beyond the white-paneled doors, but he couldn't wait to see the expression on Charlie's face when she discovered what he'd been up to.

Once his mother had been banished to Devonshire, Max had asked Charlie to redecorate both Exmoor House and Devereux House to suit her own taste. But he hadn't yet invited her to do the same at Heathcote. Not because he didn't want her to make her mark on this particular home. Far from it. It was simply because he'd wanted to surprise his wonderful wife with some changes of his own.

He'd wanted to spoil her because she deserved it.

Drawing a deep breath, he pulled open the doors. "Happy anniversary, my love."

As soon as Charlie stepped across the threshold into the sumptuously appointed sitting room, her eyes widened in wonder.

"Oh, Max," she breathed as she crossed the rose-patterned Aubusson rug, then spun around, taking everything in. The crystal chandelier and intricate plasterwork above her head, the amber damask curtains at the windows, and the delicate cherrywood armchairs and chaise longue upholstered in cream brocade. "This…this is beautiful. I'm practically speechless. I had no idea you'd been planning anything like this."

"I'm so pleased you like it," he said, watching her lovely face. Her cheeks were flushed with pleasure, and her eyes shone with delight.

"And it goes on forever…" Charlie wandered through to the adjoining bedchamber. "You've moved everything about. Combined the rooms."

"I might've," he said as he followed her toward the

enormous tester bed. "We always share the same bed, so I didn't see much point in maintaining separate bedchambers. Do you mind, though?" He grimaced. "I know I snore sometimes."

Charlie picked up one of the cushions from the elaborate arrangement at the head of the bed and hugged it to her bosom. "Of course I don't mind. I think it's an eminently sensible idea. And your snoring doesn't bother me at all. It's music to my ears."

"Ha ha, my love. I'm certain you're lying," he said with a soft chuckle. "But I do appreciate the fact that you are happy to sleep beside me every night."

Charlie met his gaze over the gold brocade counterpane. "There's no place I would rather be."

Her voice was low and soft and as rich as silk, and Max's loins tightened with longing. "I feel exactly the same way," he murmured.

Ignoring the urge to crawl across the bed and pull her down into his arms, he held out his hand instead. "Come, I have something else to show you."

He led Charlie past their new dressing rooms and into a brand-new addition to Heathcote: a high-ceilinged bathroom that resembled an airy conservatory. The dome above them was constructed from glass and wrought iron, and there were a series of tall arched windows that looked out upon the lawns and the lake. Gauzy curtains provided a modicum of privacy during the day, and heavier curtains of silk damask could be drawn at night. Everywhere one looked, there were fragrant white blooms, leafy green palms, and ferns.

But the main attraction—aside from the elegant white marble fireplace and a chaise longue at one end piled with snowy white towels—was the large sunken bath in the center of the room. As per Max's directions, it had already been filled with steaming hot water.

"Max…" Charlie pressed her hands to her cheeks. "This room, the bath, it's all simply stunning. But how on earth have the servants managed to fill such an enormous tub with hot water? It would have taken them all day."

"That's a very good question," said Max with a grin.

"I consulted the architect Sir John Soane, who installed a similar tub for Lord Hardwicke at Wimpole Hall. Water is pumped in from the lake and after it's passed through a filter, it's heated via a boiler beneath the floor."

"That's…I'm amazed." Charlie turned and threw her arms about his neck. "Max, this is the most wonderful surprise. Thank you. I'm overwhelmed with gratitude. This is the best, indeed the most magnificent gift I've ever received."

He laughed at that. "I'm glad you approve."

Her eyes were soft with love as she said, "I do."

"Well, shall we make use of it, my sweet wife?"

A wicked smile played about her fulsome lips. "We shall."

It didn't take them long to divest all of their clothes, then Max assisted Charlie down the short set of wide, porcelain-tiled stairs into the water.

As soon as Max sat on one of the steps, he gathered Charlie into his arms. Her warm, wet skin slid against his, and the desire that was already flowing through his veins headed straight to his groin.

"The temperature of the water is perfect," murmured Charlie, sliding her hands over his shoulders. "It reminds me of that time we visited those Turkish baths in Brighton last year."

"Yes. In any event, this is much better than naked sea bathing in Brighton."

Charlie laughed, and her breasts with their succulent nipples bobbed in the water in the most tantalizing way. "I agree. Sea bathing wasn't how I imagined it would be. Even though it was July, the water was freezing." She gave an exaggerated shiver, and when her breasts jiggled again, Max couldn't help but groan.

Cupping her face, he whispered in a voice frayed with lust, "As much as I'd love to spend time lathering soap and fragrant oil all over your delicious curves, sweet Charlotte, I don't think I can wait a moment longer to be inside you."

Her gaze locked with his. "I want you inside me too,"

she murmured. "Only…I want to share my anniversary gift with you first."

Anticipation curling through him, Max began to rub his thumb in idle circles over one of her nipples. The tip immediately stiffened into a tightly furled peak, tempting him to take it between his lips. "I have you, my love. That's the only gift I need."

"That's very sweet of you, but no matter how much you taunt me with your wicked fingers, I will not be deterred." Charlie clasped her hands about his neck, and an emotion he couldn't quite place lit her honey-brown eyes. "Maximilian Devereux," she murmured with grave sincerity, "you and I are going to have a baby."

Max blinked. His breath hitched. When he spoke, his voice was little more than a rasp. "Charlie, do you mean it? Are you sure?"

She touched his jaw, and her mouth curved with a tender smile. "Of course, I'm sure, my darling husband. Haven't you noticed that my bosom is a little larger and my waist is a little thicker?"

"I…I suppose…" He frowned. "Actually, no, not really." And then his vision blurred as the most incredible feeling of unadulterated joy flooded his heart. Closing his eyes, he leaned his forehead against Charlie's. "My darling. My love. This news…I can barely speak. I'm practically incoherent with happiness."

"So am I."

When Max lifted his head, Charlie's beautiful, tear-bright eyes gazed back at him. "Make love to me, Max."

Despite the fact his cock was still hard and ready, a frisson of worry slid through him. "Are you sure it's safe?"

She smiled. "Of course it is, you darling, silly man. None of my friends have remained celibate during their pregnancies. I mean, can you imagine any of *your* friends going without for so long? Aside from that, I recently spoke with a midwife Arabella recommended, and she also confirmed that all will be well."

He gave a soft chuckle. "You make a compelling argument." His hand slid to her belly, and he caressed her silken skin beneath the warm water. "When is the babe due, do you know?"

"I'm only eight weeks along, so it will be a while yet, but both Arabella and the midwife think he or she will arrive around Christmastide."

"I can hardly wait," Max whispered. And then, because he could no longer contain all the wondrous feelings brimming inside him, he kissed Charlie, the duchess of his dreams.

Desire surged again, hot and insistent, yet Max resisted the impulse to take Charlie hard and fast. He wanted to make these glorious moments last.

He wanted to celebrate their love.

His tongue slid softly between Charlie's lips, tasting her sweet warmth. Her soft sighs and the way she stroked him back with her own tongue made him ache to possess her even more.

He settled his mouth upon one breast, and while he suckled, he slipped his fingers between her thighs. The delicious moan that spilled from her throat as he teased her slick sex made his cock jerk with appreciation.

"Max, I need you," she whispered huskily. She rose, straddling him, the water lapping at her hips. With her face flushed with desire and her damp chestnut curls clinging to her neck, she looked exactly like a goddess. Like Venus rising from the sea.

"Sweet Jesus, Charlie," he groaned as she gripped his throbbing shaft and took him—all of him—inside her. He cupped her delicious derriere. How well she filled his hands. How well she clasped his thick, throbbing length. So hot. So wet and silken. Tighter than a fisted glove. He would never grow tired of her. Of this.

He tightened his arms about her, and she undulated her hips, gently loving him with her body and her eyes. Her whispered words and breathy moans.

Max couldn't hold back as urgent lust pulsated through his veins. Gripping her waist, he pumped his hips until pleasure claimed them both in a great rush. As he cried out Charlie's name, her fingers twisted in his hair, and when she was spent too, she collapsed against him, her sweet breath fanning against his neck.

Max wrapped his arms about his wife. His chest was so full of love, he didn't know how his body could possibly contain it.

Drawing back, he caught her drowsy, sated gaze. "How I love you, my darling," he said, his voice filled with tender awe. "You bring me so much joy, I'd give you the whole world and everything in it if I could."

Charlie's eyes glowed, and when she smiled, he basked in the warmth of it. "Oh, Max, I love you too," she whispered. "With my entire heart. And you don't need to give me the world, or even the moon and the stars, because when I'm with you, I'm in heaven."

And then she kissed him, and Max knew without a shadow of a doubt that they'd both find everything that they'd ever want or need right here in each other's arms.

AUTHOR'S NOTE

From what I can fathom, John Anster's poem, *The Ever-lasting Rose*, wasn't published until August 1819 in *The London Literary Gazette*, although it may have been in private circulation prior to this. In any event, the quote that appears at the beginning of Chapter Eleven, fit my story so well, I just had to use it. I hope readers can forgive me using a little poetic license.

Likewise, John Keats's well-known love sonnet to Fanny Brawne, *Bright Star*, wasn't published until 1838, quite some years after the poet's death, but there are accounts that he perhaps began to pen an early version of the poem in April 1818. Mr. Keats's words are just so beautiful, I couldn't resist including a quote in my book.

Lastly, all of the artworks mentioned in the story (apart from Madame de Beauvoir's two entirely fictional paintings) actually do appear in the 1819 Royal Academy of Arts Exhibition's guidebook. The quote by Sir Francis Bacon at the beginning of Chapter Twenty-three is featured in the 1819 guidebook as well.

THANK YOU FOR READING!

If you enjoyed ***How to Catch a Devilish Duke***, please help other readers find it too. Consider leaving a review wherever you bought the book.

And don't forget the other books in the Disreputable Debutantes Series!

ALSO BY AMY ROSE BENNETT

Visit Amy Rose Bennett's website for all the purchase links...

www.amyrosebennett.com

STEAMY HISTORICAL ROMANCE TITLES

The Byronic Book Club Series

Up All Night with a Good Duke, Book 1

Curled Up with an Earl, Book 2

Disreputable Debutantes Series

How to Catch a Wicked Viscount, Book 1

How to Catch an Errant Earl, Book 2

How to Catch a Sinful Marquess, Book 3

How to Catch a Devilish Duke, Book 4

Scandalous Regency Widows Series

Lady Beauchamp's Proposal, Book 1

The Ice Duchess, Book 2

A Most Unsuitable Countess, Book 3 (Coming 2023)

Improper Liaisons Novella Series

An Improper Proposition, Book 1

An Improper Governess, Book 2

An Improper Christmas, Book 3

Highland Rogue Series

The Master of Strathburn, Book 1

The Laird of Blackloch, Book 2

Wicked Winter Nights Novella Series

My Lady of Misrule, Book 1

My Lord of Misrule, Book 2 (Coming 2022)
A Wicked Twelfth Night Wager, Book 3 (Coming 2023)

∼

SWEET REGENCY ROMANCE TITLES

All She Wants for Christmas
Dashing Through the Snow

∼

STANDALONE TITLES
Long Gone Girl

ABOUT THE AUTHOR

Amy Rose Bennett is an Australian author who has a passion for penning emotion-packed historical romances. Of course, her strong-willed heroines and rakish heroes always find their happily ever after. A former speech pathologist, Amy is happily married to her very own romantic hero and has two lovely, very accomplished adult daughters. When she's not creating stories, Amy loves to cook up a storm in the kitchen, lose herself in a good book or a witty rom-com, and, when she can afford it, travel to all the places she writes about.

Amy loves to hear from readers. You can contact her via her website or other places she hangs out on social media —links below. You can sign up for her free newsletter via her website too.
www.amyrosebennett.com

CPSIA information can be obtained
at www.ICGtesting.com
Printed in the USA
BVHW040232280223
659383BV00004B/51